MW00855933

OVERKILL

ALSO BY J.A. JANCE

ALI REYNOLDS MYSTERIES

Edge of Evil
Web of Evil
Hand of Evil
Cruel Intent
Trial by Fire
Fatal Error
Left for Dead
Deadly Stakes
Moving Target
A Last Goodbye (A Novella)
Cold Betrayal
No Honor Among Thieves (A Novella)
Clawback
Random Acts (A Novella)
Man Overboard
Duel to the Death
The A List
Credible Threat
Unfinished Business
Collateral Damage

JOANNA BRADY MYSTERIES

Desert Heat
Tombstone Courage
Shoot/Don't Shoot
Dead to Rights
Skeleton Canyon
Rattlesnake Crossing
Outlaw Mountain
Devil's Claw
Paradise Lost

Partner in Crime

Exit Wounds

Dead Wrong

Damage Control

Fire and Ice

Judgment Call

The Old Blue Line (A Novella)

Remains of Innocence

No Honor Among Thieves (A Novella)

Random Acts (A Novella)

Downfall

Field of Bones

Missing and Endangered

Blessing of the Lost Girls

J.P. BEAUMONT MYSTERIES

Until Proven Guilty

Injustice for All

Trial by Fury

Taking the Fifth

Improbable Cause

A More Perfect Union

Dismissed with Prejudice

Minor in Possession

Payment in Kind

Without Due Process

Failure to Appear

Lying in Wait

Name Withheld

Breach of Duty

Birds of Prey

Partner in Crime

Long Time Gone

Justice Denied

Fire and Ice

Betrayal of Trust

Ring in the Dead (A Novella)

Second Watch

Stand Down (A Novella)

Dance of the Bones

Still Dead (A Novella)

Proof of Life

Sins of the Fathers

Nothing to Lose

Girls' Night Out (A Novella)

Den of Iniquity

WALKER FAMILY MYSTERIES

Hour of the Hunter

Kiss of the Bees

Day of the Dead

Queen of the Night

Dance of the Bones

Blessing of the Lost Girls

POETRY

After the Fire

OVERKILL

J.A. JANCE

GALLERY BOOKS
NEW YORK AMSTERDAM/ANTWERP LONDON
TORONTO SYDNEY/MELBOURNE NEW DELHI

G

Gallery Books
An Imprint of Simon & Schuster, LLC
1230 Avenue of the Americas
New York, NY 10020

First Gallery Books hardcover edition April 2025

Interior design by Erika R. Genova

Manufactured in the United States of America

10 9 8 7 6 5 4 3 2 1

Library of Congress Control Number: 2024946269

ISBN 978-1-6680-3578-8

ISBN 978-1-6680-3580-1 (ebook)

For Sophia, another Pima Hall girl who made good

PROLOGUE

SEDONA, ARIZONA
MONDAY, MARCH 13, 2023
2:00 P.M.

Most of the time the door to Ali Reynolds's office at High Noon Enterprises was wide open. That was not the case during the first two weeks of March. The fifteenth of that month was the deadline for putting together and handing over all the numbers to the accountant so that company tax documents could be prepared in time to comply with Uncle Sam's April fifteenth deadline.

Growing up, Ali had never seen herself as a numbers person. What she had wanted was to be a journalist—specifically a television journalist, and she had done so for a number of years. At the top of her game she had been a high-profile local news anchor for an L.A. station until, in her early fifties, she'd been booted from her desk because the new and much younger news director deemed her "too old" to be on TV.

At that point, she had bailed on L.A. and come back to her hometown, Sedona, in central Arizona's Verde Valley, and that's when her life had changed direction. After a short foray into the world of law enforcement, she had met and married a tech entrepreneur named B. Simpson, a guy who had abandoned his given name, Bartholomew, in junior high due to unrelenting teasing about his being the real Bart Simpson.

Ali had been in on the ground floor as B. founded his cybersecurity company, High Noon Enterprises. He was the tech genius in the family. What Ali didn't know about high tech could have filled volumes, but it turned out that, although she really didn't care for numbers, she was good at them, and that's how she had eventually morphed into being High Noon's CFO.

In the world of cybersecurity, High Noon was the David to everyone else's Goliath. With fewer than ten full-time and mostly long-term employees, the company was fast making an international name for itself. One of those employees was Lance Tucker. As a high school kid in San Leandro, Texas, he and his computer science teacher had created a piece of groundbreaking encrypted software they called GHOST, which made it possible for High Noon to prevent unauthorized incursions into clients' computer systems while, at the same time, being able to track bad actors back to their original source.

When Ali's phone rang at 2:45, she saw it was B. on the line. He and Lance had flown out of Phoenix the night before and were currently in Washington, DC, working with their attorney to secure a patent on the next version of GHOST.

"How's it going?" Ali asked.

"It's going," B. said, sounding a bit gloomy. "Dealing with attorneys isn't exactly my favorite pastime. I'm guessing it's going to take the rest of the week to get this all sorted. How are things on the home front?"

"Pretty much the same," she replied. "My having to deal with tax season is on a par with your messing around with attorneys."

"Sounds about right," B. replied with a short laugh. "Did Cami get off all right?"

Camille Lee, High Noon's outside salesperson, was spending the entire week in California doing meet and greets with both new and existing customers. By far the most important of those get-togethers would be a high-profile meeting with the head of a Japanese conglomerate, Dozo International.

"Yes, she landed in L.A. a couple of hours ago," Ali answered. "She's planning on spending all day Thursday studying the dossiers Frigg prepared on all the Dozo company execs who will be in attendance at the dinner that evening."

Frigg was the pet name of an AI owned by one of High Noon's key employees, Stu Ramey. Dossiers prepared by the artificial intelligence were incredibly thorough, enough so that Cami would walk into the meeting knowing far more about her guests than any of them suspected.

"It'd be wonderful if Cami could reel Dozo in," B. said. "It would be a huge feather in her cap, and in ours, too. Oh, wait. Lance is giving me the high sign. I have to go."

"Okay," Ali said. "Talk to you later."

GRAYS, UK
TUESDAY, MARCH 14, 2023
9:00 A.M.

The text exchange was brief and to the point:

Is everything in place?

Yes.

Good. Happy hunting. You'll get the rest of your money once she's well in hand. Keep me posted.

With that, Adrian Willoughby shut down his computer and headed home. At long last, things were finally in motion. Once this was all over, he'd be out of here for good.

CHAPTER ONE

EDMONDS, WASHINGTON
MONDAY, MARCH 13, 2023
8:30 A.M.

That Monday morning, Donna Jean Plummer pulled her Toyota RAV4 into the driveway and used her clicker to open the garage door. Both of her employers' cars were parked inside—Mr. Brewster's sleek black BMW and Mrs. Brewster's red Camaro. Mrs. Brewster used her car so seldom these days that it was covered with a layer of dust, but Donna Jean was surprised to see the BMW. That was usually gone long before she arrived.

Donna Jean worked for the Brewsters two days a week. Mr. Brewster had turned sixty over the weekend, and they'd had a big celebration on Sunday. Donna Jean had spent most of Friday getting the house ready for the festivities. Mrs. Brewster wasn't much of a cook, so the party had been professionally catered. Nonetheless, since Mrs. Brewster wasn't any better at tidying up than she was at cooking, Donna Jean expected that the place would be an ungodly mess.

With that in mind, Donna Jean glanced at her watch. Monday morning was garbage day in Edmonds, Washington, and one of Donna Jean's duties was making sure the trash containers were all moved out to the curb before the trucks showed up. She wanted to have today's garbage loaded into the bins in time to be hauled away.

Donna Jean paused in the garage long enough to break down the accumulated assortment of shipping boxes and put them into the recycle bin. Mrs. Brewster had two major hobbies—drinking and shopping online. The booze came from a local liquor store that delivered her standing order to the front porch every Monday afternoon.

Mrs. Brewster spent a fortune each month on stuff she never used. Once it came into the house, Donna Jean usually hauled it upstairs to the master bedroom where Mrs. Brewster spent the bulk of her time. Once the shipping boxes were empty, Donna Jean took them down to the garage.

As for whatever Mrs. Brewster bought? When she was done with an item, it was banished to one of the other bedrooms on the second floor. At this point, all three were packed wall-to-wall with junk, most of it brand-new. As a result, what had once been a four-bedroom home was now essentially a one-bedroom. Donna Jean had no idea why Mr. Brewster put up with his wife's shopping nonsense, but she kept her mouth shut. After all, it was none of her business.

With the boxes broken down and in the recycling bin, Donna Jean used her key to let herself into the house via a door from the garage that opened into the laundry room. She expected the alarm to sound, but it didn't. That wasn't surprising, because Mrs. Brewster for sure, and maybe even Mr., had tied one on during the party. Once their guests took off, neither of them had bothered to reset the alarm.

As expected, the place was disgusting. Not as bad as the aftermath of a fraternity party, but close. The kitchen counter was loaded with the caterer's collection of disposable bamboo serving trays and platters, along with all the leftover food. Dirty dishes—Mrs. Brewster's collection of delicate china and crystal glassware, all of which would need to be hand-washed—were scattered on every flat surface throughout the ground floor.

Expecting Mr. Brewster to come downstairs at any moment, Donna Jean started a pot of coffee. Then, glancing at her watch, she grabbed some clean trash bags from under the kitchen sink and began her search-and-destroy mission. She began by clearing the kitchen counter of the caterer's leavings. Just the mess in the kitchen was enough to fill two trash bags. Armed with a third, she made her way through the rest of the house collecting trash, then went out onto the patio, where, along with gathering more trash, she emptied a number of overflowing ashtrays.

The leavings in some of the ashtrays told Donna Jean that some of the previous evening's guests hadn't limited their smoking choices to cigars and cigarettes. She had reason to believe that, with or without Mr. and Mrs. Brewster's knowledge, a certain amount of recreational drug use had been added to the party's agenda, but Donna Jean's job was to clean up the mess, not to point fingers.

By the time she managed to get all the accumulated trash out of the house and loaded into the bins, she dragged them down to the curb just as the garbage truck was turning onto the street.

Back in the house, as she collected dirty dishes and glassware, there was still no sign of Mr. Brewster. It was unusual for him to sleep so late. But then again, he did a good deal of traveling. Maybe he had been called out of town unexpectedly and had taken a limo or an Uber to the airport. That would explain why his car was still in the garage. As for Mrs. Brewster? She generally didn't show her face until around noon, when she finally would venture downstairs for what passed for breakfast—usually coffee and toast and maybe some cold cereal.

Not wanting to let that fresh pot of coffee go to waste, Donna Jean decided to take her morning coffee break early. After having a cup, she set about washing dishes, many of which had been soaking in the sink. Then, on her next pass through the downstairs and out onto the patio, Donna Jean collected all the soiled linens, which would need to be washed, ironed, and returned to their assigned drawers.

As she brought the last of the dirty linens in from the patio, she attempted to latch the slider. For some reason, the door wouldn't close properly. On her second try, she noticed that the cork from a wine bottle had somehow ended up in the track of the slider between the patio and the family room. Clutching her load of linens in one arm, she bent down, retrieved the errant cork, and dropped it into the pocket of her apron. Then, with the slider properly closed and latched, she headed for the laundry room.

As Donna Jean washed, dried, stacked, and put away all of Mrs. Brewster's prized china and crystal, she found herself humming under her breath. Creating order out of chaos was something she found immensely satisfying, and being able to do so without a homeowner under foot and getting in the way was even better. Mr. Brewster was never a problem on that score, but Mrs. Brewster? When she was around, she tended to issue orders left and right, and nothing was ever done quite to her satisfaction.

Donna Jean had just moved the load of linens from the washer to the dryer when her cell phone rang. Extracting the phone from her apron pocket, she spotted her daughter's smiling face on the screen.

"Hey, Amy," she said. "How's it going?"

"I wanted to be sure that you're still good with picking up Jacob's birthday cake from Safeway on your way home tonight."

Today was her grandson's sixth birthday. A joint party with one of his friends from school would be on a Saturday later in the month, but this evening's celebration would be family only—his folks, his baby sister, and his grandmother—gathering for dinner and dessert.

"Of course," Donna Jean replied. "No problem at all."

Still, with afternoon traffic between Edmonds and Seattle, Donna Jean reminded herself that she'd need to finish work in time to head out a few minutes early.

Back in the kitchen, she was in the process of wiping down the countertops when she noticed for the first time that one of the knives—the largest one in fact—was missing from the knife block. For someone whose cooking consisted mostly of heating food in the microwave, Mrs. Brewster was exceptionally fussy about her knives. If one of those had disappeared, Donna Jean knew there would be hell to pay.

She did a quick search through all the utility drawers, thinking someone from the catering company might have mistakenly put the missing knife away in the wrong place, but after a thorough search, she realized there was no such luck. The knife was gone, and no matter who had misplaced it, Donna Jean knew she was the one Mrs. Brewster would hold responsible.

By eleven the downstairs was squeaky clean. As Donna Jean started on the ironing, she was beginning to worry that if Mrs. Brewster didn't wake up pretty soon, Donna Jean would be hard-pressed to have the master bedroom done before it was time for her to do the family's weekly grocery shopping, which she did every Monday afternoon. Fortunately, since the other bedrooms were packed full of junk, the master bedroom was the only one she had to deal with upstairs. Donna Jean was a dozen or so napkins into the ironing process when she heard a bloodcurdling scream.

Heart pounding in her throat, she abandoned the ironing board and raced toward the horrific sound. Halfway through the living room, she looked up the stairs and skidded to a stop. Mrs. Brewster stood on the landing at the top of the stairway screeching wordlessly at the top of her lungs. That was bad enough, but the woman's ghastly appearance took Donna Jean's breath away. Her nightgown was covered with blood. So were both hands, one of which held a bloodied knife.

"What happened?" Donna Jean demanded as she clambered up the stairway.

"It's Chuck," Mrs. Brewster managed, speaking intelligibly for the first time. "I must have stabbed him. He's dead." With that, she collapsed onto her knees, sobbing but still holding the knife.

Pausing halfway up the stairs, Donna Jean grabbed the phone out of her pocket and somehow managed to dial 911.

"What is the nature of your emergency?" the operator asked.

"Someone's been stabbed," Donna Jean replied. "He may be dead."

"Is he breathing?"

"I don't know. I haven't seen him. He's in the bedroom. I'm outside on the stairs."

"What is the address?"

Donna Jean reeled it off.

"First responders are on their way to your location."

"Thank you," Donna Jean said.

Reaching the top of the stairs, Donna Jean dropped to her knees next to the distraught woman who was sobbing brokenly.

"How could this have happened?" Mrs. Brewster demanded, frantically waving the bloodied knife in the air. "How could I have done this?"

Afraid the woman might accidentally harm herself, Donna Jean gently eased the weapon out of the her hand and slid it safely out of reach. At that point Donna Jean realized that the blood she was seeing on both the nightgown and the knife was completely dry.

"It's going to be okay," Donna Jean murmured over and over. "It's going to be okay."

That wasn't true, of course, because nothing was going to be okay, but she didn't know what else to say.

At that point Mrs. Brewster folded herself over until her forehead was touching the hardwood floor. That's when Donna Jean saw something red come streaking out through the bedroom door and onto the landing. It took a moment for her to make sense of what she was seeing. The guided missile turned out to be Mrs. Brewster's precious kitty, a snow-white longhaired cat named Pearl. Now as bloodstained as her mistress, Pearl raced across the landing and dove under Mrs. Brewster's heaving chest where the animal vanished from view.

In all the years Donna Jean had worked for the family, that was the first time she'd ever seen Pearl emerge from the master on her own. That's where the cat lived—in the bedroom suite. On those rare occasions when she'd had to visit the vet or go to the groomer, she was always transported through the rest of the house in a cat carrier. Obviously the poor animal was as frantic and traumatized as her owner.

Mrs. Brewster continued to sob. "It's all right," Donna Jean murmured again and again. "I called 911. Cops and EMTs are on their way."

"It's too late for EMTs," Mrs. Brewster managed. "They won't be able to save him. Chuck's dead. I must have killed him."

The next hours were a nightmare. The EMTs and uniformed officers showed up almost simultaneously, but the EMTs were forced to wait outside until the cops came through, clearing the house to make sure the killer was no longer inside.

Eventually Donna Jean was escorted to a patrol vehicle, where she was placed in the back seat and questioned in detail by one of the first officers on the scene. Some amount of time later, still from that vantage point, she watched as a man and a woman—detectives most likely—led Mrs. Brewster from the house, still wearing her nightgown and with her hands cuffed behind her back. A blanket had been tossed over her shoulders, presumably to hide the bloodstains, but as she moved, Donna Jean still caught glimpses of red. By then a large crowd had gathered out on the street. No doubt everyone there saw the bloodstains, too.

CHAPTER TWO

EVERETT, WASHINGTON
MONDAY, MARCH 13, 2023
9:00 A.M.

As Adam Brewster and his partner, Joel, waited at Paine Field for their flight from Seattle back to California, Adam was in a world of hurt. He had a hell of a hangover, which was unusual for him because, unlike his long-estranged father and his father's friends and associates, Adam wasn't much of a drinker. But yesterday, faced with seeing his father and stepmother in the flesh for the first time in close to two decades, his nerves had gotten the best of him. Every time a server had offered him a drink, he had taken it and tossed it down. As a result, he had been way beyond tipsy when Joel had called for an Uber to take them back to their hotel.

The party had been a lavish, catered affair in honor of his father's sixtieth birthday. When he and Joel had walked up onto the still familiar front porch to ring the bell, Adam had actually been holding his breath, preparing himself for being greeted by either his father or his stepmother. Instead, the door had been opened by someone in a catering uniform. It was only after they stepped out of the vestibule and into the living room that his father had caught sight of him. Whereupon, drink still in hand, his father had made his way through the crowd and greeted Adam with an enthusiastic hug.

"Thank you so much for coming," he said. "It's good to see you in the flesh after all this time."

At that point, his father had turned to Joel with his hand extended in welcome. "And you must be Joel," Charles Brewster had added. "Welcome. I'm glad to meet you."

His father's greeting had left Adam thunderstruck. Things had been far different back when he was a senior in high school. The situation at home had been tough. For one thing, his mother had been diagnosed with breast cancer. Treatments for breast cancer back then weren't nearly what they are now, and it was clear from the start that she was terminal. Adam had dealt with it by absenting himself from the house as much as possible. That had resulted in his being involved in his first ever romantic relationship with a guy named Daniel Herndon, someone several years older than Adam.

At the time, Adam had been too naive to realize what was really going on. Dan had claimed to be working toward a career as a professional photographer, and when he had suggested that they take a few titillating photographs of each other, it had seemed like a playful part of their blossoming sex life. It wasn't until they broke up a year or so later that the reality had hit home. Sextortion is all too familiar these days, but back then it had come as an unwelcome surprise that Danny had sought Adam out primarily because he was a rich man's son.

After the breakup Danny had threatened to send some of the photos to Adam's father unless Adam forked over five thousand bucks.

"Have a ball," Adam had told him. "Do your worst." That's what he had said, but he hadn't believed that Danny would actually go through with it.

In the meantime, Adam had begun noticing that with his mother so ill, Clarice Simpson, his mother's best friend and the wife of his father's partner, B. Simpson, was spending a lot of time at their house, most of it at his mother's bedside. Back then, Adam had really admired Clarice's kindness to his mother and appreciated her loyalty to a dying friend.

But then Dan had carried through on his threat. Once the packet of photos showed up at the house, all hell broke loose. Adam's father had been absolutely livid at the very idea that his son might be queer. His father hadn't actually ordered him out of the house. Adam left of his own accord, and fortunately, he'd had somewhere to go—his grandmother's place. It turned out his mother's mother was a lot more open-minded about homosexuality than her son-in-law. She had noticed that her grandson was "different" while he was still in grade school, and she had always been nothing short of loving and supportive. Gran had taken Adam in without a moment's hesitation and no questions asked.

Two weeks later, when Adam had gone back to the house in Edmonds to collect the rest of his stuff, he had let himself in with his key. On the way to his room, he had poked his head into the master, hoping to say hi to his mom, but she had been sound asleep, with her faithful housekeeper, Donna Jean Plummer, dozing in the recliner next to the bed. Rather than disturb either of them, Adam shut the door and let them be. But when he opened the door to what had been his own room, he had been in for a shock when he found his father and his mother's good friend, Clarice Simpson, getting it on in what had formerly been Adam's single bed.

Stark naked, his father had come roaring off the bed with both fists raised in the air as if prepared to knock Adam into next week, but Adam had stood his ground.

"Go ahead and hit me, you asshole," Adam had snarled at his father. "You can't hurt me any more than you already have." Then, pulling the door shut behind him, he fled the house. The rest of his stuff remained exactly where he'd left it because he'd never gone back to retrieve it.

That was the last time Adam and his father had spoken for the better part of twenty years. Adam had attended his mother's funeral two months later, but during the course of that, he and his father hadn't exchanged a word.

It turned out that, in his late teens, Joel Franklin, Adam's husband, had lived through similar circumstances. He, too, had been banished from the family home. To Joel's profound regret, his father had died before there had been any kind of resolution between them. Joel was the one person in Adam's life who had urged him to try reconciling with his own father before it was too late.

A little over a month ago, Adam had finally decided to take that advice. Screwing his courage to the sticking place, he had picked up his phone and dialed the number listed for his father's Seattle-based company, Video Games International.

When the person answering the call asked if she could tell Mr. Brewster what this was all about, Adam came close to hanging up the phone, but he hadn't.

"I'm Chuck Brewster's son," he had said. "I'd like to talk to him."

When his father got on the line a few seconds later, he had sounded ecstatic to hear his son's voice.

"Oh, Adam," he exclaimed. "Adam, Adam, Adam! This is an answer to a prayer. I'm thrilled to hear from you! Where are you living? What are you doing with yourself? How are you?"

Adam had been genuinely surprised by his father's effusive greeting, and that initial phone call had lasted more than an hour and a half. Before it ended, Adam and Joel had been invited to Chuck Brewster's sixtieth birthday party coming up a few weeks later on Sunday, March 12.

Lost in thought, Adam was startled when Joel poked him in the shoulder. "They just called our flight," he said. "Time to board."

Adam and Joel were seated in first class. Adam made it through watching all the economy passengers file to their seats in the back of the aircraft. He managed to listen to the droning safety measure announcement. And he was still awake when the flight attendant came through taking drink and breakfast orders. Adam assured her that the only thing he wanted was not to be disturbed. Then, once the flight attendants said passengers were free to do so, he pushed his seat all the way back and fell sound asleep. The next thing he knew, that same flight attendant was shaking him awake and saying that they were preparing to land and he needed to raise his seat back to its full upright and locked position.

Once on the ground, they made their way to long-term parking and drove to their spacious home on Churchill Drive in Huntington Beach's Holly-Seacliff neighborhood. Adam had showered, changed clothes, and was ready to head for the office when the doorbell rang. A glance at the front door surveillance screen showed him that two uniformed police officers were standing on the porch.

"Good afternoon, Officers," Adam said, opening the door.

"Are you Adam Brewster?"

"Yes, I am. How can I help you?"

"We're sorry to have to tell you this, but your father was found deceased in his home earlier today. The investigator in charge of the case is Detective Raymond Horn of the Edmonds Police Department in Edmonds, Washington. He'd like you to give him a call at your earliest convenience. Here's his contact information."

Adam was floored. He had seen his father yesterday for the first time in decades and now he was dead?

"Are you s-sure?" he stammered as the officer handed him a piece of paper. He stared at it but could hardly make sense of what was written there. "How did this happen?"

"I'm so sorry for your loss, Mr. Brewster, but we don't have any details at this time. For those you'll need to speak with Detective Horn."

"Yes, of course," Adam said. "Thank you."

With that, he backed away from the open doorway, shut the door, and then staggered over to the living room sofa.

"Who was that?" Joel asked, emerging from the bedroom while tying the belt of his robe around his waist.

"It was the cops," Adam answered unsteadily, "about my father. He's dead. They came by to tell me and gave me the name and number for a detective in Edmonds."

"Oh, no," Joel said. "How's that even possible?"

"I don't know," Adam said, shaking his head.

"Are you okay?" Joel asked

"I'm not okay," Adam answered, fighting back tears. "Just when I'm supposedly getting my dad back, now I've lost him for good."

"Oh, babe," Joel said. "I'm so very sorry. How can I help? What can I do?"

"Call the office and let them know I won't be coming in this afternoon after all. While you do that, I'll give that detective a call."

Reading from the piece of paper the cops had given him, Adam dialed the number with trembling hands. "Edmonds PD Homicide," a voice answered. "This is Detective Raymond Horn."

Homicide? Adam thought. *Does that mean Dad was murdered?*

"This is Adam Brewster," he said, taking a deep breath. "I understand you wanted me to call you."

"Have uniformed officers stopped by to see you?" Detective Horn asked.

"They just left," Adam replied. "They told me he was dead, but they didn't say how or why. What happened?"

"All I can say at the moment is that earlier today your father was found deceased at home under suspicious circumstances and with obvious signs of homicidal violence," Detective Horn replied. "When did you last see him?"

"Late last night—I'm not sure of the time—when my husband and I left Dad's place in Edmonds. There was a big party for his sixtieth birthday party. We left as it was starting to break up."

"By 'we' you mean you and Joel Franklin?"

"Correct."

"Are you back home in California?"

"Yes, in Huntington Beach. That's where we live. We only got back to the house an hour or so ago."

"Would it be possible for the two of you to come in for a formal interview?" Detective Horn asked. "We're attempting to locate and speak to as many of the party guests as we can."

"That's not really an option right now," Adam answered. "I'm an architect with a multimillion-dollar project that's going out for permits by the end of this month. That's why we flew in for the party late on Saturday and came home on the earliest possible flight today."

"Will you be returning to Washington for the funeral?"

"I suppose," Adam allowed. "When will that be?"

"Depends on when the ME finishes up with the autopsy."

"When's that?"

"Sometime in the next day or two."

"Project or no, I'll for sure be in town for the funeral," Adam agreed. "Will that be soon enough for us to do the interview?"

"It'll have to do," Horn said reluctantly. "In the meantime, did you or Mr. Franklin notice anything off about your father's behavior during the party? Or your stepmother's behavior either, for that matter?"

As a kid, Adam had idolized his father. Before their big blowup, they'd been close. Adam understood that, in going to the birthday party, he had hoped to regain some of that closeness. Knowing now that was impossible, he had to swallow the lump in his throat before he could answer.

"Detective Horn, Saturday was the first time I'd seen either one of them in more than twenty years, so I'm not someone who could tell if something was off or not. I did notice that Clarice probably drank a lot more than she should have, but that wasn't any of my business. By the time she left the party to go upstairs to bed, she was far enough under the influence that Joel actually had to help her negotiate the elevator."

"Did your father and stepmother seem to be at odds about anything? Were there any obvious signs of tension between them? Any sharp words?"

Adam thought about that. Beyond a single perfunctory hug from Clarice when he and Joel had first arrived, he'd had very little further interaction with her. Nor had he observed any exchanges, angry or otherwise, between Clarice and his father. But he had been shocked by his stepmother's appearance. In fact, he'd barely recognized the woman. Back when she'd been his mother's best friend, Clarice Simpson had been a real beauty—nothing short of a blond bombshell. Now she was past her prime and more than slightly overweight. Her facial features had been distorted by too much plastic surgery, and the wig on her head could have used some work.

She'd been at the party, of course, but not really a part of it. She'd spent most of it sitting in isolated splendor in a recliner next to the fireplace in the living room with servers stopping by from time to time to offer various canapés and beverages. Adam had been relieved when Joel, another odd man out as far as the festivities were concerned, had dragged a nearby chair over to where she was sitting and begun chatting with her. That was pure Joel Franklin. The man was kindness personified. But when it came to answering Detective Horn's questions, Adam chose his words carefully.

"I never saw anything out of line," he said. "They weren't especially lovey-dovey during the party, but then why would they be? They've been married close to twenty years. Besides, it was Dad's big day. Maybe Clarice didn't want to steal any of his limelight."

"I've been given to understand that you and your father had been estranged for quite some." Detective Horn suggested. It was a statement, not a question.

Adam sighed. "My leaving home was pretty much a mutual decision. He didn't approve of my lifestyle choices and I didn't approve of his."

"But you'd recently reconciled?"

"Not exactly. I called him at work a number of weeks ago out of the blue, just to test the waters. At the time I had no idea what his reaction would be. Turns out he seemed thrilled to hear from me. Much to my astonishment, he ended up inviting both my husband and me to his upcoming birthday party. But that's the only time we spoke at any length—during that initial phone call. The party was crowded and busy. He introduced me to people—business associates mostly, but it wasn't the time or place for a long-winded father/son chat."

"So you have no idea if there was anything troubling him or worrying him?"

"None at all."

"Were you aware that he had recently consulted with a divorce attorney?"

"No, I was not."

There was a slight pause in the conversation. "So you'll still need me to come in for a formal interview while I'm there for the funeral?" Adam confirmed.

"By all means."

"And how will I know when that is? I had my dad's phone numbers, but I don't have Clarice's."

"You wouldn't be able to reach her by phone even if you had her numbers," Horn replied. "She's currently being held in the King County jail on suspicion of first-degree murder."

Adam was shocked. "Wait, you think Clarice did it?"

"She hasn't been charged yet, but I expect she will be," Detective Horn answered. "Once funeral arrangements are in place, I'll let you know the details so we can set up a time for the interview. I'll also need to speak with Mr. Franklin. If he helped your stepmother onto the elevator late that evening, it's possible he's the last person who was with her during the party."

The call ended then. Adam could hear Joel in the other room, talking to someone on the phone. Meanwhile, Adam Brewster sat alone on the couch and wept, not simply because of what had just happened, but also because of what would never be. He had always thought that someday he'd have his father back in his life. Now he never would.

CHAPTER THREE

SEATTLE, WASHINGTON
TUESDAY, MARCH 14, 2023
9:00 A.M.

Donna Jean Plummer sat in her tiny Wallingford apartment waiting for the cops to show up. They had called her first thing that morning, asking if she would be willing to come to the station to be interviewed.

Since this was a homicide investigation, she couldn't very well say thanks, but no thanks, so naturally she had said yes, even though it meant having to call her Tuesday customers, Mrs. Applebaum and Mrs. Wilson, and let them know that she wouldn't be coming in today.

The TV was off. She'd watched as much of the morning news as she could stomach. Gritting her teeth, she had sat through the first part of a local station's segment concerning the murder—a repeat from the previous evening's newscast—one where the street outside the Brewsters' house was still blocked off with crime scene tape and cop cars were parked every which way. When the reporter started to introduce Mrs. Homewood—the nosy old battle-ax who lived next door to the Brewsters, Donna Jean had switched it off. Dead tired, almost numb from lack of sleep, and with her heart filled with dread concerning the upcoming interview, she simply sat and waited.

Pearl was nowhere to be seen. Donna Jean expected that the cat was hiding under the bed in her bedroom, but at least she was quiet for now, and that was a huge improvement. The poor animal had howled to the high heavens most of the night. No wonder Donna Jean had barely slept.

Sitting in the back of a patrol car, Donna Jean had watched the action unfold in Edmonds the day before. Shortly after Mrs. Brewster had been driven away in an unmarked car, a van marked Animal Control had turned up on the scene. When Donna Jean realized they were about to take poor Pearl away to the pound, she had intervened, telling them that she'd take the distressed animal home with her.

"Fine with me," the guy from the pound had said with a shrug.

At that point the house had been a designated crime scene, and Donna Jean wasn't allowed back inside. A cop had gone in and collected her purse and jacket from the laundry room so she could drive herself home, but they had drawn the line at bringing out any supplies for Pearl. As a result, Donna Jean had been forced to stop off at PetSmart on her way home to pick up a carrier, a litter box, food, and litter for the displaced and still nightmarishly blood-stained kitty. Knowing how skittish the cat was, once she was parked outside her apartment, Donna Jean stuffed Pearl into the carrier before opening the car door.

It had taken time for Donna Jean to lug Pearl and all her gear up two flights of stairs to her third-floor apartment. Once finished with that, she had called Amy, letting her daughter know that she wouldn't be attending the celebratory dinner that night after all, and that someone else would need to retrieve Jacob's birthday cake.

"What's wrong, Mom?" Amy asked, her voice filled with concern. "Are you not feeling well?"

"Something happened at work today," Donna Jean said. "Mr. Brewster died last night."

"Mr. Brewster?" Amy repeated. "Oh, my goodness! You've worked for him for years."

"Yes, I have, and I'm heartsick about it. Please tell Jacob I'm sorry, but I'm just not up to it."

"Of course not," Amy agreed. "I know Jacob will understand, but are you all right? Do you need any help?"

"No," Donna Jean said. "I'm fine."

It turns out she was wrong about that. When it came to bathing Pearl, she really had needed help.

Aware of how skittish the animal could be, Donna Jean didn't open the carrier until they were both inside the bathroom with the door closed behind them and with a bottle of No More Tears shampoo readily at hand. Closing the door had been a good decision. Realizing she was about to be placed in a tub full of water, Pearl had gone into an absolute frenzy—fighting, biting, and doing her best to scratch Donna Jean's arms and hands. Fortunately, Donna Jean had been smart enough to put on a pair of rubber gloves and her long-sleeved bathrobe before tackling the project.

Once covered with shampoo, Pearl had escaped Donna Jean's grasp and leaped out of the tub. After a five-minute chase and with the aid of a bath towel, Donna Jean was at last able to capture the elusive animal and return her to the tub for a final rinse.

Almost a full hour after entering the bathroom, the two of them emerged with the still dripping cat wrapped snugly in yet another damp towel. Exhausted by her part in the ordeal, Donna Jean sank gratefully into her recliner where, upon examination, she was forced to admit a partial defeat. Even now Pearl's ears remained a pale shade of pink. Eventually the cat fell asleep in Donna Jean's lap. At that point, she had mistakenly assumed that the worst was over. Unfortunately, it wasn't, not nearly.

At bedtime, Donna Jean left the litter box and an open-doored carrier in the bathroom, but the moment she closed the door, the animal had launched off into an earsplitting chorus of ungodly yowls. Ten minutes later, with Pearl still howling piteously in the background, Donna Jean's phone rang. The name showing in caller ID was that of Sylvia Portillo, Donna Jean's next-door neighbor. Although the two women knew each other, they weren't exactly the best of pals.

"What the hell's going on over there?" Sylvia demanded. "It sounds like someone's being murdered."

Although the comment came several hours after the fact, it was nonetheless a little too close to the truth for comfort, because someone had indeed been murdered.

"I brought a cat home from the Humane Society," Donna Jean sputtered into the phone. "I'm fostering her."

"How about if you try fostering the damned thing a little more quietly?" Sylvia demanded. "Otherwise I'm not going to get a wink of sleep."

In the end, the only solution had been for Donna Jean to take the bereaved animal into her bed.

By morning, Pearl had vanished. Donna Jean finally located her under the bed. She had been on her knees, using a dish of cat food to try and coax the cat out, to no avail, when Amy called.

"Mom," Amy said excitedly. "I just saw on the news that Mr. Brewster was murdered. Why didn't you say that in the first place?"

Donna Jean thought for a moment before she answered. "I didn't want to wreck Jacob's birthday."

"Are you all right?"

"I'm fine."

That was a lie, but evidently Amy didn't notice.

"All right, then," she said. "Jacob wants to talk to you before he goes to school. Hang on."

"Hey, Grammy," the boy said when he came on the line.

"Happy birthday," Donna Jean said. "Sorry I missed your party."

"That's okay," Jacob replied. "It was only the family party. The big one, the one with all my friends from school, is on the twenty-fifth at the Woodland Park Zoo. Do you want to come to that one?"

"I'll have to see about it," Donna Jean said, "but if I can make it, I will."

"Okay," Jacob said. "Bye."

The next words out of Amy's mouth were addressed to her son. "Go get ready, sweetie. I'll be there in a minute." Then she came back on the line. "I know you usually work for the Brewsters on Fridays and Mondays. Were you there when it happened?"

Donna Jean took a breath. "Not when it happened, but I was there when Mrs. Brewster found the body, and I'm the one who called 911."

"Are you serious?"

"Yes."

"How awful for you. That must have been dreadful. Are you sure you don't want me to drop by?"

"No," Donna Jean said quickly. "No, please. I'm fine."

One of those statements was true. One was not. She certainly didn't want her daughter to be on hand when the cops showed up, but she was anything but fine.

"You go on to work now," Donna Jean said. "I don't want you to be late for school on my account. We'll talk soon."

CHAPTER FOUR

SEATTLE, WASHINGTON
TUESDAY, MARCH 14, 2023
10:00 A.M.

Not surprisingly Detective Monica Burns had arrived on time at ten on the dot. "Ready?" she asked.

"Just a minute," Donna Jean replied without inviting her in. "I have to check on the cat."

She closed the door. In the bedroom she found that the food dish she'd left next to the bed was now empty, but Pearl herself was nowhere to be found. Donna Jean tried calling her but soon gave up. Besides, maybe locking her in the carrier was a bad idea. What if Pearl started yowling again? The last thing Donna Jean needed was to have Sylvia Portillo back on the warpath.

"You be good now," Donna Jean admonished the invisible cat before heading for the door, all the while hoping Pearl would have brains enough to find her way into the bathroom and the litter box.

"How's the kitty doing?" Detective Burns asked as they started down the stairs. "She was in pretty rough shape yesterday."

"She's still upset," Donna Jean replied. "I gave her a bath. She hated it, but she looks a lot better without all the blood on her."

"I'll bet that was fun," Detective Burns observed, opening the back door of an unmarked patrol car and gesturing for Donna Jean to enter.

"Not very," Donna Jean replied.

She crawled into the vehicle and fastened her seat belt. The first thing she noticed was that the doors in the back had no interior handles. This was a police car after all, and she was in the back seat. She had been confined in the same kind of vehicle all those years earlier, and the memory of it made her feel queasy.

Detective Raymond Horn sat in the driver's seat. "Good morning," he said.

"Good morning," Donna Jean responded, but she was thinking *Which one of you is the good cop and which is the bad one?*

This was mid March, so it was rainy and cold in Seattle. No surprises there. They talked about the weather for a moment or two, then Detective Horn, clearly the bad cop and the guy who was evidently in charge, launched into it.

"How long did you work for the Brewsters?" he asked.

Donna Jean understood exactly what was going on here. During the ride to the station they would engage her in seemingly meaningless conversation, every bit of which would be recorded by the vehicle's interior camera. Later they would analyze everything she'd said to see if there were any discrepancies between what she was saying now and what she said later during their "informal" interview. And no matter what they claimed, she understood that both conversations counted as interviews. Donna Jean also knew that, even though no one had bothered to read her her rights, anything she said could and would be used against her in a court of law.

"For a long time," she answered finally. "Over twenty years. I started working for Mr. Brewster before his first wife passed away."

"So you were already working Brewster when he married Clarice Simpson?"

"Yes, I was," Donna Jean replied.

That's when she noticed that her hands were trembling. Donna Jean folded them together and placed them in her lap, hoping that would reduce the involuntary movement, and it helped some.

"Do you have any family?" That seemingly innocuous question came from Detective Burns again. Donna Jean knew that detectives didn't ask questions without already knowing the answers, so they had probably already scoped out her family situation.

"A daughter and a grandson," she answered. "Yesterday was Jacob's sixth birthday. I missed his party."

And I didn't pick up his birthday cake, either.

From her apartment, driving straight up Aurora was the most direct route to Edmonds, but this time around the trip seemed to take forever. The detectives fired off one question after another, with Donna Jean limiting herself to one- and two-word answers wherever possible. For her part, Donna Jean didn't bother asking any questions about the progress of the investigation. She understood that no meaningful answers would be forthcoming.

By the time they let her out of the car and led her through police headquarters and into an interview room, Donna Jean's hands were still shaking, and beads of sweat were forming on the back of her neck.

"The time is ten forty-six a.m.on March 14, 2023," Detective Horn announced formally once they were settled on chairs in the bare bones interview room. "Present today are Detectives Raymond Horn and Monica Burns, along with Ms. Donna Jean Plummer. Ms. Plummer is a witness in the Charles Richard Brewster homicide. This is an informal interview. How exactly are you connected to Clarice and Charles Brewster?"

"I'm their . . . " Donna Jean paused before continuing. "I *was* their housekeeper."

"Let's start by having you walk us through what you did yesterday."

Donna Jean sighed. "I arrived at work around eight-thirty."

"I notice you used the word 'worked', in the past tense."

Donna Jean nodded. "With Mr. Brewster dead and Mrs. Brewster in jail, they don't exactly need a housekeeper at the moment."

Her response seemed to tickle Detective Burns. A frowning Detective Horn, on the other hand, was not amused. Donna Jean went on to describe the remainder of the morning in as much detail as she could remember.

"When you arrived, did someone let you into the house?" he asked.

"I used the garage door opener in my car," Donna Jean told him. "Then I let myself into the house through the door from the garage that leads into the laundry room."

"You used the code to turn off the home's security alarm?"

"I didn't have to," Donna Jean replied. "The alarm wasn't on."

That response seemed to take Detective Horn by surprise. "You're saying the alarm wasn't engaged?"

"Yes."

"Was that unusual?"

"Not really," Donna Jean said. "Sometimes they forget."

Not wanting to speak ill of the dead, she didn't go on to explain that not engaging the security alarm or the outdoor surveillance cameras was business as usual during and after occasions when the Brewsters entertained. She suspected that Mr. Brewster did so prior to parties so his guests wouldn't be caught on camera doing something that was either inappropriate or illegal. As for the alarm? Under the circumstances, it wasn't all that unusual that they'd forgotten to reset it.

"What did you do once you gained entry into the house?"

I'm a housekeeper, Donna Jean wanted to say. *What do you think I did?*

"I cleaned up," she answered aloud. "There had been a big party, so the place was a mess. I took care of the leftovers, gathered up all the trash, and dragged it to the outside garbage bins. After that I loaded the dishwashers, washed and dried whatever required hand-washing. Then I did the laundry. I had just started on the ironing when I heard Mrs. Brewster screaming."

"Did you notice anything unusual while you were doing those chores?"

That came from Detective Burns. Considering Donna Jean was seated in a police interview room with two homicide investigators, she sure as hell wasn't going to bring up the butcher knife that was missing from the kitchen.

"Nothing in particular," she answered.

There it was. She had just out-and-out lied to a cop in the course of a homicide investigation. Wasn't that a crime—a felony even? A new bead of sweat ran down the back of her neck and soaked into the collar of her shirt. The trembling in her hands that had plagued her during the car ride up to Edmonds had abated briefly. Now it returned with a vengeance. Fortunately, since she wasn't in the interview room as an actual suspect, her hand wasn't cuffed to the top of the table. She put both hands in her lap once more so they were safely out of sight.

Detective Horn consulted his notes. "It says here that you placed the 911 call at 11:19 a.m. on the morning of March 13. Is that correct?"

Donna Jean nodded. "I was in the laundry room ironing. As soon as I heard Mrs. Brewster scream, I dropped everything and ran to the bottom of the stairs. That's when I saw her. She was standing at the top of the stairs, covered with blood, waving a knife around, and screaming at the top of her lungs."

"What did she say to you?"

"She said that Chuck—Mr. Brewster—was dead, that she had stabbed him."

That was the first thing Mrs. Brewster had said—that she had stabbed him. Later, Mrs. Brewster had said she must have done it, which meant that she didn't really remember any of it. Did that mean she had done it in her sleep? Yes, she had been holding the damned knife, but Donna Jean knew from things Mr. Brewster had said on occasion, that by the time Mrs. Brewster went to bed at night, she was often too smashed to walk straight. That's why he'd had the elevator installed, so she wouldn't have to navigate the stairs while under the influence. If she'd been that drunk on the night of the murder, she might not have remembered exactly what had happened, but how could someone that inebriated have been steady enough on her feet to stab someone to death? And once she did it, how the hell could she fall back asleep as though nothing had happened?

"What came next?"

"I ran up the stairs. When I got to her, she was waving the knife around like crazy, so I took it away from her and put it out of reach."

"You're saying you actually handled the murder weapon?" Detective Horn asked. "With your bare hands?"

Donna Jean nodded. "I was afraid someone was going to get hurt."

"When officers arrived on scene, were you the one who allowed them into the residence?"

"Yes."

"Did they enter through the garage or through the front door?"

"The front door."

"Was it locked or unlocked?"

"Locked," Donna Jean answered. "There's a dead bolt. The key was right there in the door, but I had to go downstairs to let them in."

"At the time, besides you, was Mrs. Brewster the only other individual in the home?"

"Yes," Donna Jean answered.

"Where was she while you were doing all that cleaning?"

"Upstairs, asleep. At first I thought Mr. Brewster was sleeping, too, because his car was still in the garage. But as time went on, I thought maybe he'd gone out of town and taken a limo to the airport. That's what he usually does. As for Mrs. Brewster? She's a night owl. She goes to bed late and wakes up late."

"Our officers saw no signs of forced entry. Did you?"

That's when Donna Jean remembered the bottle cork, the one she'd found in the track of the patio slider. Until Detective Horn asked about it, she had forgotten about it completely. That could explain the lack of forced entry. But at the time Donna Jean found it, she had simply slipped the cork into the pocket of her apron, and that's where it remained. If she mentioned it now, would they think she was somehow involved in what had happened? And if she didn't mention it now and they found out about the cork later, would they accuse her of concealing evidence? And if she told them about it, what if her fingerprints were the only ones to be found on it, what then?

"No, I didn't," Donna Jean allowed. "I didn't see anything like that."

Another tiny trickle of sweat dribbled down her neck. She'd just told another lie.

"Tell us about the Brewsters' relationship. Did you ever witness any quarrels between them?" Detective Horn asked.

"Never," Donna Jean said. That was the truth, but most of the time when she was there, Mr. Brewster had been at work and Mrs. Brewster had been asleep and wouldn't appear downstairs until after Donna Jean finished her cleaning and was headed to the grocery store.

"Were you aware that Mr. Brewster had recently consulted with a divorce attorney?"

That one took Donna Jean by surprise. Clarice was a difficult woman, and Donna Jean had often wondered why Mr. Brewster put up with her nonsense, but no one had ever mentioned the possibility of an impending divorce.

"I had no idea," Donna Jean replied. "If that was the case, I knew nothing about it."

"Isn't it likely Mrs. Brewster would be better off as a widow than she would be as a divorcée?" Detective Horn asked.

"I suppose," Donna Jean said thoughtfully, although being a widow had never done her a bit of good.

"What was your relationship with Mr. Brewster like?"

"Mine?" Donna Jean asked. "I cleaned his house and did the weekly grocery shopping. That's the extent of our relationship. I was his employee, and he gave me a paycheck."

"But isn't it true that he also gave you a vehicle?" Detective Burns asked with a bit of a gotcha smirk. "And a brand-new one at that. Doesn't that strike you as being overly generous?"

Just before Christmas the previous year, when the whole Seattle Metro area had been encased in a thick layer of ice, Donna Jean had been on her way to work one morning, driving slowly and carefully in her aging Prius, when a nutcase in a junky four-wheel drive Jeep Cherokee had come sliding through the red light at an intersection and slammed right into her. Donna Jean wasn't hurt, and neither was the driver of the other vehicle, but her car was totaled. Naturally the guy driving didn't have a valid driver's license, and he didn't have any car insurance, either.

When she had called Mr. Brewster to tell him what happened, he'd actually left work to come pick her up. For the next two weeks, she'd taken the bus to and from Edmonds—a grueling hour and a half commute each way. By then the insurance company had given her a check for the full Bluebook value of her dead Prius. That was a problem because Bluebook on an eight-year-old Prius didn't amount to much, especially at a time when purchase prices on used vehicles were through the roof and totally out of range of Donna Jean's limited buying power.

She had resigned herself to the fact that, for the foreseeable future, she'd be busing it, but then December 26 came along. Since Christmas had fallen on a Sunday, most people had Monday off, but not Donna Jean. Monday was her day to clean the Brewsters' house, and since they'd had a holiday extravaganza at their house on Christmas Day, she already knew it would be a busy one.

The bus had let her out on the main drag, and she'd trudged her way two steep uphill blocks to get to their house. As she walked up the driveway, she noticed a vehicle with a massive red ribbon parked in front of the garage. Her initial assumption was that Mrs. Brewster had been given a new car for Christmas, although, when she saw it was a RAV4, it occurred to Donna Jean that one of those didn't seem to be quite up to Mrs. Brewster's upscale standards.

That's when Mr. Brewster had met Donna Jean at the door, handed her a key fob, and told her the car in the driveway was hers, free and clear. She had been utterly dumbfounded.

"Why would you do such a thing?" she had asked.

"Because you've worked for me for a very long time," he told her, "and because I think you deserve it."

But now, because Mr. Brewster had given her the vehicle, did the cops somehow suspect that Donna Jean had been involved in some kind of intimate relationship with the man? Maybe they thought he'd given her the car as a bribe, as a way to keep her from spilling the beans to his wronged wife. Or maybe they thought she was blackmailing him.

"He gave it to me because he was a kind man and knew I needed a vehicle to get back and forth to work," Donna Jean declared at last, maybe a little more forcefully than she'd intended. "A guy with no insurance crashed into my car, and I couldn't afford to replace it. I think Mr. Brewster felt sorry for me because riding the bus to get to their place took so long."

"You worked for the family for more than twenty years?" Detective Burns asked.

He'd already asked that. Instead of answering aloud, Donna Jean simply nodded.

"And yet you always refer to him as Mr. Brewster," Detective Burns said. "Is there a reason for that?"

"The reason is I know my place," Donna Jean replied. "It's a sign of respect."

"It also might be a way of putting distance between the two of you."

This whole line of questioning was getting on Donna Jean's nerves. It sounded as though he was still under the impression that there had been some kind of love triangle going on here and that Donna Jean was somehow responsible for Mr. Brewster's death. The whole idea was outrageous.

"That's because there was distance between us," Donna Jean spouted back. "Lots of it."

This wasn't Donna Jean Plummer's first rodeo, as far police interviews were concerned. She was aware that she shouldn't have reacted that way. They were getting to her. She knew it, and so did they.

"So there was nothing romantic going on between you and Mr. Brewster?"

"Nothing at all."

"It says here that you told one of the responding officers that one of the knives was missing from the knife block in the kitchen. In view of the fact that the missing knife turned out to be the murder weapon, it seems odd that you would notice something like that."

"What's odd about it?" Donna Jean replied. "That's what housekeepers are supposed to do—keep track of what's there and what isn't. I was afraid someone—maybe someone from the catering crew—had either packed it up or dropped it in the trash by mistake. The problem was, by then the garbage truck had already come and gone."

"But since you handled the knife, are we likely to find your DNA on the murder weapon?"

"I already told you that I took the knife away from Mrs. Brewster. But even if I hadn't, my DNA would probably be on it anyway. In fact, I'd be surprised if it wasn't. After all, I'm the one who does the dishes, and I don't use rubber gloves for that. My DNA is probably on every knife in the house along with every plate, glass, and piece of silverware."

"How would you describe your relationship with Clarice?"

That was Detective Burns again, stepping in and changing the subject, probably in an effort to put Donna Jean at a disadvantage.

"I worked there two days a week for years," Donna Jean said firmly, "but Mrs. Brewster and I weren't friends."

Donna Jean could have added that Mrs. Brewster wasn't a particularly nice person and didn't have many friends. Most of the guests who came and went from the home were friends of Mr. Brewster, while Mrs. Brewster was more or less a hermit, but Donna Jean held her tongue on that score.

"What was her reaction when her husband gave you that new car?"

"I don't remember her reacting one way or the other."

By then Donna Jean was losing patience. She'd already been in the interview room for the better part of two hours. Why the hell were they putting her through the wringer? She was a witness, for Pete's sake. She wasn't the one who had been found holding a murder weapon and covered in blood. Were the cops trying to claim that she was the actual perpetrator?

"Am I under arrest?" Donna Jean asked.

"No," Detective Horn said. "Of course not. We're just gathering additional information."

"So can I go now?" Donna Jean asked.

"Of course, if you wish," Detective Horn said. "But if you don't mind, would you be willing to give us a DNA swab so we'll be able to eliminate you as a suspect?"

There was no reason Donna Jean had to make life easy for them. "No," she said firmly. "I don't believe that would be in my best interests."

"What about a lie detector test? Would you consider taking one of those?"

The idea of taking a lie detector test was terrifying. She'd taken one of those once, and even though she'd told the absolute truth, the operator had told her she'd been found to be "evasive."

"Absolutely not. And I'm not turning my phone over to you, either. If you're going to arrest me, do it, but I'm not saying another word without my attorney being present."

Expecting to be placed under arrest, she stood up and looked Detective Horn straight in the eye. He blinked first. "Very well," he said before adding, "The interview concluded at one forty-five p.m."

The drive back to Donna Jean's apartment took every bit as long as the one to Edmonds had, but this one was conducted in absolute silence. Not one of the three individuals riding in the vehicle said a single word.

Back in her apartment, worn to a nub, Donna Jean sank into her easy chair and dropped her purse on the floor at her feet. She was sitting there with her eyes closed when Pearl silently leaped into her lap.

"Thank you," she said, holding the animal close. "I really needed that."

It turns out Pearl did, too. A minute or so later, she settled into Donna Jean's lap and began to purr.

CHAPTER FIVE

HUNTINGTON BEACH, CALIFORNIA
WEDNESDAY, MARCH 15, 2023
6:00 P.M.

On Wednesday afternoon, when Adam finally made it home through the nightmarish traffic on the 405, he drove into the garage and was greeted by the welcome aroma of a charcoal fire burning in the Weber grill out on the patio. Joel was grilling steaks for dinner, and after two nightmarish days of fighting a never-ending permit battle, a medium-rare New York strip was just what the doctor ordered.

Adam found Joel in the kitchen, slicing and dicing veggies for a salad. "How'd it go today?" he asked cheerfully, handing Adam a glass filled with a dark red cabernet.

"We're still not there yet," Adam said. "The permit deadline is the end of next week. After that, there will be a whole new set of code changes. If we end up having to comply with those, we won't be able to start construction on time."

"You'll get there," Joel assured him. "You always do."

"How's the writing going?" Adam asked in return.

"Medium," Joel replied. "One step forward, two steps back."

Joel Franklin was a trained RN. That was how he and Adam had met. When Adam's first long-term partner, Michael Lafferty, had been diagnosed with ALS, Michael had been determined to spare Adam the inevitable burden of caregiving that was barreling down the road at them. Before he'd even told Adam about the diagnosis, Michael had gone online looking for a private-duty nurse who would function as their live-in assistant. Joel, a recent arrival from Texas who had yet to be licensed as an RN in California, had filled the bill admirably. Joel had helped care for Michael over the awful course of the next several years, but then, once Michael was gone, Joel had stayed on.

Joel was the real reason Adam had finally broken down and called his father after all that time—because now he understood all too well what must have happened to his father. In the face of losing his wife, Chuck Brewster had turned to Clarice for comfort and solace. Having done exactly the same thing with Joel after Michael's passing, Adam felt he was no longer in any position to cast stones.

Michael had earned a fortune as a screenwriter in Hollywood. After Michael's death and Adam's and Joel's subsequent marriage, it soon became clear that it wouldn't be financially necessary for Joel to resume his nursing career. At that point, he, like countless other Southern Californians, had set his sights on writing a screenplay. Although Joel and his writing partner, a guy named Marc Atherton, worked on the project every day, Adam had yet to see so much as a rough draft. Joel claimed it wasn't yet ready for prime time, and Adam understood that, too. When he was designing a home or an office building, he didn't like showing the project to anyone until he had brought the project to a point where Adam himself was satisfied with it.

They had finished dinner and were in the process of cleaning up when a call came in on Adam's cell phone from an unidentified number in Edmonds, Washington.

"Adam Brewster?" the caller asked.

"Yes, who's this?"

"Detective Horn again with Edmonds PD. I wanted to call and give you an update."

"What's going on?"

"This morning at her preliminary hearing, your stepmother pled not guilty to the charge of first-degree murder in regard to your father's death. She was denied bail on the grounds of being a flight risk and is being held in the King County jail. I just got off the phone with Bill McCreedy of the McCreedy Funeral Home here in Edmonds. Your father's funeral service will be held at two p.m. on Tuesday afternoon."

Adam allowed himself a deep breath. Ever since he'd heard about what happened, he hadn't been able to get his head around the idea that Clarice Simpson Brewster could possibly be a cold-blooded killer, but if she was being held without bond, she probably was.

"What was the cause of death?"

"He was stabbed in the back—seventeen times."

Seventeen, Adam thought, remembering how drunk Clarice had been. *If she could barely walk, how could she possibly have done something like that?* But then, after a pause, he asked. "Who made the funeral arrangements?" Adam certainly hadn't been consulted.

"Your father's attorney was in charge of those," Horn replied. "Can I expect that you'll be in attendance?"

"Yes," Adam replied. "Joel and I will both be there."

"Once you make your travel arrangements, please let me know so I can set up interviews with you both. If you can fly in early enough on Tuesday, we can get the interviews out of the way before the service."

"All right," Adam said. "As soon as we have our flight reservations, I'll let you know."

"What flight reservations?" Joel asked once Adam was off the phone.

"That was the detective from Edmonds. Dad's funeral will be on Tuesday afternoon at two p.m. Since Detective Horn wants to interview both of us, I told him we'll be there, hopefully in time to do the interviews before the funeral so we can fly home once that's over. So after dinner, how about if you jump on the computer and check for tickets? In the meantime, I'd better lock myself in the office and go to work. Those permits aren't going to get themselves submitted on their own."

CHAPTER SIX

SEDONA, ARIZONA
THURSDAY, MARCH 16, 2023
4:00 P.M.

Ali Reynolds filled in the last line of the pdf she was working on and hit save. Then, with another few strokes on her keyboard, she flattened the document, typed in the CPA's email address, and pressed send. With that, and more than an hour before the five o'clock deadline, the most onerous task of her CFO job at High Noon Enterprises was done at last. The tax documents were out of her hair and in the hands of their CPA. As the whoosh of sent mail sounded in her ears, she leaned back in her chair, closed her eyes, and allowed herself to relax, seemingly for the first time in weeks.

With B. away in DC for the next two days, she fully expected to go home and reward herself by spending some quality time in her soaking tub before heading out to watch her granddaughter's basketball game later on that evening. Because she'd been so focused on getting the package off to the accountant, her office door was still closed. Now a light tap on the door roused Ali from her momentary reverie.

"Come in," she said.

The door cracked open, and Shirley Malone, High Noon's longtime receptionist/secretary, poked her head inside. Ali could tell at a glance that the woman was upset.

"Is something wrong?" Ali asked.

"There's an operator on the phone saying that someone named Clarice Brewster is calling collect from the King County Correctional Facility in Seattle, Washington," Shirley said.

Ali's whole body snapped to attention. Clarice Brewster wasn't someone Ali knew personally, but she certainly recognized the name. Clarice had been B.'s first wife.

Why would she be calling here? Ali wondered. *What the hell is going on?*

"Thank you, Shirley," Ali replied aloud. "I'll take the call in here, but please close the door."

Ali's voice may have sounded unruffled, but as she picked up the receiver, her hand was trembling.

"Yes," she said to the operator. "I'll accept the charges." Then, when the call went through, she added, "This is Ali Reynolds speaking. How can I help you?"

"I asked to speak to B."

"He isn't here at the moment, but I'm his wife," Ali replied calmly. "What seems to be the problem?"

"My husband's dead, and I'm in jail, suspected of first-degree murder," Clarice shot back. "That's the problem!"

Ali allowed herself a moment to process that information. As far as she knew, Clarice's second husband was Chuck Brewster, B.'s former partner at VGI—Video Games International, a company the two of them had founded together years earlier. Ali knew about B.'s first marriage, of course, but it wasn't something he dwelled on. So, although Ali was familiar with the broad strokes of what had happened, she was thin on details. The marriage had ended and his partnership with Brewster had been dissolved when B. discovered that Chuck and Clarice had been carrying on an affair behind his back. But all that had happened years earlier. Why would Clarice be reaching out to B. now?

"Where is he?" Clarice continued. "He's the one I need to talk to."

Ali remembered B. telling her once that Clarice had always been pushy. Seemingly that was still the case, but if the woman was calling looking for someone to post bail, Ali was the person she needed to talk to.

"Unfortunately, B.'s out of town on business and currently unavailable," Ali replied calmly. "What exactly is your situation?"

"Didn't you hear what I said?" Clarice responded. "I'm in jail and charged with a murder I didn't commit. I pled not guilty at my preliminary hearing, but the judge refused to grant bail. My attorney suggested that if they offer me a plea deal down to murder in the second degree, that I might be better off taking it than rolling the dice with a jury. That's why I need to talk to B."

"As I said," Ali responded, "he's out of town at the moment, and I won't be able to speak to him until later tonight."

"Give me his number, then," Clarice said. "I'll call him directly."

Like hell you will, Ali thought. *No way am I passing his number along to you!*

"I'll discuss your situation with him later," Ali repeated firmly. "Please call back tomorrow and ask for me. My name is Ali."

"But . . . " Clarice objected.

"Sorry," Ali said. "I have another call coming in. We can speak again tomorrow."

Needless to say, there was no other call. Once the receiver was back in its cradle, Ali sat staring at the phone on her desk as though it had suddenly turned into a coiled and lethal reptile. It took several minutes for her to pull herself together.

With Clarice in jail and accused of murder, this was indeed something she needed to discuss with B. sooner rather than later, but not until she knew a whole lot more about the situation than she did right now. It was 6:00 p.m. in DC. She knew that B. and Lance had plans for that evening. Rather than call B., she picked up her cell phone and keyed in the code that offered her direct access to Frigg, Stu Ramey's pet AI, still operating out of the vast array of GPUs that occupied most of the floor space in Stu's Village of Oak Creek bachelor pad.

"Good afternoon, Ali," Frigg said when she came on the line. "I hope you're having a pleasant afternoon."

Not exactly, Ali thought. "Thank you," she said aloud, "but I could use some help."

"How can I be of assistance?"

"I'd like you to research the homicide of someone named Charles (Chuck) Brewster somewhere in the Seattle area."

"Date of death?" Frigg inquired.

"No idea, but it must have occurred fairly recently. Clarice Brewster has just been arrested and charged with murder."

"Her relationship to the deceased?"

"She's his wife."

"Statistically speaking, that's not surprising," Frigg reported. "As far as homicides are concerned, spouses are often found to be the perpetrators. Where do you wish me to send the material?"

The last thing Ali was interested in right then was hearing more statistical information on spousal homicides.

"Please forward the information to my cell," Ali said. "But don't send it along until I give you the go-ahead. I'm going to a basketball game tonight, and I don't want my phone blowing up while I'm sitting in the gym."

"Very well," Frigg replied. "Go Scorpions."

That made Ali laugh. The AI had only recently become aware that human beings often took a personal interest in school sporting events and rivalries. While sorting through applicants for two open positions at High Noon, the individuals Frigg had unknowingly placed at the top of her list—and the ones who were now High Noon's newest employees—happened to come from schools that were longtime athletic rivals—Arizona State University and the University of Arizona. When the outcome of their traditional Thanksgiving game had caused some uproar in the lab, Stu had directed Frigg to do a quick study into both the histories of enduring collegiate and high school sports rivalries in the U.S. As a result of that latest bit of deep learning, the AI was now aware that athletic teams at Sedona's Red Rock High School were referred to as the Scorpions.

"Thank you," Ali said. "I'll be there cheering them on."

A few minutes later and in somewhat better spirits, Ali turned off the lights in her office and left. It was late enough in the day that Shirley's desk was already empty. That was a relief. Until she knew more about the situation in Seattle and had brought B. into the picture, Ali was happy to escape without having to provide any further information about that unsettling phone call.

After parking in the garage at their home on Manzanita Hills Road, Ali let herself into the kitchen and was struck by the dreadful silence that greeted her. Ten years earlier, during the lead-up to B. and Ali's wedding in Vegas, Ali's twin grandkids, Colin and Colleen, had been instrumental in rescuing a stray dog found wandering in the casino's parking lot, a long-haired miniature dachshund they had subsequently named Bella.

For the past decade, Bella's scampering paws clicking on the kitchen tile had welcomed Ali every time she returned home. Two weeks earlier, at an age estimated to be sixteen or seventeen, the dog's genetic back deterioration had suddenly left her a paraplegic, and Ali and B. had been forced to make the difficult decision to have their beloved pet put down. Her cremated remains were now in an urn and tucked into the corner of their garden Bella had loved the most—a shady spot under the gnarled trunk of the aged wisteria that covered their front porch.

With B. out of town, Alonzo Rivera, their majordomo, had asked if he could take a few days off to visit relatives in Phoenix. As a result, Ali had the house completely to herself. She made her way into the home's master bath and turned on the faucet in the soaking tub. A few minutes later, as she eased herself into the steamy water, it wasn't quite the relaxing, soothing experience she had anticipated. Instead, she spent the whole time puzzling over the call from Clarice.

Being arrested for murder was certainly serious, but she and B. had been divorced for ages, so why would Clarice be calling him for help? Ali knew for sure that B. regarded his failed marriage and the simultaneous loss of his best friend as one of the worst disappointments of his life, but as far as Ali knew, her husband had had nothing to do with his former wife for years. If B. had wanted Clarice to be able to contact him directly, he would have given her his number. But before Ali mentioned anything about the situation to B., she wanted to have Frigg's assessment of the situation in hand.

After the tub water cooled, rather than reheating it, Ali climbed out, dried off, and got dressed, topping her outfit with a purple, silver, and black Red Rock High signature sweatshirt. As she headed for the gym, Ali was determined to put the issue of Clarice Brewster out of her head for the time being.

Once grandkids had shown up in her life, Ali had done her best to be part of their lives, and that included attending school and sporting events whenever possible. Colleen was the athlete in the family. Although only a freshman in high school, she was already the star for Red Rock's varsity girls' basketball team where her mother, Athena, was head coach.

When she was little, Colleen had served as the team mascot for the girls' basketball program. She'd even had her own uniform—number 000, but she didn't remain a bystander for long. By the time she was in fifth grade, Colleen could dribble as well as any of the girls on the freshman team. Once her dad put up a hoop in their driveway, she spent hours every day shooting baskets.

Colleen's twin brother, Colin, was her exact opposite and didn't have an athletic bone in his body. He preferred hanging out around his father's art studio to playing ball of any kind. The eight-inch-tall metal dinosaur that stood in pride of place on Ali's desk at work was a creature Colin had crafted out of leftover bits of metal he'd gleaned from the floor of his father's studio.

That night, while Athena's husband, Chris, and Colin did their best to keep Colleen's five-year-old little brother, Logan, from racing out onto the court, Ali sat there enjoying the game without giving Clarice Brewster a single thought. The game turned out to be a nail-biter. Sedona won by a single point when Colleen sank a three-pointer from mid-court in the last two seconds of the game. Once the game was over, and Colleen finished being hugged by her ecstatic teammates and shaking hands with her opponents, she trotted over to the sidelines to hug Ali.

"Thanks for coming, Gram," she beamed. "You're the best."

There were a lot of things Ali Reynolds was thankful for, and being somebody's beloved "Gram" was very close to the top of that list.

CHAPTER SEVEN

LOS ANGELES, CALIFORNIA
THURSDAY, MARCH 16, 2023
6:00 P.M.

Camille Lee was a bundle of nerves. For the past three years she had been running point on outside sales for High Noon Enterprises. She'd been drafted into the position when, just prior to the pandemic, her boss, B. Simpson, had been sidelined by a serious automobile collision. Unexpectedly, she had been forced to pinch-hit for him at an important international cybersecurity conference in London, and she had come away a clear winner. Not only had she dazzled her fellow attendees at the conference, she'd brought home some brand-new customers as well.

Once aware that Cami was more than capable of producing sales results, B. had persuaded her to assume the company's outside sales responsibilities, allowing him to step away from what had been years of constant travel. Now he was back in the lab doing what he loved most: creating new technology.

These days, Camille Lee was the one racking up frequent flyer miles while bringing home the business. During the pandemic much of her customer interaction had been done virtually. Now that Covid was becoming less of a threat, she was doing more work on a face-to-face basis, not only as far as new customers were concerned, but also for touching base with established ones. That's what she had been doing all week in Southern California—staying in the Lancaster Hotel, a boutique establishment near LAX, and doing meet and greets with old customers as well as prospective ones. Tonight was going to be one of the latter—in spades!

In a little under an hour she was scheduled to go downstairs and host a lavish dinner with her most influential potential clients to date—a delegation of executives from Dozo International, a sprawling conglomerate based in Japan.

Over the past several years, the entire world had been plagued by cases of ransomware attacks in which gangs of black hats hacked into computer networks large and small, disabling them, and then demanding cash payments in order to restore the systems. High Noon had established quite a reputation for repelling this form of cyberterrorism. Their proprietary GHOST technology allowed them to track ransomware demands back to their original sources, where they were able to disable any devices or networks involved in such attacks.

The previous year, Dozo International, after being targeted in a ransomware incident, had coughed up a cool million euros in order to regain the use of their computer system. Now they had made tentative approaches about coming to High Noon for help. If Cami could reel them in, Dozo would be her largest new account ever. With that in mind, this evening she was hosting a private dinner for a delegation of eleven Dozo company executives who had flown in from Tokyo specifically for the meeting.

The Lancaster, a privately owned hotel gem, had become Cami's home away from home in the L.A. area. It was a relatively small place with seventy-five guest units, all of them junior suite rooms, and with a reputation for first-class service. The hotel came complete with a top-notch restaurant along with an assortment of conference rooms and fitness facilities. Its proximity to the airport made it perfect for hosting international clients. By now Cami had stayed there often enough that she had befriended almost all the staff, including the hotel's head chef, Robert Chin.

Cami's grandfather, Liu Wei Ling, had been a well-known and highly respected restaurateur in San Francisco's China Town, an establishment Robert Chin had often visited with his parents as a child growing up in the area. When Robert learned that Cami was actually Louie Ling's granddaughter, he'd been blown away, and they had become friends. Cami and Robert were on the same page in terms of language, heritage, and background. Whenever Cami turned up on the hotel's room reservation list, Robert saw to it that she was treated like visiting royalty.

With the Dozo execs coming to town, Cami knew that offering them Japanese food prepared by a Chinese chef wasn't going to cut it, so earlier that week she and Robert had put their heads together and devised a deluxe American steakhouse dining experience, which would be served in one of the hotel's several conference rooms.

Appetizers would include Dungeness crab cakes, spicy buttered shrimp, and seared foie gras. Then, after a table-side-prepared Caesar salad, the entree course would include individually prepared eight-ounce USDA prime filet mignons accompanied by a lobster tail, lobster mashed potatoes, and crispy Brussels sprouts. Dessert would consist of cherries jubilee, again prepared table-side. Naturally there would be an open bar.

But the upcoming dinner also explained why Cami was a nervous wreck. She needed everything to go right in a situation where countless things could easily go wrong. She dressed in a conservative navy-blue suit with a demure white blouse, although there was nothing conservative about her four-inch-high heels. Finally, properly attired and made up, she headed downstairs, making a pass through the kitchen on her way to the conference room that had been transformed into a private dining room.

Chef Robert greeted her arrival in his kitchen with a passable wolf whistle accompanied by a fist bump.

"Not to worry," he told Cami on her way past. "We've got this."

The hotel staff were all on full alert. As soon as Cami showed her face in the lobby, she was escorted to the reserved room, arriving a good ten minutes early. Her guests, on the other hand, arrived ten minutes late, making their way across the terrazzo-tiled lobby in a tightly knit group. They wore almost identical suits and walked in a kind of lockstep that made them look like a single creature with many legs. That thought alone meant that the smile Cami wore when she stepped into the lobby to greet them was completely genuine.

She had devoted the entire day to studying the dossiers Frigg had prepared on each of her expected guests. Based on the accompanying photographs, she recognized the leader of the pack, Koichi Kawamura, on sight. Dozo's CEO was a man in his mid-fifties with a degree in engineering from the University of Tokyo, as well as an MBA in executive education from the Harvard Business School. He was the divorced father of two. His son, Kenji, was a media sensation in Japan, known for his three-dimensional sidewalk art, while his daughter, Suki, was a third-year resident at the Johns Hopkins School of Medicine.

"Good evening," she said, as they came within speaking distance. "I'm so glad you could join me."

The group stopped as one. After handing Cami a business card, Mr. Kawamura replied in Japanese with a murmured greeting, "Thank you for having us."

As part of her new outside sales responsibilities, Cami had spent a good deal of the Covid shutdown studying both Japanese and German, adding those to the roster of languages she spoke fluently, including French and Chinese. On the road, her language skills made her a force to be reckoned with. She understood at once what Mr. Kawamura had just said to her, but at that point, a young man who was at least a good decade Cami's junior stepped forward and offered a quick translation. Cami recognized him from Frigg's dossiers as Yoshi Mashima, a recent graduate of UCLA, who was attending the dinner as the visitors' official translator.

With a Harvard MBA under his belt, Cami suspected Mr. Kawamura spoke perfect English and had no need of any translation assistance, and neither did she, but with the possibility that some of the other guests weren't as skilled in English as the head honcho was, Cami accepted the translator's presence with good grace. After studying the business card respectfully, she bowed in Mr. Kawamura's direction, smiled, and said in English, "Please, do come in."

She greeted each of the remaining guests in a similar fashion. Once everyone had entered the room, she followed suit. People had arranged themselves around the large square cherrywood table on which sat a floral centerpiece and place mats with a cherry blossom motif. Mr. Kawamura was seated with his translator on his left. Cami's designated chair was to Mr. Kawamura's right.

During the course of the dinner, conversation between Cami and Mr. Kawamura consisted mostly of inconsequential pleasantries. Where did she live? How long had she worked for High Noon? Was she married? Did she have any children? Had she ever traveled to Japan? She returned the favor by asking about his education and his family situation, as well as his long background with Dozo International.

As the meal progressed, the cumbersome and entirely unnecessary translation process made it possible for Cami to eavesdrop on other strings of conversation around the table, all of which were conducted in Japanese. Unaware that Cami understood every word, several guests didn't hold back on taking issue with the food, and they were critical of Cami as well. Why were they dealing with such a young girl? Wasn't their business important enough for Mr. Simpson himself to be here in person? Dozo should be dealing with a real decision-maker rather than someone's know-nothing secretary.

Cami's disgruntled dinner guests were by no means the first of Cami's business acquaintances to make the mistake underestimating her and blithely assuming that, since she was American, Cami Lee spoke nothing but English. As she continued her cordial three-way conversation with their boss, Cami had no difficulty maintaining her composure because she knew that when it came time to make the official proposal, she'd be adding in an extra percentage or two and chalking it up to their indiscretions.

It wasn't until after the table-side cherries jubilee had disappeared and the scotch and sake came out that the meeting finally turned serious. That's when Mr. Kawamura finally broached the subject of Dozo International's ransomware problem, once again with the entire conversation being conducted through the interpreter.

"That must have been very costly," Cami observed.

Kawamura nodded. "It was," he admitted. "We're in the process of holding our current cybersecurity provider liable for some of the damages, but they were completely outmaneuvered when it came to dealing with the problem. We had no choice but to pay up."

"Which is why you're now coming to High Noon?" Cami asked.

Kawamura nodded. "We want to know what you have to offer and how that differs from what other cybersecurity firms are able to provide."

"What we have is proprietary technology that makes it possible for us to track ransomware demands back to their original sources and then turn the tables on the perpetrators. If they don't release the targeted material, we're capable of disabling their equipment and blasting them out of existence."

"So you blackmail the blackmailers," Mr. Kawamura commented.

Cami smiled. "More or less. And once our clients have their networks back up and running, we turn what we've learned over to law enforcement. Our first order of business is getting our customers back on track. We leave it up to the authorities to put the perpetrators out of business permanently."

It was after eleven when Mr. Kawamura called a halt to the meeting. "This has all been very interesting," he said. "What kind of information would you need from us in order for you to make a formal proposal?"

Clearly the other guys in attendance had been brought along strictly for show. They were not part of the decision-making process. Mr. Kawamura was the one in charge.

"I'll be happy to send you an email tomorrow morning outlining our requirements," she replied with a smile.

"Very well," he said, once Yoshi had translated. "Please do so. And thank you for your hospitality. The meal was splendid."

"You're very welcome," she replied. "I'm so glad you enjoyed it."

Once he rose, everyone else did as well, but the other guests waited until Cami and Mr. Kawamura had left the room before filing out themselves. Their departing gestures, the formal bowing and smiling, were every bit as insincere as their initial greetings had been. Cami couldn't have cared less because she knew she had won that round fair and square.

Once the Dozo crew left the hotel, Cami went directly to her room. Normally she would have gone back downstairs to visit the hotel's fitness center before going to bed, but not this time. Knowing she had three additional appointments the next day, she went straight to bed.

Unfortunately, sleep eluded her. Like Eliza Doolittle in *My Fair Lady*, she was too wound up to sleep. After a couple of hours of tossing and turning, she got up, opened her laptop, and sent Mr. Kawamura an email laying out what information would be needed in order for High Noon to provide a detailed proposal. By the time she finished, it was close to 3:00 a.m. Finally, she was able to go back to bed and fall asleep.

CHAPTER EIGHT

SEDONA, ARIZONA
THURSDAY, MARCH 16, 2023
9:00 P.M.

Ali was on her way home from the game when B. called from his hotel in DC. He sounded tired.

"Are you okay?" she asked.

"It's a lot later here than it is back home," B. responded. "Once Lance got talking with that roomful of high-powered geeks, wild horses couldn't drag him away."

"I'll bet," Ali said with a laugh.

Shortly before the pandemic, Lance had married Lauren Harper, who had then been a deputy with the Yavapai County Sheriff's Department. She had since been promoted to the rank of detective.

"When you have a toddler at home and a wife on maternity leave with baby number two, being able to sit around and hash things out with a bunch of brainy tech guys probably felt like being on vacation."

"Exactly," B. replied. "So how did the game go? Did the Scorpions win?"

"Colleen pulled it out with a three-pointer from mid-court with two seconds to go. They won thirty-one to thirty."

"That's my girl!" B. replied.

B. had no children of his own, but anyone seeing him interact with Chris and Athena's kids would never have suspected that they weren't blood kin. His attachment to them was undeniably genuine.

"Speaking of capable girls," B. continued, "any word on how Cami is doing with the Dozo people?"

Ali glanced at her watch. "The dinner wasn't scheduled to start until seven, so it's still too early to hear from her. She believes in being prepared, however, and I know she intended to spend most of the day studying the dossiers Frigg prepared on Dozo itself and on all the people expected to show up this evening."

"Then we'll just have to hold our respective breaths," B. said.

"Yes, we will," Ali agreed, "but in the meantime, there's something else I have to tell you about."

"What is it?" B. asked.

"You're not driving, are you?""

"Driving? Of course not, I'm in my room, sitting on the bed. Why? What's wrong?"

Ali sighed before launching into it. "You had a call from Clarice today."

Her statement was followed by a moment of stunned silence. "Clarice, as in my ex-wife, Clarice?" he asked at last.

"Exactly," Ali returned. "The very one."

"Are you frigging kidding me?" B. demanded. "After all these years, why on earth would she be calling me?"

"Because her husband is dead, and she's being held in jail on a charge of first-degree murder."

"Chuck's dead?" B. inquired in disbelief. "Murdered? How? When? Why?"

That string of one-word questions could have come straight out of the syllabus for any self-respecting class in Journalism 101.

"I don't know any of the details," Ali told him. "After the call, I asked Frigg to research the situation. I told her to send me whatever she's found after the game. Why don't I have her put us on a conference call?"

"Good idea," B. said. "Where are you now?"

"Almost home," she said. "Just turning onto Manzanita Hills Road. As soon as I'm there, I'll dial up Frigg. That way we'll find out what we're up against together."

Inside the house, Ali made straight for the library and turned on the gas log fireplace. Then with her customary glass of merlot in one hand and iPad in the other, she summoned Frigg.

"Good evening, Ali," Frigg responded. "I hope you enjoyed the game. I understand the Scorpions won."

"Yes, they did, thank you, but this is about my earlier phone call. Have you been able to obtain any further information on the Brewster situation?"

"Of course."

"Then please contact B. via his iPad so you can brief both of us at once."

"One moment, please," Frigg replied.

The connection was made a moment later. "All right, Frigg," B. said. "Let's see what this is all about."

"It's probably best to start with media coverage," Frigg replied. "Here's a segment from a five o'clock news broadcast from a Seattle television station on Monday, March 13. I'm only sending one because all the local coverage is virtually the same."

The screen filled with a pair of news anchors, one male and one female, seated side by side at a glossy desk, both of them smiling broadly into the camera while the male read from the teleprompter.

"Shocking news out of Edmonds this morning, where millionaire video game entrepreneur Charles Richard Brewster, age sixty, was found stabbed to death in his Edmonds home. KOMO News Reporter Lacey Collins is on the scene. What can you tell us, Lacey?"

When Lacey appeared on the screen, she didn't look to be much older than the girls on Colleen's varsity basketball team. The location of the standup was all too familiar to former TV reporter Ali Reynolds. Lacey stood in the middle of a tree-lined street blocked off by ribbons of yellow crime scene tape. On the far side of the tape was a collection of haphazardly parked law enforcement vehicles—a CSI van and a Medical Examiner van, along with any number of patrol cars. The reporter's timing was perfect. As she spoke, a gurney, one presumably holding the victim's body, was being wheeled out of the house, down the sidewalk, and out into the street.

"The body of Mr. Charles Brewster, co-founder and currently CEO of Video Games International, was discovered deceased in his home in this quiet Edmonds neighborhood late this morning. A call from the residence reporting the incident was received by the 911 call center at 11:19 a.m. Police officers and EMS responded within minutes, but the victim was pronounced dead at the scene.

"I've spoken to a number of people from the neighborhood who witnessed the aftermath of the incident. According to them, a female individual was led from the home, wrapped in a blanket and wearing handcuffs. Reportedly she was taken to police headquarters for questioning. Witnesses have identified her as the victim's wife, Clarice Lorraine Brewster, although that has not yet been confirmed by officers on scene.

"The Brewsters were longtime residents of the neighborhood, and no one reported seeing or hearing anything unusual overnight. Several say that footage from nearby Ring cameras has already been collected by detectives investigating the incident.

"I've been speaking to Ms. Nancy Homewood, the Brewsters' next-door neighbor. This is what she has to say."

The camera switched over to an elderly white-haired lady leaning on a cane. "I can't believe such a dreadful thing could happen, and right next door, too."

"Did anything seem unusual or out of line?"

"They had a party of some kind yesterday evening with lots of cars parked up and down the street, but that's not unusual. They've always done a good deal of entertaining. This morning, the Brewsters' cleaning lady showed up right on time at eight thirty. She comes two days a week, Mondays and Fridays. I saw her hauling the trash bins out to the street while I was having my second cup of coffee. You just never know what to expect, do you?"

"That's all from here," Lacey concluded cheerfully, cutting the woman off before she had a chance to say anything more. "Back to you in the studio."

The clip ended. "So, Clarice was the person taken into custody at the scene?" B. asked.

"That is correct," Frigg replied, "although her name wasn't released to the media until after she was officially charged on Wednesday. She pled not guilty and was denied bond. She's being held in the King County jail."

"It sounds as though she was the immediate focus of the investigation," Ali suggested.

"With good reason," Frigg replied. "This photo is a still taken from the body cam of the first officer to arrive on the scene."

Ali didn't want to ask how Frigg had gained access to body cam footage. It was better not to know. Nonetheless, she watched the video with interest. In it, two women sat clutching each other at the top of a flight of stairs. One of them, presumably Clarice, was clad in what appeared to be a long-sleeved white nightgown. The front of the gown was covered with blood, from the middle of her chest to her knees. There appeared to be blood on her hands as well. She seemed to be crying, and in this particular frame, her facial features were so distorted that it looked like she was wearing a grotesque Halloween mask.

"I stabbed him," she murmured over and over. "I don't remember doing it, but I must have."

Next to her sat a second woman, one whose long graying hair was pulled back in a ponytail. She wore an apron over what appeared to be a pair of sweats and was holding something in both arms. "Is that the cleaning lady?" Ali asked.

"Correct," B. supplied. "I know her. That's Donna Jean Plummer. She's worked for Chuck for years. She was working for him back when his first wife, Melinda, was dying of cancer."

"But what's that she's holding?"

Frigg enlarged the photo.

"A cat?" Ali asked. "It looks like it's covered with blood, too."

"Not surprising," B. muttered. "Clarice always had a thing for cats."

"According to the police reports, officers were preparing to remove the cat from the scene and turn her over to Animal Control. Officers eventually collected bloodstained fur from the feline's coat and then allowed Ms. Plummer, the housekeeper, to take the animal home with her. The cat's name is Pearl, by the way," Frigg added. "She was apparently in a good deal of distress, and investigators think it likely that she witnessed the homicide."

"Thank goodness she didn't end up going to Animal Control," Ali said.

A new photo appeared on the screen. In this one, the bloodied nightgown had disappeared, and Clarice Brewster was clad in jailhouse orange. Ali knew Clarice to be somewhere in her fifties at this point, but she looked older.

"No more photos, Frigg, please," B. said. "Can you just give us a summary?"

"The medical examiner noted seventeen different stab wounds to Mr. Brewster's upper and lower back, at least three of which could have been fatal. There were no signs of a struggle and no defensive wounds. He was apparently asleep at the time of the attack and lying under a duvet. Pieces of fiber removed from his body were consistent with having come from the duvet. The toxicology report says his blood alcohol level was .32."

Ali breathed out, not wanting to know exactly how Frigg had gained access to the ME's autopsy results, either. That issue, however, went right over B.'s head.

"In other words, he was probably dead drunk when he was attacked," he observed. "Not too surprising. Back in the day, Chuck was quite the drinker. That's something he and Clarice had in common."

"The number of stab wounds would generally be indicative of overkill," Ali said, "which points to a close personal connection between perpetrator and victim, as well as a good deal of rage. No wonder Clarice is suspect number one."

"Investigators have learned that Mr. Brewster was considering filing for a divorce, so he may have been involved with another woman at the time of his death," Frigg continued.

"I wouldn't be surprised," B. said bitterly. "He was having an affair with Clarice while Melinda was still alive. Now he's cheating on Clarice. No wonder she went berserk and killed him."

"She told me she didn't do it," Ali said quietly.

"She was probably lying," B. replied. With that he abruptly ended his portion of the call.

Ali signed off with Frigg and called B. back. "Where did you go?"

"I couldn't take any more. Once upon a time, Chuck Brewster was not only my partner, he was also my best friend. First Clarice killed the friendship and the partnership, and now she's killed him, too. What the hell does she expect me to do about it? Defend her somehow? What she needs is a good defense attorney."

"I believe she has one of those," Ali told him. "But maybe she needs a better one. This one seems to be suggesting that if the prosecutor offers her a deal to plead down to murder in the second degree, she should probably take it."

"I think so, too," B. said. "I'm done."

With that he hung abruptly up again. Ali didn't blame him for hanging up a second time. This was clearly a terrible blow, and B. would need some time to process it. In the meantime, the best thing for Ali to do was give him space.

After the phone call ended, Ali puttered around the house some. The situation didn't just affect B., because Ali was upset, too. It would have been nice to have Bella to cuddle about then, but thinking about Bella only made matters worse. Ali knew that if she tried going to bed right then, she would most likely simply toss and turn. So she poured a second glass of wine and read the latest Dan Silva book for a while. It was almost midnight when she finally started getting ready for bed. When she plugged her cell phone into the bedside charger, the clock was showing 11:59 p.m., March 16, 2023.

Not exactly the Ides of March, Ali thought to herself, *but close enough!*

CHAPTER NINE

SEDONA, ARIZONA,
FRIDAY, MARCH 17, 2023
8:00 A.M.

Normally Ali gave herself a day off after finishing her tax preparation duties, but not this year. With Lance, Stu, and B. all out of the office, she felt duty bound to be there. Besides, it would give her a chance to catch up on all the things she had put off tending to while focusing on the IRS.

Expecting a call would be coming in from Clarice at any time, she dialed up Frigg on her thirty-minute commute from home to Cottonwood.

"Good morning, Ali," Frigg greeted. "I hope you have an outstanding day."

"Me too," Ali said, "but I'm expecting a phone call from Clarice Brewster later today. Before then, I'd like to have as much information as possible on the Charles Brewster situation. Anything new?"

"Only this: The crime lab has now confirmed that Mrs. Brewster's DNA was found on the murder weapon. I've also tracked down the terms of Clarice's divorce from Mr. Simpson. Rather than cash in hand, she was given half of Mr. Simpson's portion of Video Games International, giving her one-quarter ownership in the company. That arrangement, written into a prenup agreement at the time she married Mr. Brewster, remains in effect.

"Investigators have learned that Chuck had recently begun exploring the possibility of obtaining a divorce. Chuck and Clarice's prenup agreement meant that, in the event of a divorce, Clarice would have walked away with a substantial settlement. Since the two were still married at the time of his death, it's likely she stood to inherit the whole shebang. That would have been a big payday."

"No wonder she's the prime suspect," Ali murmured.

"Except," Frigg added, "if she ends up being convicted of committing the murder, she'll get nothing. And as far as suspects go, she's not the only one."

"Wait, are you saying the cops don't think she acted alone?"

"Based on the interviews they've conducted so far, investigators seem to believe that Donna Jean Plummer, the housekeeper, may have acted as Ms. Brewster's accomplice. For one thing, she was there when the body was found, and she's also the one who made the 911 call. For another, the whole house was immaculately clean, suggesting that there might have been some effort to clean up and destroy evidence before law enforcement was called to the scene. The housekeeper claims she was at home asleep at the time of Mr. Brewster's death, but since she's a widow who lives alone, there may not be a way to verify her alibi. Investigators don't seem to be looking at anyone else, but I'm beginning to wonder if both women are being trained."

"Trained?" a mystified Ali repeated. After a moment she made the connection. "Railroaded, you mean?"

"Yes," Frigg replied. "That is correct. I believe it's possible neither of them is responsible."

"What makes you say that?"

"I've discovered a puzzling inconsistency. An examination of the murder weapon revealed traces of a substance that turns out to be Nivea."

"That's a hand cream," Ali supplied. "A moisturizer I put on my hands and feet every night before I go to bed."

"Why would someone intent on stabbing a victim to death cover his or her hands with a moisturizer prior to committing the crime?" Frigg asked. "My understanding is that in the course of bloody stabbings, perpetrators often injure themselves, but that doesn't seem to be the case here. The only DNA found on the body came from either the victim himself or his wife. However, Ms. Plummer's fingerprints were also found on the murder weapon."

"She works there," Ali objected. "It stands to reason that her prints would be on items found inside the house."

Suddenly Ali found herself thinking about Mateo Vega, a guy who had spent sixteen years in prison for a crime he hadn't committed. When his then girlfriend had died after the couple had quarreled during a holiday picnic, the cops had immediately focused on Mateo and no one else. Due to tunnel vision, detectives on the case had failed to do the basic kind of investigation that might have revealed the actual killer to be someone who had attended the same picnic.

Is it possible this is the same thing? Ali wondered.

What if Frigg was right and Clarice hadn't done it? Everyone else seemed to think so, including Clarice's defense attorney, to say nothing of B. Simpson, her ex-husband.

Based on what B. had said the night before, Ali thought it unlikely that he would change his mind about that, no matter what Frigg had uncovered to the contrary.

"Go ahead and continue looking into this," Ali advised the AI at last. "Keep me posted on whatever you find, but I'd prefer that any information on this issue be kept between the two of us."

"Of course," Frigg said, "Mother's the word."

"That would be 'Mum's the word,'" Ali corrected after a momentary smile. "Mum can mean 'mother,' but it also means 'to keep quiet.'"

"Of course," Frigg replied. "Thank you for that useful information."

Once at her desk, the first email Ali opened was a long one written late at night by a still-giddy Cami Lee giving Ali a blow-by-blow description of her outstandingly successful dinner with the Dozo people. Knowing how much bringing home that new account would mean to Cami, Ali quickly sent back a congratulatory note. Minutes after finishing that, her phone rang. Stu Ramey's name appeared on caller ID.

"She's gone," he blurted as soon as Ali picked up. "Aunt Julia is gone."

Stu Ramey may have been high functioning, but he was definitely on the spectrum. As far as computers were concerned, he was brilliant. However, interpersonal relationships and emotions, including his own, were a complete mystery to him. Ali could tell from the sound of his voice that he was devastated by the loss. Stu's mother's sister, Julia Miller, had been his last living relative.

"I'm so sorry," Ali said. "Is there anything I can do?"

"I think I need help."

"Of course. What kind of help?"

"Someone called the funeral home and had them come by the hospital to collect her body. The hearse just left. I'm supposed to go see the funeral director later today, but I've never planned a funeral before. I don't know what to do."

"Did your aunt leave behind any directives?"

"Directives?" Stu repeated, as though the word was entirely foreign.

"Did she give you any hints about her preferences as far as final arrangements are concerned?"

"We never talked about things like that," Stu said. "I guess I thought she would live forever."

"Did she have an attorney?"

"Yes," Stu replied. "I know I met her once, but I don't remember the name."

Ali could tell Stu wasn't firing on all cylinders. "How much sleep have you had?"

"Not much," he admitted. "I've been spending most of my time in her room here at the hospital until . . . " The remainder of that sentence went unfinished.

"Do you have a hotel room there in town?" Ali asked.

"No. I've been going back and forth between the ranch and hospice."

"Get a room in Payson. After you let me know where you're staying, try to rest," Ali advised him. "I have some things I need to clear up here first, but once I'm finished, I'll head over to Payson to help sort things out."

"Thank you, Ali," Stu murmured. "I really appreciate it."

Once the call ended, Ali sat for a moment puzzling over the issues involved. She and B. had met Stu's Aunt Julia on occasion and had made several tax-deductible donations to Racehorse Rest, the shelter Julia Miller had established to care for retired racehorses. Qualifying as a 501(c)(3) organization would have required the services of an attorney, so Ali turned back to Frigg.

"Is there something more you need on the Charles Brewster situation?" Frigg inquired.

"No," Ali answered. "This is something else. Stu's Aunt Julia passed away earlier today. He's at a loss concerning her final arrangements, which means I need your help."

"How can I be of assistance?"

"We need the name of Julia Miller's attorney. Stu doesn't remember the attorney's name, but it should be on the legal documents surrounding the formation of Racehorse Rest."

"The ranch located in Gila County, correct?" Frigg asked.

"Yes."

"One moment, please."

There was a pause of only a minute or so before Frigg's voice came back online. "Racehorse Rest was incorporated as a 501(c)(3) charitable organization on May 6, 2007. The attorney who prepared the documents on Ms. Miller's behalf was one Louise Corman of Corman Law LLC, located on West Main Street, in Payson, Arizona. Would you like the phone number?"

"Please," Ali said.

Ali dialed the number as soon as the call to Frigg ended. "Corman LLC," a voice answered. "How may I help you?"

"I'm looking for Louise Corman," Ali answered.

After a slight hesitation the voice on the phone said, "I'm sorry to have to inform you of this, but Ms. Corman passed away from Covid in 2022. Is there anything else I can do for you?"

Ali swallowed her disappointment. "I believe she had some dealings with a woman named Julia Miller in the past. Julia passed away earlier this morning. I'm calling on behalf of her nephew, Stu Ramey."

"Oh, my goodness," the woman said before Ali could continue. "I'm so sorry to hear this. Of course I knew Ms. Miller. We all did. She's a longtime client. She and Louise were friends from grade school on. Would you like to speak to Karen?"

"Who's Karen?"

"Louise's daughter. She's taken over the practice now. I assume you're looking for documents concerning Ms. Miller's final arrangements?"

Ali was relieved beyond words. "Exactly," she said.

"One moment, then."

A few seconds later another voice came on the line. "Karen Corman speaking, and you are?"

Ali introduced herself and explained the situation.

"I had no idea Julia was even ill," Karen Corman said. "I'm surprised no one let me know. And yes, we have the originals of all the documents her nephew will need. Just have Mr. Ramey stop by our office at his convenience."

"He's a bit overwhelmed at the moment," Ali said. "Would it be all right if I accompany him?"

"Of course," Karen said. "Julia told us that he's very smart but that he has some social challenges. If he has no objection to your coming, I certainly don't."

The fact that Karen was so knowledgeable about Stu's situation made Ali realize that there was a much closer connection here than she had anticipated.

"I take it you knew Julia Miller, too?" she asked.

Karen laughed. "She and my mother were thick as thieves and more like sisters than friends. Although we may not have been blood relations, Julia always seemed like my Aunt Julia, too."

Somehow knowing that made Ali feel better, and she suspected Stu would agree.

"When I spoke to Stu a little while ago, he was worn out. I suggested he rent a hotel room and try to get some sleep. He's staying at the Payson Inn. I'm in Cottonwood at the moment and have some things to clear up here before I can head over. Once I get there, Stu and I will stop by your office to touch base, but probably not until later this morning."

"My morning is completely booked," Karen said, "but my afternoon is relatively open."

"Good," Ali said. "See you then."

Off the phone, Ali went out to the front desk to let Shirley know what was going on.

"Poor Stu," Shirley said. "Is he okay?"

"Not really."

"Please tell him that he has my condolences."

"I will," Ali said.

Forty-five minutes later, Ali headed out. She had just passed Cordes Junction when the phone call she had been dreading came through.

"I have a collect call from Clarice Brewster in the King County Correctional Facility in Seattle, Washington. Will you accept the charges?"

Ali took a deep breath. "Yes, I will," she answered.

"Why am I still talking to you instead of B.?" Clarice demanded. "Doesn't he want to talk to me?"

That was precisely the case, but Ali didn't want to go into any of that. "He's on an airplane right now." That wasn't true. B.'s flight from DC wasn't scheduled to depart for several hours yet, but the ploy worked.

"There's no point in talking to you," Clarice said.

"B. thinks you need to be sure you have a top-drawer defense attorney."

"Really?" Clarice asked. "You mean he believes I didn't do it?"

Not exactly, Ali thought. "He just thinks you need more effective representation."

Of course that wasn't true, either. B. didn't believe anything of the kind.

"All right, then," Clarice said. "That'll be my next call. I'll fire my first attorney's ass and go looking for someone whose first advice isn't for me to plead guilty to a murder I didn't commit."

CHAPTER TEN

LOS ANGELES, CALIFORNIA
FRIDAY, MARCH 17, 2023
7:00 A.M.

Cami had flown into L.A. early on Monday morning with an appointment scheduled for that afternoon and three each on Tuesday, Wednesday, and Friday. Thursday she had devoted entirely to the Dozo dinner. But on Friday afternoon, by the time the last appointment ended, her tail feathers were dragging due to lack of sleep, and she was looking forward to the next day's midmorning flight that would have her back home in Cornville by early Saturday afternoon.

On the way to her first appointment in Pasadena that morning, Cami's boyfriend, Mateo Vega, had called as she made her way through crawling traffic on the 110.

"How was the dinner?" he asked.

Mateo was the only person with whom Cami had shared both her qualms and her hopes for the meeting with Dozo. Pulling those accounts into High Noon's cybersecurity fold would mean a huge win for High Noon's reputation, to say nothing of its bottom line.

"It was great," she answered. "I've already sent them a request for the information necessary to give them an official proposal. I think we're going to sign them."

"Congrats," Mateo said, "but why didn't you call me once it was over?"

Cami flushed. "We didn't break up until after eleven, and I knew you had to be at work early today. I didn't want to wake you up."

"I wouldn't have minded," Mateo said. "You're welcome to wake me up anytime."

Mateo had come to work for High Noon after languishing in a Washington state prison for years for a crime he hadn't committed. Not only had Ali and B. given him a job, they had been instrumental in having his conviction overturned and his record expunged. He and Lance Tucker often joked about being High Noon's resident jailbirds.

Cami's position at High Noon had already been well established when Mateo came on board, but he had worked there for several years now, living in a small bungalow in Cottonwood that he shared with his widowed mother, Olivia.

Mateo was five years older than Cami. He'd been in prison the whole time she was in college and while she was starting out at High Noon. In terms of romantic entanglements, however, they were both relative newbies. When Mateo began showing up at Cami's Krav Maga sessions at a gym near work, she had mistakenly assumed he was interested in Krav Maga. In actual fact, he'd been far more interested in her than Krav Maga, but once she realized she shared those same feelings, the gym had functioned as cover for their blossoming but work-related romance.

They had managed to keep their relationship a secret for several months, but recently it had come to light. It turns out their gym hideaway was located in the same strip mall as the hair and nail salon frequented by fellow High Noon employee Shirley Malone. After noticing Cami's and Mateo's vehicles parked side by side at the gym parking lot on several occasions, Shirley had come to work and blown the whistle on them. The revelation had engendered all kinds of teasing, but the first time the two lovebirds had publicly acknowledged their relationship had been at the company's Valentine's Day potluck a few weeks earlier. At the event, instead of showing up with her usual Chinese fare, Cami had delivered a tray of homemade tamales that she had prepared under Olivia Vega's patient tutelage.

Even though everyone at work now knew they were in a relationship, Cami's parents remained in the dark. They were both Chinese and proud of it. They were also both tenured university professors. They had never approved of their daughter's leaving California in favor of going to a small town in Arizona of all places, nor did they like the idea of her being totally preoccupied with her work. Cami had no doubt that her parents would both go ballistic when they learned that not only was her boyfriend Hispanic, he was also an ex-con.

"How are things in the lab?" she asked. "And how did it feel to be running the show?"

Stu Ramey, B.'s second-in-command, was usually in charge of the lab, but he was currently off on leave, looking after his Aunt Julia who had suffered a catastrophic stroke and was currently in a brick-and-mortar hospice facility in Payson. With B., Lance, and Cami all out of town, Mateo had been left at High Noon's helm for the first time ever.

"All right," Mateo said. "There was an attempted breach in the UK last night, but with Oscar's help, we were able to stomp it out in short order."

Oscar was the name of the company's new High Noon–specific AI. For years, whenever the services of an AI had been required, the company had relied on Stu Ramey's Frigg. Now that the company had an AI of its own, they used Oscar exclusively for High Noon–related purposes. Those that were of a more dubious nature—gaining unauthorized access to homicide investigations, for example—went through Frigg. Oscar was definitely a white hat. Frigg was more or less a gray hat rather than a black or white one.

"Good work," Cami said.

"But you probably haven't heard about what's going on with Stu."

"Tell me," Cami said.

Mateo briefly brought her up-to-date about Aunt Julia's death.

"Poor Stu," Cami said. "How's he coping?"

"Not that well. Ali's driving over to Payson to give him a hand. But what's the rest of your day like?" Mateo wondered.

"Two more appointments after this first one. Then I'm going to go back to the hotel, have a quiet dinner, do a workout in the fitness center, and hit the hay early. I didn't get much sleep last night."

"What time do you fly in tomorrow?"

"If I can make that first shuttle from Sky Harbor, I should be home in Cornville by one thirty or two. But I've just now arrived at my destination and am pulling into the parking lot."

"Okay, then," Mateo said. "I'll let you go. Have a good one."

The appointments had all gone well, but Cami was grateful to head back to the hotel reasonably early. The previous night, in an effort to be a good hostess, Cami had eaten far more rich food at the dinner than she usually consumed. That had probably contributed to her difficulty in falling asleep. It also meant that she hadn't felt hungry all day long and hadn't bothered to eat.

It wasn't until evening when she was back at the Lancaster that she suddenly realized she was famished. After going up to her room and dropping off her stuff, she went down to the hotel dining room. It was certainly nice enough, but not nearly as posh as the conference room extravaganza she and Chef Robert had created in honor of the Dozo dinner.

Cami had barely sat down and was beginning to peruse the menu when Chef Robert himself appeared at her table. "How'd we do?" he asked.

"Terrific," she answered. "The guy who mattered loved every morsel. Meantime, the guys who didn't matter, the ones who were just along for the ride, griped about everything—in Japanese, of course. They'd be mortified if they knew I heard every derogatory comment."

"You speak Japanese?" Chef Robert asked.

"I certainly do," Cami replied with a smile, "along with French, Chinese, German, and now, thanks to my boyfriend and his mother, a smattering of Spanish."

Unlike Cami's parents, Olivia Vega wasn't at all opposed to Cami and Mateo's burgeoning romance.

Chef Robert laughed aloud at that. "So what is our lady's dining pleasure this evening?" he asked, changing the subject. "And what language will she be using?"

"I'll be using American English," Cami replied, "and even though it's not on the dinner menu, I'd really appreciate having a grilled cheese sandwich accompanied by a Caesar salad."

"You've got it," Chef Robert said. "And what to drink?"

"Plain water," she answered.

"All right, then," Chef Robert said. "Coming right up, and your dinner tonight is on the house."

Except for the waitstaff, the dining room had been totally empty when Cami arrived, but shortly after Robert returned to his kitchen, a couple entered. The man, middle-aged and stocky, was accompanied by a much younger woman with long black hair. She was movie-star gorgeous but didn't seem at all happy. As the hostess escorted them to their table, Cami noticed that the man was studying her. Instantly she was on full alert.

Years earlier, she had been kidnapped and held captive by the disgruntled tenant of one of High Noon's business park offices. She had managed to escape, but only by propelling herself out of the back of a moving vehicle. Physically, Cami had come away from that near-death experience with a broken leg and plenty of scrapes and bruises, as well as a profound sense of situational awareness. On this trip in particular, her danger warning lights had been flashing relentlessly.

During her stay in L.A., especially while driving to appointments, she'd felt as though she was being watched. She hadn't spotted anyone actually tailing her, but even taking evasive maneuvers hadn't reduced her growing sense of unease. Back at the hotel, once the valet had delivered her rental car to the parking garage, she had gone so far as to don a pair of jeans and a sweatshirt so she could clamber under the vehicle, a Honda Pilot, to see if she could spot a GPS tracker of some kind. Her careful search had come up empty.

As soon as the couple entered the dining room, Cami was once again on needles and pins. When seated in restaurants, she made it a point to position herself with her back to a wall while facing the entrance, allowing her to keep track of everyone coming and going. That's how she had spotted the couple in the first place, but with the man now seated with his back to her, she was able to study him from behind. The suit he wore was expensive and had obviously been made to order, since it fit his massive shoulders perfectly. Nonetheless, as he sat down, she caught the telltale bulge that told her there was a concealed weapon under that well-tailored jacket.

The presence of a concealed weapon raised her concern level to a new high and made her study him in even greater detail. He had a natural belligerence about him. He wasn't particularly tall—five ten or so—but powerfully built. He had a full head of hair—straight and black with no hint of gray. At his age, that probably meant his hair color was a dye job. His swarthy complexion and blunt facial features suggested he might be of Eastern European descent rather than Hispanic.

When the server came to take the couple's order, she addressed the young woman, asking what she wanted, but the man answered her inquiry, ordering for both of them. When their food came, the man downed his with gusto, while the young woman merely picked at hers. The idle chitchat that passed between them during their meal was done in a language Cami didn't recognize.

As for Cami's own meal? She forced herself to choke it down, all the while trying to convince herself that she was letting her imagination get the best of her. After all, other than that first glance in her direction, the man had shown no further interest in her. By the time her sandwich and salad were half gone, Cami had more or less succeeded in convincing herself that she'd made the whole thing up. With that, she signed the ticket for her dinner to her room and headed upstairs.

When Cami was on the road and wanting to stay in shape, she usually made use of hotel fitness facilities. Up in her room, she decided that she wasn't going to let the guy in the dining room keep her from doing her customary workout. With that in mind, a little after eight and wearing a track suit, Cami made her way down to the Lancaster's second-floor fitness center, one Cami especially liked. The angled mirrors hung on the walls just under the dropped ceiling, making it possible for her to be facing forward and jogging on a treadmill, while still keeping the entire room in clear view.

In public gyms, Cami preferred using the treadmill nearest the entrance. Tonight, however, that one was already occupied by a gray-haired, somewhat overweight woman trudging along with the grim determination of someone on a death march. Otherwise the room was empty, and Cami settled for the next treadmill over. She was going through her warm-up routine when the woman noticed she was there.

"I'm getting my ten," she announced. "My ten thousand steps, that is. My name's Grace. What's yours?"

Cami often visited hotel fitness centers during dinnertime so she could have them to herself. Not tonight.

"Camille Lee," she answered, "but people usually call me Cami."

"Are you from around here?" Grace asked.

Cami was from California originally, but her answer to the question clarified for her that things had changed. "I'm from Arizona," she said. "Sedona."

"That's the place with all the red rocks, isn't it?" Grace asked.

Cami smiled. "It certainly is."

She stepped onto her treadmill, but instead of turning it up to her usual jogging pace, she set it much lower, staying in sync with her neighbor.

"I always wanted to go to Arizona," Grace continued, "but Hank wasn't big on travel."

"Hank?" Cami asked.

"My husband," Grace replied. "My late husband, that is," she corrected. "He always told me there'd be plenty of time for us to travel once he stopped working. Except he was wrong about that because he never stopped working. He had a massive stroke and died right there at his desk, the SOB."

Cami had been about to express her condolences, but she stifled the words.

"The ME brought me his personal effects," Grace went on, "including his cell phone, which was in his pocket when he croaked out. He'd always been very private about that phone. I didn't know his password, of course, but I tried his birthday, and I was right. That's when I discovered that he'd been screwing around on me for years with one woman after another. He never wanted to travel with me, but he sure as hell liked to travel with all his lady friends. Business trips, my ass!"

Obviously Grace wasn't someone who minced her words. During the pause that followed, Cami struggled to find an appropriate comment, but Grace soon picked up her story again.

"He was always griping about my putting on weight, so after he died, I started working out, just to spite him. I've lost thirty pounds so far by eating right and exercising, but I'm traveling, too. I board a cruise ship tomorrow afternoon in San Pedro for a round-the-world cruise, first class all the way. I'll be on board for eighty-nine days total in my own private cabin. That's the first thing I bought when his group insurance paid off—my cruise ticket."

Cami stopped listening right then because, at that moment, the door to the fitness center opened, and the man from the dining room, alone this time, stepped inside.

CHAPTER ELEVEN

LOS ANGELES, CALIFORNIA
FRIDAY, MARCH 17, 2023
9:00 P.M.

By the time the guy walked past, Cami had the phone to her mouth and was apparently studying the screen. In reality, she was using her camera app to capture a video of the new arrival's image as reflected in the overhead mirrors while he moved past. She immediately replayed the video and was gratified to see that, as he walked behind her, he had turned in her direction. Fortunately, he hadn't looked up and caught her examining him in the mirror at the same time. But that frame was the one Cami needed. When it came to doing a facial rec search, it would work perfectly.

She immediately forwarded the video to Frigg, using the bright red script that identified the message as a howler, one that required the AI's immediate attention. Grace, seemingly realizing that Cami was now preoccupied with her phone, had finally quit talking. That allowed Cami to insert her ear buds.

"Good evening, Cami," Frigg said in greeting. "I hope you had a pleasant day. How can I be of service?"

"*Konbanwa*," Cami said, returning the greeting in Japanese and using her brightest and most cheerful tone of voice.

The seamless switch over to Japanese was a calculated risk on Cami's part. She was reasonably sure that neither of the people present in the room would be able to understand her. Since Frigg had helped tutor Cami in Japanese, she was bound to understand, but for the briefest of moments, even the AI seemed baffled.

"Is there a reason you are now speaking Japanese?" she asked.

"I need help," Cami said urgently again in Japanese. "I need facial rec on the guy in the video I just sent you."

"On it," Frigg said.

Cami ended the call and removed her ear buds. "Who was that?" Grace asked.

"My boss," Cami answered.

"What language were you speaking?"

"Japanese."

"Your boss is Japanese?"

Cami nodded. "He lives in Tokyo."

"Boy," Grace said with a laugh, "back when I was working, I would have loved having a boss who lived on a different continent or even on a different planet." With that, she stopped walking, switched off her treadmill, and held up her phone in triumph. The green numbers on the phone read 10,002. "I'm done," she announced. "I've got today's ten."

There was no way Cami intended to be left alone in the fitness center with the gun-packing guy who was now diligently lifting weights and apparently not paying the least bit of attention to them. This was Cami's chance to get the hell out of there, and she intended to take it.

"I'm beat, too," she said to Grace. "If you're signing off for the night, so am I."

Moments later, the two women exited the room one after another and headed toward the elevator that was next door to the fitness center. The Lancaster was laid out as a long L. The fitness center was located next to the elevator, which was at the near end of the long part of the L. Next door, on the short part of the corridor, was a supply room and a laundry facility. Beyond that was the stairwell.

Cami hurried into the elevator and pressed the button for her floor, number ten. "What floor?" she asked.

"I'm on five," Grace returned.

Then, just as the door was about to close Cami reversed course and exited the elevator. "I almost forgot," she said over her shoulder. "I need to stop by the front desk. You go on up. I'll catch the next one."

With that she darted off the elevator, around the corner, past the supply room and laundry, and into the stairwell. Holding her breath and hoping her pursuer hadn't caught sight of her, Cami raced down a flight of concrete stairs. She had just reached the landing on the ground floor when an overhead door slammed open, followed by heavy steps pounding in the stairwell. Much to Cami's relief, the steps were headed up instead of down.

Holding her breath, Cami silently let herself out on the ground floor, easing the heavy door shut behind her. Then, rather than heading for the lobby, she made straight for what she knew to be the service entrance in and out of the kitchen. Slipping soundlessly into the noisy mayhem, Cami went looking for Chef Robert. As soon as she caught his eye, he hurried over to her, obviously registering her concern.

"What's going on?" he asked.

"Someone's after me," she told him tersely. "I need a place to hide."

"Really?" he asked in astonishment.

"Really."

Gesturing for his second-in-command to take over, Chef Robert grabbed Cami's hand and led her into the tiny cubicle that served as his private office.

"What's wrong?" he demanded, slamming the door shut behind them. "Are you in danger?"

She nodded.

"Do you want me to call 911?"

"Oh, no," she told him. "Please don't do that."

"What do you want me to do, then?"

"Just let me sit here and think for a minute," she said. "Go back out there before anyone realizes something is wrong. I have your number. I'll call you once I figure it out."

In actual fact, Cami already had something in mind. Years earlier, on a business trip to London, there had been good reason to believe that both Ali and Cami might be in some kind of danger. To counteract that, B. had called on one of his longtime associates, Sonja Bjornson, whose company, Wonder Woman Security, provided bodyguards and security details for any number of high-profile female clients. Naturally the company headquarters was in L.A., where WWS operatives oversaw the comings and goings of many of Hollywood's female A-listers. Once Cami had headed out on the road on her own, B. had given her WWS's contact information and directed her to connect with them directly if she ever felt she was in any kind of jeopardy.

I'm in jeopardy now, Cami thought.

With surprisingly unsteady fingers, she fumbled her phone out of her pocket, located Sonja's number in her contacts list, and dialed.

"This is the WWS answering service. To whom am I speaking?"

Great, Cami thought. *The last thing I need is to be stuck talking to an answering machine.* Nonetheless, she continued. "My name is Camille Lee, Cami for short."

She heard the rapid clatter of fingers on a computer keyboard. Obviously this was a person as opposed to an answering machine.

"Would you be the Camille Lee who's employed by High Noon Enterprises?" the voice on the other end of the line inquired.

The efficiency of that took Cami by surprise. "Yes, I am," she answered.

"Are you currently in danger?"

"I believe so, yes," Cami said. "I'm at a hotel in L.A. Someone wearing a firearm appears to be following me. The first time I saw him was tonight at dinner when he turned up in the dining room. Then, a little while ago when I was in the fitness room, he showed up there, too. When I left, I'm pretty sure he tried to follow me."

"Tried?"

"I was spooked when I left the fitness center, so I used the stairs instead of the elevator. I heard someone enter the stairwell on the floor above me. Luckily, he ran up instead of down. Otherwise he would have caught me."

"Where are you now?"

"In the hotel kitchen. The head chef stowed me in his office."

"Which hotel?"

"The Lancaster."

"One moment."

Cami waited, trying not to hold her breath. Seconds later the operator came back on the line. "I have the Lancaster's layout right here in front of me. There's a loading dock at the back of the building that opens onto an alley. I can have a car and driver at your location within the next ten to fifteen minutes. Is that acceptable?"

Help was coming far sooner than Cami dreamed possible. "Absolutely."

"One moment, please." Once again the line went silent.

"I have a male driver named Jake on duty right now," the operator said once she returned. "Once he arrives on scene, he'll wait near the stairs at the far end of the loading dock. After he arrives, he'll text you on this number. His text will say, 'Jake's here. Jake, from State Farm.' Stay where you are until you know he's there. When you come out onto the loading dock, he'll blink his lights twice. If the text is wrong or if the lights don't blink twice, don't get in the vehicle. Do you understand?"

"Yes, ma'am," Cami said. "Jake from State Farm and two blinks."

"Once you're safely in the vehicle and out of harm's way, we'll determine what to do next."

With that, the call ended so abruptly Cami wasn't even able to say thank you. In the interim that followed, she could have called any number of people—Mateo, Ali and B., or even her parents. Instead she called no one at all. She simply sat there taking deep, steadying breaths and trying to get her frayed nerves under control.

A minute or so later, Chef Robert popped into the room. "Are you okay?" he asked.

Cami nodded. "Someone's coming to pick me up. The driver will text me from the loading dock."

"All right, then," he said, "but I still think I should call the cops."

"Please don't," she said. "The less fuss the better. The driver will let me know when he's outside."

"Okay," Chef Robert replied, "but I don't like it."

The "Jake from State Farm" text arrived five minutes later. When Cami opened the door to the office, Chef Robert left the line and personally escorted her out to the loading dock. As soon as they stepped outside, headlights flashed twice.

The vehicle turned out to be a hulking black Escalade. Chef Robert handed Cami up into the back passenger seat.

"You take care now," he told her.

"Thank you," she said. "I will. You've been a huge help."

"Not enough," Chef Robert replied. "Not nearly enough."

A relieved Cami settled into her seat and closed her eyes as the Escalade began to move. A few blocks later, she noticed that "Jake" was using the same evasive techniques she had used during the week in order to make sure they weren't being followed.

"Where are we going?" she asked finally.

"My orders are to take you straight to headquarters," he said.

WWS headquarters happened to be in a splashy mansion located somewhere in the Hollywood Hills. "Jake" handed her out of the Escalade inside an empty bay of a six-car garage and led her over to a lovely, silver-haired woman who stood waiting nearby. She stepped forward and gathered Cami into her arms.

"I'm Sonja," she said. "You're safe now, and I'm so glad to meet you. Are you all right?"

Cami nodded. "Tired but fine, thanks to you," she said. "All I need is a new rental so I can drive myself home to Arizona."

"Nonsense," Sonja Bjornson replied. "You'll do nothing of the kind. What you really need is a stiff drink and a good night's sleep. I've been in touch with B. He's arranging for a private jet to pick you up tomorrow at ten a.m. from Lindbergh Field in San Diego. He already sent me the tail number. Leaving by way of San Diego should keep you away from any unwelcome scrutiny in L.A. I've made arrangements for someone to stop by the Lancaster to clear out your room and pack up your things. Your luggage will be waiting for you at the airport. They'll also make sure your rental car is returned. Now come inside. What will you have to drink?"

Thanks to Mateo, Cami had a whole new beverage of choice, but she wasn't sure that was on the menu. "Could I have a margarita?" she asked.

"Of course," Sonja said. "Coming right up." Then later, as Cami was sipping her drink, Sonja asked, "Do you have any idea who the attacker was?"

Cami shook her head. "None at all, but I got his photo." She opened her phone and located the video of the man walking behind her into the fitness center. Then with his image frozen on the screen, she handed the phone to Sonja.

Sonja studied the screen for some time before handing the device back. "Send that to me, please," she said. "I'll run it through our facial rec."

Cami nodded. "The more the merrier," she said.

CHAPTER TWELVE

PAYSON, ARIZONA
FRIDAY, MARCH 17, 2023
10:00 P.M.

It was almost ten that night before Ali finally left Payson to head home. Fortunately, the Stu Ramey she had left behind was in far better shape than the one she'd met up with earlier in the afternoon, and Ali was grateful that she had been there to help him navigate a complex process that he'd never encountered before.

Their first stop that afternoon at Karen Corman's law office had been a revelation. Although Julia Miller may not have discussed her long-term plans with Stu, clearly a good deal of thought had gone into her arrangements, and her nephew was at the center of all of them.

She had directed that there was to be no funeral or memorial service, and no urn, either. Her body was to be cremated, and the ashes scattered in a small grove of pine trees at the far northeast corner of Racehorse Rest, so there was no need to waste money on an urn, and the whole cremation process, container included, was entirely prepaid.

With that information in hand, Ali had expected they'd leave the law office immediately and head for the mortuary. Not so. Since Stu was Julia's only heir, Karen Corman suggested that they go ahead and read the will. The ranch itself, all of her investments and financial accounts, as well as control of the charity went to him. Stu could choose to continue to operate the ranch as a rescue or sell it. That decision was his alone to make.

"Why didn't she ever talk to me about any of this?" Stu asked when the reading of the will ended.

"I believe she didn't want to worry you," Karen told him. "She was also afraid that if she gave you too much advance notice that you'd make your decisions about the ranch based on what you thought she'd want rather than going by what you want."

Stu considered that for a moment. "Aunt Julia was very opinionated," he said at last.

Karen laughed aloud. "Do you think?" she asked.

After leaving the attorney's office, the mortuary was the next stop. The last time Ali had set foot inside a funeral home had been in the aftermath of her father's death, and she was dreading the visit almost as much as Stu was, but when they headed inside, Ali was relieved to see that Stu had pulled himself together enough to face down whatever was coming.

The funeral director, a Mr. Jonathan Castor, met them at the door. "How may I help you?" he asked.

"We're here about Julia Miller," Stu replied.

"You must be Mr. Ramey," Castor said, extending his hand. "I'm so sorry for your loss."

Stu nodded. "Thank you," he muttered.

"Please call me Jonathan," Mr. Castor said before turning his attention to Ali. "And would you be Mrs. Ramey?" he asked.

"This is my friend Ali Reynolds," Stu interjected. "She's here to help."

"Very well," Mr. Castor said. "Please come this way."

He led them into a private office where a file labeled Julia Miller was the only item on an otherwise pristine desk.

"Your aunt was very particular about how she wanted things to be handled," Jonathan Castor began. "And most of the expenses have been paid in advance."

"Most?" Stu asked.

"Transportation expenses, of course," Castor replied, "and the cremation cost itself. If you wish to have a viewing, however, the cost of that would not be included."

"Viewing?" Stu inquired.

"It's a public gathering so friends can stop by the funeral home, see her, and pay their respects."

"She's dead," Stu said flatly. "I already saw her after she died. Why would anyone else want to?"

Why indeed? Ali thought.

Mr. Castor seemed taken aback by Stu's direct response. Ali was not. Over the past few years, in part due to bonding with the horses at Racehorse Rest, the quality of Stu's human interactions had improved immeasurably, but they seemed to regress when he was under stress.

"How long will this take?" Stu asked. "The cremation, I mean."

"Since there's no need for an autopsy, the ashes should be ready for pickup by tomorrow afternoon, if that's convenient. And if you'd like an urn, we have a whole selection—"

"No urn," Stu interrupted. "I want a box, preferably a cardboard box with a cover on it, so I can open it and scatter her ashes the way she wanted."

"Of course," Castor said, "as you wish."

Ali caught the hint of regret in the man's voice. No doubt he had hoped to add in a few extras that would have brought in a bit more cash than the amount Julia Miller had previously paid. Ali noticed the reaction, but she was sure that part of the discussion had flown right over Stu's head.

"What time?" he asked.

"Shall we say two?" Castor suggested.

"That'll be fine," Stu said, standing up. "I'll see you then."

Ali followed Stu out of the office and out of the mortuary as well. He paused on the sidewalk just outside the door. "There's a pizza place just up the street," he said. "Let's go there."

Under similar circumstances, most people wouldn't have gone in search of pizza, but for Stu Ramey, pizza was comfort food—the more toppings the better.

"Sounds good," Ali told him.

The pizza Stu ordered was good, but so overburdened with toppings that the crust collapsed under the excess weight. As a result, they ended up having to eat their slices with a knife and fork. While they ate, and for more than an hour afterward, Stuart Ramey talked, spilling out more words than Ali had ever heard him utter. He mostly talked about Aunt Julia, and how much she had meant to him, and about how much he had enjoyed being a part of Racehorse Rest. Julia Miller may not have wanted a memorial service, but she had one that afternoon anyway, and Ali Reynolds was honored to be a part of it.

At last Stu pushed himself away from the table. "We need to go to the ranch," he said. "I have to let the people there know that she's dead, and I want them to understand that nothing will change—that they'll still have their jobs and their places to live. I want them to know that everything is going to be okay."

That's where they went next—to Racehorse Rest. There were five full-time employees—the foreman, three ranch hands, and Martha, Aunt Julia's longtime housekeeper/cook. Stu summoned everyone to the ranch house. As they gathered in the living room Ali sensed the growing uncertainty. Stu delivered the news that Julia was dead with the same directness he had used with the funeral director. Clearly, the fact that Julia Miller was dead didn't come as a surprise to any of them, but Ali caught the palpable sense of relief that went around the room as Stu assured them that, from then on, he would be in charge. Clearly, his was a known and trusted presence.

Listening to Stu reassure that room of grieving people, Ali wished that B. could have been there, too. Years earlier, B. was the one who had rescued an abandoned and broken but very smart young man from the homeless shelter where he was living and had put him back together. The process had taken decades.

B. Simpson had no sons of his own, but in a very real way, he had fathered not only Stu Ramey but also Lance Tucker and now Mateo Vega. Seeing Stu come into his own like this, far away from the safety of High Noon's computer lab, should have been B.'s well-deserved reward. Instead it was Ali's.

Once the meeting ended, Stu went out to spend some time with the horses in their corrals. Ali attempted to take her leave, but Martha insisted that she stay for dinner. Although the pizza feast wasn't nearly far enough in the rearview mirror, Ali went ahead and accepted the invitation, and once dinner was over, she stayed even longer. As a result, she finally headed for Sedona much later than she had intended.

Over the course of the day she had been in touch by phone with both B. and the people at High Noon so everyone was now aware of what was going on with Stu. Ali had also learned that after a long flight delay on the ground in DC, B. and Lance were back home.

Wary of having a nighttime encounter with stray livestock or a wandering elk, Ali made no effort to call the house until she turned onto I-17 at Cordes Junction, but once she did, the moment she heard B.'s voice, she knew something was amiss.

"What's going on?" Ali asked.

"I just got off the phone with Sonja."

Ali's heart skipped a beat. "Sonja Bjornson? What's wrong?"

"Some guy tried to come after Cami at the hotel fitness center tonight. She got away from him and hid out in the hotel kitchen where she ran up the flag to WWS."

"Was she hurt?"

"No, she's fine. She got away clean. Sonja's people sent a car to pick Cami up and take her to Sonja's place. Someone from WWS will stop by the hotel and pack up her stuff so she doesn't have to go back there. I've chartered a jet to pick her up from Lindbergh Field in San Diego tomorrow morning. Chances are, if whoever's behind this knew she was staying at the Lancaster, they also know about her original flight arrangements. I don't want her going anywhere near an L.A. airport."

"Good thinking," Ali murmured. "But who would do such a thing?"

"No idea," B. replied. "I haven't spoken to Cami directly. Sonja says she gave her a killer margarita and sent her to bed. According to Sonja, however, Cami had suspected someone might be keeping track of her while she was in L.A, but she never caught anyone red-handed. Then tonight at dinner, she noticed a guy wearing a concealed weapon giving her the eye. When he showed up again later while she was working out at the fitness center, she decided it was time to split. We don't know for sure that she was targeted, but she was right to get the hell out."

"Is there surveillance footage?" Ali asked.

"We thought so," B. replied, "but when Frigg tried accessing the hotel's security system, she was late to the party."

"It had already been wiped?"

"Completely, but it turns out Frigg has been able to ID the guy anyway. His name is Bogdan Petrov. He's Bulgarian and is thought to have connections to people involved in Eastern European human trafficking."

"If the hotel's surveillance footage was wiped, how did Frigg ID him?"

"Cami used her phone to video him as he walked through the fitness center," B. explained. "She sent that to Frigg and asked for a facial rec on him. Frigg is currently compiling a dossier on the guy."

Ali thought about that for a time. "So, because of Cami's quick thinking, nothing really happened, and we're not even sure she was targeted."

"Exactly, but we need to respond as though she was."

"I'm pretty sure she's due to head out to the UK on Monday afternoon," Ali said thoughtfully. "Shouldn't we have her cancel?"

"Let's make that decision tomorrow, once we have her safely home. Where are you at the moment?" B. asked.

"Coming up I-17, just south of the Sedona exit."

"All right," B. said. "See you when you get here."

As the call ended, Ali realized that she hadn't mentioned a word about what was going on with Clarice Brewster. Given everything else that was happening, she wasn't likely to do so any time soon.

CHAPTER THIRTEEN

SEDONA, ARIZONA
SATURDAY, MARCH 18, 2023
12:30 P.M.

As the car service Escalade pulled up next to the CJ1 parked on the tarmac outside the FBO at Lindbergh Field, a uniformed co-pilot stepped up to open the door.

"Next stop Sedona?" he asked.

Nodding, Cami handed over her ID.

"I've never flown into SEZ before," he said. "I understand it's supposed to be the most scenic airport in the country."

Set on a mesa on the outskirts of Sedona, the municipal airport was surrounded by the town's signature bright red cliffs. Cami wasn't looking forward to seeing the scenery. She was looking forward to being home.

"Most of your luggage had been delivered to the FBO before we arrived, so it's already on board the aircraft. Is there anything else?"

"Nope," she told him, pulling the cell phone out of the pocket of her day-old track suit. "This is all I have at the moment."

Less than two hours after arriving at the airport in San Diego, the plane was on the ground in Sedona, and the only scenery Cami was interested in seeing was Mateo's silver Subaru Outback sitting in the parking lot. He stood waiting on the tarmac as she deplaned. When she had called Mateo early that morning, he and everyone else at High Noon had already been briefed about what had happened the night before.

"I'm glad you're home and glad you're safe," Mateo said, taking her into his arms and holding her close.

"That makes two of us," Cami murmured into his chest.

"We're supposed to stop by B. and Ali's place on the way home," Mateo told her. "Frigg has put together a dossier on your assailant."

"My alleged assailant," Cami corrected. "What if I was mistaken? What if I overreacted? What if the guy, whoever he was, had nothing at all to do with me?"

On the plane, Cami had read through Frigg's report on Bogdan Petrov. He had been born in the city of Dobrich in Bulgaria in 1979. After finishing school he had joined the military. In the early 2000s, he had served in Iraq before being dishonorably discharged. He had done several stints in prison on drug charges. He was known to have associates in the world of human trafficking, although he himself was not known to have participated in that kind of activity. His website described him as a security consultant, but there was no hint about what kind of consulting was actually being provided. *And how many consulting jobs like this did it take*, Cami wondered, *to pay for that custom-made suit?*

But the other news from Frigg left Cami feeling uneasy. Petrov's ID had come from the images captured on the video Cami had shot in the fitness center. Those were the only available images of him because the hotel's video surveillance system had been wiped clean of data. Cami understood the kind of technical know-how required to pull off that kind of a hack, and she doubted that a one-man consulting firm would have had the financial wherewithal to make it happen.

At B. and Ali's place, their majordomo, Alonzo Rivera, was back on duty, and the brunch he provided was a crusty egg, ham, and cheese casserole fresh out of the oven. The comfort food was sustaining, but Cami found the discussion that accompanied it troubling. Mateo, Ali, and B. were all convinced Cami had been targeted, but the more they talked, the more Cami found herself becoming less certain.

"What if I was totally mistaken about all this?" she asked. "I'd spent several days feeling as though someone was keeping an eye on me, but

I never laid eyes on an actual tail. When I saw this guy, I panicked, but what if he had nothing to do with me?"

"And what if he did?" Ali countered. "Your instincts are usually on the money. Given what's happened, I think you should cancel next week's trip to the UK and not go there until we find out more about who this guy is and what he's really up to."

"Cancel it?" Cami echoed in dismay. "Are you kidding? I'm in sales. Seeing clients is my job—that's what you pay me to do."

"Not if it puts you in danger," Ali said firmly. "And I also think that, for the time being, it might be best if you bunked at Stu's place for a night or two instead of going home to Cornville."

"No," Cami declared. "No way in hell. Now that I'm here, I want to be home in my own place instead of camping out in Stu Ramey's bachelor pad. If somebody is dumb enough to come after me there, you can bet I'll have my Glock in hand and be locked and loaded."

"Not in London you won't," Ali replied. "We both know you can't take your Glock to the UK, and I still think you should cancel the trip until a later time."

Cami remained adamant. "I went to a lot of trouble to set up five and a half days of back-to-back appointments. Postponing and then rescheduling them is out of the question."

With the two women seemingly at loggerheads, B. stepped into the fray. "You're both right. We don't have any proof that Cami was actually targeted, but we should probably proceed as if she was. However, Cami is also right in saying that canceling those previously scheduled appointments isn't a good idea. I say she makes the trip as planned, but that we have Sonja provide her with a security detail while she's there. All in favor?"

B. and Mateo both raised their hands at once. After a moment or two of reflection, Ali and Cami did, too. Then, for the next while, the four of them studied the detailed dossier Frigg had compiled on Bogdan Petrov. There was no sign of technical training in the man's education or military background that hinted at his having any kind of cyber skill set. None of his readily accessible financial records indicated that he'd have the funds necessary to purchase that kind of assistance in the open market. So who was he? If Petrov wasn't acting on his own, who was he working for? And was he targeting Cami individually or was High Noon itself caught in someone's crosshairs?

For the next several hours, they examined everyone involved in Cami's book of business, up to and including Dozo International. They looked at the customers she had brought on board, as well as at possibly disgruntled companies that had lost valued accounts when their business had moved over to High Noon. Nothing stood out, however, and nowhere was there any hint of a connection that led back to Bogdan Petrov.

"This isn't getting us anywhere," Cami said at last. "I'm ready to go home, change out of this damned track suit, and put my feet up."

Cami and Mateo left the house a few minutes later, but once they were in his Outback, Cami began grumbling.

"I don't need a babysitter," she said.

"You needed one last night," Mateo suggested mildly.

Cami glared at him. "I spotted a potential threat and took measures to counteract it."

"True," Mateo agreed. "But what if the next threat isn't quite so obvious? Maybe having a countermeasure already on the scene instead of having to call one in isn't such a bad idea."

"Now you're ganging up on me, too?" Cami demanded.

"I certainly am," Mateo said mildly, reaching over and taking her hand in his. "As your boyfriend, that's what I'm supposed to do. Now, what are your plans for dinner?"

"I don't have any, why?"

"Mom made her world-famous green chili tamales. How about if I drop you off at your place for a while so you can unwind. Then I'll come pick you up when it's time for dinner."

The fact that Mateo understood Cami's need for alone time was one of the things she appreciated about him.

"Sounds like a plan," she said. "Do you have to work tonight?"

"Nope, B. told me they have things covered."

"So can you come back to my place after dinner and stay over?"

He grinned back at her. "I thought you'd never ask."

Several hours later, as Mateo escorted Cami up the front steps to his place in Cottonwood, a smiling Olivia Vega was standing in the front doorway, waiting to greet them.

"*Bienvenida*," she said, gathering Cami into a smothering hug. "*Eres una chica tan valiente*." Welcome. You are such a brave girl.

When it was just the three of them, they spoke only in Spanish.

"*Gracias*," Cami replied, freeing herself from Olivia's embrace. "*Más afortunado que valiente*." More lucky than brave.

"*Afortunado y valiente*," Lucky and brave, Olivia beamed back at her.

Cami had been raised by highly critical parents, both of whom were distant and aloof. Olivia Vega was neither. At first Cami had been uncomfortable around the older woman's genial personality, but by now she was not only accustomed to it, she had come to appreciate it. And the fact that Cami was willing to speak Spanish in Olivia's presence made the younger woman an all-around winner as far as Olivia was concerned.

Compared to outside, the interior of the house was toasty warm, and it was alive with the aromas of flavorful cooking. A stack of freshly made tortillas sat on a plate next to a platter of green corn tamales, while Olivia's signature enchilada sauce simmered on the stovetop. It hadn't been that long since breakfast at B. and Ali's place. Nonetheless, Cami felt famished.

Over the scrumptious dinner that followed, Cami shared with Olivia some of the details of the previous night's dangerous encounter. As she related the story, Cami was aware that just over twenty-four hours had passed since then.

Yes, Cami thought to herself. *I was incredibly lucky then, and I'm incredibly lucky now, too.*

CHAPTER FOURTEEN

SEDONA, ARIZONA
SUNDAY, MARCH 19, 2023
2:00 P.M.

Ali and B. took it easy on Sunday morning, starting with a leisurely breakfast. After that, while B. headed to the office to go over whatever he had missed while out of town, Ali devoted herself to finalizing the security arrangements for Cami's upcoming trip. Her first choice had been for Cami to cancel completely, but considering one of Sonja Bjornson's agents would be looking out for her, Ali felt they had come up with an acceptable alternative.

Ali was considering going out for a walk when a voice message came in from Frigg, starting with her customary greeting.

"Good afternoon, Ali. I hope you're having a pleasant day."

"I am," Ali replied.

"Would now be a convenient time to update you on the situation in Washington?"

Ali had told B. that she'd stay away from whatever was going on with Clarice, but with B. in Cottonwood, what could it hurt to hear what Frigg had to say?

"Now's fine," Ali said aloud. "What have you got?"

"The first document I'll be sending is the video of a formal interview with Donna Jean Plummer."

"Donna Jean," Ali repeated. "The housekeeper? Is she now considered to be an official suspect?"

"Possibly, but this interview isn't related to Chuck Brewster. It's from a previous homicide investigation."

"Another homicide?" Ali asked faintly. "Whose?"

"The 1992 shooting death of one Kenneth Leroy Plummer, Donna Jean's estranged husband. The homicide occurred in Seattle, so the investigating agency was the Seattle Police Department. Homicide detectives Paul Kramer and Rich Little were assigned to the case."

The quality of the black-and-white video was so grainy she could barely make out the faces, and the audio wasn't much better.

"This is an old VHS recording," Ali objected. "How did you even gain access to it?"

"Sorry about the quality of the video," Frigg apologized. "Someone from Seattle PD copied the VHS tape onto a CD and sent it along to the detectives investigating the Brewster homicide. They uploaded it to a DVR file containing the other interviews related to the Brewster homicide."

Once again Frigg was up to her old tricks of gaining unauthorized access to details of ongoing investigations, but for once Ali voiced no objection.

"All right," she said. "Let's take a look."

The investigator in charge, a Detective Paul Kramer, opened the interview by announcing the time and date—1:30 p.m., June 8, 1992—as well as who all was present in the room—another Seattle PD cop named Rich Little and the suspect, Donna Jean Plummer, who appeared to be in her twenties. The tape began with Kramer reading the Miranda warning.

"Given all that, are you still willing to speak to us?"

Donna Jean nodded. "I just want to get this over with."

"Then tell us about yesterday."

"I shot him," she said simply. "He said he was going to kill me, so I shot him."

"By him, you mean your husband, Kenneth Leroy Plummer?"

"My estranged husband," she corrected, "but yes."

"What led up to this?"

"He hit my daughter. He hit Amy. Earlier in the afternoon, I needed a few things from the store. I don't usually leave her with Kenny, because I don't—I didn't—trust him to look after her. Turns out I was right. When I came home, she was crying like crazy and had a huge red handprint on her face. He told me she spilled his beer. That's why he hit her."

"What happened then?"

"I grabbed Amy and we left. I went to my folks' place. I told them about his hitting Amy, but I also told them about the rest of it—that he'd been beating on me the whole time we'd been married. They said I needed to file for a protection order and get a divorce. I knew they were right, but I decided to go home and grab some of our stuff. All Amy and I had with us were the clothes we were wearing. Mom begged me not to go, but I didn't listen. Daddy walked me out to the car, and that's when he gave me the gun—for protection."

"Is your father licensed to carry a weapon?"

"My f-father?" Donna Jean stammered. "Is he going to get in trouble for this, too?"

"Does he have a license to carry a firearm?" Kramer repeated.

"I don't know. I doubt it. He's had the gun for a long time—for as long as I can remember. I think his father gave it to him when he turned sixteen."

"What did you do with the weapon when he gave it to you?"

"I put it in my purse."

"So you concealed it?"

"I needed to put it somewhere. It was too big to fit in my pocket."

"What happened then?"

"I went home and started packing."

"Was Kenneth there?"

"No, but he came back as I was getting ready to leave. When he found out the door was locked and he couldn't get in, he went nuts."

"It was locked from the inside?"

Donna Jean nodded. "A dead bolt with a key, but he pounded on the door so hard that it made the whole house shake."

"Did you ever think about picking up the phone and dialing 911?"

"I was too scared. That's when he said he was going to go to his truck, get his sledgehammer, and break the door down. I looked out through the peephole and saw he was headed for his truck. That's where he keeps—he kept—all his tools. That's when I unlocked the door and opened it. Then I got the gun out of my purse and pulled the trigger. When I saw him fall, I couldn't believe I'd hit him. I'd never fired a gun before, but I hit him the first time out."

"What did you do then?"

"I called 911."

"Too bad you didn't do that before you shot him," Kramer said. "Ms. Plummer, we're now placing you under arrest for the murder of your husband." With that he concluded the interview.

"That detective's a jackass," Ali muttered under her breath.

"I'm assuming you're not referring to the four-legged kind," Frigg observed.

Ali laughed in spite of herself. "Definitely not," she agreed. "Had any previous domestic violence reports been made against Kenneth Plummer prior to the shooting?"

"Not that I can find," Frigg answered. "He did, however, have several DUI citations and one drunk and disorderly. That's about it."

That came as no surprise. Frigg was nothing if not thorough. Had there been a history of domestic violence reports, Donna Jean's use of a deadly weapon might have been more defensible. But since the investigators in the Brewster case had called this previous one into consideration, Ali had an idea that the case hadn't ended well.

"Before her husband was shot, did Donna Jean herself have any prior interactions with law enforcement?"

"None that I could find."

If Frigg couldn't find them, they didn't exist.

"How old was Donna Jean at the time of her arrest?"

"Twenty-three."

"And her daughter was how old?"

"Five."

"If Donna Jean was that young with no priors, no wonder she didn't know to ask for a lawyer before being questioned," Ali said. What happened next?"

"I believe it's safe to say that the prosecutor in this case was also what you would refer to as a jackass. He charged Donna Jean Plummer with first-degree murder. Eventually she went to trial and agreed to testify in her own defense. Would you care to see that portion of the trial transcript?"

"Not really," Ali replied somberly, "but I think I'd better."

CHAPTER FIFTEEN

SEDONA, ARIZONA
SUNDAY, MARCH 19, 2023
3:00 P.M.

The transcript from the King County courtroom of Judge Randall Crowell was dated July 9, 1993.

As soon as Ali noticed that, she got back to Frigg. "What was the date of that previous interview?"

"That would be 1:30 p.m., June 8, 1992."

"Was she allowed out on bail?"

"No. Her bail was set for five hundred thousand dollars. Neither she nor her parents were able raise that amount."

"So she sat in jail for over a year while awaiting trial?"

"Correct."

"What happened to the daughter?"

"She went to live with Donna Jean's parents."

Ali returned to the transcript. All Frigg had sent her was the defense portion of the trial.

JUDGE CROWELL
IS THE DEFENSE READY TO PROCEED?

CHRISTINE MAXWELL
WE ARE, YOUR HONOR.

JUDGE CROWELL

VERY WELL. YOU MAY CALL YOUR FIRST WITNESS.

CHRISTINE MAXWELL

THE DEFENSE CALLS DONNA JEAN PLUMMER. GOOD AFTERNOON, MRS. PLUMMER.

That one caught Ali's attention. It was unusual to have the defendant testify on her own behalf.

DONNA JEAN PLUMMER

GOOD AFTERNOON.

CHRISTINE MAXWELL

YOU WERE MARRIED TO THE DECEASED, KENNETH LEROY PLUMMER?

DONNA JEAN PLUMMER

I WAS.

CHRISTINE MAXWELL

HOW LONG WERE YOU TOGETHER?

DONNA JEAN PLUMMER

EIGHT YEARS ALTOGETHER. WE DATED FOR THREE AND WERE MARRIED FOR FIVE.

CHRISTINE MAXWELL

HOW OLD WERE YOU WHEN YOU MARRIED?

DONNA JEAN PLUMMER

WE GOT MARRIED ON THE DAY I TURNED EIGHTEEN. MY FOLKS DIDN'T APPROVE. . . .

ASSISTANT COUNTY ATTORNEY JACK MORRISON

OBJECTION. IS ALL THIS HISTORY NECESSARY?

CHRISTINE MAXWELL

IT IS, YOUR HONOR. THIS TESTIMONY PROVIDES BACKGROUND

AS TO HOW THE RELATIONSHIP BETWEEN THE VICTIM AND THE ACCUSED EVOLVED, AND PROVIDES CONTEXT AS TO WHAT LED UP TO THE ACTUAL INCIDENT.

JUDGE CROWELL

OVERRULED. YOU MAY CONTINUE, MS. MAXWELL, BUT KEEP IT MOVING.

CHRISTINE MAXWELL

YOUR PARENTS DIDN'T APPROVE OF THE RELATIONSHIP?

DONNA JEAN PLUMMER

NO, THEY THOUGHT HE WAS TOO OLD FOR ME AND TOO CONTROLLING.

CHRISTINE MAXWELL

WAS HE CONTROLLING?

DONNA JEAN PLUMMER

I GUESS. BUT I THOUGHT IT WAS BECAUSE HE LOVED ME. AND I THOUGHT MY PARENTS WERE JUST BEING . . . WELL . . . PARENTS.

CHRISTINE MAXWELL

WHEN WAS THE FIRST TIME HE BECAME VIOLENT WITH YOU?

DONNA JEAN PLUMMER

ON OUR WEDDING NIGHT. HE'D HAD TOO MUCH TO DRINK. I OFFERED TO DRIVE. WHEN WE GOT TO THE HOTEL, WE WALKED INTO THE ROOM, AND THAT'S WHEN HE HIT ME.

CHRISTINE MAXWELL

YOU SAY HE HIT YOU. LIKE, SLAPPED YOU?

DONNA JEAN PLUMMER

NO, HE PUNCHED ME WITH A CLOSED FIST, RIGHT IN THE GUT. HE TOLD ME THAT JUST BECAUSE WE WERE MARRIED DIDN'T MEAN

I GOT TO BOSS HIM AROUND. HE TOLD ME THAT IF I EVER TOLD ANYONE THAT HE HAD HIT ME, HE'D KILL ME, AND I BELIEVED HIM. I NEVER TOLD ANYONE.

CHRISTINE MAXWELL
WERE YOU PREGNANT AT THE TIME?

DONNA JEAN PLUMMER
I WAS.

CHRISTINE MAXWELL
WAS HE AWARE OF THE PREGNANCY?

DONNA JEAN PLUMMER
YES.

CHRISTINE MAXWELL
WERE YOUR PARENTS AWARE OF IT?

DONNA JEAN PLUMMER
NO.

CHRISTINE MAXWELL
THE ABUSE CONTINUED AFTER THAT?

DONNA JEAN PLUMMER
YES.

CHRISTINE MAXWELL
DID YOU EVER REPORT IT TO LAW ENFORCEMENT?

DONNA JEAN PLUMMER
NO, I WAS AFRAID TO.

CHRISTINE MAXWELL
DID YOU TELL ANYONE ELSE?

DONNA JEAN PLUMMER
NO.

CHRISTINE MAXWELL

WHY NOT?

DONNA JEAN PLUMMER

I DIDN'T THINK ANYONE WOULD BELIEVE ME. HE NEVER HIT ME WHERE IT WOULD SHOW.

CHRISTINE MAXWELL

WHAT HAPPENED PRIOR TO THE INCIDENT IN QUESTION?

DONNA JEAN PLUMMER

IT WAS SUNDAY AFTERNOON. MY DAUGHTER, AMY, WAS TAKING A NAP, AND I NEEDED TO GO TO THE STORE. I THOUGHT I'D BE HOME BEFORE SHE WOKE UP, BUT IT TOOK LONGER THAN EXPECTED. WHEN I GOT BACK, SHE WAS CRYING AND I SAW A HANDPRINT ON HER FACE. I ASKED WHAT HAD HAPPENED. KENNY TOLD ME THAT SHE'D SPILLED HIS BEER AND HE HIT HER.

CHRISTINE MAXWELL

WHAT HAPPENED THEN?

The remainder of Donna Jean's direct testimony was almost exactly the same as what she'd said earlier in her interview with the detectives, so Ali skimmed through to the spot where the prosecutor began his cross-examination. At that point, Ali could tell things were going to go south.

JUDGE CROWELL

MR. MORRISON? ARE YOU READY TO PROCEED?

ASSISTANT COUNTY ATTORNEY MORRISON

WE ARE, THANK YOU, YOUR HONOR. NOW, MRS. PLUMMER, WHEN YOUR HUSBAND FIRST CAME TO THE DOOR AND STARTED THREATENING YOU, WHY DIDN'T YOU DIAL 911 THEN?

DONNA JEAN PLUMMER

I DON'T KNOW. I GUESS I WASN'T THINKING STRAIGHT.

ASSISTANT COUNTY ATTORNEY MORRISON

COULD YOUR NOT CALLING HAVE HAD ANYTHING TO DO WITH THE FACT THAT YOU KNEW YOU WERE ON THE OTHER SIDE OF THAT LOCKED DOOR AND ARMED WITH A DEADLY WEAPON?

CHRISTINE MAXWELL

OBJECTION.

JUDGE CROWELL

SUSTAINED, THE JURY MAY DISREGARD THAT QUESTION.

ASSISTANT COUNTY ATTORNEY MORRISON

WHILE YOU WERE SPEAKING TO YOUR HUSBAND, WHERE WAS THE WEAPON?

DONNA JEAN PLUMMER

IT WAS IN MY PURSE ON A SIDE TABLE NEXT TO THE DOOR.

ASSISTANT COUNTY ATTORNEY MORRISON

AND WHERE EXACTLY WAS YOUR HUSBAND WHEN YOU OPENED THE DOOR?

DONNA JEAN PLUMMER

HE WAS WALKING DOWN THE STEPS TOWARD THE SIDEWALK.

ASSISTANT COUNTY ATTORNEY MORRISON

WAS HE WALKING TOWARD YOU OR WALKING AWAY?

DONNA JEAN PLUMMER

AWAY, BUT HE WAS GOING TO THE TRUCK TO GET HIS—

ASSISTANT COUNTY ATTORNEY MORRISON

AND YOU STILL FELT AS THOUGH YOU WERE IN MORTAL DANGER?

CHRISTINE MAXWELL

OBJECTION. ASKED AND ANSWERED.

ASSISTANT COUNTY ATTORNEY MORRISON

I'LL WITHDRAW THE QUESTION. AT THE TIME YOU PULLED THE TRIGGER, WAS KENNETH PLUMMER ARMED WITH ANY KIND OF WEAPON?

DONNA JEAN PLUMMER

NO, BUT—

ASSISTANT COUNTY ATTORNEY MORRISON

AND WHERE EXACTLY DID YOU SHOOT HIM?

DONNA JEAN PLUMMER

IN THE BACK, BUT—

ASSISTANT COUNTY ATTORNEY MORRISON

NO FURTHER QUESTIONS FOR THIS WITNESS.

JUDGE CROWELL

MS. MAXWELL?

CHRISTINE MAXWELL

NOTHING AT THIS TIME.

JUDGE CROWELL

VERY WELL, THE WITNESS MAY STEP DOWN.

Ali sighed. She had little doubt that the only information the jury would have taken away from that portion of Donna Jean's testimony was that Kenneth Plummer had been unarmed and walking away from her when he was shot in the back.

"What was the verdict?" she asked Frigg.

"The jury found Donna Jean Plummer guilty of voluntary manslaughter. She was sentenced to seven to ten years, with the sentence reduced by time served. She was in lockup for a total of eight."

"Three years longer than she was married to the creep who beat her up on her wedding night," Ali muttered. "What happened to her little girl?"

"Ms. Plummer's parents raised her. Amy Plummer is now Amy Plummer Robbins. She's currently thirty-four years of age. She graduated cum laude from the University of Washington and teaches seventh-grade math at Madison Middle School in West Seattle. She has one child, a six-year-old son named Jacob."

"How did Donna Jean end up cleaning houses?"

"When she was released on parole, she went to work for a company that employed a team of workers. When that company went out of business a couple of years later, Donna Jean started her own cleaning service. The Brewster account was a carryover from her previous employer. She's worked for the Brewsters on an individual basis two days a week for more than twenty years."

Ali thought about what Frigg had just told her. Yes, Donna Jean had been at the Chuck Brewster crime scene, but had any of her blood or DNA been found on the victim? And since the Brewsters were clearly good customers of hers, what would be her motivation? Was Donna Jean's previous conviction the reason the cops were seemingly determined to drag her into this investigation?

Ali posed that very question to Frigg.

"Most likely," the AI answered.

"Are the investigators looking at anyone else?"

"They are in the process of contacting the people who attended the party. Mrs. Brewster claims not to have access to the complete guest list since most of the people in attendance were connected to her husband's work. One of the guests was Mr. Brewster's son, Adam. He was on a plane heading back to L.A. when the body was discovered. I'm not sure when he'll be returning."

"I wasn't aware there was a son," Ali said.

"They were evidently estranged for some time and had only recently reconciled."

Ali thought about that for a moment. "The Brewsters are anything but broke," she said. "What happens to their money if Clarice is convicted of murdering her husband?"

"Would you like to see the applicable statute?" Frigg asked.

"Yes, please."

Seconds later the following turned up on Ali's iPad:

The murderer will be deemed to have predeceased the victim under the WA slayer statute:

RCW 11.84.030

Slayer or abuser deemed to predecease decedent.

The slayer or abuser shall be deemed to have predeceased the decedent as to property which would have passed from the decedent or his or her estate to the slayer or abuser under the statutes of descent and distribution or have been acquired by statutory right as surviving spouse or surviving domestic partner or under any agreement made with the decedent under the provisions of RCW 26.16.120 as it now exists or is hereafter amended.

Ali read through the statute several times before she spoke again. "Blood and DNA notwithstanding, I hope whoever's working this case is smart enough to follow Chuck's money. If it's not going to Clarice, you'd better believe it's going to his son. What's going on with her, by the way?"

"Clarice Brewster is still in police custody," Frigg reported. "She pled not guilty at her preliminary hearing, but the judge refused to grant bail."

"So although she's in lockup, the cops are still looking at Donna Jean?"

"Evidently," Frigg replied.

That's when it occurred to Ali that perhaps Frigg had been correct to begin with. Maybe both Clarice Brewster and Donna Jean Plummer really were being railroaded, and the cops working the case couldn't be bothered with looking at anyone else.

CHAPTER SIXTEEN

SEDONA, ARIZONA
SUNDAY, MARCH 19, 2023
9:00 P.M.

By nine that night, Ali and B. were cozily ensconced in the library, watching PBS. B. may have been watching TV, but Ali wasn't connecting with what was happening on the screen. Most of the time, there was total transparency between Ali and her husband. Tonight there was an invisible elephant in the room. When they had first heard about Chuck Brewster's murder, B. had been absolutely adamant about not wanting to be caught up in the drama surrounding his former wife. Now, with Frigg's assistance, Ali was knee-deep in it.

"What's going on with you?" B. asked finally. "It's like you're on another planet. Are you still worrying about Cami?"

Ali took a deep breath. It was time to come clean. "No," she said finally. "I'm sure Cami will be in good hands. It's something else."

"What?"

"It's Clarice. She's been charged with murder. She pled not guilty at her preliminary hearing and was denied bail on account of being a flight risk. Her housekeeper, Donna Jean Plummer, is suspected of being her accomplice."

For a long moment, B. said absolutely nothing. Finally, he asked, "You know all of this how?"

"Frigg has been looking into it at my request."

"Why?"

"Because I think there's a good chance that neither is responsible."

"Why on earth . . . ?" B. began.

"We're talking about Edmonds PD," Ali answered. "That's the same department that put Mateo Vega behind bars for sixteen years for something he didn't do. Their investigators had tunnel vision back then, and that may be the case here, too. Chuck's long-estranged son, Adam, has recently come back into the picture. If Clarice goes down for the murder, he'll most likely get everything."

"And deservedly so," B. said. "I knew Adam from the time he was born. He was a good kid who thought the sun rose and set on his dad. Estranged or not, he wouldn't do something like this, not in a million years."

"Well then," Ali said, "if Clarice and Donna Jean didn't do it, and if Adam didn't do it either, then I'd like to be sure that whoever did is held accountable."

B. frowned. "You're not going to give up on this, are you?"

"Probably not," Ali answered.

"Then leave me out of it," B. said, rising to his feet. "This may be your problem, but it sure as hell isn't mine! I don't want to have anything to do with it."

With that, B. Simpson stormed from the room, leaving Ali sitting alone, stewing in her own juices. She felt as though she had inadvertently crossed some invisible line, and she wasn't at all sure the damage could be undone.

CHAPTER SEVENTEEN

COTTONWOOD, ARIZONA
MONDAY, MARCH 20, 2023
5:30 A.M.

Things still weren't exactly hunky-dory between Ali and B. when she awakened the next morning. B. had left for Cottonwood by the time she crawled out of bed. That wasn't a good sign. They usually commuted back and forth to Cottonwood together. Whenever her mother, Edie Larson, had been busy minding everybody else's business, her dad had always said she was Edieing it. Obviously, Ali was a chip off her mother's old block, and B. regarded her involvement in his former wife's homicide case with a disdain similar to Bob Larson's attitude toward his own wife's being "too full of business."

"Mr. Simpson's already gone," Alonzo Rivera observed as he handed Ali her first cup of coffee.

"I noticed," Ali said with a nod. "I'm afraid his nose is a little out of joint with me at the moment, so I'll go to work, keep my head down, and hope it all blows over."

"Is there anything I can do to help?"

"Yes," Ali answered. "As a matter of fact, there is. Please make meatloaf for dinner. That always puts him in a good mood."

"Aye, aye, ma'am," Alonzo said with a smile and a mock salute. "Will do."

At the office, Ali was amazed to find Stu's Dodge Ram pickup parked in its assigned place.

"I had no idea Stu would be coming back to work today," Ali said to Shirley as she walked past the reception desk.

"Neither did anyone else," Shirley replied.

"I distinctly remember telling him that he should take the next few days off."

Shirley smiled. "In my experience, Stu Ramey isn't very good at taking suggestions."

Ali made her way through the office to the lab, where she found Stu at his workstation. "I thought you were going to take some time off. Don't they need you at the ranch?"

"Why would they?" he asked. "Everybody there knows what they're doing. Besides, I scattered Aunt Julia's ashes yesterday, just like she wanted me to. I'm better off being here working than I would be sitting at home brooding."

"Okay, then," Ali replied. "Work to your heart's content."

In response to Stu's dismissive wave, Ali took her leave and returned to her office. She eased into her chair and took a deep breath. Cami was on her way to the UK and maybe walking into danger, but it was comforting to know that one of Sonja Bjornson's top operatives, someone named Rachel Bloom, would be waiting for her at Heathrow.

According to Rachel's CV, she was a former intelligence officer for the Israeli Defense Forces where she had worked in cybersecurity. She was also a top marksman and trained in martial arts, including Cami's favorite—Krav Maga. Cami had objected to being handed over to the care of a babysitter. Ali hoped their relationship might morph into something resembling a friendship.

After spending all of Friday dealing with Stu's Aunt Julia situation, Ali's desk was the same disaster it had been when she had shipped the tax packet off to the accountant on Thursday. In other words, all the things she'd let slide during the tax season were still waiting for her. She started by clearing her desk and taking care of anything that was actively ticking. At the bottom of the heap was something she was actually looking forward to handling—a file folder marked AMELIA DOUGHERTY SCHOLARSHIP, 2023.

For the past ten years, in addition to her CFO duties at High Noon Enterprises, Ali had been in charge of administering the Amelia Dougherty Scholarship Program, the Verde Valley–based nonprofit from which she herself had once benefited. One of their full ride scholarships had allowed her to go on to college.

At the time Ali first began overseeing the scholarship program, it had been limited to girls only and gave out only one scholarship a year. After some strategic fundraising on Ali's part, there were now two winners per year, and both boys and girls were welcome to apply.

As applications came in, Ali read through them, setting aside the ones that really caught her attention. She wasn't necessarily looking for kids with the highest GPAs or for those whose athletic abilities made them A-listers. She tended to focus on kids who were slightly out of the norm—ones who exhibited a spark of spunk and ambition and whose family's financial situation clearly wouldn't support their sending a child off to college.

This year's application deadline had been March 1. Each applicant had been asked to provide a copy of their school transcripts along with two letters of recommendation. They were also required to write an essay on one of three topics: What Family Means to Me; The Most Important Person in My Life; and Where I Hope to Be in Twenty Years.

During her tax prep ordeal, Ali had scanned through the paperwork and read all the essays as they came in, setting aside those that touched her. Out of more than fifty essays, only two had made the final cut and landed in the second, much-thinner folder inside the first. Now, sitting alone in her quiet office, Ali reread those two essays, starting with one from a boy named Daniel Knowles.

My parents never went to college. My dad's an electrician. My mom's a housewife who takes care of her mother. They don't understand why I want to go to college and run up an armload of college debt just to become a teacher when I could sign up for an apprenticeship program and earn money while I'm learning how to become an electrician. Dad says I'll make way more money doing that than I will teaching school, but teaching is still what I want to do, and that's because of the most important person in my life—Mrs. Donner.

From first grade on, I hated school. The other kids were able to learn how to read. I wasn't, so I turned myself into the class clown. I was always in trouble and spent a lot of time in the principal's office. I flunked first grade and third grade, too. Finally, in fourth grade, they put me in special ed. That's when I met Mrs. Donner. She was the one who finally figured out that I couldn't read.

One day, she kept me in during recess. I thought I had done something wrong. Instead, she came over to my desk, gave me a Superman comic book, and told me, "This is how you're going to learn to read."

And I did. I could see what was going on in the pictures, but I wanted to know what the characters were thinking and saying. To do that, you had to understand what was in the bubbles. One bubble at a time, she taught me how to read.

This is Mrs. Donner:

Below was a hand-drawn sketch of an older woman and a young boy. The smiling woman was white-haired and holding a Superman comic book. The boy was grinning from ear to ear. The words in the woman's bubble said, "Danny, you can learn to read."

If a picture is worth a thousand words, that one did it for Ali. Yes, it was a cartoon, but she suspected that the skillfully done drawing closely resembled the real Mrs. Donner, and the words in her bubble spoke volumes about her and about the student whose life she had transformed for the better. The fact that a personal letter of recommendation from Mrs. Donner was included in Daniel's scholarship packet all these years later testified to the fact that kids lucky enough to be Mrs. Donner's students, remained her students for life.

By fifth grade, she said I was caught up enough to be placed back in a regular classroom. When that happened, the kids who always used to call me stupid still did, but I knew better. That's when I started drawing, and I haven't stopped. This year some of my drawings will be included in the high school yearbook.

Since my parents are against my going on to school, I haven't applied anywhere because I don't know how I'd pay for it. I still stay in touch with Mrs. Donner, and she's the person who said I should apply for this scholarship. She said that if I become a teacher, I could spend my summers off writing graphic novels. If I do that, maybe someday I can help some other dyslexic kid learn how to read.

Like Daniel's parents, neither of Ali's folks had attended college, but unlike Daniel's parents, they had never tried to discourage her from going. It had been Ali's mother's twin sister—her Aunt Evie—who had put Ali in touch with the Amelia Dougherty Scholarship program. In Daniel's case, it had been his very perceptive fourth grade teacher. *Go Mrs. Donner*, Ali thought.

Setting Daniel's essay aside, she turned to the one from Susan Rojas.

The most important person in my life is my great-grandmother, Emelda Moreno. Five years ago, she was a widow in her seventies and living on her husband's Social Security when my mother died of an overdose. When that happened, we were living in a homeless shelter. I came home from school one day and found Mom asleep in her bed. At first I thought she was taking a nap, but hours later I figured out she was dead.

I grew up in a totally dysfunctional family. I never knew my father, and both my mother and her mother were deep in drugs. After

Mom died, when the social workers were looking for someone to take care of me, my mother's grandmother, Grandma Moreno, stepped up.

For years, she and Grandpa Moreno managed an RV park in Oak Creek. Their mobile home washed away in a flash flood in 2015. At that point, someone offered to let them live in an old RV on their property outside Cordes Junction. That's where they were living when Grandpa died two years later, and that's where we're still living now. It's hot in the summer and cold in the winter, but it's better than living on the street.

We have to pay for utilities, but we don't pay any rent. Some money comes in from my mother's Social Security, but that will stop once I turn eighteen. Then all Grandma Moreno will have to live on is Grandpa's Social Security. She makes tamales each week, and I sell them at the farmers market, but what we make from those doesn't go very far.

My teachers keep telling me that I'm smart enough to go to college. That's why I'm writing this essay, because my school counselor made me promise I would. But I've done some research on Amelia Dougherty Scholarships. They go to people who can pursue higher education on a full-time basis. I can't. Grandma is almost eighty now. She looked after me when I needed it, and now I need to look after her.

If a scholarship from you would allow me to take college courses online, that would be a huge blessing.

Ali finished reading Susan's essay with a lump in her throat. She had no doubt that Susan Rojas, like Daniel Knowles, needed to go on to college, but the scholarship program didn't take into account caring for elderly relatives. And encouraging this young woman to opt out on her self-assigned responsibility for looking after her great-grandmother wasn't something Ali was prepared to do.

By then Ali was sure that her first impression of the letters had been the right one, and her decision was made. She wasn't sure how, but one way or another, Daniel and Susan would be this year's winners. By then, it was almost quitting time. Putting the essays back into the file, Ali picked up her purse, shut off the lights in her office, closed the door, squared her shoulders, and went in search of B.

The lab where he and Lance were working on GHOST's latest upgrade was just down the hall. Ali had learned that once they got caught up in a project, they both loved what they were doing so much, the two of them lost all sense of time. On this occasion, however, she was unsure of her reception.

"Okay," she announced, opening the door to the lab. "Work's over. I'm about to pull the plug on both of you. Time to go home."

"Do we have to?" B. whined, doing his best to imitate an intransigent kid who doesn't want to go to bed.

"Yes, you have to," she insisted. "Alonzo's back. He's making meatloaf for dinner, and we shouldn't be late."

"Speaking of Alonzo," B. said as they left the building to walk to the parking lot. "He sent me a text earlier this afternoon. He said he'd like to have a chat with us after dinner. I suggested he join us for dinner instead."

Alonzo usually prepared and ate his own meals in the fifth wheel RV that served as his residence, which was parked on the far side of their garage. The RV had belonged to their previous majordomo, Leland Brooks. Ali and B. had taken it off his hands when he had retired and returned to the UK. Alonzo had lived there the whole time he had worked for them.

Ali felt her heart fall. "Oh, no," she said. "I hope he's not quitting."

"I do, too," B. said. "Having him around makes both our lives so much easier."

When they reached the parking lot, B. paused. "My car or yours?" he asked.

The fact that B. was suggesting they ride home together made Ali hope that all was forgiven.

"How about yours?" Ali asked. "I'm sorry about last night—"

"And I'm sorry I stormed out," B. interrupted. "I know you well enough to understand that once you get your teeth into something, you're like a dog with a bone, and you're not going to let go. So do what you do, but please leave me out of it. All this brings up too much bad stuff for me, and I'm not ready to go there. Fair enough?"

"Fair enough," Ali agreed.

With that they headed home in B.'s Audi.

"Now that the taxes are done, what were you up to today?" B. asked.

"It's scholarship time," she reported. "I've picked my two winners, but there are a few bumps in the road that will need to be sorted."

"Care to talk about it?"

"Still at the thinking stage," she answered.

"I've been thinking, too," B. said. "Alonzo's been spending a lot more time in Phoenix recently. I'm wondering if he has a girlfriend."

"A girlfriend?" Ali repeated. "He told us he's a confirmed bachelor."

B. shot her a look. "Every guy's a confirmed bachelor, right up until he meets The One," he said with a grin. "Look what happened to me. I had no intention of ever marrying again, and then you came along."

"Right," Ali agreed grudgingly. "If that turns out to be the case, I'll be sure to wish them well."

Upon entering the house, they were greeted with two tantalizing aromas—the scents of freshly baked bread and Alonzo's incomparable meatloaf.

"Dinner's in about half an hour," he told them as they stepped into the kitchen. On the way through the dining room, Ali noticed that the table was set for three, with wineglasses a part of each place setting.

This is more than just a chat, she thought.

She was right. As soon as dinner started, B. went straight to the heart of the matter.

"So what's the deal, Alonzo?" he asked. "What do we need to talk about?"

Alonzo came right out with it. "I'm getting married," he said.

Fortunately, Ali had had enough advance warning that she wasn't caught completely off guard.

"Congratulations," she said at once. "That's wonderful. Who is the lucky lady? How did the two of you meet? How long have you known her? And when's the big day?"

Alonzo took the barrage of questions in good humor. "Her name is Gwen Wright. Her mother's place is next to my aunty's place in Glendale. She's been living in California and moved back to Phoenix last summer. We met when my Aunt Rose hosted a birthday pool party for Gwen's seven-year-old niece. She does medical transcriptions, so she was working remotely long before the pandemic. We want to get married, but I can't very well ask her to come live in the RV. I know my living rent-free has always been part of my compensation, but . . . "

Suddenly Ali felt as though a lightbulb had exploded in her head. Here was the answer to her Susan Rojas problem—a way for Susan to go on to school while not abandoning her great-grandmother. What was needed was an RV, an almost pristine one at that, and one of those was already in hand. If Alonzo went to live somewhere else, his RV could be moved to a convenient location near whatever college campus Susan Rojas chose to attend.

"In that case," Ali said, interrupting Alonzo in mid-sentence, "it sounds as though you'll need a raise. How much?"

Alonzo seemed flustered by Ali's direct approach. "We can't afford to buy, of course," but I found a nice apartment in Cottonwood that's two thousand dollars a month, utilities included."

"Done," Ali said. "No problem. We'll give you a raise to cover that as of this month, and if the apartment you like is still available, I suggest you grab it. When's the wedding?"

Now it was B.'s turn to be gobsmacked. Ali saw the astonished expression on her husband's face, but he made no objection.

"In a few weeks, maybe?" Alonzo suggested dubiously. "We're thinking of eloping to Vegas to tie the knot."

"Getting married in Vegas certainly worked for us," Ali told him with a smile, "and the wedding package at Treasure Island was great. We'll be glad to help any way we can. Just let us know."

With that she got up, walked around the table, and gave Alonzo a hug. "You've been worth your weight in gold and still are. I don't know how we would have gotten through the pandemic without you, and we can't wait to meet Gwen."

"How about next weekend?" Alonzo suggested tentatively. "Saturday for dinner, maybe?"

"Sounds perfect."

"Here, here," B. said. "I believe a toast is in order."

And it was.

Later, when dinner was over and B. and Ali were settled in the library, B. gave her a sidelong look. "You're not much of a negotiator," he said. "You gave away the store without even waiting for him to ask."

"No problem," Ali said. "It seemed like a fine negotiation to me. I got everything I wanted."

"Everything you wanted?" B. repeated with a frown.

"Remember how, on the way home, I told you I had a scholarship problem? Being able to use Alonzo's RV for student housing is going to make it possible for a very deserving young woman to go on to school while also caring for her eighty-year-old great-grandmother."

"Wait," B. said. "You're expecting an eighty-something-year-old woman to live in an RV with a college student?"

"She's currently living in a much older and probably smaller RV with a high school student," Ali said. "Since they were given the one they're living in for free a number of years ago, I'm guessing it's not in nearly as good condition as the one Alonzo has been using. As for Alonzo? He deserves to have a personal life, and now's a good time for him to do it. As far as I'm concerned, it's a win-win."

B. shook his head in mock exasperation. "Next you'll probably be offering to pay for the wedding package," he grumbled.

Ali grinned back at him. "That's the wonderful thing about being the CFO. I know exactly how much money we have coming and going. As far as Alonzo's raise is concerned, I know we can afford it, and although I hadn't really thought about paying for the wedding, now that you mention it, that sounds like a great idea."

CHAPTER EIGHTEEN

LONDON, ENGLAND
TUESDAY, MARCH 21, 2023
11:00 A.M.

By the time Cami's British Airways flight landed on Tuesday morning, she was a rag. She had slept for most of the flight from Sky Harbor to Heathrow, so her body was beyond confused. After clearing customs, she had walked into the terminal dreading the idea that she was about to meet her minder for the duration. She expected that Rachel Bloom would approach her discreetly and then lead Cami out of the terminal to a nearby parking structure.

The WWS operatives she had met before had all been statuesque beauties, and that's what she expected this time around. Instead, the purple-haired, stockily built woman who rushed forward to greet Cami was anything but a fashion plate. Her smiling face was full of piercings, and a collection of tattoos covered her arms and legs. She was dressed in a bright orange muumuu and a pair of yellow Crocs, and although Rachel wasn't much taller than Cami, she was strong as an ox.

"Oh, Cami, Cami, Cami," she squealed in seeming delight, grabbing Cami into a bone-crushing hug, lifting her off the floor and swinging her around in a complete circle. "It's so good to see you again. I've missed you so much. This is going to be our best vacation ever! Come on. Let's go get your luggage."

For a moment, Cami had been taken aback, but then she understood. No one witnessing that over-the-top exchange between them would ever suspect that the wildly dressed, whirling dervish of a woman of being a fully trained and possibly deadly bodyguard. All the way through the terminal and while collecting Cami's luggage, Rachel chatted away, giving every appearance that the two of them were old best friends getting together for the first time in years.

"You don't look much like your photo," Cami observed as they headed to the luggage carousels.

Rachel laughed. "The wig comes off. Once the studs come out, the holes disappear in a couple of weeks. As for the tattoos? They're guaranteed to last for two weeks. After that, they scrub right off. The thing is, no one looking at someone like this suspects I'm a bodyguard."

"You're right about that," Cami said with a laugh of her own. "You could have fooled me."

"For ease of doing my job, we have connecting rooms at the Portlandia," Rachel explained. "It's a hotel WWS has used before and one where the doorman and most of the hotel staff won't regard me with suspicion. That'll make it easier for me to keep an eye on you."

With luggage in hand, Rachel led the way to a parking structure where a cab was waiting to drive them from Heathrow to the Hotel Portlandia on London's Great Portland Street. Although the vehicle looked like the genuine article, it was clear from the conversation between Rachel and the driver that both he and his pretend cab were part of Sonja Bjornson's organization.

"How was your trip?" Rachel asked as they settled into the back seat for the forty-five-minute drive into the city.

"It was fine," Cami answered.

"I've been briefed on you," Rachel continued, "but I'd like to hear more from you about exactly what went on in L.A. last week. That way I'll have a better idea of what to look for in terms of doing threat assessment."

Cami recounted the whole ordeal in as much detail as she could remember, with Rachel hanging on every word.

"All right," Rachel said when she finished. "Sonja sent me several photos of Mr. Petrov. As far as we can tell, he hasn't left the U.S., so if there's a threat, it's unlikely to be from him. Not to worry, though. I'll be keeping an eye on you every moment of every day.

"As you may have noticed, I'm not exactly svelte," Rachel continued. "In the Defense Forces, guys called me Tank for obvious reasons. People often underestimate me, but they seldom make that same mistake twice. From what I've heard, the same thing is true for you. I think we're going to make a great team."

For the first time, Cami felt the same way. Maybe having a minder wasn't going to be such a problem after all. It might even be fun.

"By the way," Rachel added, "we've notified the Lancaster about what went on. Considering their clientele, they're eager to keep the incident out of the public eye, so they've been very cooperative. They were dismayed to learn that their surveillance footage for Friday night had been tampered with, but surveillance for the remainder of the week was pretty much intact.

"Mr. Petrov was a frequent visitor to the hotel last week, but he wasn't a registered guest. On Monday of that week, the same day you arrived, a young woman named Marina Ivanova, a Bulgarian immigrant associated with a well-known Los Angeles escort service, arrived at the hotel and booked a weeklong stay in a suite on the tenth floor."

"The same floor I was on," Cami said.

"Exactly," Rachel agreed. Pulling out her phone, she turned it on and then scrolled through it until she found what she was looking for. When she handed her phone to Cami, the picture showing on the screen was someone Cami had seen before.

"She's the same woman who was in the dining room with Bogdan Petrov just before he came after me."

Rachel nodded. "And we don't believe it's a coincidence that her suite was three doors away from yours. As I said, he wasn't a registered guest, but he frequently visited Ms. Ivanova's suite, and we've found surveillance footage from earlier in the week of him using a key card to gain entrance to her room."

"So he knew exactly where I was staying and even what floor?" Cami asked.

"Yes," Rachel replied. "We've found evidence that suggests that the Lancaster's reservation system as well as their surveillance system were both hacked in advance of your arrival. But that's not all. When Ms. Ivanova arrived on Monday, she didn't use valet parking or a bellman. Instead, she drove into the parking garage to unload her luggage."

Once again, Rachel scrolled through her phone. This time when she handed it to Cami, a video was playing. The camera was located at some distance from the action, so it wasn't easy to make out details, but a female figure was busily unloading an SUV of some kind. She lifted out two smaller pieces of roller luggage and one very large one.

The two smaller ones were evidently stackable. The larger one was not. After closing the back gate on the SUV, the woman collected her bags and started toward a nearby elevator.

"Watch how she handles the luggage," Rachel advised.

Having spent a lot of time on the road, Camille Lee was well acquainted with handling luggage. Heavily loaded bags required not only steering but also a certain amount of aiming. Lightweight ones rolled along almost of their own accord. As the woman approached the elevator, she struggled to ram the two stacked pieces over the lip between the floor of the elevator and the floor of the garage. When it came to the larger one, however, she picked it up and lifted it inside one-handed.

"It looks like the big bag is empty," Cami observed.

"Exactly," Rachel Bloom agreed, "and it was still empty on Saturday morning when Marina loaded it into her car as she was leaving the Lancaster. Unfortunately, WWS has encountered that same piece of luggage before on occasion. If someone is small in stature and totally sedated, it's possible for them to be crammed into a bag like that and removed from a crime scene without anyone being the wiser."

Cami gave herself a minute to digest what had just been said. "Wait a minute. Are you saying that big roller was intended for me?"

Rachel nodded. "I am indeed."

That admission was enough to take Cami's breath away. Her previous kidnapping episode still haunted her, and it appeared that this second one had come way too close for comfort. Just the thought of it left her feeling sick to her stomach.

"But why would someone do that?" she asked. "And why me?"

"That's what we have to figure out."

"And what about Petrov?" Cami asked. "Where's he during all of this?"

"The last time he was seen coming or going from the Lancaster was on Thursday evening. All of Friday's surveillance footage vanished, taking Mr. Petrov's subsequent comings and goings with it, but hold on while I bring up another video."

Once the new footage started playing, Cami saw they were once again in an underground parking garage with a view of an elevator lobby. The time stamp said Monday, March 13, 2023, 11:35.06 p.m. As the video began, the elevator doors opened and a woman emerged. This time the camera was close enough for Cami to recognize Marina Ivanova.

The woman stepped out of the elevator and looked both ways before setting off. She went directly to a vehicle, walked up to the front of it, and then bent over it. She stayed in that position for only a moment or two before straightening up and heading back to the elevator.

"Wait a minute," Cami said. "Isn't that my car? Did she just put a GPS tracker on it?"

"Yes, she did," Rachel replied. "She shoved it inside the front bumper so it was completely out of sight. We contacted the car rental company. Fortunately, the vehicle was back on the lot, and we were able to locate the device."

"So in all the excitement, they forgot to retrieve it," Cami said. "But I was right. Someone really was following me."

"Yes, they were," Rachel answered with a smile. "But now, not only do we have the device in hand, we also have all the phone numbers it was connected to."

"Does that mean you know where Petrov is?"

"It means we know where he was. The last time the phone pinged was on Saturday morning in a desert area outside San Bernardino, California. As far as we can tell, it was turned off at that point and hasn't been back on since."

"What would a guy from Bulgaria be doing in San Bernardino?" Cami asked.

"Good question. Now that we have the phone number, we're trying to gain access to the call history. We're working on it, but it hasn't happened yet."

Looking out the window of the cab, Cami could see they were close to their destination.

"What now?" she wanted to know.

"I'm glad you asked," Rachel replied. "Since we know that we're dealing with a serious opponent, I think we need to up our game. I know you're here on business and that you have a number of appointments lined up, but the less you're out and about the better."

"What are you saying?"

"I took the liberty of reserving a conference room for the length of your stay. Instead of going out to visit clients at their places of business, they're going to have to come to you."

"But what if they don't want to?" Cami objected.

"You're staying at the Portlandia," Rachel told her. "That's name brand, my dear. Tell them there's been a slight change of plans, and then invite them to join you for breakfast, lunch, dinner, or even for tea. Afternoon tea at the Portlandia is a thing of beauty. Trust me, your clients will be thrilled to come to you."

Cami thought about that for a moment. Then she thought about being out and about in London with some unknown individual targeting her for who knows what.

"Sounds like a good idea," she conceded at last. "I'll go to work on revising the schedule wherever possible."

"Great," Rachel said with a smile. "I didn't think you'd be so easy to convince."

"Usually I'm not," Cami said, "but you're very persuasive. And I'm grateful to know people used to call you Tank."

"So am I," Rachel said with a grin. "As they say, if you've got it, flaunt it."

CHAPTER NINETEEN

HUNTINGTON BEACH, CALIFORNIA
TUESDAY, MARCH 21, 2023
5:30 A.M.

After the call from Detective Horn, Adam had pulled himself together and spent the whole weekend working in his at-home office almost around the clock on the permit issue. By the time he and Joel left for John Wayne Airport on Tuesday morning, he felt like a zombie, but the thorny permit situation was under control at last, and the plans were ready to be submitted.

Joel had booked their flight late enough that they hadn't been able to have seats together, but that was okay. Adam didn't need to talk nearly as much as he needed to think. Once on the ground, they would go straight to Edmonds PD for their interviews with Detective Horn. Adam's was scheduled at ten a.m. Joel's would follow his. Not knowing how much time they would have between the interviews and the funeral, he and Joel were dressed to go straight from Edmonds PD to the mortuary.

As far as the funeral was concerned, Adam didn't know what to expect. With his father a homicide victim, there was bound to be a press presence, but he had no idea who would be there. Most likely some of the people he'd met at the party the week before would be in attendance, but he had no way of knowing who else would show up. He doubted Clarice would be allowed out of lockup long enough to attend.

The plane was still on the ground when the woman seated next to him tried to strike up a conversation. "I'm going to Seattle to visit my sister," she said. "Are you going for business or pleasure?"

Adam didn't want to talk to her right then, any more than he wanted to talk to Joel. "I'm going to my father's funeral," he said.

"Oh!" she exclaimed. "I'm so sorry."

"So am I," he said. He regretted being so terse, but it was enough to keep her from asking any more questions. Once the aircraft reached cruising altitude, Adam leaned his seat back and pretended to be asleep. Instead of sleeping, he was thinking about his father and Clarice.

He had barely interacted with her at the party, but he remembered her sitting there alone most of the night. And he'd caught a glimpse of her as Joel walked her over to the elevator to accompany her upstairs. Even clinging to Joel's arm, she had been unsteady on her feet. How could she possibly have been strong enough or coordinated enough to stand at her husband's bedside and deliver that many fatal stab wounds? But she must have been, and the cops must have had plenty of evidence against her if they'd been able to convince a judge to hold her without bail.

But on the off chance Clarice hadn't killed his father, who else would have? Adam had no idea about his father's situation in the days leading up to his death. Horn had mentioned something about a pending divorce. Adam didn't have a clue as to who the other woman might be, but was it possible his father's death was the result of a love triangle? Was there an irate husband or ex-husband in the picture?

And was there a will? If his father's attorney had known enough about Charles Brewster's business to go ahead and make funeral arrangements, he probably also knew whether or not there was a will. Presumably there was one. And just then, for the first time, Adam wondered if, despite he and his father's long estrangement, he himself could possibly be a beneficiary under the will?

Adam had been sitting with his eyes closed, pretending to be asleep for the benefit of his chatty seatmate, but that realization was enough to make his eyes pop open. He thought he and Joel were being interviewed right along with all the other party attendees. But what if that wasn't the case? What if Detective Horn was looking at Adam as a possible suspect?

"Are you okay?" his seatmate asked.

"I'm fine," he said.

Despite what he'd just said, suddenly his heart filled with dread. Adam had never been involved in any kind of criminal activity, but now, for his first time at bat, he was a possible homicide suspect? That was unthinkable.

The rest of the flight seemed to take forever. By the time the plane landed, Adam was a nervous wreck. They had traveled only with carry-ons, so they headed straight for the car rental desks.

"What's wrong with you?" Joel demanded once they were in their rental and headed for I-5.

"What if the cops think I did it?" Adam asked.

"You?" Joel returned.

"Yes, me," Adam answered.

"You've got to be kidding! We were both at the hotel when the homicide happened. Surely the hotel will have security footage that can prove it. And if there's no film, the cops will be able to ping your phone. That will show we left the party and went straight back to the Hilton Garden Inn in Bothell. Besides, why would you be a suspect? You reconnected with your father for the first time only a few weeks ago. What would be the motive? Surely your dad wouldn't have suddenly up and added your name to his will based on that one phone call."

"You're right about that," Adam agreed eventually. "My father was never someone who made snap decisions. What was I thinking?"

"You were thinking like a man whose father was just murdered and whose stepmother is the prime suspect," Joel replied, reaching over and placing a reassuring hand on Adam's knee. "Just answer the questions."

In the interview with Detectives Horn and Burns, Adam did just that. He answered whatever questions were posed to him to the best of his ability. Since the questions were general in nature and not the least bit accusatory, Adam's case of nerves evaporated. When had he and Joel arrived at the party? When had they left? Where had they gone after the party? What time did they get back to the hotel? During the party, had Adam noticed anything out of the ordinary? Had there been any kind of disagreement between his father and his stepmother?

"I guess there was something strange," Adam said. "Although Clarice was the nominal hostess, she wasn't really involved with any of the guests—didn't interact."

"You're saying she was alone in the crowd," Detective Horn confirmed.

Adam nodded. "And more than slightly drunk. I was grateful when Joel went out of his way to visit with her. But that's Joel for you—kindness personified. She bailed on the party early on—around nine or so. When she went upstairs to bed, Joel helped her navigate the elevator."

At that point, the interview changed direction, focusing less on the party and more on Adam's relationship with his father. How long had they been estranged? What had prompted their recent reconciliation?

That last question gave Adam pause. "It wasn't really a reconciliation," he answered. "It was more like we were becoming reacquainted. There wasn't enough time for an actual reconciliation."

Much to his surprise, Adam ended up telling Detective Horn about his mother's death and about how losing Michael had led him to Joel in the same way losing his wife must have led his father to Clarice. Maybe he told that part of the story as much for his own benefit as for the detective's. It was as though, by forgiving himself for what had happened between him and Joel after Michael was gone, Adam was finally coming closer to forgiving his father for what had happened between him and Clarice.

The interview ended with Detective Horn asking for a DNA sample and fingerprints, assuring him that was standard procedure for anyone who had attended the party. Adam was happy to provide both, but relinquishing his phone was another matter entirely.

"You're welcome to examine it to your heart's content, but can you maybe clone it and the same for Joel's?" he asked. "We'll be heading back to L.A. later this evening. I have a lot going on at work this week, and I really need my phone."

"Of course," Detective Horn said genially. "If you don't mind turning it on for me, I'll hand them over to our tech unit. I'm pretty sure they can make that work."

CHAPTER TWENTY

COTTONWOOD, ARIZONA
TUESDAY, MARCH 21, 2023
8:00 A.M.

With the Clarice situation settled between them, Ali and B. rode to work together on Tuesday morning. Going in, Ali expected to spend the day focused on scholarship business. However, she had barely arrived at her desk when an email came in from Cami.

Arrived in London in good shape. Rachel met me at Heathrow. She doesn't look the least bit like security detail material, but I'm glad to have her.

WWS has been following up on what happened in L.A. They have reason to believe that Petrov's intent was to kidnap me rather than murder me, but it seems unlikely he was acting alone. As far as anyone knows, Petrov is still in the States. WWS has learned that the last ping on his phone was from somewhere near San Bernardino, California. That tells us he's unlikely to be a threat here in the UK, but that doesn't rule out threats from someone else.

At Rachel's suggestion, I'm in the process of moving all my appointments from on-site visits to ones here in a hotel conference room. We'll probably be eating most of our meals here, too. Expensive, yes, but better safe than sorry.

I know I wasn't wild about having a bodyguard, but thank you for insisting. Don't worry about me. I'm being careful, and Rachel is definitely on the job. Now let's see if I can get any of these people to sign on the dotted line.

In other words, I'm glad we didn't cancel.

Cami

After reading Cami's email, Ali wasn't so sure. Cami had indeed been in danger in California, and to Ali's way of thinking, she was still in danger in the UK. Pocketing her phone, Ali left her office and hurried down the corridor to B. and Lance's lab.

She handed her phone to B. and then to Lance so they could both read Cami's message.

"But why would someone want to kidnap Cami?" a puzzled Lance asked, handing the phone back to Ali. "Her folks are both professors. They're reasonably well off, but they wouldn't have access to the kind of money that would make them good targets for ransom demands."

"Maybe the ransom targets weren't members of her family," B. suggested. "What if they expected High Noon to pay up?"

As soon Ali heard the words, she knew that made absolute sense. When it came to an ability to meet ransom demands, Cami's employer made a far better target than Cami's parents.

"It sounds as though whoever it is was really targeting High Noon," Ali said.

"Seems like," B. agreed, "and they may try again. For right now, Cami has twenty-four-hour protection, but going forward, we're going to have to take this kind of threat into consideration."

Both Ali and Lance nodded in agreement.

"Furthermore," B. continued, "so far there's been no law enforcement involvement in what may or may not have happened to Cami, correct?"

Lance and Ali nodded again.

"Let's try to keep it that way," B. continued. "Instead of calling the cops in on this, let's use Frigg. If High Noon was the ultimate target, it stands to reason that the culprit is most likely one of our competitors or else closely connected to one."

"If we use GHOST to take them down," Lance added, "they'll never know what hit them."

Because GHOST, a groundbreaking encrypted software, originally created by Lance Tucker and his high school computer club advisor, allowed High Noon to prowl through the internet while leaving behind no trace of any incursions.

"That's true," Ali agreed, "but we have to find them first."

Back in her office, Ali summoned Frigg and put her on the case.

"Once I find whoever targeted Cami," the AI declared, "I'll do my best to make them Shetland up," the AI replied.

"Shetland up?" a puzzled Ali repeated. "I don't understand."

"Doesn't that mean to hold a wrongdoer responsible?"

It took Ali a moment to sort it, but finally she caught on. "You mean 'pony up,'" she explained. "Shetland is a kind of pony, but pony up means 'to make someone pay up.'"

"Very well," Frigg said. "I'll do what I can to make them pony up."

Having turned the problem over to Frigg, Ali turned to her next order of business—Danny Knowles and Susan Rojas. Her plan was to notify each of them privately today. It was early spring, but college enrollment season was well underway. Danny and Susan needed to have enrollment handled long before the public announcement of their scholarship awards was made. That traditionally happened at an afternoon tea hosted by B. and Ali each year in early June.

Having determined who this year's winners would be, it was past time for Ali to arrange the celebration, starting with setting a date and arranging the caterer. The identity of the caterer was no mystery. Raphael Fuentes, a previous Dougherty Scholarship winner, usually did the honors. The only concern was whether he still had dates available in early June.

Raphael's lifetime dream had come true after he became the first male recipient of an Amelia Dougherty Scholarship. He had used the award to attend Le Cordon Bleu College of Culinary Arts in Scottsdale. Now an established caterer in the Phoenix metropolitan area, he'd handled Ali's annual scholarship teas for several years now. Because she had Raphael's direct number, Ali was able to get right through to him.

"Hey, Ali," Raphael said when he answered the phone. "Is it already that time of year again?"

"It certainly is."

"What date are you looking at?"

"Does Saturday, June third, work for you?"

"We'll make it work. The usual time?"

"Yes, four to six."

"Any idea of what you want?"

"Suit yourself," Ali told him. "You always make good choices."

"Same number of people—fifty or so?"

"You've got it."

"Okay, then. It's on my calendar. I'll work up a proposed menu and email it to you."

"Great. Thanks."

Easy peasy, Ali thought as the call ended. Next she needed to track down the proposed guest of honor who, also by tradition, was a previous recipient. This year Ali hoped that role would be filled by someone dear to Ali's heart.

Years earlier, Ali had been instrumental in rescuing a large number of abused women and children from a polygamous cult called The Family, located outside Colorado City in northern Arizona. The victims who had suffered the worst treatment were those who had attempted to escape but had been recaptured. Once returned to the cult and designated as "Brought Back Girls," they had been regarded as pariahs. Rather than being allowed to stay in dormitories or houses like other cult members, they had been charged with caring for livestock and banished to live in barns and sheds with the animals they were expected to care for.

Poorly educated and with almost no marketable skills, most of the women who had emerged from The Family had been ill-equipped to deal with a modern world. Surprisingly enough, the Brought Back Girls had fared better than the others, because the skills they had developed while working with the animals were indeed marketable.

A women's shelter in Flagstaff had been ground zero when it came to placing the Colorado City refugees, and the search for housing and jobs had included all of Arizona. A veterinarian from southern Arizona, Dr. Sophia Kaluznaicki, owner of the Green Valley Animal Hospital, had responded to the shelter's call for help. Sight unseen, she had agreed to hire one of the Brought Back Girls, Meredith Glenn, to be her new kennel girl.

Dr. Kaluznaicki's practice specialized in large animals, and Meredith had spent years caring for The Family's livestock. Meredith's new employer soon recognized the young woman's natural abilities when it came to dealing with large animals, and although Meredith hadn't received a traditional education, she was a teachable quick learner.

Eventually Dr. Kaluznaicki had taken Meredith in hand and encouraged her to dream big. To begin with, she had wanted to become a veterinary assistant, which eventually morphed into her wanting to become an actual vet. That had required her enrolling first at Pima Community College and later at the University of Arizona. This year, with the help of an Amelia Dougherty Scholarship, Meredith would be part of the first class to graduate from the University of Arizona's new College of Veterinary Medicine, which was why Ali wanted her to be the guest of honor. She would be the Amelia Dougherty Scholarship Program's first-ever vet.

After obtaining Meredith's number, Ali gave her a call. "How's it going?" she asked, after identifying herself.

"Coming down to the end," Meredith answered. "Graduation isn't until the end of May, but I already have two job offers."

"If you accept one of those, please tell them you can't start until after the third of June."

"Why not?" Meredith asked.

"Because I'd like you to be the guest of honor at this year's Amelia Dougherty Tea, if you wouldn't mind doing it."

"Would I be able to bring Sophia along?" Meredith asked.

"Absolutely."

"Then count me as a yes," Meredith said.

Two down, two to go, Ali told herself. With that handled, she hit the road.

In years past she had included parents and/or guardians when making these initial announcements, and as a general rule, the recipients' relatives were thrilled to hear the news. This time things were different. Danny's father was adamantly opposed to the idea of his son going on to school, and Susan's great-grandmother might be reluctant to pull up stakes and go live somewhere else. With those two situations in mind, Ali decided to approach her winners privately while they were still at school.

Mingus High School, which Ali herself had once attended, was right there in Cottonwood. She drove there, pulled into a visitor parking place, and then made her way unassisted to the principal's office, where she asked to speak to the school counselor, a Mrs. Woods. Since Mrs. Woods had written one of Danny's two letters of recommendation, she was delighted to meet Ali and thrilled to be able to call Danny's third-period teacher and ask that he report to her office. He did so immediately.

"This covers everything?" Danny asked in disbelief, after Ali delivered the news.

Ali nodded. "The works," she said. "Tuition, room and board, and books, along with a small monthly stipend to cover other expenses."

"But it's not a loan?"

"Definitely not a loan," Ali told him, "and it's renewable for all four years as long as you carry a full load of classes and maintain a 3.0 or better GPA. Have you chosen where you'd like to go?"

"Northern Arizona University," Danny said at once. "I got an admission application from there, but I didn't see any point in filling it out."

"There's definitely a point now," Ali said, "so you'd better get to it, but are your folks going to be okay with this?"

"They'll be fine," Danny assured her. "My dad's big issue was my having to take out a bunch of loans. He'll be glad I won't have to. Thank you."

"Don't thank me," Ali said. "Thank Mrs. Woods and Mrs. Donner. By the way, that drawing you did of Mrs. Donner is what put you over the top."

Ali's next stop was close to an hour away in Mayer. At the high school there, Ali was disappointed to learn that Susan Rojas had been marked absent for the day. Worried that something might have happened to Susan's great-grandmother, Ali drove several miles east to Cordes Junction. Armed with a street address, she followed a dirt road past a mobile home and pulled up next to a moldering RV that was parked some distance away. The vehicle had clearly seen better days.

As soon as Ali stopped the car, a young woman darted out the door and hurried up to the driver's-side window. From the anxious look on her face, Ali could tell that unexpected visitors most likely weren't welcome inside.

"Can I help you?"

"Are you Susan?" Ali asked.

The young woman nodded.

"I'm Ali Reynolds with the Amelia Dougherty Scholarship program. I'm here about your application."

Susan's expression darkened. "If you read my essay, you already know there's no way for me to go on to school. I have to look after my nana. That's why I'm absent today. Nana wasn't feeling well last night, and I didn't want to leave her alone."

Ali's heart constricted. Caring for an elderly relative was heavy duty for anyone, but for someone so young, it had to be a terrible burden. Given that, Ali couldn't help but wonder if Susan's grandmother would still be part of the equation once school started in the fall.

"Your nana is very lucky to have you looking after her," Ali said, reaching over and pushing open the passenger door. "Hop in. Let's talk."

Reluctantly, Susan did as she was told. They talked for the better part of an hour. Gradually Susan's mood changed from one of wariness to one of hope.

"You mean Nana would be able to live there with me?"

"That's exactly what I mean."

"I'd want to go to NAU, then," Susan said. "ASU is too close to my mother's family in Phoenix. I don't want to be anywhere near them. Neither does Gran. But you're saying everything I need will be covered—tuition, books, food, and everything?"

"The works," Ali said. "That's what 'full ride' means. I'm giving you the news now so you can start the enrollment process, but the public announcement won't be made until early June at an afternoon tea, so are you in or out?"

"Definitely in," Susan said.

"All right, then," Ali said. "That's all I need to know."

"Thank you," Susan added faintly.

"You're welcome," Ali replied. "And congratulations."

She left shortly after that, driving back to Sedona feeling as though she had put the scholarship matter to bed one more time. Someday, she'd need to pass the Amelia Dougherty torch on to someone else, but for right now, she still found it incredibly rewarding. And for today, at least, it had helped take her mind off whoever the jerk was who was targeting Cami Lee and High Noon Enterprises.

CHAPTER TWENTY-ONE

SEATTLE, WASHINGTON
TUESDAY, MARCH 21, 2023
2:00 P.M.

Despite the fact that it meant canceling two of her regular housecleaning jobs for the week, Donna Jean had called in sick so she could attend Mr. Brewster's funeral. It wasn't as though she'd been invited. No one had bothered to notify her of where it would be or even when. Amy was the one who had gone on the internet and tracked down the time and location.

The media was there en masse. The murder was still big news in the Seatttle area, and the reporters were most likely hoping Mrs. Brewster would show up at her husband's funeral in an orange jumpsuit and handcuffs. She hadn't.

Donna Jean had no idea that the funeral was an invitation-only affair. She was at the door to the mortuary, trying to explain to the person in charge that she had worked for the Brewsters for years and that she needed to come pay her respects. He was in the process of turning her away when a miracle happened. Adam Brewster showed up and recognized her on sight.

"Why, Donna Jean," he said pleasantly. "It's so good to see you again. Thank you for coming."

Adam, always the gentleman, immediately offered Donna Jean his arm. As they started inside, the doorkeeper held up his hand. "Your invitation, sir?" he inquired.

Adam favored the man with a sharp-eyed glare. "I'm Adam Brewster, Chuck Brewster's son, and this is Joel, my husband," he said, gesturing toward the man standing just behind him. And this," he added, patting Donna Jean's hand, "is Donna Jean Plummer, my parents' longtime housekeeper. I don't believe any of us needs an express invitation to attend my father's funeral."

Taken aback, the man quickly pulled a walkie-talkie out of his suit pocket and spoke into it briefly before holding it up to his ear and nodding as he listened.

"Pardon me, Mr. Brewster," he said once that crackly conversation ended. "I'm so sorry. Mr. McCreedy will be here momentarily to escort you to the private family seating area. Your father's service is scheduled for the third chapel on the right."

"A private seating area won't be necessary," Adam replied. "Joel and I will sit wherever Ms. Plummer is seated."

Donna Jean felt a tremendous rush of gratitude as Adam led her down a long corridor lined with several closed doors. Door number three stood open. The expensive floral arrangement on a nearby tripod announced that they were at the right place.

An usher quickly stepped forward to greet them. Adam accepted two of the proffered programs, passed one to Donna Jean, and then waved the usher aside. "We'll manage on our own," he said. "Thanks anyway."

That was how Donna Jean attended Chuck Brewster's funeral. She had always wondered if Adam was gay. Now she knew for sure, but that didn't change the way she felt about him. She had loved him as a little boy and wept for him as he lost his mother. Now, official invitation or not, she was proud to be sitting next to him.

During the service, several people went up to the lectern to say what a wonderful man Charles Brewster was—how kind he had been and how civic-minded. Donna Jean didn't know much about his being civic-minded, but she could have told that roomful of people about how kind he had been to her. Still, she was a little surprised when the pastor asked if anyone else had something to add. She fully expected

Adam would stand up at that point and say something about his father, but he didn't, and neither did she.

When the service ended, Adam asked if Donna Jean was interested in attending the reception. "No, thank you," she told him quickly. She had already crashed the funeral. She had no intention of barging in on the reception as well. Besides, she didn't feel like attending a party. She wanted to be back in her apartment with Pearl in her lap.

Donna Jean fled the funeral home immediately after the service and went straight home. Several hours later there was an unexpected knock on her door. Once she opened it, there stood Detective Raymond Horn.

"Good evening, Ms. Plummer. If you don't mind, I'd like you to come with me."

Donna Jean did mind. She minded with every fiber of her body, but clearly saying no was not an option. She couldn't imagine why the cops were still coming after her. What did they think she could tell them?

"Why?" she asked. "What's going on? Has something happened?"

"Just a few more questions," he said. Once she gathered her coat and purse, Detective Horn escorted Donna Jean to his vehicle, telling her as they went, "Detective Burns will meet us back at the station."

As he opened the back door to his vehicle and motioned Donna Jean inside, she tried to suppress the sudden wave of panic that rushed through her body.

"Am I under arrest?" she asked, once Detective Horn was in the driver's seat.

"Not so far," he answered, "but you very well could be."

Donna Jean took that as a threat and didn't respond. Fortunately, she was sitting down. Had she been standing up, her legs might have given way under her. Since it was rush hour, naturally the drive to Edmonds took the better part of an hour.

"Do you still have the cat?" he asked while they waited at a red light.

"Yes," Donna Jean replied.

"Is she okay?"

Donna Jean knew he was trying to draw her into conversation, but she didn't want to play that game. It was all designed to put her at ease and make her think that he was on her side—that he had her best interests at heart, but that wasn't true.

"Pearl's fine," she answered.

"Have you heard from Mrs. Brewster?" Horn asked. "Has she made any effort to contact you?"

Why would she? Donna Jean wondered. "No," she answered.

"Not even to ask about her cat?"

She has other things to worry about, Donna Jean thought. "No," she said again.

"I saw you at the funeral in the company of Mr. Brewster's son."

"Yes," she said. "As far as I could tell, Adam was always a good boy—kind and thoughtful. He probably still is, but he and his father had a big blowup about the time his mother died. Until today, I hadn't seen him since."

"Did you know he attended his father's birthday party?"

"I had no idea."

"I saw you at the funeral but not the reception. The reading of the will happened shortly after that, and you weren't there for that, either."

"I'm not good at socializing," Donna Jean said. "As for the reading of the will? I had no reason to know about that and no reason to be there, either."

"You had no idea that under the terms of Mr. Brewster's will, you're one of his beneficiaries?"

"Me?" Donna Jean asked faintly. "Not that I know of."

"Well, you are," Horn replied. "It turns out Mr. Brewster left you a cool hundred and fifty thousand dollars, but of course those funds can't be distributed until after we've concluded our investigation."

Donna Jean could barely believe what she'd just heard. For someone who struggled each month to pay the rent, keep the lights on, and buy groceries, a hundred and fifty thousand dollars sounded like an astronomical amount of money, but she also understood Detective Horn's underlying message. As long as she was still a suspect in Mr. Brewster's homicide, she wouldn't see a dime of it.

Once they finally arrived at Edmonds PD, Donna Jean was again led into an interview room—a different one this time—where Detective Burns was already seated.

"Good to see you again," she said.

Donna Jean nodded but said nothing. There was nothing good about it. She was fully expecting that this time one of the detectives would deliver a Miranda warning, but neither of them did. Supposedly that meant she was still a person of interest rather than an actual suspect, but was that true? Were they just leading her along, hoping that she'd say something to implicate herself?

Once the interview began, Detective Horn charged right in. "As I told you on our way here, Mr. Brewster's will was read earlier today."

He paused as though expecting Donna Jean to say something. She simply nodded.

"You told me that you had no idea you were a named beneficiary in that document. Is that true?"

"Mr. Brewster never mentioned anything of the kind."

"That seems like a lot of money for him to hand over to a part-time employee," Detective Horn continued. "Do you have any idea why Mr. Brewster would do that?"

That made it sound as though the detectives were back to thinking there had been some kind of illicit relationship going on between Mr. Brewster and Donna Jean. Or maybe they thought she was blackmailing him.

She shrugged. "I have no idea why he'd give me anything. I worked for him for a long time. When his first wife was dying, I took care of her every day. Maybe that's why—as a way of saying thank you."

"The thing is, Donna Jean," Horn said, "I'm wondering if that's true. I've seen murders where the amount of money involved was less than a hundred fifty K, so why don't you tell us again exactly where you were on the night Mr. Brewster was murdered."

"I already told you. I was at home, asleep in my apartment. You can check my phone. It was right there on its charger on the nightstand next to my bed."

"Just because the phone was there doesn't mean you were. You're a person with unlimited access to the Brewsters' home. That means you have opportunity. You're due to receive a hundred fifty thousand dollars. That gives you motive. You also had easy access to the murder weapon. In homicide investigations, that counts as a royal flush. In addition, your DNA was found on the murder weapon. It doesn't get much better than that."

"I already told you how my DNA got on that knife. When I found Mrs. Brewster, she was out of her head—frantic—and waving it around in the air. I was afraid someone was going to get hurt. That's why I took it away from her."

"By the way," Horn continued. "Mrs. Brewster is the other beneficiary under the terms of her husband's will. Was she aware of your previous homicide conviction?"

"I'm not sure. She may have been, but I don't think we ever discussed it. It's not something I'm proud of, and I don't like talking about it. I worked for Mrs. Brewster. I cleaned her house, washed her dishes, did her laundry. We didn't sit around talking about my personal history."

"Mrs. Brewster is the primary beneficiary of the will and is due to inherit most of his estate. If Mr. Brewster had gone through with his plan to divorce her, she would have received far less. If she was aware of your previous conviction, perhaps she turned to you for help."

Donna tried unsuccessfully to stifle her outrage. "She didn't, and even if she had, I would never have murdered Mr. Brewster."

"If you really had nothing to do with what happened then," Detective Horn offered, "why not take a lie detector test? That would prove once and for all that you're telling the truth."

But Donna Jean Plummer wasn't about to fall for that one. She'd been down this road once before, and she wasn't going to make the same mistake twice. When the cops had been investigating Kenny's death, the lead detective had been a guy named Kramer. She thought that she had forgotten his name long ago, but much to her surprise, in that moment it came back to her. He had told her the same thing in almost the same words—that taking the lie detector test would rule her out once and for all.

Then, during the test, the examiner had asked her if she had ever wished her husband would die. She had answered yes, and that was the truth. On more than one occasion, when Kenny was out drinking, she had wished he'd plow into a tree or a telephone pole or something on his way home and not come back—ever. At the very least, it would spare her that night's torment and it might even keep her from having to face up to doing anything about it—like getting a divorce. She had a feeling that she wasn't alone in thinking like that. There were probably plenty of unhappily married women out there who were in the same fix.

But then the operator had asked her the next question—the one about whether, on the drive from her parents' place to her own, had she planned on shooting him. She hadn't exactly planned it, but she had certainly thought about it, telling herself that if Kenny came after her, she was going to pull the trigger. But she was already sitting in a police interrogation room, and it seemed stupid to come right out and admit that she had reached that conclusion.

"No, of course not," she had answered.

But that was a lie, and this was a lie detector test. No matter what she had said, it wouldn't have been admissible in court, but it was enough for the operator to tell her at the conclusion of the examination that she had been found to be "evasive."

Once the ordeal was over, she had found Detective Kramer and his partner waiting outside the examination room. She could still see the triumphant look on his face as he held up a pair of handcuffs.

"Hands behind your back," he had said. "You're under arrest for the murder of Kenneth Plummer."

After that, Donna Jean had been hauled off to jail, and the rest was history.

At that point she looked Detective Horn full in the face. "No," she said aloud. "Once and for all, I am not doing a lie detector test."

"Is it possible you've already had some unfortunate dealings with one of those?" Detective Horn inquired.

Donna Jean felt her soul shrivel within her. There it was. That's what this was all about—her previous conviction for Kenny Plummer's death.

With a superhuman effort, she pulled herself together. "I'm done here," she told him. "Either arrest me or let me go, but I'm not saying another word without having an attorney present."

"Very well, Ms. Plummer," he said. "Suit yourself, but if I were you, I wouldn't plan on leaving town anytime soon."

CHAPTER TWENTY-TWO

LONDON, ENGLAND
THURSDAY, MARCH 23, 2023
5:00 P.M.

After two and a half days of being locked in a hotel conference room doing back-to-back phone calls and meetings while taking all meals in the hotel's dining room, Camille Lee was more than ready for a break. The weather was drippy, but this was London, after all. She had hoped she and Rachel would be able to go for a brief walk, but Rachel nixed that idea. With the failed kidnapping attempt in mind, she agreed they could go out to dinner—to one of the best curry places in all London, but only if they traveled to and from the restaurant in Wonder Woman's faux cab.

Cami had changed out of her work attire and into something more comfortable when someone knocked on the door of her suite. It wasn't the kind of discreet tap you'd expect from room service or housekeeping. No, this was far firmer than either of those.

Knowing Rachel was grabbing a shower, Cami went to the door in her bare feet and peered out the peephole. Three men clad in suits and ties stood in the corridor. One she recognized as the Portlandia's assistant manager. The other two were most likely police officers, since one of them was holding up a badge.

"Who is it?" Cami asked.

"Detective Inspector Howard Wallace and Detective Sergeant

Matthew Frost of the Essex Police," the one with the badge answered. "Are you Camille Lee?"

Essex police? Cami wondered in dismay. *What do they want with me?*

"Yes, I am," she replied aloud. "How can I help you?"

"We're investigating a mysterious death, and we'd like to speak to you."

"One moment, please," she said. "Let me finish dressing."

Back in the suite's bedroom, she slipped on her shoes. She didn't really need to be wearing shoes in order to speak to the detectives. What she really needed was a moment to gather her thoughts. She considered calling in Rachel for reinforcements but decided against it.

A mysterious death, she wondered. *Whose? And since the crime had obviously occurred somewhere in the UK, if not in London proper, what could it possibly have to do with me?*

Back at the door, she took a deep breath and put on a welcoming smile before swinging it open. "Won't you come in and have a seat?"

While the hotel manager melted into the background, the other two men entered and settled on the suite's love seat, while Cami sat in the easy chair across from them. DI Wallace appeared to be somewhere in his early fifties. DS Frost was a good fifteen years Wallace's junior. The younger man was carrying a satchel-like briefcase that he set down on the floor near his feet. Presumably Wallace was in charge, and Frost was there to fetch and carry.

"You mentioned a mysterious death," Cami said, directing her statement in Wallace's direction. "Who's dead, and why is it any concern of mine?"

"Before we go into that," he replied, "please tell us the nature of your relationship with Adrian Willoughby."

Adrian Willoughby? That was a stunner, and Cami couldn't have been more astonished. A few years earlier, Willoughby had been a supposedly up-and-coming tech blogger who presented himself to the world as an impartial observer. His supposedly unbiased media posts had often cast High Noon in a bad light. Eventually it had surfaced that, while writing those derogatory postings, Willoughby had been receiving under-the-table payments from one of High Noon's major competitors.

Just prior to the pandemic, B. Simpson, Cami's boss, had been scheduled to deliver a paper at a high-powered international cybersecurity meeting in London. When he was seriously injured in a car wreck shortly before his scheduled departure, Cami had been sent in B.'s place. That was where she had encountered Adrian Willoughby face-to-face.

On the last evening of the conference, a somewhat smarmy and already very tipsy Willoughby had approached Cami in the hotel bar. Over the course of several drinks, he had invited her up to his room. By then, however, Cami had already figured out he was working for High Noon's competition, and she had decided to beat him at his own game.

By the time they left the bar, he'd been so drunk that he'd needed assistance walking. She had escorted him up to his room, where he promptly passed out face down on the bed. Left to her own devices, Cami had used the man's own cell phone to blow up his life.

An examination of his recent text messages had revealed that, not only was he caught up in a contentious divorce proceeding, but he was also involved in serious relationships with at least two other women. One believed herself to be his fiancée and was pregnant with his child. Cami had gone through Willoughby's phone, taking screenshots of any number of damning text exchanges with the other women in his life before sending them along to the attorney of Willoughby's soon-to-be-former wife. After returning the phone to the unconscious man's pants pocket, Cami had let herself out of his hotel room. The next day she had flown home to the U.S. Shortly thereafter, Willoughby's cybersecurity blogging career had come to an abrupt end. But even though Cami and Willoughby weren't on the best of terms, she certainly hadn't wished him any harm.

"Our relationship wasn't exactly cordial," Cami admitted aloud after a thoughtful pause. "On the final night of an international cybersecurity conference, he approached me in the bar, plied me with booze, and invited me up to his room. I'm sure he had delusions of grandeur about getting lucky. Unfortunately for him, by the time we left the bar, Willoughby was too smashed to walk on his own. I escorted him to his room. The last time I saw him he was dead drunk and lying fully dressed on the bed."

"When was that?" DI Wallace asked.

"Back in January of 2020," Cami answered, "prior to the pandemic."

"And you haven't seen him since?"

"No."

"Or corresponded with him?"

"No, not at all," Cami replied. "But you said you were investigating a mysterious death. Is Adrian the victim?"

DI Wallace nodded.

"When did he die?"

"In the early morning hours of Saturday, March 18," Wallace replied.

"I was still in the States," Cami objected. "I didn't land in the UK until Tuesday morning, so why are you questioning me?"

Rather than answer her question, DI Wallace turned to his partner. "The folder, please, DS Frost."

The younger cop opened his satchel and extracted a file folder, which he handed over to his superior. Wallace opened the file and removed a sheaf of photos that he passed along to Cami. As she sorted through them, cold chills sped through her body, and there was no disguising her dismay.

Cami herself was the subject of each of the photos, all of which had been taken from a considerable distance, probably by someone using a high-powered telephoto lens. What took her breath away was what she glimpsed in the background, which included the exteriors of several of the buildings she had visited the previous week. There were numerous shots of her in her vehicle entering or leaving the Lancaster Hotel's parking garage. She also recognized the clothing she'd been wearing. No doubt her growing distress manifested itself on her face.

"Is there a problem, Ms. Lee?" DI Wallace asked.

"I was in L.A. on business last week. The whole time I was there I had an eerie feeling I was being followed, but at the time I had no way of proving it," she said. "It's clear from these photos that I was."

"Did you report this suspected stalking situation to law enforcement?"

"I didn't."

"Why not?"

Cami shrugged and tried to sound more unconcerned than she felt. "It didn't seem all that serious at the time, and I didn't think the cops would believe me."

That was more or less true, but by the time she had fled the fitness center and headed for the hotel kitchen, she had known good and well it was serious. The problem was, she hadn't called the cops in then, either.

"Where did all these photos come from?" she asked. "And how did you get them?"

"We were able to obtain a search warrant for Mr. Willoughby's computer and downloaded the images from his text file. The sender was listed as unknown, but Willoughby's response was interesting."

"What kind of response?"

"A single word—GO. That was it. No idea what he meant."

Cami felt as though a bucket of ice water had just splashed over her body. She knew exactly what GO meant. With that one word, most likely to Bogdan Petrov, Adrian Willoughby had set the plot in motion, one designed to take Cami out permanently. She quickly ran the two timelines through her head. Early morning in the UK on Thursday, would still have been Wednesday night in Los Angeles. The Dozo dinner had been Thursday night, and the fitness center incident had occurred on Friday.

When Cami managed to refocus on DI Wallace, he was in mid-sentence. " . . . but the presence of this collection of photos in Mr. Willoughby's text file suggests that his interest in you goes far beyond a simple one-night stand gone bad."

At that point, Cami realized she had to come clean not only about Willoughby but probably about Bogdan Petrov, too.

"That night at the conference, when Adrian tried to put the make on me, I blew up his life," she admitted.

"You blew up his life?" a puzzled Wallace repeated. "How?"

"Adrian was a jerk. After he passed out, I checked his phone. Turns out he was going through an ugly divorce while carrying on affairs with a couple of other women. So I took screenshots of some of the texts and sent them along to his wife's divorce attorney in hopes it might help with her divorce negotiations."

"We noticed," Sergeant Frost said, speaking up for the first time. "According to correspondence we found in the desk in his office, he was way behind on his child support payments—to two separate women."

Wallace shot his junior partner a withering look before turning back to Cami. "You're saying that was the totality of your interaction with him?"

"Yes."

"Did Mr. Willoughby know that you were the one who had been in contact with his estranged wife's attorney?"

"I certainly didn't tell him, but he may have figured it out."

"And maybe became obsessed with you?"

"Possibly," Cami replied. "But you said you were investigating a mysterious death, not a homicide. How did he die?"

"I'm afraid that was something of a misstatement," Wallace admitted. "His death has been ruled a homicide. According to Mr. Willoughby's Apple Watch, he passed away at 9:46 p.m. on Saturday night. He had purportedly been out of town on a business trip to Edinburgh and was due to return on Sunday evening. When he didn't turn up, his wife reported him as missing on Monday morning. His body was found floating face down in one of the lakes in the Chafford Gorges Nature Park earlier today. There was some blunt trauma to his head, but the coroner has ruled his cause of death as drowning. He was likely alive but unconscious when he was placed in the water. Our subsequent investigation has revealed signs of a struggle at Mr. Willoughby's office in Grays. We believe the office is where the initial attack occurred, while the nature park was the dump site."

Cami had never heard of the Chafford Gorges Nature Park and had no idea where that was or where Grays was, either, for that matter. Just then a text message came in on DI Wallace's phone. He pulled the device out of his pocket and glanced at the screen before saying, "The coroner has just completed the next-of-kin notifications and has now released the victim's name to the public."

He studied Cami for a long moment before adding, "The afternoon prior to his death, Adrian Willoughby booked a single one-way ticket from Heathrow to Malé-Velana International Airport in the Maldives. His current wife knew nothing about that scheduled departure. His flight was due to depart Heathrow on Sunday evening. Would you have any idea why he might be traveling to the Maldives?"

"None whatsoever," Cami replied. "But there's one thing more you should know."

"What's that?"

The whole time they'd been talking about Adrian Willoughby, Cami's thoughts had been in turmoil. Thanks to Frigg, she knew exactly who had sent those telltale photos, and this was now a homicide investigation. From where she sat it seemed likely that revealing that information at this point would be better than concealing it.

"I believe I know the name of the man who sent those photos to Adrian Willoughby."

Wallace seemed surprised. "You do?"

"As I told you, the whole time I was in L.A. I felt as though I was being followed, but I couldn't catch anyone in the act. On Friday night, while I was in the dining room, a man walked past me. When he gave me the once-over, it caught my attention. When he was seated, I realized he was carrying a concealed weapon under his suit coat. That set my alarm bells ringing, so when he showed up again later in the fitness room, I managed to grab a photo of him as he walked past my treadmill. After that I made a run for it, leaving the hotel without even returning to my room."

"You felt you were in imminent danger?"

"Absolutely," Cami answered. "I asked an associate of mine to run the fitness center photo through facial rec. It came back as someone named Bogdan Petrov, a Bulgarian, I believe, but I had no idea who he was or why he would be coming for me."

"And you still didn't report the incident to the police?"

"I didn't. I had my suspicions that he'd been following me but no actual proof."

There was a knock on the connecting door between Cami's room and the one next door. Moments later, Rachel poked her head inside.

"Sorry," she said quickly when she spotted the two detectives. "I didn't realize you had company."

"This is my friend Rachel Bloom," Cami explained. "We have dinner reservations. This is Detective Inspector Wallace and Detective Sergeant Frost with the Essex Police."

Both men rose as one. "We were just going," DI Wallace said quickly. "When are you planning on returning to the U.S.?"

"I'm due to fly home on Saturday."

"You might want to consider delaying your departure a day or two, just to give us a chance to finish up with our inquiries, because we may wish to interview you again." DI Wallace handed over a business card. "And if you happen to remember anything else, please be sure to give me a call."

Cami simply nodded before ushering the two men out of the room and into the corridor.

"Were those homicide detectives?" Rachel demanded as soon as the door closed behind them.

Cami nodded.

"What have you gotten yourself into while my back was turned?"

"It's a long story," Cami answered, grabbing her jacket. "I'll tell you while we're at dinner. Now, let's go have some of that curry."

"We're not going anywhere, and we're not having curry, either," Rachel told her. "You're going to have to settle for room service."

"Why?"

"Because I just had a call from Sonja. A farmworker in Southern California found a dead body in an irrigation ditch yesterday morning. That body has just been identified as that of Bogdan Petrov. The victim was shot in the back of the head execution style, and the death has been ruled as a homicide. With Petrov out of the picture, in terms of threat assessment, I have no idea who or what I should be looking for in order to protect you. In other words, it looks to me as though we're stuck at the Portlandia for the duration."

CHAPTER TWENTY-THREE

COTTONWOOD, ARIZONA
THURSDAY, MARCH 23, 2023
8:00 A.M.

Ali and B. drove to the office together the next morning. She had barely settled in at her desk when a text came in from Frigg.

Can we talk?

That was odd. Ali sent an immediate reply:

What's going on?

Mr. Brewster's will was read on Tuesday, Frigg replied. I'm sending two more videos.

While waiting for the videos to arrive, Ali found herself shaking her head. *How on earth could Frigg have gained access to the reading of Chuck Brewster's will?*

Thinking the reading of the will would have occurred in an attorney's office with a wall filled with legal tomes forming the background, Ali was surprised when the video opened in what was clearly a police interview room. The detectives Ali knew to be Horn and Burns were seated across the table from a clearly distressed Donna Jean Plummer.

"This interview is starting at six twenty-three p.m. on Tuesday, March 21, 2023," Detective Horn announced. He was clearly in charge, and his smug attitude rubbed Ali the wrong way. "Present in the room are

Detectives Monica Burns and Raymond Horn of the Edmonds Police Department, along with Donna Jean Plummer."

Unlike Detective Horn, Donna Jean seemed uncomfortable and beaten-down. During the course of the interview she seemed totally floored when she learned that she was a named beneficiary in Chuck Brewster's will. She didn't seem fazed by the idea Detective Horn seemed to think that her inclusion in Mr. Brewster's will might have motivated her to participate in his sudden death, and that he believed Donna Jean had known about it well in advance of Chuck's death. She denied it, of course, but without any visible reaction. What really seemed to bother her was Horn's suggestion that she submit to a lie detector test. That was when she abruptly ended the interview.

At the time Frigg had brought those previous interviews to Ali's attention, she had expressed concern about the possibility that both Clarice and Donna Jean were being railroaded. Based on what Ali had seen in this one, it occurred to her that the AI's assessment of the situation was correct and that now both women were in Detective Horn's crosshairs.

Ali went back and watched the interview again from beginning to end. As far as she could tell, nothing in Donna Jean's behavior was off. She was understandably distressed at being hauled into a police interview room for a second time, and who wouldn't be, especially since it involved an on-going homicide investigation? Ali knew how that felt. In the aftermath of her second husband's murder, she herself had been considered a suspect and remembered exactly how being cast in that role had felt. At the time, she had been utterly mystified to find herself dealing with something so devastating, and Donna Jean Plummer appeared similarly lost.

As for her reaction to learning that Chuck Brewster had left her with what must have seemed like a huge amount of money? From Ali's point of view, the woman's response was totally in keeping with someone who was astonished by that news. Detective Horn's reference to a polygraph test taken during the course of the investigation following Donna Jean's husband's death suggested to Ali that Donna Jean's previous conviction for that had a lot to do with Detective Horn's current laser focus on her as a suspect.

Detective Horn had not yet gotten around to placing Donna Jean under arrest and charging her. If and when he did that, Ali guessed Donna Jean would then qualify for the services of a court-appointed defense attorney. Ali also knew how well that had worked out for Mateo Vega in this very same jurisdiction—Edmonds, Washington. Mateo had ended up spending sixteen years of his life in prison for a crime he hadn't committed, and Ali worried that Donna Jean might be looking at a similarly grim outcome.

Ali called Frigg back. "Thanks for sending that," she said. "Let me know if there are any further developments."

"You haven't watched the second video," Frigg reminded her.

Ali sighed. Her desk could wait. "All right," she said. "Go ahead and play it."

As soon as the video began to play she realized that this was probably the same room she had seen before during Donna Jean's interviews, only this time, with Adam Brewster in the room, the atmosphere was entirely different. The time stamp read 10:00 a.m., on Tuesday, March 21, 2023. Detective Horn was once again running the show, but where he had appeared to be overbearing and almost threatening while dealing with Donna Jean Plummer, with Adam Brewster his behavior was almost deferential. And unlike Donna Jean, who had appeared to be beyond stressed, the well-dressed thirtysomething young man seated opposite the two investigators seemed completely at ease.

"Thank you for stopping by to speak to us," Horn said. "With the funeral scheduled for later today, I'm sure it's been a very challenging time for you."

"Yes, it has," Adam agreed. "There was a crisis at work last week, and we weren't able to get back any sooner."

"Please accept our condolences on the loss of your father, Mr. Brewster," Detective Horn began.

Adam replied with what appeared to be a rueful half smile. "Actually," he said, "my father and I lost each other a long time ago. We were estranged for a number of years. I finally reached out to him by phone only a few weeks ago in late January. We talked for far longer than I ever expected. Before the call ended he had invited both of us to his upcoming sixtieth birthday party."

"By 'us' you mean you and Joel Franklin?" Horn inquired.

"Yes," Adam replied. "My husband. We flew in from L.A. for the party and were on our flight home by the time the body was discovered. I had a number of things going on at work and wasn't able to return until today."

"Tell me about the party," Horn suggested.

"Except for my dad and Clarice, I didn't know anyone there," Adam began. "Clarice was the nominal hostess, but I got the feeling that she didn't know many of the guests, either. When she found out I was there, I thought she was going to faint dead away. I don't believe she had any idea that Dad had invited me."

"How did you and your father come to be estranged?" Horn inquired.

"I was still in high school and my mother was dying of cancer when I found out that my father was screwing around with Clarice behind Mom's back. Not long after that, my father figured out I was gay. At that point we came to a mutual parting of the ways."

"A parting that lasted this long?" Detective Horn asked.

"After spending some time walking in my father's shoes, I began to rethink some of what happened back then. My first partner, Michael Lafferty, was twenty years older than me. We were together for ten years. When he was diagnosed with ALS, it came as a huge shock."

"ALS," Detective Horn repeated. "Lou Gehrig's disease?"

Adam nodded. "His initial prognosis was two to five years. He was a fighter and refused to give up. He made it all the way to six, but the last two years were pure hell. Joel is the RN Michael had hired to be his live-in nurse. After Michael was gone, somehow Joel never left. It was like the two of us had been through a war together.

"That's when I finally began to have some real understanding of what my father must have gone through when my mother was dying. When you're stuck in a lose/lose situation like that, you end up being really isolated. You crave companionship and solace. I suppose he and Clarice started out as friends back then, but eventually it turned into something more. The same thing happened to me with Joel. We started out as friends and ended up falling in love.

"After we married, Joel was the one who encouraged me to get back in touch with my father. Joel's family was a lot like mine, but his father died before the two of them had a chance to mend fences. Joel didn't want me to make the same mistake."

"How long ago did you and your father bury the hatchet?" Detective Horn asked.

"Only a few weeks—the end of January maybe? I finally worked up enough courage to reach out to him at work. I wasn't sure if he'd even take my call. When he invited Joel and me to come to his big party, you could have knocked me over with a feather."

Watching the video, Ali was struck by Adam's visible emotion when he told about how recently he and his father had become reacquainted and his obvious regret that there hadn't been enough time for them to effect a real reconciliation. She saw him swallow a lump in his throat before answering and heard the wistfulness in his voice. She also noticed a tear beginning to form in the corner of his eye, one he quickly dabbed away. At that point Ali paused the video, rewound it, and then played that portion of the interview again.

In police interviews following homicides, guilty parties often resort to over-the-top hysterics. Those are easy to spot, especially when no tears are present. But in Ali's experience, real regret is hard to fake, and that's what she was sure she was seeing here—a man whose chance of reestablishing a relationship with a long-estranged father had been snatched away from him forever. Would someone like that viciously slaughter his father only a matter of hours after arriving at the family home for the first time in decades? That made no sense.

The interview ended with Horn asking for fingerprints and a DNA swab, both of which Adam Brewster provided with no objection. Those weren't the actions of someone with something to hide, either. So if Adam hadn't killed his father, and if neither Clarice Brewster nor Donna Jean Plummer were responsible, who was?

Ali was sitting there staring at her computer screen and puzzling over that when Frigg's voice came back on the line.

"Somebody's lying," she said.

"Who?" Ali asked. "It sounded to me as though he was telling the truth—like he didn't do it."

"Either Adam is lying or his husband is," Frigg replied. "Or maybe both of them are. According to Adam, he was motivated to reach out to his father due to a similar situation that had occurred in Joel Franklin's life in which he, too, had been ostracized by a father who died prior to the two of them having any kind of reconciliation. The problem is, Marvin Franklin, Joel's father, is alive and well and living in Hammond, Indiana."

"That's a surprise," Ali said. "What do we do now?"

"I don't know what you're going to do," Frigg replied, "but I'm going to start by doing a more thorough inquiry into Joel Franklin's background."

CHAPTER TWENTY-FOUR

COTTONWOOD, ARIZONA
THURSDAY, MARCH 23, 2023
10:00 A.M.

Off the line with Frigg, Ali sat at her desk trying to make forward progress on her to-do list, but the circumstances surrounding Chuck Brewster's homicide kept derailing her ability to concentrate. She was about to go to the break room for a cup of coffee when her phone rang with Cami's face showing in caller ID.

"Hey, Cami," Ali said cheerfully. "Good to hear from you. How's it going?"

"Not so well," Cami said. "I just had a visit from the cops."

"The cops?" Ali echoed. "How come?"

"Two homicide detectives from the Essex Police. Adrian Willoughby's body was found floating face down in a lake somewhere in Essex early this morning."

The name Adrian Willoughby didn't ring any bells as far as Ali was concerned. "Who?" she asked.

"Adrian Willoughby. Remember back in 2020 when a blogger kept giving us all kinds of bad press?"

That did sound faintly familiar. "Oh, him," Ali said. "I had forgotten about him completely. He's dead?"

"Yes, not just dead but murdered. He died Saturday night. They know the exact time of his death because he was wearing an Apple Watch."

"But what does that have to do with you?"

"He had pictures of me on his computer," Cami explained. "Candid photos that were taken of me last week while I was in L.A. The authorities here used facial rec from those to figure out that I had entered the UK at Heathrow on Tuesday morning."

Ali did a sharp intake of breath. "Are you kidding? Were the photos taken by Bogdan Petrov?"

"Most likely," Cami answered. "And Willoughby responded to the text containing my photos with a single, one-word reply. It said GO—all caps."

"As in do it?"

"That's what it sounds like to me."

"Does this mean Willoughby sent Petrov after you?"

"Maybe, maybe not. Willoughby's finances were in the tank, and the kind of tech Petrov had at his disposal—his ability to wipe the Lancaster's surveillance system, for instance—would have cost a lot of money. But speaking of Petrov, that's the other thing Rachel just told me."

"What about him?"

"Sonja Bjornson's people managed to retrieve a tracking device from my rental car and traced that to Petrov's phone. The last time it pinged was somewhere near San Bernardino. His body was found yesterday morning in an irrigation ditch near there. It's just now been identified."

Ali was aghast. "So he's dead, too?"

"Apparently."

"Of what?"

"Shot in the back of the head, execution style."

"So Willoughby sent Petrov after you, and now both of them are dead. That means someone is cleaning up after them, but why on earth would Adrian Willoughby target you in the first place?"

Cami sighed. "I'm afraid I gave him some pretty good reasons," she admitted.

For the next several minutes, Ali listened in astonishment while Cami recounted how, back in 2020, in the aftermath of that conference in

London, Willoughby had made an unwelcome pass at her. In return, she had wreaked havoc in the smarmy creep's personal life.

"All right," Ali said when Cami finished, "what you did wasn't exactly according to Hoyle, but it was also little more than a prank. I can't imagine why he'd be motivated to send a hit man after you three years later."

"Maybe he was doing someone else's bidding," Cami suggested. "You do remember who he was working for back then, don't you?"

The early months of 2020 were pretty hazy for Ali. With B. out of commission due to serious injuries from an automobile crash and with the pandemic bearing down on everyone, she'd had her hands more than full.

"I don't remember much," Ali admitted.

"He was a well-known blogger in cybersecurity circles," Cami said, "and a lot of what he wrote showed High Noon in a very bad light. It wasn't until later that we figured out that George Smythe of Cybersecurity International had been paying Adrian under the table."

The name George Smythe certainly jogged Ali's memory. He had attended the same conference where, in B.'s absence, Cami had delivered a paper to the assembled group. After her presentation, Smythe—seemingly the perfect English gentleman—had approached Ali. While praising Cami's presentation, Smythe had gone on to suggest that he hoped High Noon would make better use of her talents than keeping her locked away in a computer lab. That conversation was one of the things that had led to Cami's being put in charge of outside sales.

"When we were trying to identify problematic people on Saturday," Ali said once Cami finished, "ones who might have had issues with you, why didn't either one of those names come up?"

"Because it didn't dawn on me that either one of them would be involved," Cami replied. "Nothing about them seemed important enough to mention."

"Well, they've been mentioned now," Ali said. "As soon as we're off the phone, I'll turn Frigg loose on both of them. Give me the names of those Essex detectives."

"Detective Inspector Howard Wallace and Detective Sergeant Matthew Frost."

"All right," Ali said as she jotted down the names. "And if you can, send along the number of that cell phone WWS located for Bogdan Petrov. Let's hope Frigg has enough bandwidth to monitor three separate homicide investigations on two different continents at the same time."

"Three?" Cami echoed. "What do you mean three? Who else is dead?"

Obviously Cami wasn't the only one who had left a bit of critical information out of that lunchtime meeting on Saturday. Somehow Chuck and Clarice Brewster's names hadn't come up, either.

Let he who is without sin . . . Ali thought.

"With all the uproar going on," Ali said aloud, "I must have forgotten to mention that B.'s former partner, Chuck Brewster, was murdered somewhere in the Seattle area last week while you were in L.A. We're looking into the situation on behalf of B.'s ex-wife who may or may not have been involved in the homicide."

"That's a lot to deal with," Cami said after a moment. "Are you sure you want me to have WWS send you that phone number?"

"I'm sure," Ali said. "I'll turn it over to Frigg and see what she turns up."

CHAPTER TWENTY-FIVE

SEDONA, ARIZONA
THURSDAY, MARCH 23, 2023
12:00 P.M.

After asking Frigg to focus on the Adrian Willoughby case, Ali made her way down the hall and spent her lunch hour huddling with B. and Lance over this latest wrinkle.

"I've run into Smythe several times," B. said. "At one point he was interested in purchasing High Noon outright. I told him I wasn't interested. That's about the time Willoughby's disinformation campaign started."

"Did you know Smythe was the one behind all that negative press?" Ali asked.

"I may have suspected as much, but once Willoughby went dark, I figured it wasn't that big a deal, and I forgot all about it."

"Forgot about it so completely that you never mentioned it to me?" Ali asked.

B. nodded. "Sorry about that," he said, "but do we have any proof that Smythe was still in contact with Willoughby prior to his death or if he's ever had any dealings with Bogdan Petrov?"

"I've got Frigg looking into it," Ali replied. "But this is a police matter now, and that means we're going to have to come forward and bring them into the picture sooner or later."

"Starting with Cami's attempted abduction?" B. asked.

"I think so," Ali replied.

"To which jurisdiction?"

"Let's see what Frigg turns up before we make a determination on that, but I'll make sure that whatever she finds from this point on is going to have to stand up in court. I'll also let Cami know that we're looking into the possibility that Smythe may be behind the failed attack on her."

"Fair enough," B. agreed.

Glad that everyone was now on the same page, Ali headed back to her office and did just that, letting Cami know in an encrypted text that George Smythe would now be at the center of Frigg's investigation. Then she summoned Frigg and told her the same thing.

"I'll get right on it," the AI said, "but are you interested in the latest news from King County?"

"What now?" Ali asked.

"Clarice Brewster has a new defense attorney who requested and was granted a second bond hearing. As of ten o'clock this morning, Clarice Brewster was released to house arrest on a million-dollar bond. Since her home is still considered a crime scene, she'll be staying at a local hotel at her own expense. She's required to surrender her passport and wear an ankle monitor."

"Thank you," Ali said.

"There's one thing more," Frigg added. "I know you asked me to focus on Adrian Willoughby, but there's something else I just learned about Joel Franklin. I'm unable to find any record of his being licensed as a registered nurse in the state of Texas."

"That's very interesting," Ali said. "So saying his father was dead isn't the only lie he told Michael Lafferty and Adam Brewster. There may be more."

"Agreed," the AI said. "I'll keep looking."

Off the call with Frigg, Ali sat there and thought about what she'd just learned. Obviously Clarice had taken Ali's advice after all, and it had paid off. While out on bond, staying in a hotel would be more comfortable than being locked up in jail. And if she could cough up enough money for a million-dollar bond, Ali had no doubt that Clarice had been able to spring for a top-drawer defense attorney. But what about her supposed accomplice? What kind of representation could Donna Jean Plummer afford?

That was the last thing the woman had said to Detective Horn in their most recent interview—that she wanted an attorney, but Ali knew that a public defender couldn't be appointed until Donna Jean was actually charged with a crime. During that last interview, Detective Horn had made it clear that, although they weren't yet ready to indict her, she was still under suspicion. Ali was concerned about what might happen in the meantime.

Sitting there, Ali thought again about what had happened to Mateo Vega when he, too, had been targeted and eventually wrongfully convicted. When the situation had been brought to Ali's attention, she'd turned to and received help from a guy connected to an all-volunteer cold-case organization. She remembered that he was a retired Seattle homicide cop, but it took a moment for her to recall his name, until finally it came to her—J.P. Beaumont.

One of the things that helped her remember was the fact that, like B. Simpson, Mr. Beaumont went by his initials rather than his given name. Without allowing herself time to reconsider, she located his number in her phone's contacts list and pressed call. The last time she had spoken with him had been several years earlier. Maybe the number wouldn't even work.

But it did. A moment later a male voice answered. "Why, Ali Reynolds. Long time no hear. How the hell are you?"

"I'm fine," she said. "And you?"

"I'm fine, too. What about Mateo? How's he doing?"

Ali was a little surprised that he remembered. "You came up with his name right off the top of your head."

"Of course I remember his name," J.P. said with a laugh. "I spent my whole career putting killers in prison. Mateo happens to be someone who should have never gone to prison in the first place, and I was able to aid in his exoneration. That makes him pretty memorable in my mind. To what do I owe the honor of this call?"

"I'm asking for help again," Ali said. "Are you familiar with the murder of someone named Charles Brewster? He died in Edmonds a little over a week ago."

"You mean the video game guy?" Beau returned. "Sure, the story's been all over the news. I hear they have one suspect in custody, the victim's wife, and another person of interest who is still under investigation."

"You're a bit behind the times," Ali told him with a laugh. "The victim's wife and prime suspect, Clarice Brewster, was released earlier this morning after posting a million-dollar bond. The person still under investigation is the Brewsters' longtime housekeeper, Donna Jean Plummer."

"Wait, wait, wait," Beau interrupted. "You're still in Sedona, right?"

"Yes."

"And all this is going on in the Seattle area?"

"Correct."

"What's your connection?"

"Chuck Brewster was my husband's former business partner. Clarice is my husband's former wife."

"Okay," Beau said after a pause. "A double whammy, then. What do you need?"

"I need the name of a good criminal defense attorney who might be willing to take on a case temporarily on a pro bono basis. As I said, the housekeeper, Donna Jean Plummer, is still under suspicion. I think she's an unlikely candidate, but the cop in charge seems to be suffering from a case of tunnel vision. He's interviewed her several times. Unlike Clarice, she can't afford a high-powered criminal defense attorney. Once she's officially charged, she'll probably qualify for a public defender, but between now and then, I think she could use some help."

"As an ex-cop, I'm not exactly on a first-name basis with many criminal defense attorneys," J.P. said, "but I might know someone who is. Hang on. Let me check my contacts list. Okay, here it is. The organization is called Justice for All. Think Innocence Project but on a smaller scale. Rosalie Whittier was the lead defense attorney on a wrongful conviction case I encountered in Arizona. Would you like her contact information, or would you like me to ask her to give you a call?"

"Sending my number to you now," Ali reported, "and please send me hers as well, but since you're someone who actually knows her, having an introduction from you will probably work better than a cold call from me."

"Okey doke," Beau said. "I'll get right on it."

Much to Ali's relief, Rosalie Whittier called her back a mere twenty minutes later. "Ali Reynolds?" she asked.

"Yes."

"Rosalie Whittier here. I understand from a mutual acquaintance that you're interested in preventing a possible miscarriage of justice."

"Yes, I am," Ali said.

She spent the next half hour explaining Donna Jean's situation in some detail, and that wasn't easy. After all, Ali had no direct connection to anyone involved, including the homicide victim and both suspects. But her mention that the detective involved might be suffering from a case of tunnel vision seemed to grab Rosalie's attention, especially when Ali told her about Donna Jean's previous homicide conviction.

"You believe he's focused on her as a repeat offender?"

"That's how it looks to me."

"All right, then," Rosalie said. "I have a colleague in the Seattle area who might be willing to help. If you can give me Ms. Plummer's contact information, I'll have her reach out to see if we can be of service."

"Thank you," Ali said.

"And if she requests to have representation from us, can we come back to you in case you have any additional information?"

"Her attorney certainly can," Ali answered. "We'll do everything we can to help."

As the phone call ended, Ali ran both hands over her eyes. "And that," she said to herself, "is taking Mom's Edieing to a whole new level."

CHAPTER TWENTY-SIX

SEATTLE, WASHINGTON
THURSDAY, MARCH 23, 2023
7:00 P.M.

By the time Donna Jean got home that night, she had put in a full ten-hour day. She had cleaned both of her Thursday houses and managed to make up part of one of the two she had missed on Tuesday. Too tired to even put a frozen dinner in the microwave, she settled at the kitchen table with a bowl of Cheerios and a carton of milk.

Mrs. Brewster had called around noon to let Donna Jean know that she was out on bail and being held under house arrest at the Hotel Sorrento in Seattle. Donna had never set foot inside the Sorrento. It sounded expensive, but no doubt Mrs. Brewster could afford it.

"It's pet friendly," Mrs. Brewster reported, "but I can't imagine Pearl would be happy here, so if you don't mind looking after her . . ."

"It's fine," Donna Jean said quickly. "She's pretty much settled in. I'll be glad to keep her as long as you need." *Unless I end up going to jail, too*, she thought.

"And about the house," Mrs. Brewster continued. "It's still considered a crime scene at this point, but once they release it, I'm planning on having some renovations done, so I don't have any idea when I'll need you to come back."

Somehow Donna Jean had always known that would be the eventual outcome. The problem was, some of her other customers, assuming correctly that she might be the unnamed person of interest in Mr. Brewster's homicide, had already told her they no longer needed her services, either. As a result, Donna Jean was currently on the prowl for replacement customers, so far without success.

"I'll pay you a hundred bucks a month for taking care of Pearl," Mrs. Brewster offered.

Donna Jean knew that most pet-sitting services cost far more than a hundred dollars a month, but that didn't matter.

"No need," Donna Jean had said. "I like having her here."

At that moment, when Donna Jean was down to the last of her Cheerios, Pearl emerged from the bedroom and gave Donna Jean's leg a soft nudge on her way past. The cat had already figured out correctly that if she did that trick at mealtimes, she was usually given a treat, and it worked this time as well. Donna Jean placed her almost empty cereal dish down on the floor, where Pearl made quick work of the last few spoonfuls of milk at the bottom of the bowl.

That's when her phone rang with a call from an unknown number located in Bellevue. Donna Jean didn't know anyone living on the far side of Lake Washington, but on the off chance that it might be someone looking for a new cleaning lady, she went ahead and answered.

"Hello."

"Donna Jean Plummer?" an unfamiliar female voice asked.

"Yes, who's this?"

"My name is Moesha Jackson. I'm a criminal defense attorney with Justice for All. A woman named Ali Reynolds contacted us earlier today indicating that it's possible you're being unfairly targeted in a homicide investigation, and that you might be in need of legal representation."

Donna Jean was mystified. Who was this woman? How had she gotten her number? How did she know Donna Jean needed an attorney? And who the hell was Ali Reynolds?

The silence on the phone must have lasted longer than expected. "Are you still there, Ms. Plummer?"

"Yes, I'm here," Donna Jean said quickly. "I just don't know how . . . "

"Justice for All is in the business of trying to undo miscarriages of justice. In this case we might be able to prevent one. Would it be possible for us to get together tomorrow to discuss your situation?"

"Miss . . . " Donna Jean began.

"Ms. Jackson, but you can call me Moesha."

"I appreciate your calling," Donna Jean said quickly, "but I'm in no position to hire an attorney."

"Justice for All works pro bono," Moesha explained. "That means there is no charge for our services, but in order to look into your case, I'll need you to sign a document saying you're accepting me as your attorney. That's why we need to get together in person—for you to sign the document. After that, you can tell me what's going on and make a determination about whether you'd like us to go to work for you. So what time tomorrow would be convenient?"

With the Brewsters permanently off Donna Jean's calendar, Friday mornings were now wide open.

"Where?" she asked.

"How about at my office?"

"Where's that?"

"In Bellevue on Northeast Eighth," Moesha replied.

For Donna Jean, crossing one of the Lake Washington bridges to go to Bellevue was like going to a different planet. But what would a Bellevue attorney think of her shabby apartment? In the end, though, that seemed like the lesser of two evils.

"I really don't know my away around Bellevue," she admitted. "Would it be possible for you to come here?"

"Sure, would ten a.m. work?"

"Yes," Donna Jean agreed before she had a chance to change her mind. "Ten will be fine. Do you need the address?"

"Oh, no," Moesha said. "I already have it. See you then."

How does she know where I live? Donna Jean wondered. *How does she know so much about me? And how many other people do, too?*

At that point, she was so upset that she left the kitchen just as it was—with her dirty bowl right there on the kitchen floor. In the living room, she dropped heavily into her easy chair and allowed herself a moment of absolute despair. But just then, Pearl came over to her chair, hopped up into her lap, and curled herself into a tight ball.

Somehow that made everything better.

CHAPTER TWENTY-SEVEN

SEDONA, ARIZONA
THURSDAY, MARCH 23, 2023
10:00 P.M.

B. was already in bed and Ali was thinking about joining him when Frigg sent her another message:

Would now be a good time for an additional briefing?

Yes, please. Call me.

Moments later the call came through. "Good evening, Ali. I hope you've had a pleasant day."

"Not exactly," Ali said. "I'm glad it's almost over. What have you found?"

"I decided to press the easy button," Frigg said.

That made Ali almost laugh out loud. Frigg's conversational abilities were becoming more and more human all the time.

"How so?"

"By pinging cell towers," Frigg replied.

Ali happened to know that procedure generally required search warrants, but for Frigg it was just a matter of sorting through numbers, something the AI was exceptionally adept at doing.

"Even if a phone isn't actively in use," Frigg continued, "it still registers with nearby cell towers. That's what I did. I started pinging phones registered off the cell towers closest to the Brewster residence in Edmonds, Washington, on the day of the party. At approximately six p.m. on Sunday, March 12, 2023, three cell phones with Huntington Beach area codes—prefixes 562, 567, and 714—all pinged off towers near the Brewster residence at the same time. The 562 number is registered to Adam Brewster, and the 657 is registered to Joel Franklin. The 714 is a burner. All three devices arrived in the area at the same time and departed simultaneously four and a half hours later."

"Having a burner may sound suspicious," Ali interjected, "but it isn't exactly against the law."

"No, it's not," Frigg agreed, "but please bear with me. I continued to analyze all devices registering on that tower throughout the evening, from the time the party started until three hours after what the medical examiner estimated to be Charles Brewster's time of death. There was a mass exodus of phone numbers around ten p.m."

"That would be about the time the party broke up," Ali said.

"Correct," Frigg agreed. "As the night wore on, the number of devices registering on the tower dwindled because there was almost no traffic. The remaining IP addresses appear to belong to neighborhood residents."

"I'm sure the cops did the same thing," Ali said.

"Perhaps they did," Frigg agreed, "but they might not have been quite as thorough. I went above and beyond. I analyzed all numbers pinging off those towers over several days both before and after the party. On Friday, March 10, I found a second Huntington Beach area code, another 714, registering on that same set of towers. This one is registered to someone named Marc Atherton. It first pinged off the Edmonds cell towers at eleven fifteen p.m. on Friday and departed at twelve forty-five a.m. on Saturday.

"Since that seemed like an odd time for someone to be visiting the neighborhood, I looked into Marc Atherton's background. He was born Richard Mansfield in Bend, Oregon. At age twenty he was involved in a hit-and-run automobile accident, in the course of which passengers in the other vehicle were seriously injured. He spent six years in a Portland area prison. He changed his name after moving to California and lives in Huntington Beach where he's a bartender at a local establishment called the Meet and Greet. I think there's a good possibility Atherton is involved in all this, and that Saturday night visit was for recon purposes."

"What makes you say that?" Ali asked.

"Remember that unidentified burner phone that showed up at Mr. Brewster's birthday party? The call history on Mr. Atherton's phone shows a steady stream of calls and texts between those two devices, his phone and our unidentified burner. Many of the texts have to do with a screenplay the two individuals seem to be writing together."

Ali knew that Frigg shouldn't have been able to hack into anyone's cell phone, but it was hardly surprising that she had. As for why people resorted to using burners? Because they didn't want people to know what they were doing.

"So who owns the burner?" Ali asked. "And did you find anything incriminating?"

"I'm quite sure the burner belongs to Mr. Franklin. As for finding something incriminating? Perhaps. On the night of Mr. Brewster's birthday party, at 9:03 p.m., I found an incoming text from the burner on Mr. Atherton's text history."

"One word?" Ali repeated. "What did it say?"

"'Done!'" Frigg replied.

"Done what?" Ali asked.

"There's no further explanation," Frigg answered. "It's the 9:03 timing that makes it possibly incriminating. That's approximately the same time when Adam Brewster said that Joel helped an inebriated Clarice Brewster negotiate the elevator when she made her early exit from the party."

From the start, Ali had wondered how Clarice, lying in the same bed, could possibly have slept through the violent attack on her husband.

"Wait, are you suggesting Joel may have drugged her?" Ali asked.

"I believe that's possible," Frigg answered, "but since no blood work was done on her the following day, without an admission of guilt on someone's part, that will be difficult to prove. And the question remains—was Adam Brewster involved?"

Ali thought about that, remembering Adam's demeanor during his interview with Detective Horn as he spoke about reconnecting with his father after their long estrangement. The regret in his voice in the aftermath of the homicide had seemed genuine.

"My gut says no," Ali answered. "He seemed thrilled about finally having his father back in his life. There's no way he would have been involved in murdering him. But if Marc Atherton and Joel Franklin are responsible, what have they got to gain?"

"Everything," Frigg answered at once. "If Clarice pleads guilty to or is convicted by a jury of murdering her husband, she will be assumed to have predeceased him and won't be eligible to inherit his estate."

Ali nodded to herself. "At that point, Adam Brewster, Chuck's only son, might very well inherit the whole shebang."

"The what?" Frigg asked.

"Shebang," Ali repeated. "It means 'all of it.' And if something were to happen to Adam after that, Joel Franklin, as his spouse, would be next in line. Are you suggesting that maybe Joel Franklin and Marc Atherton are playing a long game—murder Chuck, frame Clarice, and subsequently get rid of Adam?"

"Exactly," Frigg replied. "Strategic planning is my specialty."

"Yes, it is," Ali agreed. "Unfortunately, Detective Horn seems permanently stuck on convicting Clarice and Donna Jean Plummer. So what do we do now?"

"We wait to see if his investigation catches up with ours."

At that point, Ali changed the subject. "Any luck on the Adrian Willoughby case in the UK or Bogdan Petrov's in San Bernardino?"

"So far interviews and progress reports from the Essex Police are somewhat more challenging to access than those in the States, but I'm working on it," Frigg replied. "As for Petrov? His time of death is estimated to be sometime in the early morning hours of Saturday, March 18."

"In other words, he died shortly after Cami's foiled kidnapping," Ali said. "Isn't that the same day and about the same time Adrian Willoughby died?"

"It would be except for the time difference," Frigg replied.

"So if Petrov and Willoughby were both involved in the attempted kidnapping, whoever was really behind it didn't waste any time covering their tracks by taking them both out. How was Petrov killed?"

"Shot execution style in the back of the head. A nine-millimeter slug was extracted from his skull but was too damaged to obtain any further information. No casings and no footprints or tire tracks were found at the scene."

"So no physical evidence," Ali breathed.

"And no surveillance videos, either," Frigg added. "I'm pinging nearby cell towers for the number retrieved from the GPS locater found in Cami's rental car, but I'm not making any progress there. However, I'm seeing numerous calls on that phone between Petrov and Willoughby—between them and no one else."

"Okay," Ali urged. "Keep working."

"We will," Frigg replied. "My CPUs and I never sleep."

And now neither will I, Ali thought as the call ended. Rather than going to bed right then, she sent a quick email to Cami, giving her an overview of what Frigg had just told her. That way Cami would have the information first thing in the morning when she awoke in London.

With that done, Ali went to bed and really did go to sleep. Tomorrow would be another day.

CHAPTER TWENTY-EIGHT

LONDON, ENGLAND
FRIDAY, MARCH 24, 2023
8:00 A.M.

Sitting down to her room service breakfast, Cami opened her phone and found Ali's most recent message. It didn't provide much more information than she'd already gathered. Moments later, she was startled by the ringing of the landline phone on her bedside table.

"Hello?"

"Ms. Lee?"

"Yes."

"Detective Inspector Wallace here. I was wondering if you'd be available to come into police headquarters for a formal interview later on this morning. There have been a number of new developments in the case, and we'd like to discuss them with you."

"Where is your headquarters located?"

"In Chelmsford," he answered. "We're about thirty miles from where you're staying."

Cami thought about all the appointments she had set for today, but with both Petrov and Willoughby dead, this was now a double homicide with international implications. Unfortunately, she was the one common denominator in both cases. No wonder DI Wallace wanted a second interview.

"Okay," she said, "but in order to do that, I'll need to move some appointments around. The best I can do will be early afternoon."

"That'll work. Do you need the address?"

"No, we'll be able to find it."

"Who's we?" Wallace asked.

"My friend Rachel and I," Ali said. "You met her last night. She knows her way around the UK far better than I do."

"All right," Wallace said. "Let's plan on one o'clock."

Off the phone, Cami hurried over to the connecting door between her room and Rachel's and tapped on it. "Slight change of plans," she said.

Rachel opened the door, still in her PJs. "What kind of change?" she asked.

"DI Wallace wants to do a formal interview with me at the Essex Police headquarters in Chelmsford early this afternoon."

"Under caution or not?"

"He didn't say."

"What did you tell him?"

"That I'd be there around one."

"I take it he knows Petrov is dead?" Rachel asked.

"Yes, he does."

"You shouldn't go into that interview without a solicitor," Rachel said. "I can call someone."

"No, don't bother. I'll be fine. What I need to do now is move today's appointments around and postpone them until Monday, if at all possible, and that means I'm going to have to change my departure date."

"I'll see if WWS's faux cab is available," Rachel replied. "We sure as hell aren't going to Chelmsford and back on public transportation. We'd be sitting ducks."

After changing her return flight to Tuesday, Cami spent the remainder of her morning canceling her Friday appointments and moving them around. Then, before going downstairs to meet up with Rachel, she sent an encrypted text to both Frigg and Ali:

> Changed the departure for my return flight to Tuesday. Going to an interview with DI Wallace concerning Adrian Willoughby's homicide. No calls or texts until I let you know otherwise.

Once the message was gone, she sat there staring at the screen on her phone. She was quite sure that if her phone was put through a forensic examination, the hidden texts back and forth would be undetectable, but what if there was something that investigators would expect to be there but wasn't—like the one containing the screenshot of Petrov in the Lancaster fitness center that she had sent to Frigg in a Howler form? Fortunately, she had given the screenshot to Sonja Bjornson by hand. Maybe she'd be able to make DI Wallace believe that High Noon had come by their copy the same way.

The distance from the Portlandia to the Essex Police Headquarters in Chelmsford may have been only thirty miles, but the drive took close to an hour. On the way, Cami noticed that both the driver and Rachel were on full alert, watching for any kind of tailing vehicle. Cami, on the other hand, was wondering why Wallace was bringing her in for another interview. Before entering the room, just to be on the safe side, she set her phone to block all incoming calls and messages until further notice.

"The time is 1:23 p.m.," he announced once everyone was seated. "I am Detective Inspector Wallace. Present in the room with me is Detective Sergeant Frost and a U.S. citizen named Camille Lee. Ms. Lee, you do not have to say anything, but it may harm your defense if you do not mention something when questioned that you later rely on in court. Anything you do say may be given in evidence."

In that moment, Cami knew she wasn't here as a witness. She was here as a person of interest at least, if not an actual suspect. Rachel had been right to suggest that Cami should be accompanied by a solicitor, and Cami should have gone along with that idea.

"First off," Wallace began, "I believe you told me in our previous interview that you had identified your presumed stalker as someone named Bogdan Petrov."

Cami nodded. "That is correct."

"And how exactly did you determine that?"

"As I told you, by using facial rec, we were able to confirm his identity."

Much to Cami's relief, her use of that first person plural pronoun went right past DI Wallace without so much as a raised eyebrow.

"Are you aware he's deceased?"

Cami realized now was not the time to pull any punches. "Yes, I am," she answered. "My understanding is that his body was found on Tuesday. I believe the location was in a field somewhere near San Bernardino, California."

"How is it that you have so much information about a homicide that occurred an ocean and a continent away?"

"I work for a company named High Noon Enterprises, a cybersecurity firm," she answered. "As I told you, law enforcement wasn't notified about what went on in L.A., but my employers have been looking into it. They're the ones who learned Petrov was dead. I didn't find out about it until I read it in a text message this morning."

With that Cami opened her phone, located Ali's text, and then handed it to DI Wallace.

"Who's this Frigg?" he asked after reading it.

"One of our investigators," Cami replied.

"But you didn't feel obliged to pass that information along to me when I called you later on? Withholding information is considered a crime, you know."

"As I said, I only learned about Petrov's death this morning. When you called, asking me to come in for an official interview, he wasn't the first thing that came to mind. I was far more concerned about moving my appointments. Besides, we're talking about it now, aren't we? How is that withholding?"

DI Wallace sighed. "Okay, walk me through your day in Los Angeles last Friday, starting at the beginning."

Cami did so, from going to her Friday morning appointments, until the time she had fled the fitness center.

"Who exactly did you call for help?"

"WWS," Cami explained. "That's short for Wonder Woman Security. They're an international personal security firm owned by a woman named Sonja Bjornson. They specialize in providing personal security for high-profile women. B. Simpson, my boss, had given me the direct phone number and told me that if I ever felt I was in danger, I should call them, so I did."

"Do you consider yourself high-profile?" Wallace asked.

"I don't," Cami replied, "but evidently there are people out there who do."

"Anyone in particular?"

"There's someone we think might possibly be behind all of it."

"Name?"

"His name is George Smythe," Cami said. "His company, Cybersecurity International, is one of High Noon's largest competitors. We believe he's also the person who encouraged and underwrote the bad press Adrian Willoughby wrote about us several years ago."

"Do you have any contact information for him?"

"No," Cami answered. "His company is located here in the UK, I'm not sure where."

Wallace made a note of that information. "All right, so back to last Friday. What happened after you left the hotel fitness center?"

"WWS sent a car to pick me up and take me to their headquarters, which is located in Ms. Bjornson's house in the Hollywood Hills. I stayed there until Saturday morning when another WWS vehicle drove me to an airport in San Diego where I caught a private flight back to Arizona."

"And the people from WWS will be able to verify all of that?"

"Yes."

"I'm going to need their phone number."

"Of course," Cami said, extracting her phone from her pocket once more before locating and reading off the WWS number from her recent calls list.

"Would you mind if we turned your phone over to our tech unit so they could examine it?"

Thanks to Lance's GHOST operating system, Cami knew that all encrypted texts and emails would have vanished without a trace. "Sure," she said, handing over her phone. "No problem."

Wallace passed the device along to Detective Sergeant Frost. "Take this downstairs, have them clone it, and bring it right back."

"Copy that, sir," Frost said.

"DS Frost is leaving the interview," DI Wallace announced. "Now tell me, how did your employers become aware of Bogdan Petrov's death?"

"Shortly after our first interview," Cami replied. "WWS launched their own investigation into the stalking situation. Since I believed I'd been followed, they had someone track down my rental car. An examination of that led to the discovery of a tracking device that had been connected to a cell phone that stopped pinging somewhere near San Bernardino. When a dead body was found near that location, I believe WWS suggested to local authorities that Petrov might be their unidentified victim."

"What have you been doing since you've been here?"

"I've been at the hotel the whole time. The Portlandia's surveillance videos will verify that. Coming here this morning is the first time I've set foot outside the hotel since I checked in."

Wallace nodded. "All right, then," he said. "It's clear that Petrov and Willoughby were conspiring against you. Now they're both deceased, so why would this George Smythe want you dead?"

"I'm not sure he wanted me dead. WWS is pretty sure the crime was planned as a kidnapping, a well-funded one at that. The technical capability it took to wipe the Lancaster's surveillance system would have cost a fortune."

"A kidnapping for ransom, then?" DI Wallace asked. "How much money are you worth?"

"I don't think the guy behind this was looking for money. We believe he's trying to lay hands on GHOST."

"I beg your pardon?"

"G-H-O-S-T is a proprietary software that has put High Noon at the head of the pack in the world of cybersecurity. Previously, Smythe tried to buy us out, but my boss wasn't interested in selling. I believe kidnapping me was Smythe's backup plan for getting his hands on the software."

"Do you have any way of proving that?"

"Not so far, but we're working on it. Am I under arrest, then?"

"Not at the moment," Wallace said. "We'll try taking a look at this Smythe fellow. Are you still planning on leaving the UK tomorrow?"

"No, I've delayed my departure until Tuesday, but if you need me to, I can make arrangements to stay longer. Can I go now?"

"Tell me about Ms. Bloom," Wallace said. "Is she really your friend or is she actually your bodyguard?"

Cami was surprised that he'd sorted that out.

"The latter," she said.

"And she works for this . . . " Wallace paused long enough to consult his notes. "WWS organization?"

Cami nodded.

"We'll need to interview her as well."

Just then the door opened and DS Frost returned, carrying Cami's phone, which he returned to her.

"Find anything?" Wallace asked.

Frost shook his head. "Not so far. Nothing out of line, and our preliminary examination shows that the phone has been pinging off towers near the Portlandia from the time she checked in on Monday afternoon until she left there this morning to come here."

"All right, then, Ms. Lee," Wallace said. "You may go. Please bring in Ms. Bloom, DS Frost. Let's see if her version of events matches up with Ms. Lee's."

CHAPTER TWENTY-NINE

CHELMSFORD, ENGLAND
FRIDAY, MARCH 24, 2023
3:00 P.M.

Emerging from her own interview and expecting Rachel's would last the better part of an hour, Cami checked her watch. After taking her phone off block, she gave Frigg a call.

"Good afternoon, Cami," Frigg said. "I hope you're having a pleasant day."

It may have been morning in Sedona, but Frigg was always in step with the correct time zones.

"Not exactly," Cami replied. "I've just spent two hours being interviewed by the Essex Police in conjunction with the Adrian Willoughby homicide."

"Do they consider you a suspect?"

"He was murdered before I ever arrived in the country, but they're checking my alibi, and they've asked me not to leave the country until they've completed their inquiries. In the meantime, do you have anything for me?"

"Rather a lot, actually. Is this a good time to go over it?"

Spotting a bench in the hallway leading to the interview rooms, Cami sank down on it. "Go ahead," she said.

"In examining Mr. Smythe's finances, I discovered that in 2020 his situation was dire. It would appear that he had expanded the company too rapidly and was facing the possibility that it would go under. A massive influx of funds from Eastern Europe, Bulgaria in particular, rescued him from having to file for bankruptcy, and that gave the business time enough to recover from that over expansion."

"That's about the same time Adrian Willoughby launched his misinformation campaign against High Noon," Cami put in. "Are those two things connected?"

"Possibly," Frigg replied. "Soon after the arrival of those funds, Mr. Smythe established a second cybersecurity enterprise located in Sofia, Bulgaria. He did so in partnership with a Bulgarian national named Petar Borisov. The company's name translates into English as Data Security. That seems to be the source of most of the funds found in Mr. Smythe's offshore cryptocurrency accounts."

"So that one's making money, then?" Cami asked.

"Supposedly," Frigg replied, "but I suspect the company's actual business dealings have very little to do with cybersecurity and far more to do with money laundering, since most of their supposed customers appear to be shell companies located in Eastern Europe."

"You're saying they don't actually exist?" Ali asked.

"The companies exist only on paper, but the money moving back and forth is real enough, and it appears to come from any number of illegal activities—drugs, human trafficking, and arms sales."

"How much money?"

"Based on what appears to be George Smythe's cut, I'd estimate it's in the billions," Frigg answered. "And as far as what happened to you in L.A.? I believe I've located the smoking weapon."

"You mean the smoking gun?" Cami asked.

"Yes, of course," Frigg corrected quickly. "The smoking gun."

"What is it?"

"I'm now able to penetrate Mr. Smythe's cryptocurrency accounts and track his recent wire transfers."

"Wait," Cami said. "Aren't cryptocurrency accounts supposed to be impenetrable?"

"You can't believe everything you see on the news," Frigg replied. "At Odin's direction I cut my hacking teeth on penetrating block-chain transactions."

"What did you find?"

"In the middle of February, Mr. Smythe made a sizable payment to someone you happen to know."

"Adrian Willoughby, by any chance?" Cami asked.

"Yes," Frigg replied.

"How much?" Cami asked.

"Three hundred and fifty thousand pounds."

Cami whistled. "That's sizable, all right, but I'm not surprised. What went on in California didn't come cheap. Anything else?"

Frigg continued. "On Friday of last week there were two additional smaller transfers from Mr. Smythe's account. One of them went to a Richard Hernandez, the owner of a cannabis shop in San Bernardino, California, and the other to an English dockworker named Ed Scoggins. Scoggins lives in the town of Tilbury, right next door to Grays, where Willoughby and his wife lived. Scoggins was released from prison two years ago after serving fourteen years for a fatality drunk-driving conviction."

"So Hernandez or one of his associates was likely hired to take care of Petrov, while Scoggins, the guy in Tilbury, handled Adrian Willoughby?"

"Presumably," Frigg answered.

"When I was being interviewed by the Essex Police earlier, I pointed the investigators in George Smythe's direction, but I only had my suspicions rather than any proof. Since you were able to access those financial transactions, will they be able to do the same thing?"

"No doubt they could," Frigg replied, "but not without obtaining the proper warrants. At the moment, I don't believe they're anywhere close to having probable cause."

Even though Cami had already had her own suspicions about the man, it was shocking to realize that someone who had always presented himself as a proper English gentleman was actually an international criminal.

"Then maybe we need to figure out a way to give them some," Cami said determinedly. "And if Smythe has already targeted me once, what's to stop him from doing so again?"

"Nothing," Frigg replied. "Nothing at all."

"That's not very reassuring," Cami said.

Just then Rachel emerged from the interview room, greeting Cami with a scathing look. "Let's go," she said grimly.

Ending the call with Frigg, Cami hurried after Rachel. "What's wrong?" she asked.

Rachel spun around to face her. "Who the hell is George Smythe?" she demanded. "I'm supposed to be protecting you, so why did I have to hear about him from DI Wallace instead of from you?"

With that, Rachel once more set off down the hallway, while Cami scrambled to keep up.

"I know a lot more about him now than I did this morning," Cami said.

"Like what?" Rachel demanded.

"Like he made several wire transfers from his cryptocurrency accounts recently—one of which was a payment of three hundred and fifty thousand pounds to Adrian Willoughby."

"Wait," Rachel said. "Are you telling me you have someone who's able to track cryptocurrency transactions?"

"Not someone," Cami admitted. "Something—Frigg is actually an AI. I'm sure the authorities here could do the same, but in order to do so, they'll need to know about them to begin with, and then they'll need a warrant."

"Good luck with that," Rachel replied.

On the drive back to London, Cami told Rachel everything she knew about George Smythe. At first Rachel listened in stony silence. Gradually she softened.

"All right," she said when Cami finished. "Thanks for cluing me in, but before we sit down to figure out next steps, we're going to have something to eat. I vote we call ahead for takeout orders of some of those Indian dishes we missed having the other night, only this time, with George Smythe still on the loose, we'll be dining in the security of our Portlandia hotel rooms rather than out in public."

CHAPTER THIRTY

COTTONWOOD, ARIZONA
FRIDAY, MARCH 24, 2023
8:00 A.M.

Once at her desk, Ali tried calling Cami several more times with the same result. She was finally focused on work when a call came in from Frigg.

"I just spoke to Cami," the AI said.

"Lucky you," Ali grumbled. "I've tried calling her several times, only to find she had blocked her phone."

"No doubt that was while she was being interviewed by the Essex Police."

"Interviewed by the police again?" Ali echoed. "Why? What's going on?"

"They were questioning her in regard to Adrian Willoughby's death."

"Don't tell me they suspect her of being involved in that!"

"Presumably not since she wasn't even in the UK when the crime occurred, but they spoke to her nonetheless."

"If the situation on the ground has come to the point of bringing her to the attention of law enforcement, I want her home as soon as possible," Ali declared. "Now that her phone is working again, I'm going to call her and tell her to be on the next available flight."

"That may not be possible since she's now part of an active police investigation," Frigg replied, "but I have some additional information I'd like to relay to both you and Mr. Simpson. Would you like me to add him to this call?"

"No," Ali said. "I'll have him come here."

Once B. arrived in Ali's office, both of them listened with increasing dismay while the AI related everything she had discovered about George Smythe, including the payments that led back not only to Adrian Willoughby but eventually to Bogdan Petrov as well.

"So Smythe is caught up in all kinds of illegal activities," B. said, "but what the hell does any of that have to do with Cami?"

"To your knowledge, is Mr. Smythe aware of Mr. Tucker's GHOST operating system?" Frigg asked.

B. paused for a moment before he answered. "Since he once offered to buy it, I'm sure he is, but Lance told him straight out that it wasn't for sale."

"But having access to something like that would be very beneficial to Mr. Smythe's criminal associates," Frigg observed, "and that may have been the motivation behind Cami's attempted kidnapping as well. Perhaps Smythe was hoping to use her as a bargaining chip in order to gain access to GHOST."

"Whoa," B. said, "are you saying that's what they would have asked for as ransom—a working version of GHOST?"

"I do," Frigg replied, "because having GHOST at their disposal would make it possible for the crooks to operate with almost complete impunity."

"We can't let that happen!" Ali exclaimed.

"Agreed," B. said. "Thank you bringing this to our attention, Frigg."

As soon as the call ended, Ali dialed Cami. She answered after the first ring.

"Good to hear your voice," Ali said. "I tried calling you several times earlier, but the calls didn't go through."

"Sorry about that," Cami said. "I was going into an interview with the Essex Police and didn't want to be interrupted."

"We know," Ali said. "Frigg just told us all about that and a lot of other things as well, none of which are putting me at ease about your being in the UK. How soon can you be home?"

"I'm not sure," Cami replied. "I've moved my departure to Tuesday, but I don't know if I'll be able to leave even then. The detective said I may have to stay longer. We'll have to wait and see."

"Is Rachel taking good care of you?"

"So far so good," Cami said with a laugh. "Right now, we're back in my room at the Portlandia, dining room-service style on wonderful takeout curry."

"All right, then," Ali said reluctantly. "I'm glad to hear you're safely back at the hotel. B. and I don't want you taking any unnecessary risks."

Once off the phone, it wasn't easy for Ali to get back to work, but eventually she did. Shortly after two, Shirley came rushing into her office, carrying a thick FedEx packet.

"I thought you'd want to see this right away," Shirley said.

"What is it?" Ali asked, reaching out to take it.

"It's from Dozo International."

"This soon?" Ali asked, tearing open the envelope. "Cami's dinner with them was only a week ago. This can't possibly be good news."

But it was. As she shuffled through the pages, Ali was astonished to discover she was holding in her hand all the information necessary for High Noon to create a company-specific cybersecurity proposal for Dozo International.

She immediately called B. to pass along the good news.

"If they're moving this fast, they must be really desperate," B. said. "Or maybe their minds were already made up before they ever came to the dinner. Have you called Cami to let her know?"

"Not yet," Ali said. "I just opened the packet." She glanced at her watch. Two p.m. in Sedona meant it was just past ten in London. "But it's not too late to call her."

"Hang on," B. said. "I'll come there so we can congratulate her together."

CHAPTER THIRTY-ONE

SEATTLE, WASHINGTON
FRIDAY, MARCH 24, 2023
10:00 A.M.

Donna Jean sat in her tiny living room that morning with Pearl curled up in her lap and watched the clock on the wall tick slowly toward ten. It wasn't just any clock. It was the electric one Amy had given her that first Christmas after she got out of prison. It was a cat—a black-and-white plastic cat. With each tick the eyes moved back and forth and so did the tail. It was ugly, Donna Jean supposed, and until she became acquainted with Pearl, she'd never really liked cats, but Amy had been so excited as Donna Jean had unwrapped the gift all those years earlier, that, no matter what had been inside the box, it would have been a treasure. It still was. Not only that, but even after all these years it still worked.

As soon as a knock sounded at exactly ten o'clock, Pearl made tracks toward the bedroom, while Donna Jean went to answer the door. She opened it wide enough to see a forty-something-year-old Black woman standing in the hallway holding a briefcase.

"Ms. Plummer?" the new arrival asked, holding out her hand. "I'm Moesha Jackson."

Donna Jean opened the door wider. "Yes, please call me Donna Jean. Do come in."

Donna Jean showed her guest to the kitchen table, where, after taking a seat, she deposited her briefcase on the floor.

"How are you doing?" Moesha asked.

"I've been better," Donna Jean replied. It had only been a week and a half since she had gone to the Brewsters' home for the last time, but it felt like forever.

"I have some questions for you," Moesha said. "I'm sure you have some for me as well."

Donna Jean nodded. "Who sent you?"

"The long answer to that question is that my father was wrongfully convicted of a crime and spent eighteen years in prison for something he didn't do. An organization called Justice for All helped overturn his conviction. I went to work for them as soon as I graduated from law school. The person who brought your situation to our attention is a woman named Ali Reynolds who lives in Sedona, Arizona. Her husband is someone named B. Simpson."

Donna Jean sat up straighter. "Mr. Simpson? Really? I remember him. He was Mr. Brewster's partner at one time, but that fell apart when his wife had an affair with Mr. Brewster."

"Then Clarice and Mr. Brewster got married?" Moesha asked.

Donna Jean nodded wordlessly.

"I'm not entirely sure how or why this happened, but for some reason Ms. Reynolds, Mr. Simpson's current wife, is under the impression that you are being unfairly targeted by the detectives investigating Mr. Brewster's homicide. That's what I'm here to discuss, but before we do that, I need you to sign something."

Moesha opened her briefcase, extracted a piece of paper, and passed it over to Donna Jean along with a pen. "This is a retainer. Once you sign it, you'll be designating me as your attorney, and anything you say to me in the course of this conversation or any other is under privilege. Do you understand?"

"It means whatever I say to you is confidential," Donna Jean said, signing the document without bothering to read it, and pushing it back across the table.

"Yes, it is," Moesha agreed with a smile. "Ms. Reynolds suggested that perhaps the detectives in the Brewster homicide are targeting you based on the idea that you're a repeat offender. I've done some investigating into that case, but please tell me about your husband."

"About Kenneth?" Donna Jean asked uncertainly.

Moesha nodded. "Was he violent with you?"

"Yes," Donna Jean answered. Over the next few minutes, she went through the whole painful story one more time, ending by saying, "I'm sorry he died, but at the time it was him or me. I did that crime, and I did my time, but I had nothing to do with what happened to Mr. Brewster."

"You worked for the Brewsters for how long?"

"For more than twenty years—from before the first Mrs. Brewster died."

"What's that been like?"

"I worked for them two days a week. Mr. Brewster was always kind to me. He even left me some money in his will—a hundred and fifty thousand dollars. I think that's part of the reason that Detective Horn is so sure I did it—for the money, but I had no idea he was going to give me anything until after the will was read."

"What about Mrs. Brewster?" Moesha asked.

Donna Jean sighed. "She's always been . . . well . . . I guess 'prickly' would be the right word. Not easy to get along with, and I thought Mr. Brewster could have done better, but it wasn't my place to say so. The detective mentioned that he was looking into getting a divorce, but I didn't know anything about that."

"Tell me about your interviews with Detective Horn."

"He wanted me to tell him everything about that day, and so I did, from the time I came to work until the cops showed up."

"Now I want you to tell me," Moesha said.

Donna Jean sighed, but she told that story again, too—about getting there, taking the trash out, cleaning the house, and finally finding a bloodied Clarice at the top of the stairs and taking the knife away from her. The whole time, Moesha was taking notes in something that didn't seem to be regular handwriting.

"So Detective Horn seemed to think that there might have been some kind of romantic entanglement between you and Mr. Brewster?"

Donna Jean nodded. "He wanted me to take a lie detector test, and I refused."

"Why?"

"Because I took one of those when Kenny died, and even though I told the truth, they said I was being evasive. But this time I knew I had lied, and they were going to catch me at it."

"You told a lie?" Moesha asked. "What kind of lie?"

In response, Donna Jean stood up and walked into her bedroom. She returned holding what appeared to be a ball of tissue in her hand. Once she was seated, she unwrapped the tissue and revealed what was inside.

"What's that?" Moesha asked, frowning. "A wine cork?"

Donna Jean nodded. "I found it that morning while I was cleaning. That day, when I tried to close the slider that leads from the family room out onto the patio, this was lying in the track. I slipped it into my apron pocket without even thinking. When everything happened, I forgot about it completely. Then there was a big fuss about there being no forced entry. That and all the blood was why they thought Clarice did it. I should have mentioned the cork when Detective Horn asked me if there was anything out of place, but I didn't because I was afraid they'd think I was somehow involved."

Moesha carefully removed the tissue-wrapped cork from Donna Jean's hand.

"This would have made it possible for the assailant to gain entry into the home through the unlocked slider?"

Donna Jean nodded.

"You touched it?"

Donna Jean nodded again. "When I put it in my apron pocket. When I found it again after I got home, I used a Kleenex to take it out and put it in my dresser drawer."

"So your prints and DNA will be on it, but maybe someone else's will be as well," Moesha said. "Now that I'm aware of this piece of possible evidence, I'm duty bound to turn it over to Detective Horn."

"Do you have to?" Donna Jean asked in dismay.

"Absolutely," Moesha said, "because there's a good chance that evidence found on this cork might just lead him to the real killer."

CHAPTER THIRTY-TWO

EDMONDS, WASHINGTON
FRIDAY, MARCH 24, 2023
1:30 P.M.

Detective Raymond Horn had one hell of a headache. No surprises there. With a job like his, headaches weren't at all unusual. He kept a bottle of aspirin in his desk drawer for that very reason.

He had spent the morning reviewing the whole collection of Brewster interviews. Mr. Brewster had been considering a divorce at the time of his death, but they had been unable to locate or identify the presence of another woman in his life. He had simply wanted out. Ray and Detective Burns had succeeded in tracking down all the partygoers as well as the waitstaff, but they had come up empty there as well. No one had noticed anything out of line. Mentally pushing aside the interviews, Ray had just gulped down a couple of aspirin when his phone rang.

"Someone's here to see you," the desk sergeant told him. "Name's Moesha Jackson. She claims to be Donna Jean Plummer's attorney."

So Donna Jean has lawyered up, Ray thought. That was hardly a surprise, but talking to a suspect's attorney in the middle of the bullpen was not a good idea.

"Is the conference room available?" Ray asked.

"Yes, it is."

"Okay, put her in there. Detective Burns and I will join her shortly."

Ray beckoned to his partner. "We're wanted in the conference room," he said. "Donna Jean Plummer's defense attorney has stopped by for a visit."

In the conference room they were greeted by a Black woman with a headful of tightly braided hair.

"Good afternoon," he said to her. "I'm Detective Horn and this is Detective Burns."

Their visitor stood up and held out her hand. "I'm Moesha Jackson, Donna Jean Plummer's defense attorney."

Horn was a bit taken aback when Ms. Jackson stood up. She was exceptionally tall—six three at least, and a good two inches taller than he was. That's when he recognized her. "Wait," he said after a moment, "didn't you used to play basketball for U Dub?"

Nodding, Ms. Jackson smiled. "I certainly did," she said. "I was Moesha Rains back then. I take it we were there at the same time?"

"I was a senior when you went to the Sweet Sixteen."

"That was a great experience," Moesha said. "Once I graduated, I had a chance to go pro, but I chose law school instead."

"Good choice?" Detective Horn asked.

"No regrets," Moesha replied, before turning to the business at hand. "I have Donna Jean's signed retainer right here. Do you need to see it?"

It was Detective Horn's turn to smile. "I believe we can take your word for it, Ms. Jackson," he said cordially. "What can we do for you today?"

"I'd like to have access to whatever interviews you've conducted in regard to the Brewster homicide investigation."

Horn's smile vanished. "All of them?" he asked. "Your client's interviews, yes, but I'm not sure we can open up the whole investigation."

"I've got something here that might just sweeten the deal," Moesha said. She reached into her purse and pulled out something that looked like nothing more than a handful of wadded up tissue.

"What is it?"

Without replying, Moesha straightened out the tissues, revealing what was inside.

"A wine cork?" Ray asked peering at it.

"A wine cork," Moesha repeated, pushing both the cork and the tissue across the table until they were within Detective Horn's reach.

"And why would this be of any interest to our investigation?" he asked.

"As I understand it, in the aftermath of the homicide at the Brewsters' residence, there was no sign of forced entry, correct?"

The two detectives nodded in unison.

"When Donna Jean was cleaning the house that morning, she found this lying in the track of one of the sliders, one leading from the family room out onto the patio. She slipped it into the pocket of her apron without giving it a second thought, and didn't even remember it until you were doing that first interview with her."

"You're suggesting that's why there was no forced entry, because the house wasn't locked up after all?"

Moesha nodded.

"Why the hell didn't she say so at the time?"

"Because she wasn't thinking straight, but also because she was terrified that you'd end up believing that she was somehow involved with the crime, and it doesn't appear she was wrong about that. It seems to me as though she's being treated as a person of interest."

"If she's innocent, then why the hell wouldn't she agree to a polygraph?" Ray growled. "That would have cleared her immediately."

"You're aware of her previous homicide conviction?" Moesha asked.

Horn nodded. "Yes."

"She submitted to a polygraph in the course of that investigation and was found to be evasive—which may or may not have been true. I'm aware of situations where police officers have told suspects they've failed polygraph tests when, in reality, they hadn't. As you no doubt know, cops aren't required to tell the truth in those situations."

"Would she be willing to submit to one now?"

"I don't know," Moesha answered. "I'll have to ask her."

After a short silence, Detective Horn reached for the tissue and pulled the cork closer. "We're most likely talking about touch DNA here. Donna Jean handled this with her bare hands?"

Moesha nodded. "Yes, when she picked it up and placed it in her pocket."

"Presumably her DNA will be on the cork."

Moesha nodded in agreement. "Correct, it should be, and so should the DNA of whoever opened the bottle. With any kind of luck, however, you'll also find the DNA of the person who placed the cork in the slider during the party."

"All right," Detective Horn said. "We'll get this to the crime lab for processing right away. Thanks for bringing it in. And I'll leave word that you're to be given access to all appropriate interviews."

"One more thing," Moesha said, rising to her feet. "Have you looked into cell phone traffic on the cell towers nearest to the Brewsters' residence?"

"I'm pretty sure we've followed up on that," Horn replied. "Why?"

"If I were you, I'd go looking for cell phones with Southern California area codes pinging off those towers in the days both before and after Mr. Brewster's death. You might find something interesting."

"What are you saying?"

"Just take a look and see what turns up," she said. "I'll be going now, but if you plan on bringing Donna Jean in for further interviews, I fully expect to be notified."

Once the attorney left the conference room, Detective Horn sat there staring at the cork. "She's got a hell of a lot of nerve waltzing in here and telling us how to do our jobs," he grumbled.

Detective Burns, however, was also staring at the cork. "Depending on what the DNA shows, does this take Donna Jean off our list?" she asked.

"Hardly," Detective Horn scoffed. "In my book, coming forward with so-called evidence more than a week after the homicide occurred doesn't exonerate anybody. But just to be on the safe side, take the damned thing down to the crime lab. In the meantime, I'll get someone started looking at that cell tower data. With a case like this hanging over our heads, we can't afford to leave any stone unturned."

CHAPTER THIRTY-THREE

LONDON, ENGLAND
FRIDAY, MARCH 24, 2023
7:00 P.M.

After enjoying an outstanding dinner of Indian curries, Cami and Rachel were sitting in Rachel's room savoring glasses of chardonnay when Cami suddenly fell silent.

"What's wrong?" Rachel asked. "You seem out of sorts."

"I am out of sorts," Cami admitted. "In my interview with DI Wallace, I did my best to point him in George Smythe's direction, but I don't think I made a dent. What if Smythe ends up getting away with all of this?"

"Sometimes you have to trust the system," Rachel observed.

"What if I don't?" Cami asked in return. "What would happen if I gave the Essex Police a little shove in the right direction?"

"That sounds like interfering with a homicide investigation," Rachel said. "I don't think it's a good idea."

But Cami remained undeterred. "Remember that old saw about leading a horse to water?"

"Sure," Rachel said. "It goes something like, you can lead him to water but you can't make him drink. What about it?"

"What if I came up with an idea to make that horse thirsty?" Cami asked. "What if I offered to give George Smythe exactly what he wants?"

"What are you talking about?"

"I'm talking about GHOST, High Noon's proprietary operating system. It looks as though Smythe sent Petrov after me because he wanted access to GHOST. What if I approached him and offered to sell him a stolen copy of the software? If I could get a recording of him agreeing to buy stolen goods, that might be enough to get Wallace's attention."

Rachel was floored. "Are you nuts?"

"I want to be sure he gets caught. All I have to do is put my cell phone on Record when I talk to him. If he's willing to buy stolen goods, what else is he willing to do? And if I have a recording of him agreeing to make the purchase, that might be incriminating enough to get Wallace's attention. By the way," Cami added after a pause, "what's the deal with recording private conversations here in the UK—legal or illegal?"

"It's not illegal," Rachel responded, "but if you think that kind of recording can be used as evidence in a court of law, that's a big maybe."

"Maybe it won't need to be," Cami said, "especially if I can provoke him into saying or doing something stupid."

"What are you proposing?" Rachel asked. "If you're expecting me to go along with this idiotic scheme, forget about it. I'm being paid to protect you. That doesn't include letting you go rogue."

"In that case," Cami said, getting to her feet, "I'll have to make like the Little Red Hen."

With that, she picked up her glass, still half-full of wine, and headed for the connecting door between their rooms.

"First we were talking about a horse. Now we're talking about a chicken?" Rachel seemed genuinely puzzled.

"It's a children's story," Cami told her. "Don't worry about it."

Back in her suite, Cami sat on her love seat for a time, thinking about George Smythe—a man with an exaggerated sense of his own importance. For someone like that, exposure of any wrongdoing on his part would be anathema. In addition, as one of the movers and shakers in the UK's tech industry, every detail of his life—both business and personal—would be documented in at least one digital calendar or maybe even two. Unfortunately for him, hacking into computers was Frigg's strong suit. Without wasting another second, Cami dialed her up.

"Good evening, Cami," the AI said. "I believe you've had a challenging day."

"You could say that," Cami replied, "but now I need some help."

"How can I be of assistance?"

"I'd like to have access to George Smythe's schedule for the next several days so I can find an opportunity to engage him in a bit of private conversation."

"Is that wise?" Frigg responded.

"Not wise, maybe," Cami said, "but I believe it's necessary."

"Are Ali and Mr. Simpson aware of your intention to speak to him privately?"

"They are not," Cami replied, "and I would like to keep it that way."

"So mum's the word?" Frigg asked.

"Exactly, but since he's the CEO of Cybersecurity International, his devices are probably well-protected."

"Not to worry," Frigg replied dismissively. "Cybersecurity's algorithms aren't exactly foolproof. How soon do you require this information?"

"As soon as you have it."

"Are you sure? It's already quite late in London."

"I'm sure," Cami said. "Tomorrow's Saturday. It's officially my day off, so I can sleep in."

Off the phone with Frigg, Cami sat in semidarkness with her room lit only by London's city lights shining in through the window, watching the endless stream of traffic on Great Portland Street several stories below and worrying that maybe Rachel was right and what she was planning really was nuts.

Clearly, striking out on her own was in direct contradiction of what Ali and B. expected of her. Not only were they her employers and her friends, they were also the people who had hired a recent college graduate sight-unseen and given her a chance to grow into a job she had come to love. What she was contemplating constituted a very real betrayal of them. Once they learned that she had gone after Smythe on her own, would they fire her? Was bringing him down worth jeopardizing her own life, never mind her career?

And then there was Mateo. Of course she wanted to discuss all this with him, but she couldn't—and for the very same reason. Bringing him in on her plan might put his future on the line as well.

She was sitting there struggling with her conscience and going back and forth when her phone rang with Ali's face showing in caller ID. Cami's first thought was that Rachel had called Ali to let her know that Cami was about to go on the warpath, but it turned out that wasn't the case.

"B.'s here with me," Ali announced as soon as Cami answered. "We're calling to congratulate you."

Expecting to be hauled on the carpet, hearing that congratulations were in order came as a welcome surprise.

"Congratulate me about what?" Cami asked.

"I'm sitting here with a FedEx packet from Dozo International in my hand," Ali answered excitedly. "It contains a formal request for a quote from High Noon."

Cami was thunderstruck. Although it seemed much longer ago, her dinner with Dozo at the Lancaster had happened only a week and a day earlier. In her experience, corporate decisions usually moved at a glacial pace.

"This soon?" she asked. "Are you kidding?"

"No kidding," B. put in. "If High Noon ends up landing this one, I'm pretty sure there'll be a sizable bonus headed in your direction."

Cami was happy to accept their congratulations, but when the call ended, she continued to sit by the window, staring outside without really seeing anything and still worrying. The idea of going after George Smythe seemed foolhardy and dangerous, too, but somehow she couldn't let go of it.

So how should she proceed? For starters, she'd have to do this on her own. Finding a way to ditch Rachel wouldn't be easy. Obviously, she'd have to approach the man in public. If she put her phone on record, she'd have proof of exactly what he'd said and how he'd reacted during their supposedly private conversation.

The more Cami thought about it, the more it seemed that her original idea of pretending to sell him a copy of GHOST wasn't such a good plan after all. What then? Should she let him know up front that she had learned about his offshore finances or bring up her suspicions about the illegal money laundering activities going on under the auspices of Bulgarian-based Data Security?

Even more than that, what did she expect to gain from all this? What she needed was some kind of solid evidence that she could hand over to DI Wallace. In actual fact, she'd be poking a bear, and a very dangerous one at that. And what was the likely outcome? Maybe he'd call the cops and have her charged with attempted blackmail. Or, and this seemed far more likely, he'd send someone else after her, a hitman this time, rather than a potential kidnapper. After all, two people were already dead.

When Bogdan Petrov had come looking for her, Cami had been smart enough to evade him. But did she want to live her whole life in a similar state of watchfulness? While she remained lost in thought, an hour passed, then two, then three. It was well after one and she was finally thinking about going to bed when the call came in from Frigg.

"Good morning, Cami," the AI said. "I hope this isn't an inconvenient time."

"No, it's fine," Cami answered. "What do you have for me?"

"I believe," Frigg said, "it's commonly known as 'the full meal deal.'"

CHAPTER THIRTY-FOUR

LONDON, ENGLAND
SATURDAY, MARCH 25, 2023
1:00 A.M.

I have obtained Mr. Smythe's home addresses as well as the location of his workplace in London," Frigg began. "His private chauffeur remains at his estate in Sevenoaks, so he uses a car service for transportation back and forth to work from his residence on Prince Albert Road to Cybersecurity's headquarters on Fleet Street. His pickups for those are at seven thirty a.m. and four thirty p.m. He employs the same car service to take him back and forth between his office and his club near Piccadilly Circus, where he goes for lunch on an almost daily basis. Pickups for those are scheduled for eleven thirty a.m. and one thirty p.m. respectively."

"Can you send me the actual addresses?" Cami asked.

"Yes," Frigg replied. "Addresses, phone numbers, and email addresses will be sent via encrypted text for ease of copying. Right now I'm just hitting the tall points."

"You mean the high points," Cami corrected.

"Yes, of course," Frigg agreed, "the high points."

"Mr. Smythe's marital situation is currently in a state of flux," the AI continued. "He and Margaret, his wife of twenty-six years, are in the process of divorcing. At this point she still resides on the family estate outside the town of Sevenoaks, which is located in Kent, about an hour or so outside London. The property is currently listed for sale at 3.7 million pounds."

"Sounds like quite the estate all right," Cami said. "How did he manage to hang on to that when his finances were so bad back in 2020?"

"I believe his business dealings with the Bulgarians may have had something to do with that. As requested, I was able to gain access to his contacts as well as his calendar. This evening, it shows he will be attending a performance of *Medea* at the Soho Place Theater. Curtain time is seven thirty p.m., with a note that says pick up Elissa at home at five thirty."

"Who's Elissa?" Cami asked.

"That would be Elissa Rogers, age twenty-six. She's a high-end model."

"Of course she is." Cami said.

"She's also three years older than Mr. Smythe's twenty-three-year-old daughter, Michelle."

And suddenly, just like that, everything Cami needed arrived at what she would later describe to Mateo as a moment of divine inspiration. Frigg continued to drone on with her verbal report, but Cami was no longer listening. She suddenly knew exactly how to take down Mr. Smythe without ever needing to meet up with him in person and without putting a target on her own back.

Years earlier, Cami had essentially dismantled Adrian Willoughby's life by contacting his estranged wife's divorce attorney and letting him know, by way of an anonymous tip, about Adrian's current love life. Naturally the attorney had taken the bit in his teeth and run with it, forcing Adrian to cough up child support for all his children, legitimate and otherwise.

From a divorce attorney's point of view, George Smythe's situation would be far more interesting than Adrian's. For one thing, there were large sums of money involved, most of which, Cami suspected, his estranged wife knew nothing about. Tracking down those hidden assets was something any self-respecting divorce attorney would tackle in a heartbeat. DI Wallace might need probable cause to go digging into

George Smythe's offshore business interests and his cryptocurrency accounts. Margaret Smythe's divorce attorney most assuredly would not.

"Wait a second," Cami said, interrupting Frigg's monologue. "Stop. Do you happen to know the name of Margaret Smythe's divorce attorney?"

"Her name is Angela Baker," Frigg replied. "She's a partner in one of London's top family law firms."

"Is it possible to contact her?"

"I have her email address. Why?"

"Please forward it to me. I'm about to turn that attorney into an attack dog. Once she finds out what George Smythe has really been up to, including the money held in his cryptocurrency accounts, she'll also be privy to his wire transfers—the one to Adrian Willoughby as well as those used to take out both Willoughby and Petrov. I suspect she'll be more than happy to forward that information to Inland Revenue along with my friend DI Wallace of the Essex Police."

Cami's conversation with Frigg didn't end until after two in the morning, but even then she didn't go straight to bed. Instead she composed a long email to Angela Baker:

Dear Ms. Baker,

I am writing in regard to your client, Margaret Smythe. It has come to my attention that her husband, George, has been involved in some possibly illegal money-laundering activities that are being run through a Bulgaria-based business entity called Сигурност На данните—aka Data Security—which he operates in partnership with a man named Petar Borisov. Monies received from those ventures are being held in offshore cryptocurrency accounts in his name, the existence of which Margaret is most likely completely unaware.

At the bottom of this missive, I'll be attaching applicable identification numbers for those accounts. I suspect your passing this information along to Inland Revenue would be greatly appreciated. In addition, wire transfers made from these accounts lead back to at least two recent homicides—the murder of Bogdan Petrov in San Bernardino, California, and the death of Adrian Willoughby in Grays, Essex.

I'm sending this information to you as an anonymous tip. For various reasons, I'm unable to supply my identity. In addition, this message has been encrypted so that, within fifteen minutes of your reading it, the email and the account identifiers listed below will vanish from your mailbox. You will not be able to reply. If you're interested in following up on any of this information, please copy this message and save it to another file before that happens.

You may be wondering about my involvement in all this. I happen to be someone whose life was put in jeopardy by George Smythe but who is unable to prove it. If you can provide justice for Margaret, you will also be providing justice for me.

I'm wishing both you and Margaret the very best of luck. Just consider me an interested bystander.

Long after Cami pressed send, she sat staring at her computer screen. It was now three o'clock on Saturday morning. She had just dropped a pebble into a deep well. All Cami could do now was wait and hope that the attorney was up to the task. If she was, and if this worked, it would be more than a little ironic that the GHOST-generated email Cami had just sent could shoot down the guy who had been prepared to go to any lengths, murder included, to lay hands on Lance Tucker's handiwork.

"Couldn't happen to a nicer guy," Cami muttered aloud to herself. With that, she finally crawled into bed, where she fell asleep instantly and slept like a baby.

When she awakened hours later, her Apple Watch was dead because she'd forgotten to charge it when she went to sleep. A glance at her bedside clock told her it was 11:00 a.m.

Rachel, who had let herself into Cami's suite, was visible, camped out on the sitting room's love seat.

"It's about time you woke up," she observed. "You were so pissed off when you left my room last night, I was afraid you might have taken off on me, so I let myself into your room to check and found you sound asleep. I finally ordered up a pot of coffee along with some toast and jam. Want some?"

"Please," Cami said, crawling out of bed and pulling on her robe. Once in the sitting room, Rachel handed her a cup and saucer.

"Are you okay?" Rachel asked. "You look like hell."

"Gee, thanks," Cami said.

"Couldn't sleep?"

"Not right away. But if it's any consolation, I've come around to your way of thinking. Trying to sell an illicit copy of GHOST to George Smythe was a stupid idea. It was too risky and probably wouldn't have worked anyway."

Cami let Rachel have the win without bothering to mention that she had found a completely different way to deal with George Smythe.

"I'm so relieved to hear that," Rachel said. "As I said last night, it's time to trust the system. As for today? It's Saturday. No appointments, right?"

"None whatsoever," Cami replied.

"All right, then," Rachel said. "It's the weekend. What say we do something fun for a change?"

"Like what?"

"How about seeing if I can sort out tickets to a couple of West End shows for tomorrow night and a road trip for today?"

"Seeing a show or two might be fun," Cami said, "but what kind of road trip?"

"Have you ever been to Stonehenge?"

"Never," Cami said. "I've always wanted to see it, but when I've been here, I've always been totally focused on work."

"Time to change that, then," Rachel declared. "Stonehenge happens to be one of my favorite places on the planet, and it's only a little over two hours away. Our car and driver are available. On a trip like that, it'll be easy to spot if someone is following us. What do you think?"

Considering the stress and pressure of the last two weeks, Cami was all for it. "Sounds good to me," she said.

"Good," Rachel said. "While you shower and dress, I'll go downstairs and order up one of the Portlandia's epic picnic lunches. It's about time the two of us had some fun."

Forty-five minutes later they headed out of the city and into an emerald-green countryside bathed in brilliant sunshine and topped by bright blue skies. Relaxing in the back seat, Cami couldn't have cared less where they were going. She was grateful to be out of the hotel and able to relax.

Two hours later, when they turned off the highway onto a much smaller road, they seemed to be in the middle of nowhere. But then after a few more minutes of driving, as they topped a small rise, all was revealed. The circle of huge, ancient stones was still off in the distance, but Cami felt an immediate sense of wonder.

"It looks magical," she said.

"It is magical," Rachel agreed. "Now let's go have fun."

They did just that. They walked the circle, disappointed that they weren't actually able to touch the massive stones. Cami took a few selfies and texted them to Mateo and Ali. Later, in a quiet field on the far side of the car park, Cami and Rachel shared their picnic lunch with their driver, Fred, who turned out to be retired MI-5.

As they headed back to London, Cami felt lighter than air. A day off was exactly what she'd needed.

CHAPTER THIRTY-FIVE

SEATTLE, WASHINGTON
SATURDAY, MARCH 25, 2023
9:00 A.M.

When Donna Jean's landline phone rang at nine o'clock in the morning, her heart filled with dread. Was this going to be another summons from Detective Horn? Instead, she was delighted when the voice on the phone belonged to her grandson, Jacob.

"Hey, Grammy," he said. "Are you coming?"

She had been so caught up in everything else that the fact that Jacob's "big" birthday party was today had completely fallen out of her head. Her first instinct was to say no, that she couldn't possibly make it.

"Please," he begged. "It's going be lots of fun. We'll be inside, so even if it's raining, you won't get wet. There'll be lots of food. We'll be able to see the animals, ride on the carousel, and everything. It'll be fun."

Much to her surprise, Donna Jean found herself asking, "What time?"

"One," he answered. "Please!"

After spending this dozen or so days living in an awful limbo, Donna Jean finally felt as though she had someone on her side. She wasn't sure exactly how Moesha Jackson had come into her life, but Donna Jean was incredibly grateful she had. The woman seemed to be someone who believed her; someone who actually thought she was innocent.

"You said one o'clock?" she asked Jacob at last.

"Yes."

"All right, then," Donna Jean said, surprising herself. "See you there."

CHAPTER THIRTY-SIX

SEDONA, ARIZONA
SATURDAY, MARCH 25, 2023
10:00 A.M.

On that sunny and pleasantly warm Saturday morning in late March, Ali awakened to the aroma of baking bread. Tonight was their scheduled dinner meet-up with Alonzo's new heart-throb Gwen, and clearly he was going all out. He had told Ali that the menu would include a freshly baked French loaf, caprese salad, and lasagna, topped off by limoncello cake. With B. off on a solitary hike through Sedona's iconic red rocks, Ali headed outside, where, armed with a vase and kitchen shears, she set about creating a suitable centerpiece in honor of the occasion.

Before retiring and returning to the UK, Leland Brooks, Ali and B.'s former majordomo, had created a wonderful English garden in their front yard. It was still too early for most of the flowers to be in bloom, with the exception of the aged wisteria lining the front porch. That was covered with cascades of fragrant flowers, drooping like slender, foot-long bunches of grapes. Ali spent the better part of an hour before she finally had a combination of flowers and greenery that measured up to her specifications.

She had just placed her creation on the dining room table when a text came in from Cami. The message said: *This is what I'm doing on my day off. Wish you were here.* That was followed by a series of photographs of a grinning Camille Lee standing in front of the massive upright boulders of Stonehenge.

Considering everything Cami had been dealing with recently, it gladdened Ali's heart to see her smiling and happy.

Looks like fun, Ali texted back. You certainly deserve it.

Over the strenuous objections of her parents, Cami had come to Arizona to work at High Noon as an untried college graduate. Over the years she had matured into the caring, capable young woman she was now, and the blossoming romance between her and Mateo was clearly good for her as well. Ali had never had a daughter of her own, but she liked to think that she'd had the same kind of impact on Cami's life as B. had had in the lives of Stu Ramey, Lance Tucker, and now Mateo Vega.

Late morning found Ali curled up in her favorite chair in the library with the latest Michael Connolly mystery. That's when her phone rang with an unknown Seattle area code showing in caller ID.

"Hello?"

"Ms. Reynolds?" someone asked a bit uncertainly.

"Yes, I'm Ali Reynolds. Who's this?"

"My name is Moesha Jackson with the Seattle branch of an organization called Justice for All, a group that deals with wrongful convictions."

J.P. Beaumont managed to come through after all, Ali thought. "Yes, of course," she said aloud. "I'm familiar with JFA."

"A Seattle resident, one Donna Jean Plummer, has retained me as her defense attorney in a homicide investigation. I understand you're the one who contacted my colleague Rosalie Whittier, suggesting that we be in touch with Ms. Plummer. Is that correct?"

"Yes," Ali admitted. "Guilty as charged."

"I asked my client what her connection was with you, and she told me she had no idea, that she had never met you or even heard your name. What can you tell me?"

For the next few minutes, Ali filled the woman in on the complicated history between B. Simpson and Chuck and Clarice Brewster, including the fact that, in the aftermath of Chuck's homicide, Clarice had called on B., her longtime ex, for help.

"Did he?"

"Hardly," Ali said with a short laugh. "In fact, he refused to have anything to do with her. I'm the one who suggested that she find herself a different attorney, which she evidently did. Once Clarice was out on bail, I realized the Brewsters' part-time housekeeper was also under suspicion. Since I doubted she'd have the kind of financial resources necessary to hire a quality legal defense team, I connected with a friend of mine, a private investigator named J.P. Beaumont. Beau put me in touch with your organization."

"Why go to so much trouble?" Moesha asked.

Ali laughed again. "If you asked my husband that question, he'd say it's because I'm totally incapable of minding my own business," she replied. "I also happen to know someone who was stuck with a public defender back in the day and who did years in prison for a crime he didn't commit. I guess I was afraid Donna Jean wouldn't get a fair shake."

"Given what I've seen so far, that was probably the right call," Moesha said, "and now here we are. The investigators on the case have interviewed most, if not all, of the people who attended Mr. Brewster's birthday party the evening before he died. Several of them indicated that, at the time Clarice Brewster went to bed that night, she was so inebriated she could barely walk and needed assistance getting upstairs to her bedroom."

"If she could barely stand on her own," Ali observed, "how could she possibly be coordinated enough to stab someone to death?"

"Precisely," Moesha agreed. "And although there's no evidence that shows Donna Jean was anywhere near the Brewsters' home at the time of the homicide, the investigators seem to be stuck on the idea that she is somehow involved in what happened, based on the fact that she had unlimited access to the home and also because, due to the terms of Mr. Brewster's will, Donna Jean benefited financially from his death."

"To say nothing of her being a repeat offender," Ali put in.

"You're aware of her previous conviction?"

"I am," Ali replied. "I told you I'm incapable of minding my own business. I looked her up."

"You may be correct in thinking that Donna Jean's previous conviction is a contributing factor as to what's gone on with the Brewster investigation so far," Moesha said, "but since you've clearly given this case a good deal of thought, I'm wondering if you have any suggestions that might help me in launching my own investigation."

Ali paused for a moment, wondering how much she could say without going overboard. Finally she said, "As a matter of fact, I do. Are you aware Chuck Brewster had a son?"

"Yes, I am. I believe his name is Adam. My understanding is that he was not included in his father's will, and as a result, doesn't have an obvious motive. There was a relatively small bequest made to Donna Jean, which seems to have helped bring her into the picture as a suspect, but that doesn't quite add up. Seventeen stab wounds is a clear indication of overkill by someone with a powerful motive. That speaks to the wife far more than it does to Donna Jean."

"As far as the will is concerned, what happens if Clarice is convicted of having something to do with her husband's death?"

Moesha considered for a moment before she answered. "Under Washington law I believe she would have been presumed to have predeceased him. As the only surviving child of the deceased, Adam would be second in line, as long as there are no other named secondary beneficiaries. Are you suggesting that perhaps my investigation should focus on him as an alternate suspect?"

"Not necessarily," Ali replied. "Does Justice for All have the ability to access traffic on cell phone towers?"

"Of course. Why?"

"Our own investigation has picked up some troubling information from following the call history of several phones with Southern California area codes that pinged off the towers near the Brewster residence the weekend of Chuck Brewster's homicide. If I were you, I'd start my cell tower search several days prior to the actual murder. The killers may not have left behind any physical evidence, but as they say, digital footprints are the new DNA."

"You referred to 'our' investigation. Does that mean you're a private investigator?"

"No, I'm not," Ali said with a laugh. "I'm just the neighborhood busybody."

"But you're suggesting that perhaps Adam Brewster had accomplices?"

"I'm suggesting that Adam Brewster may not have anything to do with it," Ali replied, "but I believe that his husband, Joel Franklin, does—Joel and probably one of his close associates."

"What makes you think that?" Moesha asked.

"For one thing, Mr. Franklin is a liar. When Adam's former partner was diagnosed with ALS, he hired Joel as his private duty nurse. At the time, Joel claimed to be a registered nurse recently arrived from Texas who had not yet updated his credentials. The problem is, Texas has no record of his ever being a licensed nurse in that state. Adam became estranged from his father back when he was in high school, partly due to the fact that Adam was gay. When Joel showed up on the scene, he claimed the same thing had happened to him—that his father had disowned him on account of his being a homosexual, but that his father died prior to their being able to reconcile. That's why he lobbied so hard for Adam to reconcile with his father before it was too late. The problem is, Joel's father is still alive and well and living in Hammond, Indiana."

"Being a liar doesn't make him a killer," Moesha suggested.

"It doesn't mean he isn't one," Ali countered.

"You do realize this sounds completely far-fetched, don't you?" Moesha asked.

"Yes, I do," Ali said, "but nonetheless it may still be true."

"Can I ask how you happened to come by this . . . shall we say theory?"

"You can ask, but all I'm willing to say is that it came from a confidential source."

"What a surprise," Moesha said with a laugh, "but you've certainly given me some possible leads. You really can't mind your own business, can you?"

"Nope," Ali agreed.

"Thank you, then," Moesha said. "I really appreciate the help."

The call ended then. Relieved that she had done everything she could to help Donna Jean Plummer, Ali put down her book and headed for the master suite. She figured that, before B. came home from his hike, she had just enough time for a quiet visit to her soaking tub.

When Alonzo and Gwen showed up at the door, both Ali and B. went to greet them. After making the introductions, Alonzo announced, "Guess what? We got the apartment. The landlord is doing some painting and installing a new carpet. We get the keys two weeks from today."

Things were certainly moving faster than Ali had anticipated when she had been attempting to sort out housing arrangements for her Amelia Dougherty Scholarship nominee, Susan Rojas, but she had no complaints about that.

As Ali escorted the couple into the living room, she caught the sparkle of a diamond on Gwen's finger. "Does that ring mean congratulations are in order?" she asked.

Gwen responded with a beaming smile. "Indeed it does," she said.

"When's the big day?" Ali asked.

B., who hadn't managed to catch sight of the ring, seemed taken aback by the question. Alonzo was not.

"We're planning a Cinco de Mayo wedding in Las Vegas," he said. "You guys want to come?"

"We'll be happy to. Have you booked a hotel?"

"Not yet. That's next up," Gwen said. "Any suggestions?"

Ali sent a smile in B.'s direction. "Treasure Island certainly worked for us," she said. "And whichever hotel you decide, our wedding gift will be chipping in on the wedding package."

Dinner was a joyous affair. During the course of it they learned more about Gwen's history. Alonzo, who had spent twenty years as a submariner for the U.S. Navy, had never been married. It turned out, neither had Gwen. She had been engaged once, in her early twenties, but her fiancé had perished in a car crash weeks before the wedding.

"I always believed he was the one, and I never even looked at anyone else," Gwen told them over Alonzo's limoncello cake. "Then, at my niece's birthday party, there was Alonzo, holding court at his Aunt Rose's barbecue grill. As soon as I tasted his medium-rare rib eye, it was love at first bite."

After an enjoyable evening, when bedtime came around, Ali noticed that she hadn't mentioned anything about her long conversation with Moesha Jackson to B., and she decided that was just as well. In this instance, what her husband didn't know wouldn't hurt him.

CHAPTER THIRTY-SEVEN

EDMONDS, WASHINGTON
SUNDAY, MARCH 26, 2023
1:30 P.M.

Raymond Horn was waiting his turn to tee off on the fourteenth hole of the Nile Golf Course when the cell phone in his pocket buzzed. Usually he would have been annoyed by the interruption, but he was having a crappy game. This was his first round of the year, and the course was a soggy mess. The greens had all been aerated, and carts were restricted to cart paths only. His shots had been so piss-poor that he'd done far more walking than usual.

On this occasion, the Sunday afternoon call from the Washington State Patrol Crime Lab—especially one from Gretchen Walther, their lead DNA tech—was welcome, but for right that moment, he went ahead and let the call go to voice mail.

"Hey, guys," Ray said to the rest of his foursome. "It's work. I'm going to have to bail."

His fellow golfers, all cops, knew Ray was up against a high-profile case. As he shoved his driver back into his bag and set off for the pro shop, they waved him off without even razzing him about being a poor loser.

Gretchen had left a voice mail message, but he called her back without listening to it. "Sorry I couldn't answer when you called. Why are you working on a Sunday?' he asked.

"I was led to believe the evidence brought in for testing on Friday was a rush job," she replied.

"Have you got a profile on that cork?" he asked.

"I certainly do, three to be exact. One leads to an unknown female, one leads to Donna Jean Plummer, and the third leads back to someone named Joel Franklin. We ran all three through CODIS. We got hits on Donna Jean and Joel, but nothing on the other one."

"Nothing surprising about any of that," Raymond said. "Donna Jean Plummer is in CODIS due to a previous conviction. She was the victim's housekeeper and supposedly is the person who found the cork. Franklin is a nurse and married to the son of our homicide victim. He was also a guest at the victim's birthday party the night before."

"So the presence of those two of the DNA profiles at the crime scene can be explained away?" Gretchen asked.

"Maybe," Ray replied. "We're already looking at Plummer, but we'll look into Franklin all the same. Thanks."

But as Ray headed home, he thought about it some more. Moesha Jackson had said that Donna Jean had discovered the cork in the rail of a slider on Chuck Brewster's back patio and that had kept the door from securing properly. Interviews with party guests had indicated that the party had been a catered affair. Did that mean that the catering staff had served the beverages? If so, why would Joel have been handling one of the corks?

Edmonds was a Seattle suburb, but it was also a relatively small, close-knit community. Ray knew that his wife, Mona, and the Brewsters' caterer, Anna Rawlins, had become acquainted through PTA dealings while their mutual kids were in elementary and middle school and were still friends. Anna had already been questioned and said she had seen nothing out of the ordinary at the Brewsters' party, but now Ray wanted to ask her an entirely different set of questions.

Back at his desk at the Edmonds Police headquarters, he located Anna's interview, which contained her contact information. After reviewing the interview, he gave her a call.

"Detective Ray Horn here," he said when she came one the line. "Sorry to call on a Sunday afternoon, but do you have a moment?"

"Sure," she replied. "What's up?"

"Did you have a bartender on duty at the party?"

"Of course."

"So he would have been the one opening the wine bottles?"

"She," Anna corrected. "Her name's Lyssa. I put her on the job because she runs a tight ship. Mr. Brewster didn't want anyone being overserved."

Ray glanced through the list of interviewees. Lyssa's name wasn't among them.

"Do you happen to have her number?"

"Sure. Her last name is Owens. Here's the number."

Moments later, Ray had Lyssa Owens on the phone. They may have missed interviewing her the first time around, but that was about to be rectified.

"Sorry to disturb you at home on a Sunday, Ms. Owens," he said. "This is Detective Raymond Horn with Edmonds PD. I'm investigating the Charles Brewster homicide. Do you mind answering a few questions?"

"I left town the morning after the party and didn't hear about what happened until after I got back," Lyssa said. "Mr. Brewster seemed like a perfectly nice man. I don't know if I can help, but I'm happy to answer your questions."

"You were in charge of the bar?"

"Yes."

"What did you serve?"

"The usual—red wine, white wine, champagne, beer, the occasional cocktail, and a few nonalcoholic beverages, but not many of those."

"And you opened all the wine bottles?"

"Absolutely," she answered. "Opened them and counted them, too. That's my job."

"What do you do with the corks?" Ray asked.

"At the Brewsters, I tossed them into an extra ice bucket on the bar. I try to make a note of the bottles as I go, but I also hold on to the corks. It's a second way of keeping track. At the end of the party, the number of empty bottles and the number of corks need to match up so the client gets charged correctly.

"By the time the party was over, there were fourteen empty bottles total and a few partials. The weird thing was, I ended up one cork short. The reds were all there, so it must have been one of the whites. They were all high-end wines. I was afraid I'd end up having to pay for it, but Anna said it was okay and not to worry."

Ray was thunderstruck. It never would have occurred to him that collecting corks was a way of tracking wine inventory.

"About that ice bucket," he said. "Where was it?"

"At the end of the bar. Why?"

"Could one of the guests have accessed it?"

"I suppose, but if someone did, I didn't notice."

"Did most of the guests come to the bar for their drinks or did someone serve them?"

"About half and half."

"And, in your opinion, was anyone overserved that night?" Ray asked.

"Not by me, and definitely none of the guests, but by the time the wife of the birthday boy went upstairs, she was pretty much out of it. That wasn't on me or on any of the waitstaff. One of the guests—her stepson's husband, I believe—had been waiting on her hand and foot."

"So he collected drinks from the bar and took them to her?"

"Pretty much," Lyssa replied. "I didn't realize she'd had too much until she started to go upstairs. Fortunately, he helped her negotiate the elevator, so I didn't have to ask one of our servers to do it. I was surprised when I heard she'd been arrested. I didn't see how a person that inebriated could possibly be responsible for stabbing someone to death."

Detective Raymond Horn knew it was time to shut down the conversation. Other people had mentioned that Clarice had been drinking at the party, but no one else had recounted the real extent of it or how she'd gotten that way. Now he knew. And if Joel Franklin had been ferrying drinks from the bar to Clarice, what were the chances he'd had ample opportunity to slip something else into one of her drinks and lay hands on a used cork as well?

For the first time he wondered if he had been wrong the whole time. Maybe instead of focusing on Clarice and Donna Jean, he should have been looking at Adam and Joel. Tomorrow he intended to do just that.

CHAPTER THIRTY-EIGHT

LONDON, ENGLAND
SUNDAY, MARCH 26, 2023
11:00 A.M.

In 1973, Angela Baker had announced to her parents that she had no intention of being shipped off to a top-drawer finishing school in Switzerland. Instead, she wanted to attend Oxford and study law. Her mother, Genevieve, had been appalled by that declaration. After all, if St. Delphine's had been good enough for both her mother and her grandmother, why wasn't it good enough for Angela?

That was because Angela had seen the results. St. Delphine's had prepared Genevieve Rogers to marry well and run a household—which she had done, on the surface anyway. To all appearances, Roland James Baker III, had been quite the catch. He was someone who made money hand over fist. He had also ventured into the political arena where he had spent a number of years commuting back and forth between London and Brussels, where he had represented the UK's interests at the European Union.

Unfortunately, he was also a serial philanderer—something Angela had figured out at age thirteen when she had caught him red-handed in bed with one of the bridesmaids in the aftermath of a cousin's wedding. From then on, she began paying closer attention to her father's comings and goings. His having women on the side wasn't a one-time thing. This was long before computers and instant messaging and texting, but Angela had found his stash of telltale letters along with the batch of R-rated photos he kept as proof of his various conquests.

When she had tried to talk to her mother about it, suggesting that maybe Dad had outside interests, her mother had brushed it off saying, "It's nothing to worry about. That's just how your father is." As long as Angela could remember, there had never been a spark of love or affection between her parents, and by the time she was in her late teens, she realized the truth. Armed with her training from St. Delphine's, Genevieve had managed to find a very posh bed—one that was laundered each week and made each day by someone else. She, however, was the one who had to lie in it, because her finishing-school education had prepared her for nothing else.

At Oxford, Angela had taken a first. After graduating, passing the bar, and becoming a barrister, she had turned her laser-like focus on family law. As the years passed, she saw her mother, still trapped in a loveless marriage, withdraw more from life and into her unhappy self. At age fifty-two, Genevieve had taken her own life with an overdose of sleeping pills. Days after her mother's death, Angela had gone to her office and found that her mother had mailed a handwritten letter to her there. Written on one of Genevieve's embossed note cards, it had said: *I wish I had done as much with my life as you are doing with yours. I'm so glad you didn't take my advice*. It was signed *"Love, Mum."*

Now, matted and framed, that note hung in her office right behind her desk, along with her impressive collection of diplomas and awards. Over time, her mother's final words had become the guiding principle of her life. Through the years, Angela had gained the reputation for being the go-to solicitor for women, especially high-profile ones, exiting problematic marriages. There was nothing that gave her life more purpose than putting the screws to philandering, cheating husbands. When opposing counsel who had come up against her in court referred to Angela as a piranha, they did so with good reason.

As for her own father? Still alive, Roland James Baker III was now Angela's responsibility. Suffering from Alzheimer's, he lived in an upscale memory care home, currently paid for with the remains of his dwindling fortune. If his own money ran out, as it might well do, Angela would need to cover the cost of his care, but she no longer bothered visiting him. The last time she had done so, he'd had no idea who she was, and she hadn't gone back.

Never married and pushing seventy, Angela had no intention of calling it quits. What she did was a mission as opposed to a nine-to-five job. She took calls and responded to emails and texts, no matter the day of the week or the time of day. When she awakened that Sunday morning, it was only natural that she went scrolling through her inbox over her first cup of Earl Grey.

When she reached a message where the sender was a series of numbers and symbols rather than a name, she was tempted to delete it, but the subject line—"George Smythe"—reeled her in. One of Angela's previous clients, a satisfied one, had referred Margaret Smythe to Angela when she discovered that her husband was carrying on with a much younger woman who was only three years older than their daughter.

George had pulled similar stunts before, but never with someone that young, and for Margaret, the current mistress's age was the last straw. The couple had already gone through mediation and agreed on a settlement that left the family home to Margaret and the London flat to George. Since Margaret's job had been that of a corporate wife, George had agreed to pay ongoing maintenance until she managed to unload the family home. But that agreement had been made without Margaret's knowing about the considerable amount of funds George had possibly been amassing illegally and concealing offshore.

Not wanting to lose the anonymous message, Angela copied it and saved it under the name "Gotcha" in her computer's Margaret Smythe folder. Then she sat there wondering who this anonymous tipster was and had she really been personally threatened by George Smythe? What was the story behind that?

Out of curiosity, Angela made herself a piece of toast, poured herself another cup of tea, and waited, letting the minutes tick off on her watch. After the promised fifteen minutes, the email vanished from her computer screen. She checked her trash and junk files and found no sign of it.

She wasn't sure how the vanishing act worked, but obviously it had. Next, she reached out to Samira, her IT consultant, asking her to get back to her as soon as possible. In the meantime, she did some searching on her own, just to verify some of what the tipster had said. Angela's modest computer skills were enough for her to find the two recent homicides her tipster had mentioned. Adrian Willoughby's and Bogdan Petrov's so-far unsolved murders were currently under investigation by the Essex Police.

"And so are you, Mr. George Smythe," Angela said aloud, "and you'd best look out, because your friendly neighborhood piranha is coming for you."

CHAPTER THIRTY-NINE

EDMONDS, WASHINGTON
MONDAY, MARCH 27, 2023
8:00 A.M.

When Raymond dragged his ass into the office on Monday morning, he was much the worse for wear. The health app on his phone said he'd had only three hours of sleep, and it showed.

He'd lain awake most of the night, tossing and turning and wondering how he could have gotten things so completely wrong on what was likely to be one of the most prominent cases of his career. His homicide victim had seventeen stab wounds. If that wasn't a clear indication of overkill, what was? It also usually meant the killer was someone close to the victim and who had a clear motive—a greedy or unfaithful spouse, an angry offspring, or a rejected lover.

Clarice had checked several of those boxes, and Ray had never bought the idea that she could have been sleeping in the same bed next to her husband while he was being stabbed to death and not have heard a thing. Now, though, having talked to the party's bartender and learned that someone had been feeding her drinks all night? That changed everything. Did that someone also have reason to want Chuck Brewster dead? As for what else might have been in Clarice Brewster's drinks? Unfortunately, there was no way to tell. The tox screen for Chuck Brewster, the actual victim, had yet to come in, but in the aftermath of the murder, Clarice, who was still among the living, had never been subjected to one.

Sometime in the middle of the night, Mona had thrown off her covers, sat up on her side of the bed, and demanded, "What the hell is the matter with you? You may not be sleeping, but neither am I."

At that point, she had grabbed her iPad and flounced off to spend the remainder of the night in the guest room. That was one of the hazards of being married to a cop. When investigations went south and an officer wasn't sleeping, most likely his or her spouse wasn't, either.

Ray was at his desk nursing a cup of coffee that he had dredged out of the bottom of the break-room pot when Detective Burns showed up. She looked fresh as a daisy, which made Ray feel that much worse.

"Anything happening?" she asked. It took a few minutes for him to bring up the DNA match on the cork along with his new theory of the case—that perhaps the guy who had been feeding booze to Clarice all night might have been giving her something else as well.

"Maybe it's time we took a much closer look at Joel Franklin," she said. With that, she headed for her computer. Once there, she studied her screen with frowning concentration while her fingers flew over the keyboard at a speed Ray knew he could never duplicate.

It was only a matter of minutes before she said aloud, "Hey, I think I've got something."

"What's that?"

"Didn't Adam Brewster tell us that Joel was the guy who encouraged him to reconcile with Chuck Brewster because his own father was dead and they'd never managed to overcome their estrangement?"

"I seem to remember him mentioning something like that," Ray said. "Why?"

"Because Joel Franklin's father, Marvin D. Franklin, and his wife, Lucille, are both alive and living in Hammond, Indiana."

"Hang on," Ray said. "I'll check the video for sure."

Sure enough, close to the end of Adam Brewster's interview, he had said just that—that Joel had wanted him to reconcile with Chuck because he himself had missed doing so with his own father before the older man had passed away.

Ray was stunned. Monica Burns may not have been leading the interview, but she sure as hell had been paying attention to every detail.

Six months earlier, Smitty Howard, Ray's longtime partner, had pulled the plug and disappeared into the sunset. Ray hadn't exactly been thrilled when Monica Burns turned up as Smitty's replacement. In the intervening months, Ray had yet to give Detective Burns her head, and that fact hadn't gone unnoticed.

A few weeks earlier, Chief Nelson had pulled Ray aside. "Look," he said, "I know you're showing Detective Burns the ropes, but you need to let her take the lead on occasion. That's the only way she's going to learn how to do the job."

Ray had planned on doing just that—to start having Monica take the number-one position on a case, but his good intentions hadn't been enough to overcome his reluctance to let her do so in regard to this one. Now, however, he wondered if maybe the chief was right, and it really was time for Ray to change his tune.

"Good catch," he said aloud to Monica. "And if Joel lied to Adam about his family life, what else has he lied about and how come?"

Monica was still glued to her computer when Don Wilson from the Tech Unit turned up at their shared cubicle.

"Found it," he said, scattering a sheaf of computer printouts across Ray's desk. "Take a look at these."

"What am I looking at?" he asked.

"Our initial cell tower examination covered Saturday and Sunday, the day before and the day of the homicide. The phones present on Saturday were primarily ones with area codes from this general area. On Sunday, however, starting about midafternoon and over the same general time period of the party, we noted the presence of three different phone numbers bearing area codes from Southern California. One of those is registered to Adam Brewster."

"The homicide victim's son," Ray supplied.

"The second leads back to a Joel Franklin."

"He's Adam Brewster's spouse," Ray said. "What about phone number three?"

"No idea," Don answered. "It's a burner, so there's no way to tell whose it is."

That's easy, Ray thought. *It belongs to whoever's got something to hide.*

"All three phones both started and stopped pinging on the towers closest to the Brewster residence at the same time," Don continued. "That suggests that all three devices were traveling together. We picked them up again a few minutes later, at the next set of towers to the south of the first one, so it's likely that when they left the party on Sunday evening, they were headed southbound. By the way, none of those devices reappeared in the general area during the time frame when the ME estimates the homicide occurred."

"So, either they weren't at the scene, or the killer or killers were smart enough not to bring their devices along with them."

"We can continue monitoring towers," Don continued, "but as you get closer to Seattle, there are more and more towers, and I don't have enough manpower here to launch that kind of digital grid search."

"That's okay," Ray said. "You've made a good start."

"Actually, there's more," Wilson said. "What I've given you so far covers the day of the party. You asked me to take a look at the same towers a day or so earlier, and I did."

By now he had both detectives' undivided attention. Unfortunately, Don Wilson was hopelessly long-winded.

"Did you find anything?" Monica urged.

"As a matter of fact, I did," Don announced with a grin. "Late on Friday night, March 10, yet another Southern California phone, registered on the tower nearest your crime scene. The first ping came in at eleven fifteen p.m. on Friday. The last one was at twelve forty-five Saturday morning."

"That's an hour and a half," Ray said, thinking aloud, "pretty late at night for a casual visitor to show up. Did you track down the owner?"

"Sure did," Wilson replied. "Name's Marc Atherton. Lives at 459 Sixteenth Street in Huntington Beach, California."

"Who's Marc Atherton, and what the hell was he doing in the area of our crime scene the morning before the homicide?"

"You'll need warrants to find that out," Don Wilson said cheerfully. "I'm glad that's your job instead of mine. TU's already done its part."

"That phone has to be connected to the case," Monica asserted. "When we canvassed the area for video footage, we made the same mistake TU did the first time around. We looked for and downloaded footage on the night of the homicide instead of two nights before. Maybe our killer was doing recon in advance of the hit."

"Time to fix that, and you're driving," Ray said, picking up the car keys and tossing them in Monica's direction. "An hour and a half is a lot shorter time frame than we were looking at before, and we already know where we're likely to find usable video."

CHAPTER FORTY

COTTONWOOD, ARIZONA
MONDAY, MARCH 27, 2023
10:00 A.M.

Ali went to work that Monday feeling lighter than air. All she had to deal with were her usual work responsibilities. There were no immediate crises awaiting her attention. The first email she opened that morning came from Cami.

What a great weekend, and boy did I need one!

That surprise trip to Stonehenge on Saturday was amazing. Hope you enjoyed the pix. On Sunday we had tickets to two plays—a matinee performance of *The Mousetrap* and an evening performance of *Les Mis*. *The Mousetrap* was a little hokey, but it's been running for seventy years. *Les Mis* was terrific.

Today I'll be working my way through the appointments that had to be canceled on Friday. At this point I'm still due to fly home tomorrow, but I'm waiting to hear from DI Wallace on that. I'll let you know for sure when I find out what he says.

So far there hasn't been any indication that someone has been paying any kind of undue attention to us. I've been glad to have Rachel with me, but I'm worried about the added expense when it may not have been necessary.

Cami

Attached to the bottom of the email was a photo showing Cami and a purple-haired young woman standing side by side and grinning for the camera under the marquee of the London Theater with the words *The Mousetrap* overhead.

Prior to Cami's trip, Sonja Bjornson had sent Ali and B. a copy of Rachel Bloom's employee file at WWS for their perusal. The accompanying photo had been of a poised, young woman—a brunette—who had looked calm, collected, and entirely capable. No one looking at the wild-haired young woman with Cami would ever guess that she was a fully trained and dangerous bodyguard.

As for Ali herself? With no updates on the progress of the Chuck Brewster homicide, all Ali had on her plate for the day was doing her actual job, and that was a welcome change.

CHAPTER FORTY-ONE

EDMONDS, WASHINGTON
MONDAY, MARCH 27, 2023
11:00 A.M.

It turns out Monica Burns was a surprisingly assertive driver. Ray Horn had a tough time keeping his mouth shut, but refraining from back seat driving was probably a good first step in giving the younger detective her head.

Back in the Brewsters' neighborhood, the two of them returned to the houses where they had previously obtained surveillance footage for Saturday night and Sunday morning. This time they downloaded footage for a specific ninety-minute period from late Friday night to early Saturday morning. In a few instances they found residents who hadn't been home for their first canvassing go-round but were there this time out. Everywhere they went, the people were cooperative and understanding. The thought that a killer might still be lurking in the area was a very real concern, and people were motivated to do whatever they could to help.

Once back at the department, Ray and Monica went to an evidence room and began sorting through the footage. The equipment there allowed them to analyze everything frame by frame. Ray was more than happy to let Monica take charge, but it was a painstaking process. Eventually they spotted a light-colored SUV seemingly prowling the neighborhood, but even on a frame-by-frame basis, there was no way to identify the make or model. It wasn't until the last video they'd collected that they finally hit pay dirt.

That footage came from a house on the street just above the Brewsters' place. Just beyond it, the roadway dead-ended at a power line right-of-way with no real turnaround. At 12:03 a.m. Saturday morning, a small, light-colored SUV came down the street. At the dead end, the driver threw the car into reverse and then backed past the nearest driveway, the one with the camera, before pulling back into it to finish executing a U-turn. Amazingly enough, the video was crystal clear. Unfortunately, the camera's angle didn't allow a view of the license plate. Monica hit the pause button and studied the image.

"It's a RAV4," she announced at last. "Probably a 2022. And that sticker in the corner of the windshield means it's a rental."

Donning his reading glasses, Ray peered at the screen. He could see the sticker all right, but everything on it was a fuzzy blur. Eventually Monica was able to isolate the sticker and enlarge it, but still it wasn't quite legible. Finally, having done as much as she could, she made a call to the Port of Seattle Police at Sea-Tac. After a short conversation, she sent the enhanced image to someone there who was able to use a specially calibrated lens to decipher some of what the human eye could not.

"It's an Enterprise rental," Monica's contact said when she phoned back. "Unfortunately, that's all I can tell you. I can't decode the rest of it, either."

"No worries," Monica told her. "We already knew that it's a RAV4. Now that we know it's from Enterprise, figuring out the rest should be easy. Thanks for the help."

"Good work," Ray Horn told Monica for the first time ever as she ended the call. Here's an idea. If I were a killer getting ready to do a middle-of-the-night hit, what would I need more than anything?"

Monica gave him a puzzled look. "A cup of coffee, maybe?"

"Perhaps," Horn agreed, "but more than that, I'd need to take a leak. How about we go looking for places where our killer might have gone looking for one or both of those essentials—coffee and a restroom—

on the night of the actual homicide, Sunday, March 12, and see if we can come up with surveillance footage of either our killer or that same rented RAV4."

"Good thinking," Monica said. "We might just get lucky."

Off they went on a second search-and-destroy mission. The two most likely establishments were located on Edmonds Way, both within a mile of their crime scene. The one to the south, a Food Mart, was closer than the one to the north, a Circle K, so they went there first. Since it was early afternoon on a Friday, the owner himself, Mr. Ranjit Bisla, was on the premises and working on payroll in a backroom office. He was happy to access and download however much of that night's video as they might want to see.

The store had seven cameras in all, three interior ones and four outside. Inside, one camera was over the cash register and one was located above the hallway leading to the restrooms and office, while the third focused on the front entrance. One of the exterior cameras was directly over the outside entrance, while a second covered the gas pumps. The two final ones were located on either side of the building and covered the remainder of the property.

After leaving the Food Mart, they traveled north to the Circle K. This time the clerk on duty wasn't able to access the footage. He tried reaching the on-call manager but ended up having to leave a message for him to call Detective Horn at Edmonds PD at his earliest convenience.

Having skipped lunch, Ray and Monica stopped off long enough to pick up Subway sandwiches on their way to the department. Back in the evidence room, they queued up the footage and settled in for what they anticipated to be a long ordeal. Thanks to the cellular tower data, for Friday's video search they'd had a definite timeline. This time they had no such thing. Just to be on the safe side, they had asked for and received separate downloads from each of the seven cameras starting at 8:00 p.m. and ending at 6:00 a.m.

"Let's start with the footage from the camera covering the exterior front entrance," Monica suggested.

This time she was able to fast-forward, slowing the video only when a light-colored vehicle of any kind came into view. Several light-colored vehicles came and went, but they were definitely not the one in question. Then, with the time stamp in the corner of the screen reading 1:09:43 a.m., 3-10-2023, Monica brought the video to a full stop.

"Got it!" she said. "That's a RAV4."

Truth be told, after his sleepless night, Ray had nodded off in front of the computer screen and Monica's voice startled him awake. She paused the video long enough to make note of the time stamp before rewinding the recording for thirty seconds or so and then pressing the play button.

Excited as bloodhounds catching a scent, Ray and Monica stared at the screen. The video was in black and white, so the vehicle appeared to be white. It rolled past the entrance camera between the front door and the gas pumps before turning right toward the parking area on the north side of the building. For several seconds after it turned the corner, headlights glowed brightly from that direction, but eventually they must have switched off.

After that, Monica and Ray waited with bated breath until finally a man dressed in dark clothing and wearing a hoodie over his head rounded the corner and strode purposefully toward the sliding doors at the entrance. As he stepped under the camera, the hoodie concealed his face. Then, immediately thereafter, he disappeared from frame.

"Can you switch cameras?" Ray asked.

"Give me a minute."

As soon as Monica located the correct time stamp on the interior entrance cameras, they watched the hoodie-clad figure—a male probably six feet tall with a medium build—walk into the building. With his head still ducked to hide from the camera, he took only half a dozen steps before turning sharply to the right and disappearing down one of the aisles.

"See there?" Ray Horn crowed. "I was right. He's headed for the restrooms."

It seemed to take forever for Monica to locate the correct camera and time stamp. This time they waited for close to three minutes before their target reappeared. When he did so, they were in luck. While in the restroom, he had evidently dropped the hoodie. Realizing his mistake, he quickly pulled it back into place, but not before he'd momentarily revealed his face.

"Can you freeze that?"

"Already did," Monica said. "Froze it and sent it to the printer!"

"This may not be the first time a pee stop has solved a homicide," Ray muttered, "but if this works, it'll be a first for me."

"Switching over to the gas pump cameras now," Monica said. "Let's see if we can tell which way he goes."

The RAV4's turn signal indicated he was turning northbound on Edmonds Way, but instead of merging into traffic, he immediately turned right again, into the next parking lot. At that point both headlights and taillights disappeared.

"Any idea what's there?" Horn asked.

"I'm not sure," Monica answered. "A small strip mall, I think."

"Which means none of the businesses are open at night," Ray said. "And that'll be our next stop. Let's hope somebody there has cameras."

By then it was after four. Worried that the businesses might close at five, they wasted no time. Edmonds Way Center contained five storefronts—a dry cleaners, a chiropractic practice, a physical therapy office, a feline veterinary clinic, and a hearing clinic, and all of them appeared to have cameras. Monica and Ray headed for the dry cleaners—the business at the southernmost corner of the mall.

The footage there existed, but with an inexperienced teenager at the counter and no manager on the premises, it took the better part of two hours to gain access to it. Finally, with the required footage in hand, they went back to the department where the evidence room they had been using still awaited them.

After uploading the video, Monica quickly fast-forwarded to the one a.m. time stamp. At 1:14:28 a.m., 3-10-2023, a pair of headlights entered the parking lot from the south. Although the lot was completely empty at that hour, the car stopped well away from the building, and the headlights switched off. Moments later, in the darkness, a figure emerged from the driver's side and headed northbound, walking along Edmonds Way.

"Do we need to go back out and look for more footage?" an exasperated Monica asked.

"No," Ray said. "We'll stick with this one. Let's keep watching until those headlights come back on. This is how far from the Brewsters' place?"

"About a mile," Monica answered.

"Supposing it takes him thirty minutes or so to walk that far, half an hour to commit the crime, and another half to get back. Fast-forward to two thirty and start watching there."

Monica did as requested. They waited in silence as the somber realization sank in that during that interval of fast-forwarding, Charles Brewster was likely being stabbed to death. When Monica slowed the video once more, the SUV was still visible, parked in the distance. The minutes crawled by with nothing happening, but then at 2:46:57 a shadowy figure emerged from the darkness and walked on a diagonal from the far corner of the parking lot directly to the RAV4. The driver's-side door opened, the interior lights flashed on, the shadowy figure climbed inside, and the door closed. Moments later the headlights flashed on. Then something unbelievable happened. In the process of making a U-turn to exit the parking lot, the SUV came straight toward the camera.

"Got the plate!" Monica crowed, freezing the frame.

"Time for a road trip," Ray said. "We're better off doing this in person rather than trying to talk to someone over the phone. Are you up for a rush-hour trip to SeaTac?"

"You bet," Monica said, "but let's shut down here before we leave. I have zero intention of coming back tonight."

After clearing out of the evidence room, they left the department and headed south, once again with Monica at the wheel.

"So Atherton's phone and the RAV4 were both in the area on Friday night, but the phone was missing on Sunday. That means the killer was smart enough to leave his phone turned off the night of the actual homicide, but not when he was scoping out the neighborhood. What I want to know is how the hell Moesha Jackson was smart enough to figure that out."

"With a traffic tie-up on I-5, they took Highway 99 to get from Edmonds to SeaTac's Consolidated Car Rental facility. Once there, they went straight to the Enterprise desk, where Ray bypassed customers waiting in line and approached the counter via the exit.

"I need to speak to a supervisor," he announced.

"I'm sorry, sir," a frowning desk attendant told him. "You'll need to wait your turn."

Ray flashed his badge. "This is a homicide investigation," he growled back. "I need to see a supervisor now!"

The flustered desk clerk made a quick phone call. Shortly thereafter, a woman wearing a tag that said "Eileen" emerged from a door behind the counter and beckoned for Ray and Monica to follow her.

"What seems to be the trouble, Officers?" Eileen asked after seating herself behind the computer on a well-worn desk.

"We're investigating a homicide that occurred in Edmonds the weekend of March 10," Ray explained. "We believe the killer drove himself to the crime scene in one of your rental vehicles, a light-colored RAV4. Here's the plate number," he added, handing her the piece of paper on which Monica had jotted down the information. "We need whatever information you can give us regarding the person who rented this vehicle."

The woman glanced at the paper in her hand and then looked back at Ray. "Do you have a warrant?" Eileen asked.

He sighed and leveled an unblinking stare in her direction. "A man was murdered—stabbed to death in his own bed while he was fast asleep. We're trying to catch his killer," he said. "This is information you can give us with a few clicks on your computer keyboard. Yes, we can go to a judge and get a warrant, but do we really need to waste the time it'll take for us to get one? Couldn't you give us a little help here without making us jump through hoops?"

Eileen wavered for a moment before caving. Less than a minute after she started typing, the printer on a counter behind her began spitting out pages. When the print job finished, she gathered the pages of the rental agreement and handed them to Ray. Marc Atherton's name was right there, front and center. He had rented the vehicle at 5 p.m. on Friday, March 11, 2023 and returned it at 8 a.m on Monday, March 14, 2023. Ray passed them over to Monica, who glanced at them and nodded.

"There you go," Eileen said, without adding the implied *Now get the hell out.*

"Thanks," Ray said. He was in the process of getting to his feet, but in a true Columbo moment, Monica didn't budge. "Are your rentals equipped with GPS?" she asked.

Eileen sighed. "Of course," she said.

"Where is this vehicle right now?"

Eileen replied with another spurt of typing. "It's in the garage being cleaned. It was returned an hour and a half ago and is due to go out again at seven in the morning."

"I'm afraid you're going have to find a replacement for that morning rental," Monica said.

"Why?"

"We believe a killer drove this vehicle during the commission of a crime. We're going to have to impound it and have it towed to our garage for a forensic examination."

"But this rental happened weeks ago," Eileen objected. "The car been cleaned several times since then. There can't possibly be anything left to find."

"You'd be surprised," Monica replied, because she knew that wasn't true, and so did Raymond Horn.

Stabbings are messy, even stabbings through bed coverings. Although the killer may have worn gloves or other protective clothing, that didn't mean he had walked away clean. And blood evidence, even minute droplets of it, don't go away with ordinary cleaning. If it's there, visible to the naked eye or not, Luminol tells all.

CHAPTER FORTY-TWO

CHELMSFORD, ENGLAND
MONDAY, MARCH 27, 2023
9:00 P.M.

At nine o'clock Monday night, Howard Wallace sat in his office, staring disconsolately at the phone on his desk. Camille Lee was due to fly home on Tuesday. Unfortunately, since the investigation into Adrian Willoughby's homicide was going nowhere fast, he had no reason to have her hang around any longer.

Days in, DI Wallace and DS Frost had yet to identify a single viable suspect. Under questioning, Camille Lee had pointed the finger at someone named George Smythe, but she had done so without supplying a scintilla of actual evidence. Smythe was evidently a highly respected member of the UK's cybersecurity elite. Although Wallace and Frost had done a good deal of research on the guy, they'd come up empty. Camille Lee's finger-pointing didn't qualify as anything close to probable cause. As for bringing someone that prominent in for random questioning when Howard didn't have anything to back up his suspicions? That was a surefire recipe for disaster.

They had also looked at Willoughby's wife, but like Camille Lee, she, too, had an airtight alibi. Mrs. Willoughby had been in Wales with a group of girlfriends at the time of her husband's murder. In other words, it was time for the investigators to go back to square one and start over.

Knowing he was admitting defeat, Howard picked up his phone and dialed. "DI Wallace here," he said when Camille Lee answered.

"Any news?" she asked.

"Not so far," he said without going into any further detail. "I wanted you to know that, as far as the Essex Police are concerned, you're free to fly home."

"Thanks for telling me," Camille told him. "That'll give me time to pack and notify the front desk that I'll be leaving tomorrow. I hope you catch him."

No doubt she meant that she hoped they'd catch George Smythe. Howard was glad she didn't actually speak the name aloud because he might have been forced to reply, "Not bloody likely!"

When the call ended, DI Wallace left his desk and turned off the lights in his office before closing the door. He was feeling defeated, yes, but he'd be back in the game tomorrow.

CHAPTER FORTY-THREE

CHELMSFORD, ENGLAND
TUESDAY, MARCH 28, 2023
11:00 A.M.

The next morning, as expected, DI Wallace and DS Frost went to work. They spent the morning going back to the very beginning of the Adrian Willoughby case, searching through their notes and interviews and combing for some tiny detail that might have been overlooked. DS Frost had just gone to fetch coffee when the desk sergeant showed up.

"Someone's out front asking to see you, sir," he announced. "Says her name's Angela Baker. She's a solicitor."

Wallace frowned. "Why is that name familiar?"

"She was all over the news last week after she took that MP to court. The guy thought he had his divorce agreement all tied up in a neat little bow, but she found out he had been stashing money away without his wife's knowledge. Angela Baker made mincemeat of him."

Since Howard Wallace had suffered a similar fate in his own divorce proceeding years earlier, Angela Baker's reputation for demolishing divorcing husbands wasn't a stellar recommendation.

"What does she want?" he growled.

"Claims she has information about the Willoughby case."

"Sure she does," DI Wallace muttered, "but go ahead and bring her in."

The woman who appeared in front of him a few moments later certainly looked the part of a high-powered solicitor. She was a pencil-thin older woman, dressed in a designer suit, wearing very high heels, and carrying a monogrammed briefcase. With her silver hair cut in a perfectly angled bob, she looked as tough as her vividly manicured nails.

"DI Howard Wallace?" she inquired.

"Yes, I am," he replied, getting to his feet. "And you're Ms. Baker?"

Nodding, she took a seat without waiting to be invited.

"What can I do for you?" he asked.

"I understand you're investigating the Adrian Willoughby homicide?" she inquired.

"That is correct."

"In that case, I may have some pertinent information for you."

Just then, DS Frost appeared in the doorway carrying two cups of coffee.

"This is my partner, Detective Sergeant Frost. Do you mind if he joins us?"

"Not at all."

After making the introductions and offering their guest one of the two cups of coffee—which she refused—they settled down to business.

"You have something for us about the Adrian Willoughby case?" Wallace prompted.

Angela Baker nodded before hefting her briefcase up into her lap and using a combination lock to click it open. Instead of removing any of the contents, she leveled a green-eyed stare in DI Wallace's direction.

"I've been retained by a woman named Maggie Smythe to represent her interests in a divorce proceeding against her husband, George."

Wallace's whole body stiffened as he made the connection. If Angela noticed the reaction, she ignored it.

"You may recognize the name," she continued. "His company, Cybersecurity International, is one of the top cybersecurity firms in the country."

"Yes, I know," Howard said.

At that point he was reasonably sure of the identity of Angela Baker's so-called anonymous source. Camille Lee's fingerprints were all over this. Unfortunately for him, by now she was probably in the air and headed home.

"The divorce is not exactly amicable," Ms. Baker continuued. "The couple had done mediation and had come to what we believed was an amicable agreement. However, as a result of this anonymous tip, I've recently been made aware that Mr. Smythe has been accumulating funds offshore and concealing them not only from his wife but also from Inland Revenue."

"Not a good idea," Howard said.

Angela Baker actually smiled at that.

"Indeed," she said. "Not at all. As I said, the information came to me on Sunday. One of my associates spent all day yesterday verifying it. If this were information concerning my client, it would, of course, be entirely confidential."

"But this concerns her husband," Howard offered, "so client privilege doesn't apply."

Angela Baker smiled again. "Correct," she said. "The divorce decree was due to be granted tomorrow. Since this new information is clearly a game changer, I've requested an urgent meeting with the judge in charge to delay the proceedings until these allegations can be investigated more thoroughly. Because Mr. Smythe's actions seem to be indicative of criminal behavior, I've taken the liberty of reporting our findings to Inland Revenue. I suspect they'll be more than happy to follow up."

"But that doesn't explain why you're here," Wallace objected.

"No, it doesn't," Angela Baker agreed, lifting the lid to her briefcase and removing several oversized computer printouts. "I was just getting to that. My anonymous source suggested that some of the wire transfers listed here might be connected to your investigation. Again, as an officer of the court, I feel obliged to pass them along."

With that, she handed the papers over to DI Wallace. The first page was a record of a wire transfer made a month earlier from one of Smythe's cryptocurrency accounts to one belonging to Adrian Willoughby. Howard scanned down the page until he found the amount.

"Three hundred and fifty thousand pounds?" he exclaimed. "That's a lot of money."

"Yes, it is," Angela Baker agreed. "I believe it may have been an advance payment for services to be rendered at a later date. I suspect that an examination of Mr. Smythe's electronic devices might reveal exactly what those services entailed, but of course you'd need a warrant to access those."

"Of course," Wallace acknowledged.

"In that regard, although the amounts are much smaller, the names on these next two wire transfers might also be of interest."

She handed over two additional pieces of paper. DI Wallace scanned them long enough to spot the names—Richard Hernandez and Ed Scoggins—and the amounts. The one to Hernandez was in the amount of ten thousand dollars. The one to Scoggins was for ten thousand pounds.

"Who are they?" Wallace asked.

"Mr. Hernandez lives in California in a place called San Bernardino. Mr. Scoggins lives in Tilbury, which, I believe, is very close to where Mr. Willoughby's body was found."

"And this last one?" Howard asked, holding up the final printout.

"That one is actually from Mr. Willoughby's cryptocurrency account. It's to the account of a Bulgarian national named Bogdan Petrov who, as I understand it, is also no longer with us. I believe he was recently found deceased near San Bernardino, California."

After dropping that remark, Angela Baker snapped her briefcase closed and spun the lock. "Helpful?" she asked, rising to her feet.

"Very," Wallace replied. "Thank you."

"Good," Angela said with a smile. "I thought it might be, and now

I'll be going. I'm off to have a long chat with Margaret Smythe. I'll want her with me when I speak to the judge tomorrow."

"I'm sure you will," Wallace said.

He waited until she passed the desk sergeant and was on her way to the lobby before he turned to DS Frost. "I want everything there is to be found on Ed Scoggins of Tilbury."

"On it!" Frost replied.

"With the evidence found in these money transfers, having probable cause is no longer an issue—not even for George Smythe. Once you finish looking into Scoggins, we'll drive up to London and invite Mr. Smythe in for an interview. I want to blow that sod out of the water before Angela Baker does."

CHAPTER FORTY-FOUR

LONDON, ENGLAND
TUESDAY, MARCH 28, 2023
2:30 P.M.

Shortly thereafter, DS Frost pulled over and stopped in front of the Fleet Street office building that held the headquarters of Cybersecurity International. While he waited in the vehicle, his boss, DI Wallace, stepped into the lobby where he was directed to the third floor. Once there he found a receptionist desk located just outside the elevator doors.

"I'm here to see Mr. Smythe," Wallace announced. "Is he in?"

"Do you have an appointment?" the receptionist asked.

"No," he replied, flashing his badge, "but I have this. My name is DI Howard Wallace. I'm with the Essex Police."

"May I ask what this is about?"

"It's a private matter, and I need to speak to him directly. It's urgent."

The woman looked slightly flustered, but eventually she reached for her phone. "Very well," she said. "One moment." After a brief conversation, she turned back to the detective. "Someone will be out to collect you directly."

Wallace surmised that the shapely young blonde who came to conduct him into George Smythe's private office had most likely been hired on the basis of her looks rather than her computer skills.

"This way, please."

Just past the receptionist desk was a partition with a glass door that required a badge to gain entry. Behind the door was an upscale suite of several offices. Wallace followed his escort to a closed door at the very end of the hallway, where she stopped and gave the door a light tap.

"Come in."

The blonde opened the door and allowed Wallace to enter before closing it behind him. George Smythe was seated at a sleek glass-topped desk where a phone, a single keyboard, and several computer monitors served as the only decorations. Behind him a large window afforded a view that included a tiny slice of St. Paul's Cathedral. As far as London real estate went, this wasn't the low-rent district.

Smythe rose to his feet and held out his hand in greeting as DI Wallace crossed the room. "You are?" he asked.

"I'm Detective Inspector Howard Wallace with the Essex Police."

"Please have a seat," Smythe invited, but then, resuming his own chair he echoed, "The Essex Police? What's this about?"

"I'm investigating the murder of Adrian Willoughby."

"Oh, of course," Smythe said. "I heard about that. Poor Adrian."

"I understand the two of you had some business dealings once," Wallace offered.

"Yes, we did," Smythe agreed, "but that was several years ago now. I haven't seen him for some time, but how can I help?"

Lie number one, Wallace thought. *You may not have seen him, but you've certainly been in touch.*

"We're trying to collect background information on the deceased," he said. "We thought that, as one of his former associates, you might be able to offer some insights. I'd like you to come in for a routine interview, this afternoon if at all possible."

"You're with the Essex Police?" Smythe asked. "Where are you located?"

"Chelmsford."

"That's totally out of the question, then," Smythe asserted. "I won't have time. It's miles away, and I have a dinner engagement this evening."

"Of course," Howard said with a smile. "I understand that you're a very busy man. That's why I arranged to borrow an interview room at the Charing Cross Station of the Metropolitan Police. It's only a matter of minutes from here, and I have a car and driver waiting down on the street."

By now the man was looking a bit flustered, and DI Wallace was afraid he was losing him. He needed to have the man's answers on the record today, if at all possible.

"I'd want my solicitor to be present," Smythe added.

"Oh, absolutely," Wallace said with an agreeable smile. "I'd be surprised if you didn't."

Shaking his head, Smythe picked up the phone and punched a single button. "Put me through to Peter Albers," he barked into the receiver. "Yes, I'll hold."

While Smythe waited with the phone to his ear, DI Wallace waited, too, feeling more and more anxious with every passing moment. If Angela Baker had already dropped the hammer, and if Peter Albers's firm was also handling Smythe's divorce proceedings, this could very well go south in a matter of minutes.

Mr. Albers must have come on the line. "Good to hear from you, too," Smythe said into the phone. "Yes, I need a bit of a favor. I have a policeman here from the Essex Police. He's investigating the murder of a former acquaintance of mine and wants me to come in for an interview." There was a momentary pause before he continued. "Yes, this afternoon. It's evidently routine questions only. All the same, I'd like to have you or someone from your firm with me." Another pause. "Yes, it'll be here in London. The detective has made arrangements to use an interview room at the Charing Cross Station of the Metropolitan Police."

After that there was another pause, a longer one this time. "Yes, I understand completely," Smythe said finally before turning to Howard. "Peter is busy this afternoon, but he can have one of his junior associates there in half an hour. Will that work?"

"Perfectly," DI Wallace breathed in relief. "Tell him we'll wait for him in the lobby so we can all go in together. What time is your dinner engagement?"

"Seven," Smythe answered.

"Good," Howard said. "We should be done in plenty of time."

By ten past five, four people were seated in an interview room at Charing Cross Station. DI Wallace and DS Frost sat on one side of a bare-bones table, while George Smythe and Matthew Hogan, Peter Albers's younger associate, were seated across from them.

After reading the customary caution, Howard did his best to keep the tone of the interview friendly and nonconfrontational, wanting to lock Smythe in on answers to questions that seemed to have nothing at all to do with the matters at hand.

"When and how did you and Adrian Willoughby meet?"

"It was back in the nineties," Smythe answered. "At the time, the whole idea of cybersecurity was still in its infancy. He did some consulting work for me back then. Later, he started a cybersecurity newsletter that was well respected in the industry."

"Is that newsletter still in existence?" Howard asked.

"No, a few years ago he went through some personal difficulties and that went out of business. After that, we more or less lost track of each other."

"And you've had no dealings with him since?"

"No," Smythe answered without hesitation.

Most likely the solicitor would have preferred an evasive, "No comment." DI Wallace, on the other hand, was delighted with Smythe's unequivocal no, because Angela Baker's wire transfer printout proved otherwise.

"You don't have any idea about someone who might have wished to do Adrian Willoughby harm?"

"None whatsoever."

"Have you ever heard of the name Ed Scoggins?"

Lulled into a sense of complacency, Smythe blinked in surprise before answering. "Not that I know of," he answered finally.

Knowing he'd hit solid gold, DI Wallace ended the interview. "That's all we need then," he said. "Thank you so much. You're free to go. We'll be glad to take you back to your office."

"No," Smythe said. "Not necessary. I'll catch a cab from here."

Wallace and Frost stayed where they were while the other two men left the interview room.

"What now?" Frost asked once they were alone.

"Now we go to Tilbury and find out what Ed Scoggins has to say for himself."

Before leaving for London, Frost had done some research on Ed Scoggins, who worked as a dock worker in Tilbury. Two years earlier he had been released from prison after serving fourteen years for a fatal drunk-driving conviction. He lived in a five-bedroom home on Albany Road in Tilbury, where he and four other dockworkers rented rooms from an elderly widow. He was also the registered owner of a white, ten-year-old Volkswagen Crafter.

Willoughby's office on Curzon Drive hadn't been fitted out with surveillance cameras, but Wallace and Frost had previously examined hours of surveillance video from businesses near the crime scene. At the time they had been looking for individuals who appeared to be suspicious. But now, with the possibility that a reasonably identifiable vehicle might be connected to the crime, they had asked one of their department's uniformed officers to go back through those same video segments looking for a white Volkswagen Crafter. She had succeeded spectacularly.

On Saturday, March 18, she had found a van matching that description coming and going on Curzon Drive near Willoughby's office at 7:45 p.m. on Saturday, March 18, 2023, a mere two hours prior to Adrian's time of death. The footage was too grainy to reveal the number of passengers in the vehicle, but presumably Ed Scoggins had been at the wheel. If a confrontation had occurred inside the victim's office, it would have been easy to move an unconscious victim from there and then conceal him from view in the van's windowless cargo area.

"Great work," DI Wallace told her once he heard the news. "Now see if you can find any footage of that van traveling to the Chafford Gorges."

"That shouldn't be too hard," she replied. "There aren't many direct routes, and we know the approximate times he'd be going to and from. I'll get right on it."

Less than an hour later, the CCTV footage paid off again, when at 8:36 p.m. the Crafter was spotted turning right off Mill Lane onto Warren, just south of Chafford Gorges. At that point, DI Wallace wasn't prepared to wait any longer. Based on the two connections he'd already made—the Smythe wire transfer printouts from Angela Baker and the appearance of the van in close proximity to Willoughby's office, he thought they had enough probable cause to bring Ed Scoggins in for questioning at least, and maybe even to obtain a search warrant for his vehicle. By the time he and DS Frost arrived on Albany Road, he had both warrants in hand.

The white-haired woman who answered the door wasn't thrilled to see them. "Whaddya want?" she demanded without any pleasantries.

"We'd like to speak to one of your tenants, a Mr. Scoggins," Howard Wallace said.

"Hey, Eddie," she called over her shoulder. "A couple of coppas are here to see you."

The big-boned, balding man who came to the door looked decidedly wary. "Who are you?"

Wallace pulled out his badge. "I'm DI Howard Wallace and DS Matthew Frost with the Essex Police. We'd like to ask you a few questions."

"About?"

At that point, Scoggins's landlady was still lurking almost out of sight behind the entryway wall.

"It would probably be better if we did this in private," Wallace suggested. "If you wouldn't mind accompanying us to the Grays Police Station . . ."

"Am I under arrest?"

"Of course not," Howard assured him. "Just a few routine questions."

But of course the questions weren't routine at all, and DI Wallace didn't mince words. "Where were you on the evening of March 18?" he asked for openers.

Scoggins frowned. "What day?"

"March 18 was a Saturday—late afternoon or early evening."

"No idea," Scoggins answered. "The weekend is the weekend, so I was probably at the pub with one of my roomies here. Why?"

"Does the name Adrian Willoughby mean anything?"

Scoggins shook his head, but Howard noticed the tiny pause before that happened. "Never met him?"

"No," Scoggins added after another pause. "Don't know him at all."

"So if we were to examine the VW Crafter we saw parked outside your residence, there's no chance we'd find any of Adrian Willoughby's DNA there, correct?"

"None whatsoever."

"Good," DI Wallace said. With that, he removed a document from the inside pocket of his sport coat and slapped it down on the table.

"What's that?" Scoggins asked.

"It's a search warrant for your VW van, which was seen in close proximity to two separate crime scenes involved in the death of one Adrian Willoughby who died on the night of March 18, 2023."

"Am I under arrest?"

"Not at this time," Wallace told him. "But, depending on what the forensics team finds in your van, there's a good chance you will be. So, if you're thinking of taking off in the meantime, I suggest you reconsider. As we say in our business, you can run, but you can't hide."

CHAPTER FORTY-FIVE

EDMONDS, WASHINGTON
TUESDAY, MARCH 28, 2023
4:00 P.M.

On Monday morning, when a sleep-deprived Raymond Horn went to work, he had been looking at a case that he had gotten all wrong, and which seemed to be dead in the water. As he and Monica had been chasing video footage and cell tower pings yesterday, he had thought the best they'd be able to hope for was a warrant to search the phones that had appeared on the towers prior to Chuck Brewster's death.

Now, on Tuesday afternoon and only a little over thirty hours later, he and Monica had zeroed in on an actual suspect. With an arrest warrant for Marc Atherton in hand, they were in the process of boarding an Alaska Airlines flight from Everett's Paine Field to Orange County's Santa Ana Airport.

It hadn't been an easy thirty hours. There had been all kinds of bureaucratic hoops to jump through before the RAV4 in question could be towed from SeaTac to Edmonds PD. Once in the impound yard's garage, Ray and Monica had waited on the sidelines while CSIs went through the vehicle with a fine-toothed comb. With nothing unusual visible to the naked eye, the process seemed to take forever, but eventually Luminol won the day. Nothing of evidentiary value was found in any of the obvious places—on the car seat, the steering wheel, the rearview mirror, or the gearshift. But finally, using infrared light, their careful search turned up tiny traces of blood-transfer smear on the underside of the driver's-side door handle and a similar one on the inside surface of the driver's-side seat belt.

Both stains showed evidence of having undergone additional wipe-downs by Enterprise garage attendants. Most likely they had assumed they were dealing with some kind of food spillage rather than human blood.

"So what's the deal?" Ray asked when the lead CSI came to let him know what they'd found.

"It may be easier to get a DNA profile from the stain on the fabric than the one on the door handle. What do you want us to do?"

"Remove both and take them into evidence," Ray replied, "but try getting a profile from the seat belt first, if that seems like a better bet."

"Will do. Is there a rush on this?"

"You'd better believe it. Once you have them bagged and tagged, Detective Burns and I will transport them to the Washington State Patrol Crime Lab."

They had done just that, with Monica Burns once again at the wheel. At the lab, they had handed over their evidence and were assured that it would be given the highest priority and subjected to Rapid DNA testing.

Ray Horn didn't put much store in that. He remembered all too well a time not so long ago when it had taken weeks or sometimes months to get a DNA profile. Much to his chagrin, on the way from south Seattle back to Edmonds, Ray's lack of sleep from the night before finally caught up with him, and he dozed off in the car.

It was after two in the morning when he finally got home. Mona was fast asleep when he crept into the bedroom and slipped into bed. His alarm was generally set for 7:00 a.m. Thinking he had earned a bit of a sleep-in, he turned it off before sliding under the covers. As a result, he was still out cold at 8:05 a.m. when Gretchen Walther, the crime lab's lead DNA tech, called on his cell.

"Got it!" Gretchen announced when he answered.

"Got what," Ray growled, "a profile?"

"No, silly," she shot back. "We've got a match off the seat belt!"

Ray Horn sat bolt upright in bed. "To whom?" he demanded.

"To your victim, Charles Brewster," Gretchen announced.

"You're kidding."

"Do I sound like I'm kidding?"

"No, of course not. Sorry. Thank you so much."

Before hitting the shower, Ray called Monica Burns's cell. She sounded bright-eyed and chipper. "Where are you?" he asked.

"Where do you think? It's after eight. I'm at work. Where are you?"

"Still at home. I overslept. But the crime lab just called. DNA from the seat belt is a match to Chuck Brewster."

"We've got him, then, don't we," Monica breathed.

"We've got Marc Atherton," Ray returned. "But it's pretty clear he didn't act alone. We need warrants for Atherton's phone and for that burner as well. I'm on my way in, but can you have the requests typed up by the time I get there?"

"On it," Monica said.

And Ray knew she would be. Heading out of the house, Ray passed Mona, who was up, dressed, and sitting at the kitchen table, working her daily crossword puzzle.

"Breakfast?" she asked.

"Just coffee," he said, grabbing one of their travelers.

"You've cracked the case, haven't you?" she said.

He stopped short and looked at her in surprise. "How did you know?"

"I can tell by the stupid grin on your face," she said with a smile.

"Cracked it, yes," he replied. "Now we have to finish putting the pieces together."

"In other words, I'll see you when I see you?"

"Exactly."

On his way to the department, Ray realized that when it came to handing out cop wives, he was very lucky. And once at the office, he had to admit he'd been lucky, too, in drawing Monica Burns as his partner.

By the time he got there, she had the requests for warrants typed up and awaiting Ray's signature. There were five in all—a request for an arrest warrant on Marc Atherton and requests for searches on four separate cell phones—Marc Atherton's, Joel Franklin's, and Adam Brewster's, along with that unidentified burner.

"Have you ever met Judge Gordon Parks?" Ray asked as he finished signing the last of the warrant requests.

"I've heard the name, but I've never met the man in person," Monica replied.

"Then it's high time you did," Ray said. "When you need warrants in a hurry, he's your go-to guy, so come on."

It was only a three-block walk from the Edmonds PD headquarters to the judge's chambers, where Judge Parks lived up to his advance billing. Minutes later, they came away with all the requested warrants.

"What next?" Monica asked as they headed back to the department.

"First, we turn the device warrants over to the Tech Unit so they can get started on those. Then we need to talk to the chief and see if he'll let us travel to Huntington Beach."

After a quick side trip to the TU, their next stop was Chief Nelson's office.

"You're sure this Atherton character is your guy?" the chief asked.

Ray nodded. "We believe he's the one who wielded the knife, but we don't think he acted alone. TU is working on the cell phone data right now. We're hoping that will give us a clearer picture about the identity of his co-conspirator. For starters, however, we want to go to Huntington Beach and take Atherton into custody."

"How soon?" Chief Nelson asked.

"As soon as possible."

"All right," the chief said. "Go on back to your desks. I'll call down to Huntington Beach PD and let their chief know he's about to have an out-of-town arrest team land on his doorstep."

Ten minutes later, Chief Nelson stopped by Monica and Ray's shared cubicle. "You guys are good to go," he said, dropping a Post-it containing a phone number onto Ray's desk. "Once you have an ETA, give this number a call. It's the direct number to Huntington Beach's homicide squad. Ask for Eduardo Ortega. He'll be your boots on the ground."

In the past it might have taken days or even weeks to obtain requested cell phone data. Fortunately, Don Wilson was a personable kind of guy who had developed one-on-one working relationships with folks from various phone providers. In this instance, luck was with them. By noontime, Don had obtained both call and text data for all the phones in question. The call histories themselves told an interesting tale. There were plenty of calls between Adam's phone and Joel's, and none at all between Adam's and Marc's. There were some calls from Joel's phone to Marc's, but when it came to the burner? There were dozens of incoming calls that had been placed from the burner to Marc, but none at all the other way around.

Monica was quick to note that and point out the implications. "It's straight out of the cheater's handbook," she said. "Joel was free to place calls on the burner whenever he wanted, but he didn't want incoming calls from Marc on that to arrive at inconvenient times."

"Like when Adam Brewster was at home?" Ray asked.

"Exactly," Monica said with a nod. "The same thing happened to me. I suspected my ex might be cheating, but I didn't have any proof. Then one day while he was in the shower, I checked his pants pocket and found *his* burner. Outgoing calls only when I was home. Two-way calls when I wasn't. I threw him out of the house that very day and filed for a divorce the day after that."

Ray had known Monica Burns was divorced, but he'd never before been privy to any of the details.

"You think maybe the two of them are having an affair?" Ray asked.

"I'd be willing to bet on it," Monica said, "but why would the two of them decide to murder Chuck Brewster?"

"I think Joel saw the possibility of a big payday. He knew that Adam was in the process of mending fences with his father—perhaps even pushed him to do so because Chuck Brewster was loaded. If Chuck was out of the way, and if Clarice went to prison for his murder, there's a good chance that the bulk of Chuck's estate would end up going to his biological son, which, since they're married, would also put all that wealth inside Joel's sphere of influence."

"So, motive, means, and opportunity?"

"Yup," Ray said. "Sounds like a home run to me. How soon can we be on a flight to Huntington Beach?"

Monica quickly went to work making travel arrangements—flight, hotel, and car rental. She booked them on a flight from Paine Field in Everett to Orange County leaving at 4:33 that very afternoon, and she found rooms at the airport Embassy Suites. Ray was fine with all of it.

Once the travel arrangements were in place, both detectives headed home to pack. "Remember," Monica reminded him, "as police officers, we can carry concealed weapons on the plane, but we'll need to go through an extra step of security to make that happen. See you at the airport."

By 3:30 they had filled out the proper concealed weapon forms, cleared security at Paine Field, and were waiting to board. That's when Ray finally got around to calling the phone number Chief Nelson had given him.

"Detective Ortega, Huntington Beach Homicide Squad. I'm assuming this is one of our visiting dignitaries?" he asked.

"Yes, I'm Detective Ray Horn. Sorry I didn't call earlier. Detective Burns and I will be flying into Santa Ana Airport this evening, arriving around seven thirty."

"What do you need and how can we help?"

"We have two subjects, and we'll need locations for both of them. Marc Atherton is most likely the muscle. We have an arrest warrant on him. We suspect that Joel Franklin, the husband of our homicide victim's son, is the mastermind, but we don't yet have enough for an arrest warrant on him. The thing is, once we take Atherton into custody, we'll need to make sure there's no opportunity for any communication between him and Joel."

"Gotcha," Detective Ortega replied. For the next few minutes, Ray brought his counterpart into the picture. By the time the briefing was finished, he and Monica had boarded the plane, and the flight attendants were preparing to close the doors.

"Okay," Detective Ortega said. "While you're in the air, we'll do our best to locate and put unmarked surveillance on both individuals. Give me a call as soon as you're on the ground. Will you need transportation?"

"Thanks but no thanks," Ray said. "We've got a rental. See you when we get there."

CHAPTER FORTY-SIX

HUNTINGTON BEACH, CALIFORNIA
TUESDAY, MARCH 28, 2023
4:45 P.M.

Adam Brewster was in the process of shutting down his computer to head home when a call came in from James Fisk. Jimmy—as Adam's previous partner, Michael Lafferty, had called him. Fisk had been Michael's personal banker for decades. Now, with Micheal gone, he was Adam and Joel's personal banker.

"Hey, Jimmy," Adam said when he answered. "What's up?"

"I was wondering how things are with you?"

"Fine," Adam began, then changed his mind. "Fairly fine," he amended. "My father passed away a couple of weeks ago, so things have been a bit complicated."

"I'm sorry to hear that," Jimmy said. "Had he been ill?"

"Actually, he was murdered," Adam answered. "His wife, my stepmother, appears to be the prime suspect."

"Wow," Jimmy said. "Losing a parent is tough, but losing one to a homicide has to be devastating."

James Fisk wasn't privy to the details of Adam's personal life, and Adam felt a little further explanation was necessary. "My father and I had been estranged for close to twenty years. We had just begun to reestablish contact when all this happened, so I'm still not sure what I'm supposed to feel. But what can I do for you?"

"I'm actually calling about one of your accounts—the one ending in 024."

"That's the household account," Adam said.

"There's been some unusual activity on it in the last couple of weeks, and I've just now noticed that it's overdrawn," Jimmy explained. "Your line of credit is there, so there won't be any overdraft charges, but would you like me to transfer some funds in from your investment account to put the other one back in the black?"

Adam was mystified. On the first of every month, he made a twelve-thousand-dollar deposit into the household account to cover all automatic bill-paying activity and for Joel to use to cover groceries, the landscaper, the pool guy, auto repairs, and anything else that might come up. Yes, it was close to the end of the month, but Adam had never known the account to be overdrawn.

"What kind of unusual activity?" he asked.

"In the past week or so there have been several sizable checks that came through that account. They've all been written to cash and endorsed by Joel. One for five thousand dollars cleared just a little while ago. That one, combined with the posting of the ACH on Joel's Camaro, put your balance over the edge."

"Why on earth would Joel be writing checks for cash?" Adam demanded.

"I have no idea," Jimmy replied. "As a signer on the account, the tellers had no reason to ask. The situation came to my attention due to the overdraft. Would you want me to make that transfer?"

Adam's investment account held the remainder of the sizable inheritance he had received in the aftermath of Michael's death, and he had maintained that account as his separate property. He had occasionally felt guilty about doing so, but right this minute, if Joel was doing things behind his back, that was probably a good thing.

"No," Adam said decisively. "I'm leaving for home right now and I intend to find out what the hell is going on. I'll get back to you tomorrow about making that transfer."

"Should I post a fraud alert on that account?" Jimmy asked.

"By all means," Adam said. "I want the regular bills to go through without interruption, but if Joel tries to write any more checks, can you keep those from clearing?"

"In order to do so, I'll need you to come in and sign some paperwork."

"All right, then," Adam growled into the phone. "Depending on what I find out once I get home, I'll stop by tomorrow. We can square things up then."

CHAPTER FORTY-SEVEN

COTTONWOOD, ARIZONA
TUESDAY, MARCH 28, 2023
4:30 P.M.

Ali was clearing her desk in preparation for leaving the office when a call came in from Frigg. Before answering, Ali studied the phone with some apprehension. The AI seldom called with good news, and Ali couldn't help but wonder what was wrong now. It wasn't Cami. She had boarded her flight at Heathrow hours earlier. In fact, Mateo had already left to drive to Phoenix to pick her up and bring her home.

"Good afternoon, Ali," Frigg said. "I hope you're having a pleasant day."

That depends, Ali thought. "What's going on?" she asked.

"I believe your day is about to get better," Frigg replied. "Do you remember Frank Muñoz?"

A little over two years earlier, Frank Muñoz, an ex-con bent on wreaking revenge on the people who had put him in prison years earlier, had very nearly taken B.'s life along with that of his airport shuttle driver, Hal Holden, the former Pasadena police officer who had effected Muñoz's original arrest and conviction.

"Of course," a puzzled Ali replied. "Why do you ask?"

"Remember how we located him?"

"I believe you managed to find him online and locate his home address."

"Correct," Frigg answered. "After he burned down his former wife's home, I hacked into several nearby news sites and planted a trojan so I could capture the IP addresses of all people logging in to that story, especially ones doing so repeatedly. It worked then, and it's working now. It turns out that the homicide investigators in Edmonds have finally gotten the hint."

"What hint?"

"That they need to be looking at people other than Clarice Brewster and Donna Jean Plummer. I've hacked into several Seattle area news sites capturing the names and IP addresses of everyone logging into stories connected to the Charles Brewster homicide. There was an update on KOMO News earlier this morning. According to that, nameless sources close to the investigation speaking anonymously have revealed that, although Mr. Brewster's widow is still considered to be a suspect in the case, detectives are currently following up on leads in Southern California."

"That is good news," Ali said.

"But it gets better," Frigg replied. "One of the devices logging in to that news site was the burner, logging in from an IP address on Churchill Drive in Huntington Beach, California."

Ali allowed herself a relieved deep breath. "So, it's either Adam or Joel."

"Definitely Joel," Frigg declared. "As soon as the cops lay hands on that burner and go through what's on it, let's hope they'll have everything they need to put Mark Atherton and Joel Franklin away for good."

CHAPTER FORTY-EIGHT

HUNTINGTON BEACH, CALIFORNIA
TUESDAY, MARCH 28, 2023
7:00 P.M.

Still short on sleep, Ray dozed off almost as soon as the plane was in the air and slept until the plane was preparing to land at SNA.

"Are you aware that you snore?" Monica asked as he moved his seat into its full upright and locked position.

"Sorry," Ray replied. "Mona may have mentioned that from time to time."

"Poor woman," Monica said. "Your wife must be a saint."

"Pretty close," Ray agreed.

On the ground in Santa Ana, Ray dialed Detective Ortega's number as they made their way through the terminal toward baggage claim.

"Okay," Ortega said. "Here's the deal on your suspects. We found a 2018 BMW motorcycle registered in the name of Marc Atherton. You told me that he's employed at a place called Meet and Greet, a gay bar here in town located at the corner of Beach Boulevard and Main. Since his motorcycle is currently parked behind the bar, he's probably at work. We don't actually have eyes on him, because, in a place like that, cops would stand out like a pair of sore thumbs."

"Any idea what time he'll get off?" Ray asked.

"Not really, but security footage from the business next door showed him arriving and going inside, at one p.m. Since I doubt he's scheduled to work a twelve-hour shift, he'll probably leave prior to closing time.

"What about Joel Franklin?"

"Adam Brewster arrived home at his residence in the Holly-Seacliff neighborhood at twenty past five. When he pulled his Lincoln Navigator into the double garage on Churchill Drive, Joel Franklin's Camaro was already parked inside. Since Mr. Brewster's arrival, no one has come or gone."

"That's a huge help," Ray said.

"Where are you?" Ortega asked.

"We're in baggage claim now," Ray reported. "Once we get our luggage and pick up our rental, we'll check into our hotel and then head to the bar. Does the Meet and Greet serve food?"

"Their website says yes, but it's probably not gourmet fare."

"We're cops," Ray said. "We don't need gourmet, but maybe Detective Burns and I can pass for a pair of misguided tourists who happened to stumble into the place by accident. How far is the bar from Huntington PD?"

"Only a mile or so away," Ortega said. "Happy hunting. I have an interview room reserved for your use later this evening, and I'll make it a point to be on-site when you bring your guy in."

With their luggage finally in hand, Ray and Monica located their rental, a hybrid Tahoe. After leaving the airport, they checked into their hotel before heading for the Meet and Greet around 8:30.

To his knowledge, Ray Horn had never visited a gay bar, so he wasn't quite sure what to expect. When they got there, the place was relatively full, but in a very subdued kind of way. The clientele consisted mostly of middle-aged to older pairs of men who engaged in quiet conversations over their various beverages. The music playing in the background was an endless stream of original-cast recordings of Broadway show tunes.

There were actually two bartenders at work behind the bar. Ray and Monica seated themselves at the bar close to what appeared to be Marc Atherton's station, where they ordered and downed reasonably good burgers. If Atherton thought it odd that his barstool customers stuck to straight coffee, he made no mention of it. About twenty to ten, however, he stopped by where they were seated to drop off their check.

"I'm about to go off shift," he told them, "so if you don't mind paying up . . ."

"No problem at all," Ray assured him, reaching for his wallet. While the two of them sorted out the bill, Monica sent a quick text to the Huntington PD officers who were parked outside, letting them know that their subject was about to exit the bar. The whole idea was to have Atherton in custody before he and his motorcycle made it out of the alleyway.

A few minutes later, Atherton caught the eye of his fellow server and waved as if to say he was leaving, and then he disappeared through the swinging door that led to the kitchen. Knowing there was most likely a rear entrance, Monica and Ray followed hot on his heels.

"Wait a minute," the cook shouted after them as they passed. "Where are you going?"

In reply, Ray waved his badge in the disapproving cook's direction and kept right on going. They caught up with Atherton in a back alleyway where he was standing next to a motorcycle with his back to them while donning a helmet.

"Mr. Atherton?"

The man started when Ray said his name. That was the moment when he might have simply jumped on his motorcycle and made a run for it, but he didn't.

"Yes," he said uncertainly, turning to face them. "Who are you?"

Prior to their arrival at the Meet and Greet, Ray and Monica had sorted out the strategy that they would try to convince Atherton to agree to speak to them by assuring him that their investigation was focused solely on Adam Brewster.

Still holding his badge wallet, Ray flipped it open. "I'm Detective Raymond Horn with the Edmonds, Washington, Police Department," he said, "and this is Detective Monica Burns. We're looking into the murder of a man named Chuck Brewster, and believe his son, Adam Brewster, may be responsible. I understand you're acquainted with Adam's husband, a man named Joel Franklin. Is that correct?"

Marc nodded. "Yes," he said. "Joel's a good friend of mine."

"Would you mind accompanying us to Huntington PD to answer a few questions?" Monica asked.

"Am I under arrest?"

"Not at all," she said reassuringly. "All we're doing is making routine inquiries and looking for background information."

"Okay," Marc said. "I know where Huntington Beach PD is. Can I meet you there?"

"Why don't you ride with us?" Monica suggested lightly. "Our vehicle's right out front. We'll be glad to bring you back here once we're finished."

Atherton hesitated for an indecisive moment, but finally nodded. "Will this take long?"

"Probably not. As I said, it's just a few routine questions. How long have you known Joel?"

"Several years. We're writing a screenplay together, a thriller."

"Really," Monica said, sounding enthusiastic. "How exciting! I always dreamed of writing novels. The problem is, I'm good at starting manuscripts, but I never make it beyond the third or fourth page."

"I'm the same way," Atherton said. "I'm good at writing dialogue, but Joel's specialty is plotting. While I'm still focused on the first few scenes, he's already planning the ending."

"Sounds like the two of you make a great team," Monica said as she opened the back door of the Tahoe so Atherton could climb inside. "Does your screenplay have a title?"

"It's called *Tying Up Loose Ends*," Atherton answered. "The killer is a serial strangler."

"Sounds fascinating," Monica said.

As she settled into the passenger seat, Ray started the engine. During the short drive to Huntington PD, Ray was happy to let Monica do all the talking. Her enthusiastic flattery about Atherton's being a writer was clearly working its magic, and Ray didn't want to break the spell.

In the lobby of Huntington Beach police headquarters, they met up with Detective Eduardo Ortega, "Eddie," as he liked to be called, who was waiting to escort them to their interview room. Given the evidence they had already gathered on Marc Atherton, there was no way to keep pretending he was only a person of interest. It was time to read him his rights, and once they were seated in the interview room, Monica did just that.

The abrupt change of subject seemed to jar Marc Atherton. "But I thought you said I wasn't under arrest," Atherton protested.

"You're not," Monica responded. "You're free to leave at any time, but we needed to verify that you're still willing to speak with us."

Atherton shifted uneasily in his seat. "I guess," he allowed finally.

Without missing a beat, Monica returned to their discussion of *Tying Up Loose Ends.* "Every movie has to have some kind of twist," Monica said, "so what's the twist in yours?"

Marc's momentary uneasiness evaporated. "That would be a spoiler, now, wouldn't it," he replied. "You'll have to wait until you see it to find out."

"Fair enough," Monica said. "Now how about if we go about tying up some of our loose ends?"

Enjoying the joke, Atherton grinned and nodded in agreement.

"If you don't mind," she added, "we'd also like to examine your phone." The request seemed to give him pause. He hesitated for a moment, before he said, "Sure," and handed it over.

Since they already had the search warrant in hand, she could have simply demanded it, but Monica's charm offensive made that unnecessary.

"Thanks," Ray said, accepting the phone. Then, not wanting to break the mood, he added, "If you'll excuse me, I'll pass this along to some tech guys."

Taking the phone with him, he stepped out of the room. Outside, he met up with Detective Ortega, who was observing the interview through the two-way mirror. Wanting to join him, Ray had barely settled onto a stool when Marc's phone, still in Ray's hand, began to ring. A glance at the screen revealed no name, but he recognized the number—the one to the unidentified burner.

Ray guessed that Joel probably knew that Marc would be off work by then, so why was he calling? Was he hoping for a meetup of some kind, or had Joel somehow gotten wind that the investigation into Chuck Brewster's homicide had come home to roost? After four rings, the call went to voice mail.

Unable to access the voice mail message, Ray slipped the phone into his pocket and turned his attention back to the interview room. Monica was now asking a series of nonconfrontational questions. How long had he and Joel been friends? How had he and Joel met? Joel had stopped by the bar when he first arrived in town, and they had hit it off. Had he ever met Chuck Brewster? No. What did he know about Adam's strained relationship with his father? Chuck Brewster was offended when he found out that his son was gay and had thrown him out of the house. What did he know about Chuck Brewster's financial situation?

Marc hesitated before answering that one. "Just that he was loaded," he said.

At that point Marc's phone rang again. Once again, the call went to voice mail, but Ray was beginning to worry. Maybe Joel and Marc had made plans to get together after Marc got off work, and perhaps Joel was wondering not only where Marc was, but why he wasn't answering his phone.

"Is that Joel calling?" Detective Ortega asked.

Ray nodded. "Again."

"Getting anxious?"

"Maybe."

Ortega did some amazingly fast texting. Moments later, a reply came in. "Don't worry. All's quiet on Churchill Drive. Both cars are in the garage, so everyone's still at home."

When they turned their attention back to the interview room, the mood had undergone a sea change. Marc Atherton was now on high alert.

"Tell me about your trip to Seattle three weeks or so ago," Monica said. "I believe that was the weekend of Chuck Brewster's birthday party. Were you invited to that?"

"No, I wasn't."

"We know you were in the area at that time, so if you didn't go to the party, why were you there?"

"To visit some friends."

"Which friends?"

Atherton visibly twitched. "Do I have to name them? I don't want to drag them into this."

"She's got him cold," Ortega muttered under his breath. "He's going to cave for sure."

"Maybe he is," Ray agreed, "unless the SOB decides to lawyer up."

With that small aside, they turned back to the interview.

"That's up to you," Monica was saying, "but if they can provide you with an alibi, you'd best name them. You see, we happen to have video footage of your rented RAV4 driving around Chuck Brewster's neighborhood in the early morning hours two days before the homicide occurred. Would you mind telling me what you were doing there?"

"Just driving around."

"In the middle of the night?"

"Couldn't sleep."

"We also have video of your visiting a Food Mart in Edmonds the evening of the party. We know that you parked your vehicle near a strip mall less than a mile from the crime scene. It remained there for some time and didn't leave again until after Charles Brewster was deceased. Do you have an explanation for that?"

Atherton said nothing.

"You might also be interested in knowing that, while examining your rented RAV4, we located a tiny blood smear that has since been discovered to contain Mr. Brewster's DNA. Before you say anything more, one way or the other, you need to know that, although you may have wielded the murder weapon, we don't believe you acted alone. You might want to consider that old saying "the first to squeal gets the deal. Now, if you'll excuse me, I need to visit the ladies'. Can I get you anything—coffee? A soda?"

Atherton shook his head and said nothing.

When Monica reached the door, Detective Ortega opened it from the outside. "Good time to walk away and let him spend some time stewing," he told her as she stepped into the hallway. "You've given him a hell of a lot to think about."

"I hope so," she said.

Just then, Atherton's phone rang again, and Ray glanced at the screen. "It's the burner," he said aloud.

"In other words, Joel Franklin," Monica said.

Ray nodded. "This is his fourth call. He's left several messages, but we can't hear them, and we need to before we go after him. See if you can get Atherton to give you his password."

Monica nodded. "Will do," she agreed. "If I can, I'll text it to you. While you go after Joel, I'll focus on Atherton. He's not leaving that room until I have a full confession."

CHAPTER FORTY-NINE

HUNTINGTON BEACH, CALIFORNIA
TUESDAY, MARCH 28, 2023
10:00 P.M.

When Detectives Ray Horn and Eddie Ortega left Huntington Beach PD, they did so in Ortega's unmarked Interceptor.

"Do you know where we're going?" Ray asked.

Eddie nodded. "Churchill Drive in Huntington Beach," he answered. "Do you think Detective Burns will get that confession?"

"I wouldn't bet against her," Ray replied.

They were barely underway when a radio transmission came in. "We've got movement."

"It's from the uniforms parked outside Adam Brewster's house," Eddie explained to Ray before asking, "Which car did they take?"

"Joel Franklin's Camaro."

"How many people in the vehicle?"

"Only one as far as we can tell."

"Try to keep the subject in sight, but follow at a distance," Eddie directed. "If he speeds at all, has a broken taillight, or runs even so much as a single red light, initiate a traffic stop."

"Gotcha."

"Where are you right now?"

"Eastbound on Ellis."

"Okay, we just left headquarters and are coming your way. Keep us posted."

"Will do."

Just then a text came in from Monica containing nothing but the numbers 1, 2, 3, and 4. Ray hauled out Marc's phone and typed them in. Sure enough, the phone opened right up. He went to the call app, found the voice mail messages, and played them back using the speaker.

"Hey." Joel's voice sounded casual and at ease. "You should be off work by now. Want to get together? Call me back."

Message number two said, "I thought you would have called by now. Are you working overtime?"

Message number three sounded more impatient. "I just called the Meet and Greet. They said you left a while ago. Where the hell are you? Call me back."

The fourth message contained only two words. "Screw you!"

"He sounds upset," Eddie observed. "Panicked, even."

"Doesn't he just!"

"Is he bolting?" Eddie wondered aloud. "Any chance he was able to communicate with Marc after you and Detective Burns made contact?"

"None whatsoever."

Another radio transmission came through. "Headed northbound on Goldenwest Street," the uniformed officer reported. "He's sticking to the speed limit, and so are we."

"Roger that," Eddie said.

Meanwhile Ray was mulling the problem. "They said both vehicles were in the garage, right?"

Ortega nodded. "Correct."

Suddenly Ray had a sick feeling in the pit of his stomach. "Where's Adam Brewster, then? First Joel was terribly anxious to make contact with Marc. Then awhile later, without their ever being in touch, he takes off alone for parts unknown in the middle of the night. That doesn't sound good to me. Can you ask someone to initiate a welfare check?"

"Will do."

Eddie made the call. "Uniforms are being dispatched," was the response, "but it'll take time for them to get there."

Ray understood that was only to be expected. "So if you were Joel Franklin, with a murder rap hanging over your head and wanting to make a run for it, where would you go?"

"That's easy," Eddie answered. "Mexico. Tijuana is only two and a half hours from here."

"But that's to the south, right?"

"Correct."

"So why's he heading north, and why are we?"

"Because locals know that coming from Holly-Seacliff, traveling north on Goldenwest to Warner, is the fastest way to the 405. We're on Beach Boulevard, which runs parallel to Goldenwest. Not to worry, though. Regardless of whether he heads north or south on the freeway, the guys who are tailing him have him in sight and will keep us posted."

CHAPTER FIFTY

HUNTINGTON BEACH, CALIFORNIA
TUESDAY, MARCH 28, 2023
11:00 P.M.

When Detective Burns reentered the interview room, she brought along only one cup of coffee. Marc Atherton sat with his arms crossed, staring down at the tabletop. He seemed to have recovered some of his composure, so Monica took her time, sitting down and arranging the paperwork in front of her. Once it was time to resume the interview, she took a roundabout approach.

"So how long have you and Joel Franklin been an item?" she asked.

"What makes you think we're an item?" Marc demanded. "We're writing buddies. That's it."

"Oh, come on," Monica returned. "We obtained search warrants for your phone and for both of Joel's phones as well—you know—his real one and the burner. We have a lot of reading to do as far as the actual messages are concerned, but it turns out there are literally dozens and dozens of calls between your phone and Mr. Franklin's burner. That indicates there's a lot more going on between you than a writing-buddy relationship."

Marc hesitated before he answered. "Awhile," he said, finally answering her question. "Like I said, we met at the Meet and Greet shortly after he arrived in town and hit it off. Shortly after we hooked up, Joel was hired to be the caretaker for Michael Lafferty, who had just been diagnosed with ALS. Michael's partner, Adam, worked full-time, and they needed a caretaker 24/7. Then, after Michael died . . . " He shrugged. "I guess you know about that."

"So you two have been involved the whole time, since before Joel married Adam Brewster?"

"Off and on," Atherton admitted. "We're not exactly exclusive."

"What about Adam? Does he know about you and Joel?"

"I doubt it. I come from the wrong side of the tracks. Adam and Michael were both born with silver spoons in their mouths. Considering my background, Joel thought it best for me to keep a low profile."

"By background you mean the time you spent in prison?"

Marc Atherton nodded. "Among other things. So as far as Michael and Adam were concerned, I was Joel's screenwriting partner and nothing more."

"But you're partners in more ways than just writing, aren't you," Monica asserted. "I suspect there's a mountain of material in your electronic devices, including previously deleted messages, texts, and searches that will tell us exactly that. At the moment, we've only had a chance to examine communications that were exchanged around the time of Chuck Brewster's murder. For example, on the night of Sunday, March 12, at 9:03 p.m., just hours before his time of death, you received a one-word text from Joel's burner that said, 'Done.' What did he mean by that? What had he done?"

Marc shrugged. "I have no idea." But his eyes said otherwise.

"I don't think that's true," Monica responded. "I believe you know exactly what Joel had done. We have heard from various witnesses that Joel Franklin was exceptionally attentive toward Mrs. Brewster during the course of the party—that he brought her food and beverages and chatted her up. Then later on, when it was time for her to leave, she was so inebriated that she required assistance in order to make her way upstairs. We learned Joel was the one who actually escorted her to her bedroom.

"As a result, we're wondering if maybe, in the course of bringing her all those beverages, it was Joel's job to slip her something—a sleeping potion of some kind or maybe even a smidge of scopolamine. Whatever it was, it knocked her out so completely that she slept right through what was happening while you stabbed her husband to death seventeen times."

Marc made no effort to respond verbally, but the shocked expression on his face spoke volumes.

Monica continued. "As I said, we've barely scratched the surface as far as your internet interactions with Mr. Franklin are concerned, but we did take a close look at the one immediately following the 'done' one. That one says, "Last one on the left." Is it possible that's a reference to one of the sliders on Mr. Brewster's back patio, perhaps the one leading from the patio into the family room?"

Again, Marc didn't respond, but Monica could tell that she was wearing him down. His legs were twitching nervously under the table, and so were his hands.

"So here's the deal, Mr. Atherton. We have video surveillance that shows Mr. Franklin was at the Hilton Garden Inn at the time Mr. Brewster was murdered. We can physically place you in the area of the crime scene. We found smears of Mr. Brewster's blood in your rental car. It's clear to us that you're the individual who wielded the knife, but I don't believe you acted alone, and what I said earlier still goes. The first to squeal gets the deal.

"I'm a cop not a prosecutor," Monica added. "I can't negotiate plea deals, but I can let prosecutors know when someone assists us in an investigation. So here's your last chance to help yourself, Marc. Tell me about Joel Franklin's involvement in all this, because I'm guessing this plot was far more his idea more than it was yours. Still, if you're willing to take the whole rap, that's entirely up to you."

Suddenly Marc's face crumpled and he seemed close to tears. "He hated his parents."

"Who hated his parents," Monica asked. "Joel?"

"No, Joel told me that Adam hated *his* parents. His mother died of cancer when he was in his teens. She was barely in the ground when his dad married again, this time to one of Adam's mother's good friends. That's when all the trouble started. His father and his new stepmother threw Adam out of the house because he was gay. It happens, you know. People who are treated that way learn to deal with it, but they never get over it."

"You're saying this all happened because of that long-ago betrayal?" Monica asked.

Marc nodded. "Joel said it seemed like Adam had done just that—that he was okay with it, but then just a few months ago, when his dad showed up out of the blue and wanted to be back in Adam's life, it was too much. He had, like, a PTSD episode—a complete breakdown. Adam told Joel that he didn't want to have anything to do with either his father or his stepmother. How dare his father come breezing back into his life and act like nothing happened? But then Adam realized that his father was loaded—he'd made a fortune in the video game industry, and it occurred to him that if his father died and his stepmother turned out to be the killer, he, Adam, would inherit everything."

"What happened then?" Monica asked.

"Adam asked Joel if he and I could make that happen for him. His dad's upcoming birthday party seemed like the perfect opportunity. Joel said Adam promised each of us fifty grand if we could make it work. We figured that having a hundred thou between us would give us enough money to go somewhere cheap like Idaho or Montana and start over. Joel said that as long as I wasn't carrying my phone when I did the job, nobody would be able to figure out I was involved. He also said that I needed to stab the guy a whole bunch of times so it would look for sure like the wife did it."

Monica was shocked. She had sat through Adam Brewster's interview and had never for a moment believed that he was involved in his father's murder. Was he that good of a liar? She still wasn't sure.

"Is there a chance that Joel lied to you about Adam wanting his father dead?" she asked.

"No way," Marc said, looking uncertain. "Why would he do something like that?"

"I don't know," Monica answered, "but he was certainly wrong about one thing. Phone or no phone, we were smart enough to find you. So here's a pen and paper," she added, pushing a tablet and pen across the table. "I need you to write down everything you just told me. Once you're finished, sign it. Chances are, if you're willing to testify against your co-conspirators at trial, there's a good chance the prosecutor will take your cooperation into consideration."

"Do you think that'll help?" Marc asked.

With seventeen stab wounds in the back? Monica thought to herself. *I doubt it.*

Aloud she said, "Let's hope."

CHAPTER FIFTY-ONE

HUNTINGTON BEACH, CALIFORNIA
TUESDAY, MARCH 28, 2023
11:30 P.M.

Joel Franklin may have been observing all posted speed limits on his way to the 405, but Detective Ortega definitely hadn't. As a consequence, he and Ray Horn beat both the Camaro and its tailing squad car to the intersection of Beach Boulevard and Warner by three whole minutes. When the Camaro rolled past, Ray pulled in behind it and let the squad car fall back into second place. As Franklin's car merged into the righthand lane to take the southbound entrance onto I-405, another radio transmission came through, this one from police headquarters.

"On your welfare check request at 3759 Churchill Drive, no one answered the front door and uniforms found it locked. They went around back and made entry through a patio slider. They report having found some signs of a physical confrontation in the kitchen, although it looked as though someone had put a lot of effort into cleaning up. However, when the officers cleared the residence, no one was there."

Ray turned to Eddie. "If both of them were at the house earlier, and nobody's there now, what do you want to bet that Adam Brewster is in the back of Joel Franklin's Camaro?"

"No bet," Eddie replied, "and with his life possibly at risk, we don't have to wait around for a warrant." Then, into his radio he added, "We believe someone is being held captive in the trunk of a fleeing vehicle. Initiating a traffic stop so we can do a search."

With that, Detective Ortega lit up the lights on his Interceptor. The uniformed officers in the patrol car behind them followed suit.

For a moment, Ray thought Franklin would hit the gas and make a run for it, but it was almost midnight. With freeway traffic at a minimum, Joel must have realized he had no chance of evading a police pursuit. He turned on his directional signal, hit the brakes, and pulled over onto the shoulder. Once Ortega came to a stop behind the Camaro, the officers in the patrol car rolled around to the front of it, close enough to keep it from being able to merge back into traffic.

If Joel Franklin thought this was some kind of ordinary traffic stop, he was in for a surprise. The uniformed officers approached him with weapons drawn. "Turn off the engine and step out of the vehicle!" one of them shouted.

For a long moment, nothing happened. Ray fully expected that Joel would come charging out of the Camaro with a weapon drawn, but that didn't happen, either. He simply opened the door and exited. "What's this about?" he wanted to know.

"Get on the ground!"

This wasn't Ray Horn's rodeo, and he wasn't wearing a vest, so he stayed where he was in the Interceptor until Joel Franklin was on the ground with his hands cuffed behind his back. That's when Ray leaped out of the car and sprinted for the Camaro's back bumper. It took a moment for him to locate the button that unlatched the trunk. When the lid rose, he saw a bound and gagged Adam Brewster lying there, staring up at him with a look of absolute terror on his face. As Ray removed the gag, Adam's terror morphed into relief.

"Detective Horn?" he asked. "What are you doing here?"

"Looking for you, as it turns out," Ray replied.

By then, Eddie Ortega appeared at Ray's side. "That's a lot of blood," he observed. "What happened?"

Up until then, Ray hadn't noticed that the lower part of Adam's shirt and his pants were strained bright red.

"Joel came after me with a knife," Adam answered. "He tried to stab me in the gut. I almost managed to get out of reach, but I must've tripped over something. I fell backward and hit my head. The next thing I knew, I woke up in the trunk of the car. I knew I was bleeding, so I used my hands to apply pressure. Eventually the bleeding stopped."

"It looks like you're hurt pretty bad," Ortega observed. "You'll need an ambulance. I'll make the call."

While he did that, Ray turned back to Adam and began using his Leatherman to snip through the layers of duct tape binding his hands and feet.

"Why did he attack you?" Ray asked.

"Because I'd just found out he's been robbing me blind. Our banker called this afternoon to let me know that the household checking account was overdrawn. It turns out that, instead of paying bills, over the last several days he's been writing checks out of the household account and cashing them. I came home to have it out with him. Unfortunately, he was making dinner at the time. One moment he was chopping vegetables at the counter. The next, he came after me with the knife."

Ortega returned. "EMS will be here in about ten," he said.

Ray stood there for a moment with the phone at his ear, looking down at Adam Brewster. Since the bleeding had stopped, Ray suspected that the stab wound itself probably wasn't all that serious. The trouble was, years earlier while he'd still been working patrol, he'd encountered a sixteen-year-old named Jeremy Foresman who'd been stabbed in the gut during the course of a gang-related street fight. In that case, too, the wound hadn't seemed all that bad. Unfortunately, the tip of the knife had punctured Jeremy's large intestine. By the time he was diagnosed with peritonitis, it was too late, and he had died of sepsis days later. Ray Horn worried the same thing might happen to Adam Brewster.

Just then a call from Monica came in from Ray's phone. He started not to answer it, but then thought better of it.

"What's going on?" he asked.

"I've got a signed confession from Marc Atherton," she announced triumphantly. "He claims Adam Brewster offered to pay Joel Franklin and him fifty thousand dollars each to murder Chuck Brewster and frame Clarice. And that's not all. Marc and Joel have been romantically involved since well before Adam met Joel."

All the pieces of the puzzle were finally falling into place. Not only had Joel Franklin been stealing from Adam, he'd been cheating on him as well. He'd also just physically assaulted him with a deadly weapon before kidnapping him. Based on all of that, the idea that Joel could be the mastermind behind Chuck Brewster's homicide didn't seem to be that far out of line.

"Ray," Monica was saying in his ear. "Are you there? Did you even hear me?"

"Great news," Ray replied. "I've got some, too. Huntington Beach PD just took Joel into custody. We found Adam Brewster bound and gagged in the trunk of Joel's car, with a stab wound to his gut. I'll get back to you with details, but right now I've gotta go."

He hung up. Then, switching his phone to video record, he held the device up to Adam's face. "Once they get you in the ER, it's going to be a while before I'll be able to talk to you again. Do you mind if I ask you a couple of questions and record your answers?"

"Go ahead," Adam said with a half wave.

"We have physical evidence linking Marc Atherton to your father's murder."

Adam seemed astonished. "Are you kidding, Marc Atherton? He's Joel's writing partner. I barely know the man. How would he even know my father?"

"Good question," Ray remarked. "But tonight my partner obtained a signed confession from Marc Atherton saying that he and Joel committed the crime at your request—that you offered to pay them a total of one hundred thousand dollars to murder your father and frame your stepmother."

"That can't be!" Adam declared in total disbelief. "I never did any such thing. I wanted my father back in my life. I wanted to start fresh and remember the good things. Why would I want him dead?"

"How much do you know about Marc Atherton?"

"Not much, really, other than he and Joel write together."

"I suspect they do a lot more than write," Ray suggested. With that he pulled out Atherton's phone, logged in on it, and played back those most recent voice messages so Adam could hear them.

"That's Joel's voice, but who's he talking to?"

"These are voice messages he left on Marc Atherton's phone just tonight, starting a little past ten. The thing is, we'd already taken Marc into custody by then and had possession of the phone. We heard the messages. Marc didn't. The last one came in about the time Joel's Camaro was leaving your garage with you in the trunk."

Adam seemed stunned. "Wait, are you saying they were going to run off somewhere together?"

Detective Ortega returned in time to hear the tail end of that conversation. "I don't think so," he said. "We just found a short-handled shovel in the front passenger-seat footwell of Joel's Camaro. If he'd been able to connect with Marc tonight, I suspect he would have ended up in the trunk right along with you, and neither of you would have come out of it alive."

"Oh, my God!" a clearly stricken Adam murmured. "How could he do that, and how could I have been so stupid? I thought he loved me. I really believed I'd found the one."

"That's why they say love is blind," Ray observed. "People can't see what they don't want to see."

An ambulance rolled up just then, and Ray ended the recording. By this time Detective Ortega had obtained a warrant on the Camaro, but before searching it further, he ordered it towed back to police headquarters to be properly processed. Once the ambulance headed for the hospital with Adam inside, Ray and Eddie Ortega returned to the Interceptor.

"Poor guy," Ortega said quietly as they fastened their seat belts. "I think he was completely blindsided."

Ray nodded. "So do I," he responded. "And by the time we sit down and comb through all those electronic devices, we'll have the evidence to prove it."

There was a momentary lull in the conversation before Ray asked, "Did Joel say anything as you guys were cuffing him and putting him in the car?"

"Yes, he did," Eddie answered. "Four words only, and you can guess what they were."

"'I want a lawyer,' maybe?"

"You got it," Eddie replied.

"What a surprise," Ray responded. "And if I have anything to say about it, he's sure as hell going to need one."

CHAPTER FIFTY-TWO

COTTONWOOD, ARIZONA
WEDNESDAY, MARCH 29, 2023
9:00 A.M.

When Ali went to work on Wednesday morning, she bypassed her own office and went straight to Cami's. No longer working in the lab, she had taken over B.'s former digs.

Once inside, Ali hurriedly walked around the desk and wrapped Cami in a welcoming hug. "How are you feeling?"

"Jet-lagged," Cami replied, "but glad to be home."

Ali closed the door behind her before taking a seat. "I understand from Frigg that between you and Margaret Smythe's divorce attorney, you've done a good job of putting George Smythe in a tough spot."

"I hope so," Cami said. "With Angela Baker's help I was able to use his financial connections to point the investigations into the murders of Adrian Willoughby and Bogdan Petrov in his direction. My understanding is that Inland Revenue is going after Smythe, too. I'm told they're very thorough but incredibly slow-moving."

"So we should hide and watch but not hold our breath?" Ali asked.

Cami nodded. "Exactly."

"How did Rachel Bloom work out?"

Cami laughed. "It looks as though hiring her was an unnecessary expense, but she was great."

"Purple hair and all?" Ali asked.

"That was a wig, but a very realistic one," Cami replied. "I'm pretty sure nobody suspected her of being my bodyguard. She told me that when she was in the Israeli Defense Forces, they called her Tank. Anyone who tangles with her does so at their own risk."

"Effective, then?"

"Very," Cami said. They both laughed about that.

"What about sales?" Ali asked.

"A couple of good prospects that should come through eventually, and a few more maybes, but I plan to spend today working up the proposal for Dozo International."

"Great," Ali said. "The sooner we reel in that big fish, the better. I'll leave you to it."

With that she headed for her own office. Later that morning, around eleven, Frigg called. "Big news from Edmonds, Washington," she said. "The police chief is about to do a live news conference on the Chuck Brewster homicide. It's due to start in five minutes. Should I livestream it to your phone, computer, or iPad?"

"To the desktop in my office, please."

After turning on her computer, Ali sat for the next few minutes staring at an empty lectern in a room filled with milling reporters and cameramen. Eventually a cop in a blue dress uniform stepped up to the mic. At that point the room fell silent.

"Good morning," the officer said. "I'm Richard Nelson, chief of police in Edmonds, Washington. Earlier this month our community was shocked by the brutal murder of local video game executive, Charles Brewster. This morning, I'm happy to report that, as of last night, the two individuals we now believe to be responsible for the homicide have been taken into custody in Huntington Beach, California.

"At this time I am unable to give you their names because they have not yet been officially charged. One of them, after a brief police chase on I-405 in Huntington Beach, was arrested on suspicion of assault with a deadly weapon and kidnapping, when a seriously injured man was found bound and gagged in the trunk of his vehicle. At this point, our prosecutors are preparing formal charges against both individuals in regard to the Edmonds homicide. They are also in the process of initiating extradition proceedings for both of them.

"Early on in the investigation, Edmonds homicide detectives found enough evidence to charge Clarice Brewster, the widow of the victim, as the perpetrator of the crime. We now believe that the individuals responsible for the homicide deliberately manipulated the crime scene in order to frame her for the offense. Later today, prosecutors are expected to go to court with a motion to have the charges against Ms. Brewster dropped.

"That's all I can say for now. I won't be taking questions at this time, but we will provide updates as they become available. Thank you for coming."

With that, Chief Nelson exited the press conference.

"Wow!" Ali said into her phone.

"Would you like to know the names of the two individuals who were taken into custody in Huntington Beach last night?" Frigg asked.

"I certainly would."

"Marc Atherton and Joel Franklin," the AI replied.

"You called that shot," Ali said.

"Excuse me?" Frigg asked. "Doesn't calling the shots mean 'being in charge'?"

"That may be the official definition, but in pool or billiards, it means saying which holes a ball is going to go into before the shot is made."

"You're correct about that, then," Frigg agreed after a moment. "I did call that shot."

"What about the injured man in the trunk of Joel's vehicle? Did you get an ID on him?"

"That would be Mr. Adam Brewster. He was transported by ambulance to Huntington Beach Hospital where he's in stable condition due to a stab wound."

"He's no longer considered a suspect in his father's murder?"

"Not at this time."

"Thank you for this, Frigg," Ali said. "I'm hanging up now to go tell B."

CHAPTER FIFTY-THREE

SEATTLE, WASHINGTON
WEDNESDAY, MARCH 29, 2023
12:05 P.M.

When Donna Jean's cell phone rang in the pocket of her apron, she had just finished vacuuming the carpets for her newest client, a Mrs. Upton, and was in the process of rolling up the cord to put the vacuum away. As a general rule, Donna Jean didn't take calls while she was working, but Mrs. Upton had stepped out for a walk. Besides, caller ID said that her daughter, Amy, was on the phone. Since this was a school day, Donna Jean worried there might be some kind of emergency, so she answered anyway.

"Have you seen the news?" Amy asked breathlessly.

"What news?" Donna Jean asked. "And no, I haven't. I'm working. Why? What's going on?"

"I'm in the teachers' lounge, and the noon news is on," Amy answered. "They just showed the Edmonds police chief doing a news conference. He said two suspects in California have been arrested in the Brewster homicide and that charges against Mrs. Brewster are going to be dropped later today."

Donna Jean's legs went weak under her. Barely believing what she was hearing, she sank down on a nearby chair. If the charges against Mrs. Brewster had been dropped, did that mean she, too, was no longer under suspicion?

"Are you kidding?" she whispered.

"Not at all. I thought you'd want to know. Does that mean you'll get your old job back?"

Donna Jean had managed to scrape together enough new customers to make up for one of the Brewsters' missing days, but if Mr. Brewster was no longer there, did she really want to go back to work for Mrs. Brewster?

"Maybe," Donna Jean said. Then, hearing Mrs. Upton's key in the door, she hurriedly got to her feet and added, "Thanks. I've got to go now."

As Donna Jean started on the dusting, she was still thinking about what she'd just heard. At first she'd been incredibly relieved to think that maybe the whole awful ordeal was over, but what about Mrs. Brewster? If she offered to rehire Donna Jean, would she say yes or no? And that's when the rest of it hit her. What about Pearl? Would Mrs. Brewster want her back? Donna Jean had bonded with that precious kitty, but of course there was no way around it. Pearl belonged to Mrs. Brewster, and if she wanted Pearl, Donna Jean would have no choice but to give her up.

CHAPTER FIFTY-FOUR

HUNTINGTON BEACH, CALIFORNIA
WEDNESDAY, MARCH 29, 2023
9:00 A.M.

On Wednesday morning, neither Detective Horn nor Detective Burns were at their very best. The night before, they had stayed up late while, with search warrant in hand, Huntington PD CSIs had conducted a thorough search of Joel Franklin's Camaro. The contents of the passenger compartment had been revealing. They had included a shovel, a .32-caliber Smith and Wesson revolver, a backpack stuffed full of clothing, a laptop computer, three cell phones, a passport, and an envelope stuffed with loose cash that added up to thirty-five thousand dollars.

Seeing the shovel had been especially chilling. "If we hadn't intercepted those phone calls from Joel to Marc," Ray said, "I'm pretty sure he would have ended up in the trunk of that Camaro right along with Adam. Joel may have been headed for Tijuana, but I doubt either Marc or Adam would have made it to the border. They'd have ended up buried in a shallow grave somewhere between here and there."

Joel's laptop had been handed over to Huntington PD's tech guys, but by the time Ray and Monica showed up at police headquarters, they had not yet cracked it. While they waited, the two detectives decided to divide and conquer. With two additional search warrants in hand—one for Marc Atherton's residence and one for Joel Franklin's, Ray Horn and

Monica Burns, accompanied by local officers, set out to execute them. Ray went to Joel's place, which happened to also be Adam Brewster's residence in Holly-Seacliff, while Monica headed for Marc Atherton's apartment in Huntington Beach.

Aside from a laptop computer, nothing much showed up at Atherton's place. Other than personal items—clothing, a few dishes, and a chintzy thirty-two-inch flat-screen TV—there was little else. On a guess, Monica sat down in front of the laptop and keyed in the same numbers Marc had given her as the password to his cell phone—1, 2, 3, 4. Sure enough, the combination worked on his computer as well.

She scrolled through his recent search history. She found one for driving directions from Sea-Tac Airport to the Brewsters' address in Edmonds. He had checked with any number of car rental firms before settling on Enterprise, and the confirmation date on the emailed rental reservation was dated February 22. That alone was enough to show premeditation. Hotel and flight reservations were dated the same day and led back to a credit card belonging to Joel Franklin.

Monica could barely believe her eyes. How dim could Marc Atherton be? He hadn't even gone to the trouble of deleting his search history. If this team had a mastermind, he wasn't it.

Then one of the Huntington Beach PD Tech Unit guys came over and handed her a computer printout. "What's this?"

"We cracked Joel's phone. This is his most recent search history. We're printing out texts and email correspondence as we speak."

"In the meantime, can you set me up with a computer?" Monica asked.

"Sure thing," the guy said. "Come with me."

He led her back into the TU, located an available computer, and got her logged in. Monica located Joel Franklin's last search: "Cheapest flights from Tijuana to Mexico City."

"So that's where he was headed," Monica muttered to herself.

The next one up said: "Charles Brewster Homicide, Edmonds, Washington." Monica typed that into the desktop's keyboard and up popped a link to a website called komonews.com.

The video opened with a view of the KOMO TV news desk, complete with a pair of news broadcasters, one male and one female. The caption at the bottom of the screen proclaimed KOMO MORNING NEWS.

The guy spoke first. "Since earlier this month, we've been following the case of the brutal slaying of video game executive and Edmonds resident, Charles Brewster. His widow, Clarice Brewster, has been charged in the homicide. She's currently out on bail and living under house arrest while awaiting trial, but our reporter Darla James has an update for us this morning. What do you have for us, Darla?"

The camera view switched to a young female reporter, one Monica recognized, standing outside the headquarters of the Edmonds Police Department.

"Thank you, Gary," Darla said. "You're correct. Clarice Brewster has indeed been charged in her husband's murder, but this morning, anonymous sources close to the investigation are reporting that the focus of the investigation has recently changed, and detectives on the case will be following up on leads in Southern California. I asked Edmonds Police Chief Richard Nelson about that, and he would neither confirm nor deny. If I learn anything more, I'll be in touch. Back to you."

The clip ended and Monica sat staring at the screen. Then she checked the printout. The clip may have been from the morning news, but the timing of the search indicated it had been made much later in the day, at 3:34 p.m. on Tuesday, March 28. The flight search had happened mere minutes later at 3:58 p.m.

It was easy to connect the dots. The moment Joel knew that the focus of the investigation was shifting to California, he had begun making arrangements to get out of Dodge. But had Joel called his supposed partner in crime to warn him that the jig was up? Obviously not. Joel had been busy looking out for Joel and nobody else.

Once the CSIs had turned their attention to the Camaro's trunk, they discovered Adam Brewster had been lying on a bed of clear plastic bags filled with shredded paper. Since they were more interested in the blood and DNA evidence on the outsides of the bags, they hadn't paid much attention to the contents.

But now Monica was all about the contents. Joel had probably expected he'd be able to dispose of them at the same time he got rid of Adam's body, and maybe Marc's as well. Abandoning her borrowed desktop, Monica went looking for the guy who had brought her the printouts.

"Find anything?" he asked.

"I think so," she said. "Can you help me find the evidence that was taken from Joel Franklin's vehicle last night?"

"Can do," he said. After a quick phone call, he turned back to her. "Most of it is in the evidence room, except for the bags of shredded paper. They're in a locker in the impound garage."

"Great," she said. "Take me to the impound garage. It's the shredded paper I need to see."

At her request, Monica was led to the garage's sole interview room, where one of the bags of paper had been placed on a table for her convenience. After activating the room's recording equipment, she donned a pair of gloves and then tore open a bag. Grabbing two handfuls of shredding from the topmost layer, she spread the pieces out on the table. She could tell at once that they were bits of countless sales receipts—Safeway, Walgreens, Home Depot, BevMo. Clearly these were all debit sales receipts, and she didn't need to actually piece them back together completely in order to figure out what was going on.

Rather than looking for bits of paper listing the names of products and their prices, she went searching for the ones showing subtotals and totals. And there it was. On every single shopping receipt she examined, just above the total, was a line indicating the amount of cash back—usually that turned out to be forty dollars, probably the maximum allowed.

By the time she had collected and photographed ten or so of those, she sent the photos to Ray along with the following message:

> Joel may have been writing checks to himself, but take a look at these. Here's what Joel shredded. Every time he went shopping for anything, he gave himself forty bucks. He really was robbing Adam Brewster blind.

Ray called back almost immediately. "Congrats," he said. "How the hell did you figure that out?"

"School of hard knocks," Monica told him. "I graduated with honors. My ex used to do the same thing."

CHAPTER FIFTY-FIVE

HUNTINGTON BEACH, CALIFORNIA
THURSDAY, MARCH 30, 2023
10:00 A.M.

On Thursday morning Monica and Ray showed up at the courthouse in Huntington Beach bright and early for the hearing where Joel and Marc were to be charged. Appearing with their court-appointed attorneys, they both arrived wearing orange jail jumpsuits and shackles. When it came time for their pleas, Marc, despite his handwritten confession, pled not guilty to the murder of Charles Brewster, but he waived his right to an extradition hearing. Joel pled not guilty to assault with a deadly weapon and unlawful imprisonment in addition to the Brewster homicide charge. Ray felt certain that bank fraud and theft charges would be added at a later date. Joel, however, insisted on the extradition hearing.

After a discussion with Chief Nelson, it was decided that Marc Atherton would be released into Detective Burns's custody so she could accompany him back to Seattle on the first available flight. Meanwhile Detective Horn would remain in Huntington Beach where, with some local assistance, he would pore through the mountains of digital evidence that had been obtained from the collection of electronic devices they had gathered in the course of executing their search warrants.

Once Monica and Marc Atherton were on their way north, Ray and Detective Ortega settled into the Tech Unit's conference room where mounds of computer printouts awaited them. Since Monica had managed to extract password information from Marc Atherton, there had been no need to break into his devices. Instead, they simply logged on. By afternoon they had printed out years' worth of texts, emails, contact information, and search histories from Joel's computer. However, they needed something more.

Of the devices seized by officers during the search of Joel's residence and vehicle, there were three—a laptop, an iPad, and a phone—which presumably belonged to Adam Brewster. Rather than having the techs break into them, Ray Horn placed a call to Huntington Beach Hospital.

As he dialed the number, Ray wasn't sure what to expect, but after being connected to a room, Adam answered the phone after a single ring. He sounded far better than Ray had anticipated.

"Detective Horn here," he said. "How are you doing?"

"Fairly well," Adam said. "The doctor said I was lucky. If the knife had gone half an inch deeper, it would have perforated my large intestine and that would have been a whole other ball game. The problem is, in trying to get away from the knife, I fell backward. I don't know what I hit—the wall or the floor, maybe, but it was enough to give me a concussion and a minor brain bleed, so they're treating me for that."

"How soon until they release you?"

"Probably tomorrow or the next day, but since I've been told my home is still considered a crime scene, I'll stay with friends in Santa Ana until I get the all clear. What's happening with the investigation?"

Since it was still an active investigation, there wasn't much Ray could say, but he told Adam about that shovel found in Joel's Camaro, which had suggested to investigators that Joel had intended to knock Adam off and bury him in the desert somewhere between Huntington Beach and Tijuana, where Joel had been scheduled to board an early morning flight to Mexico City.

"Do you remember what you were lying on when you were locked in the trunk?" Ray asked.

"Vaguely," Adam said. "It felt like something plastic, but it also felt soft—sort of like one of those old beanbag chairs."

"It was actually a layer of plastic bags stuffed full of shredded paper—including lots of shredded sales receipts. My partner, Detective Burns, was able to piece some of them together. Were you aware that every time Joel went out to buy groceries or anything else for your household, he always took as much cash back as possible?"

"I noticed things seemed to be a lot more expensive than they used to be," Adam replied, "but I thought it was due to inflation."

"Some of it might be," Ray said, "but I suspect the big difference is him sticking you with a surcharge. I don't know how much exactly. In order to find that out, we'd have to put all those pieces of paper back together, and that would be a huge undertaking."

"I'll bet Jimmy Fisk, my banker, can get to the bottom of it," Adam said. "Joel used a debit card to do the shopping, so the bank will have the transaction numbers. With those they should be able to go back to the various retailers and get copies of the actual receipts."

"Based on those large checks he cashed recently, Joel's already facing felony theft charges, but there is something else we need from you. Two cell phones were found in Joel's Camaro. One of them is his regular cell and one is his burner."

"Joel had a burner?" Adam asked incredulously.

"Yes, he did," Ray told him. "A phone with only one number in the call history—Marc Atherton's. We're looking at probably hundreds of texts and calls over the past number of years, many of them of a very personal nature."

"He really was cheating on me, then?" Adam asked.

"So it would appear," Ray told him. "By the way, while we were executing the search warrant of his residence, some of your devices were also seized."

"Because it happens to be my residence, too," Adam muttered.

"Correct, so if you don't mind, we'll need passwords for those."

"No problem," Adam said.

With the password information in hand, Ray returned to the TU where he and Detective Ortega went to work reading through the extracted text histories. As they did so, everything became clear. Both Joel and Marc had been up to their eyeteeth in the conspiracy, with Adam completely in the dark. Everything pointed to the idea that once Joel learned the extent of Chuck Brewster's wealth, he had become Joel's primary target, banking on the idea that Adam would be Chuck's ultimate heir. After all, any inheritance that landed in Adam's lap would eventually end up in Joel's.

"There you have it," Detective Ortega concluded, "the first commandment in the homicide cop bible—follow the money!"

"Right," Ray Horn replied, "and that's exactly what we're doing."

In Adam's text history, Ray located the week in late January and found the exact day where Adam had first contacted his father. The text time was listed as 1:41 p.m.

Adam: I did it. I finally did what you've been saying I should do all along. I worked up my courage and called my dad at work.

Joel: How did it go?

Adam: Amazing. I was afraid he'd just hang up on me, but he didn't. In fact, he sounded happy to hear from me—really happy. We talked for a good hour and a half. Before the call ended, he invited us to his upcoming birthday party in Edmonds, Washington. I'm not sure of the date, but I wrote it down. I'll get the details from him so you can put it in the calendar.

Joel: You said the invited us. Does that mean you told him about me?

Adam: I did. And if he's over my being gay, then maybe I should be able to be over him marrying Clarice.

Wait," Ortega said, shuffling through his stack of printouts. "What day was that, and what phone?"

"January 26, Joel's cell."

"Okay, I'm seeing that conversation here on Adam's cell phone, too. The only other topic I'm seeing between them for that day is . . ."

"'What's for dinner and when will you be home,'" Ray finished, using the next text on Adam's phone to complete the exchange.

"Yes, but looky here," Ortega said a moment later.

"What?"

"Here's a text to Marc's phone from the burner. It's time is 3:05 p.m."

Joel: Adam finally did it. He got off his dead ass and called his father like I've been telling him to do for years. Guess what? His dad was overjoyed to hear from him. He's ready to forgive and forget. He even invited the two of us to come to his birthday party sometime in March.

Marc: Are you going to go?

Joel: I doubt it. Adam's furious. He said he was hoping for an actual apology. He says if his father thinks an invitation to a party will make up for disowning Adam while he was still in high school or cheating on his mother while she was dying of cancer, then he's sadly mistaken.

"But that's the exact opposite of what Adam actually said," Ortega objected.

"Yes, it is," Ray agreed.

"So you think this is the beginning of the whole thing?" Ortega asked.

Ray thought about that for a moment. "I doubt it," he said. "I'm guessing that started about the same time Joel got his first hint about Charles Brewster's net worth. But this is where Joel lies to Marc to lure him into making him believe that Adam Brewster hates his father and wants him dead. These are baby steps, but they're the start, and the start of something else, too."

"What?" Ortega asked.

"A possible plea agreement. Did you read Marc's confession?"

"No, but you told me about it—that Joel told Marc that Adam Brewster hated his father and was willing to fork over a cool hundred thou to have Chuck Brewster out of the way."

"What we have here in this pile of computer printouts," Ray said, "is overwhelming evidence that Joel was the instigator who drew Marc into the plot with lies and deceptions. As far as I'm concerned, that makes Joel even more culpable than the guy who wielded the knife. If the prosecutors offer Marc a plea of second degree, he can testify against Joel, and everything we have here will corroborate what he's saying."

"What do we do now?" Eddie Ortega asked.

"Keep reading and see how early on the two of them started talking about Chuck Brewster's money."

CHAPTER FIFTY-SIX

EVERETT, WASHINGTON
THURSDAY, MARCH 30, 2023
7:00 P.M.

This was the first time Detective Monica Burns had ever escorted a handcuffed prisoner on board a commercial aircraft. In Santa Ana there had been a lot of open curiosity about the situation with Marc Atherton. She had spent the flight being grateful that they'd be landing at Paine Field. With only two gates, the airport was tiny compared to SeaTac, and she didn't expect their arrival to cause much of a stir, but she was wrong about that. When they walked into the baggage claim area, the place was crammed full of news reporters and TV cameras.

Obviously, as far as the Seattle area was concerned, Charles Brewster's homicide was still big news. Fortunately, Chief Nelson had provided a pair of patrol officers to help run interference. The uniformed officers got them through the crush of reporters in baggage claim and escorted them outside to where an unmarked Edmonds PD vehicle with another detective at the wheel waited at the curb to drive them to the Snohomish County Jail in Everett.

Monica had finished loading Atherton into the back seat and was climbing into the front when a text came in from Ray.

> Ray: Eddie and I spent the day going through
> mounds of digital evidence downloaded from

those seized devices. It's clear Joel was the guy running the show. We found no evidence that Adam bore any ill will toward his father, but that's not what Joel told Marc Atherton.

Monica: So Joel was lying to Adam about his relationship with Marc, and he was lying to Marc about Adam's relationship with his father. Is that how he got Marc to go along with the murder-for-hire scheme?

Ray: Looks like. Before you turn him over to booking, you might give him some food for thought. When Joel called Marc, offering to pick him up after work, Adam was already bound and gagged in the trunk of Joel's Camaro. If we hadn't intercepted those calls, there's a good chance Marc would have ended up in the trunk, too. Be sure you let him know that Joel had booked only one ticket from Tijuana to Mexico City.

Monica: So if they offer him a plea deal to testify against Joel, he should take it?

Ray: I'd say jump at it. A conviction for second-degree murder is a hell of a lot better than one for first. As for his testimony, it won't just be the word of one co-conspirator against another because we have digital evidence backing up Marc's version.

Monica: Will do.

Monica pocketed her phone, then she turned back to Marc. "Did I mention that Joel tried to call you after you got off work the other night while I had you in the interview room at Huntington Beach PD?"

Marc shook his head.

"He called a total of four times, as a matter of fact," Monica continued. "He was hoping the two of you could get together."

"So what?"

"The problem is, at the time he called you, he had already attacked Adam Brewster with a knife, and Adam was bound, gagged, and helpless in the trunk of Joel's vehicle. When Joel was apprehended, he was on his way to Mexico with a one-way ticket from Tijuana to Mexico City loaded into his phone."

Monica waited to let those words sink in.

"He was leaving without me?" Marc asked, sounding bewildered.

"Actually," Monica continued. "I think it was worse than that. Why would someone expecting to fly to Mexico City be traveling in a vehicle with a loaded weapon and a short-handled shovel along for the ride? And why was he so interested in having you in that same vehicle?"

"Wait," Marc said in disbelief. "Are you saying he was going to kill me?"

"Let's just say I don't believe either you or Adam Brewster would have been alive by the time Joel Franklin crossed the border into Mexico."

After that, Marc said nothing more. The brooding silence in the car stretched from one minute to two. It took all the restraint Monica could muster to keep her mouth shut. Eventually Marc spoke.

"That lying son of a bitch! Do you think he would have gone through with it?"

"What I think doesn't matter," Detective Burns said. "The real question is, do you?"

By then they were pulling up to the sally port at the Snohomish County Jail. Nothing more was said, but it didn't need to be.

Hint dropped, Monica Burns told herself. *Message received loud and clear!*

CHAPTER FIFTY-SEVEN

COTTONWOOD, ARIZONA
FRIDAY, MARCH 31, 2023
6:00 P.M.

It was Friday evening, and B. and Ali were on their own for dinner, making do with meatloaf sandwiches. Alonzo and Gwen had taken off for Vegas right after breakfast that morning. In the days after their engagement dinner, the idea of waiting around until Cinco de Mayo had gone by the wayside. They had booked the Little Chapel by the Courthouse for an 8:00 p.m. wedding. Not wanting to make a fuss, they had assured relatives and friends on both sides, that, if need be, they'd grab someone off the street to serve as witnesses. Rather than helping plan the festivities, with one last bit of Edieing it, Ali had settled for booking a two-night stay in the bridal suite at the Bellagio.

Thanks to Frigg, B. and Ali were totally up to speed concerning what was going on in the Chuck Brewster homicide investigation. Adam Brewster's husband and a close associate of his, Marc Atherton, had been arrested in the case and were both facing charges of first-degree murder. Atherton was now in the Snohomish County Jail in Everett, Washington, where he was being held without bail while awaiting trial. Joel was still in Huntington Beach with an extradition hearing scheduled for the following week. Charges against Clarice Brewster had been dropped. Ali assumed that meant Donna Jean Plummer was no longer under suspicion, either. Ali hadn't mentioned to B. exactly how deeply she and Frigg had been involved in the case, and she had no intention of doing so.

As the two of them settled down at the kitchen table, Ali could tell that B. was brooding about something.

"What's wrong?" she asked.

"I've spent all day thinking about Adam Brewster," he said. "He was a good-natured, cute little kid, and he absolutely idolized his father, at least he seemed to. Whenever we were developing a new game, he loved being one of our beta testers. I always thought that when he grew up, he'd end up being a part of VGI. I had no idea that he and his father had been estranged for years, and now, instead of being a part of the company, Adam is an architect living in California. Not only has he lost his father forever, he did so at the hands of the person he thought was his life partner. I can't imagine what he's feeling right now."

Because Ali had been privy to the police interviews, she knew far more than she should have about Chuck and Adam's estrangement.

"Yes, you can imagine it," Ali reminded B. gently. "He's probably feeling almost the same way you did when you found out Chuck and Clarice were having an affair."

B.'s troubled gaze met Ali's. "Exactly," he admitted.

"Why don't you give him a call?" Ali suggested.

"Me?" B. asked in dismay. "Call him out of the blue after all these years? What would I say?"

"Think about it," Ali said. "You're a longtime friend of the family. Obviously, Adam is aware of what Chuck and Clarice did to you. That means you probably know more about his current situation than anyone else on the planet. I'm willing to bet that most of his friends are currently tiptoeing around the situation without any idea of what to say. I believe you'll know exactly what to say because, not only are you genuinely sorry, you're someone who really understands."

"Maybe you're right," B. conceded, "but how can I call him? I don't have his number."

Ali smiled. "I'm pretty sure Frigg can rectify that situation in a matter of minutes."

In actual fact, it was less than two. Once B. keyed the number into his phone, he switched the call to speaker.

"Hello," a male voice said warily.

"Is this Adam Brewster?"

"Yes, it is. Who's this?"

"Someone who knew you a long time ago—B. Simpson."

"B.?" The tone of Adam Brewster's voice instantly brightened. "Really? I thought I'd never hear from you again."

"You were wrong," B. replied. "I heard about what happened to your dad, and I wanted to say how sorry I am."

Adam took a breath. "Thank you," he said. "So am I. Do you know who they've arrested?"

"My understanding is that it's someone with whom you were very close. That's got to hurt."

A lengthy pause followed before Adam spoke again. "You understand all about that kind of betrayal, don't you?"

"Yes," B. agreed, "I'm afraid I do. I can also tell you from personal experience that it takes a long time to get over it. I just wanted to let you know that I care. You have my number now. If you need to talk to someone who knows what you're up against, feel free to call me any time."

"Thanks, B.," Adam Brewster said with his voice breaking. "That means a lot."

With that, the call ended.

"Feel better?" Ali asked.

B. nodded. "Much," he said. "Thank you."

CHAPTER FIFTY-EIGHT

SEATTLE, WASHINGTON
SUNDAY, APRIL 2, 2023
2:00 P.M.

When Donna Jean's phone rang that Sunday afternoon, it awakened her out of a sound sleep. She had been dozing in her easy chair right along with Pearl. As soon as she saw Mrs. Brewster's name in caller ID, her heart fell. She had heard that the charges against Clarice had been dropped and that she was being released. This was the call she'd been dreading—the one where Mrs. Brewster would demand that Donna Jean bring Pearl back home.

"Hello," she said tentatively.

"Oh, good," Mrs. Brewster said. "You're there. I was worried I wouldn't be able to reach you. They just brought me home, and without that damned ankle monitor, either, thank goodness. But the house is a shambles and there's no food here at all. Can you come by tomorrow and straighten things out?"

Donna Jean could barely believe her ears. She had managed to fill up her Friday schedule, but Mondays were still open.

"Of course," she said. "What time?"

"The usual," Mrs. Brewster said. "I assume you still have your key?"

"Yes."

"Don't be surprised if you find me sleeping on the sofa in the living room. I just went upstairs and looked. There's still blood on the mattress.

I can't believe nobody bothered to clean up that mess. You'll need to make arrangements to have it hauled away and have a new one delivered."

Obviously, nothing had changed. Mrs. Brewster was still the same old Mrs. Brewster.

"Of course," Donna Jean said. "I'll take care of it. Do you want me to bring Pearl with me?"

"Pearl," Mrs. Brewster said. "I'd almost forgotten about her. Why don't you let her stay on with you for the next little while. Being at the hotel gave me something of an epiphany. I quite liked it, actually. Rather than remodeling this old place, I'm going to put it on the market. I've been reading up on cruise ship retirements. That's exactly what I'm going to do."

"What about Pearl?"

Mrs. Brewster sighed. "They don't allow pets on cruise ships, so unless you want her, I suppose I'll have to turn her over to the Humane Society."

"Please don't do that," Donna Jean said quickly. "She's no trouble at all. I'll be glad to keep her."

"Good," Mrs. Brewster said, "it's settled, then. See you tomorrow."

On Monday, Donna Jean showed up at Mrs. Brewster's place and spent most of the day taking care of cleaning up the master bedroom. She found a place that would deliver a new mattress that very day and take away the old one, too, bloodstains and all. Mrs. Brewster's Amex card worked wonders.

"Next, you'll need to clean out those other bedrooms," Mrs. Brewster told her.

"What should I do with all that stuff?"

"I don't care," she said. "Take what you want, donate the rest, or call those Got Junk people and have them come haul it away. Now that I've made up my mind, I don't want to waste any time. The sooner I list this place the better."

Donna Jean worked like crazy that day and all the next week, dropping by Mrs. Brewster's place to sort things whenever she could spare the time from her other jobs. There were plenty of secondhand stores that were more than willing to take Mrs. Brewster's castoffs, which ended up including all of Mr. Brewster's clothing and goods as well. But every night when Donna Jean came home to find Pearl awaiting her arrival, she sat down with the kitty in her lap and counted her blessings.

Two weeks later, she came home and found an envelope in her mailbox down in the lobby. The return address said LITTLE, MASON, AND DOBBS, LLC., with a street address on Madison in downtown Seattle. She waited until she was in her apartment before tearing the envelope open. Inside she found a cashier's check made out to her in the amount of one hundred and fifty thousand dollars, along with an accompanying letter:

Dear Ms. Plummer,

Now that the police investigation into Charles Brewster's homicide has concluded, we are pleased to send along the amount left to you in his last will and testament, given to you in gratitude for your many years of faithful service.

Yours Truly,
William Dobbs

Dropping both the letter and the check on her kitchen table, Donna Jean staggered over to her easy chair and fell into it. Then, after all these awful weeks, she finally felt free to let the tears fall.

"Mr. Brewster was always the nicest man," Donna Jean told Pearl when the cat leaped up into her lap. "I really miss him."

CHAPTER FIFTY-NINE

CHELMSFORD, ENGLAND
FRIDAY, JUNE 2, 2023
9:00 A.M.

At the end of March, when DI Wallace had been about to bring the hammer down on Ed Scoggins's head for the murder-for-hire homicide of Adrian Willoughby, he had been furious to be called into the chief's office and told he needed to put his arrest warrant on pause. Word had come down from on high that Inland Revenue was launching a major investigation into Mr. George Smythe, and they didn't want DI Wallace's findings in his petty little homicide to spook the man. Their people would speak to the people in charge at Essex Police when the time was right for him to take further action.

Grinding his teeth, DI Wallace had reluctantly put his arrest warrant on hold. He'd kept an eye on the man, however. Obviously, Scoggins had recently come into some money. He'd moved out of the house-sharing situation on Albany Road into a flat of his own, and he'd upgraded his aging vehicle, too, by ditching the ten-year-old VW Crafter for a model that was several years newer.

Once the old van was sold, DI Wallace made it his business to know exactly where it had gone. After locating it at a junkyard, he'd had it seized as potential evidence in his investigation, and he hadn't been wrong. The Essex Police forensic team had indeed located traces of Adrian Willoughby's DNA in the back of the discarded Crafter.

So while he and DS Frost had continued to amass evidence, they hadn't been able to do anything with it. Then, on the morning of Friday, June 2, DI Wallace was summoned into the chief's office.

"It's a go," he was told. "Inland Revenue will be taking Mr. Smythe into custody at noon today on charges of money laundering and tax evasion. The homicide charges for Mr. Willoughby's murder will be added on once he's in custody."

"So we can bring in Mr. Scoggins now?" Wallace verified.

"Indeed you can," the chief said, "the sooner the better. I'm more than ready to mark this case closed."

CHAPTER SIXTY

SEDONA, ARIZONA
SATURDAY, JUNE 3, 2023
4:00 P.M.

Ali Reynolds was having a perfectly wonderful day. Cami was on her way home from Tokyo with Dozo's signed contract in hand, and Ali was preparing to play hostess for that year's Amelia Dougherty Scholarship Tea. The caterers were there and setting things up. Both of this year's recipients, Daniel Knowles and Susan Rojas, would be in attendance. Daniel's parents, finally realizing his college education wasn't going to cost them an arm and a leg, were also expected to attend, as was Susan's great-grandmother. The event's guest of honor, newly minted veterinarian Dr. Meredith Glenn, would be there along with her mentor, Dr. Sophia Kaluznaicki.

Ali was in the bathroom putting on the last of her makeup when Frigg called. "Good afternoon, Ali," Frigg said. "I hope you're having a pleasant day."

"I am," Ali answered. "A very pleasant day."

"I have news," the AI continued.

Ali's heart fell. More often than not, when Frigg called with a news brief, it wasn't good.

"What's going on?" she asked.

"The London *Times* is reporting that London-based cybersecurity tycoon, Mr. George Smythe, was taken into custody yesterday by agents from Inland Revenue on multiple counts of money laundering and tax evasion. He is also expected to be charged in the murder of Adrian Willoughby. I will provide further details as they become available."

Ali breathed a heartfelt sigh of relief. "Thank you, Frigg," she responded aloud. "Thank you so very much. You've just made my perfect day that much better."